Miguel Najjar was born in Lebanon in 1951. He attended a French educational institution until High School graduation in 1970. The author then left for the United States and obtained a Master's degree in Electrical Engineering, graduating in 1975 from California State University at San Jose.

Ever since, the author worked in the engineering field, acquiring vast experience in Lebanon, the Gulf region and the United Kingdom, where he became a British citizen in 1987. Following retirement in 2019, the author is offering freelance consultancy support to engineering firms that are interested to enter the Gulf market. In parallel, he has written his first book *Beyond the Valley of the Saints,* and is completing his second manuscript.

This book is dedicated to my son Shadi, my daughter Rima, Roula Ibrahim, and my late work colleague Roland Raad.

Miguel Najjar

# BEYOND THE VALLEY OF THE SAINTS

AUSTIN MACAULEY PUBLISHERS

LONDON * CAMBRIDGE * NEW YORK * SHARJAH

Copyright © Miguel Najjar 2025

The right of Miguel Najjar to be identified as author of this work has been asserted by the author in accordance with sections 77 and 78 of the Copyright, Designs and Patents Act 1988.

All rights reserved. No part of this publication may be reproduced, stored in a retrieval system, or transmitted in any form or by any means, electronic, mechanical, photocopying, recording, or otherwise, without the prior permission of the publishers.

Any person who commits any unauthorised act in relation to this publication may be liable to criminal prosecution and civil claims for damages.

This is a work of fiction. Names, characters, businesses, places, events, locales, and incidents are either the products of the author's imagination or used in a fictitious manner. Any resemblance to actual persons, living or dead, or actual events is purely coincidental.

A CIP catalogue record for this title is available from the British Library.

ISBN 9781035882076 (Paperback)
ISBN 9781035882083 (ePub e-book)

www.austinmacauley.com

First Published 2025
Austin Macauley Publishers Ltd®
1 Canada Square
Canary Wharf
London
E14 5AA

I extend my sincere thanks to all those who supported me during the writing of the manuscript and to the professional team of Austin Macauley Publishers that enabled me to get the book published.

Special acknowledgement to my family members for their relentless encouragement.

I would also like to thank my brother Edgar and niece Jasmina for their input and suggestions.

# Prologue

He sat in a leather padded armchair on the marbled terrace facing Lake Albano, his past reeling before him. The present and the future woven into the turmoil of yester life; the past had been the platform of what came next. Luigi, the Pontiff, was an early riser. He usually woke up when the celestial canvas of scintillating stars would wane with the gradual advance of dawn. By then, the moon's reflection on the undulating water surface was barely noticeable. The early morning sunshine crept from the east, sweeping the surrounding hills with a gentle caress of warm light, announcing the beginning of a new day.

Now in his late sixties, spending the summer at Castel Gondolfo was an escape from Rome's suffocating heat and incessant Vatican meetings. Situated thirty kilometres away from Rome, the castle granted the Pope, peace and retreat. He could pray, reminisce and find time for himself to ponder over critical church issues that required his immediate attention.

He thought of his late mother. He really missed her presence and her comforting smile. She had been a terrific mother who stood by him, offering support, affection and advice, while avoiding any attempt to impede his choices. She had believed in him and never stood in his way, even when his decisions seemed rather rash. He had loved her so much, not just for being a great mother but because of her sincere devotion to the entire family, particularly her beloved husband Fabriano who had preceded her in death decades earlier. Luigi had also been very fond of his father even though he had known him for just ten years. He missed his parents and wished they could all be together, at least for a few moments. He needed to share things with them; to get a pat on the shoulder; a hug, and above all, gain family recognition for his deeds and achievements. Despite his age, he remained a son. Emotions had no age boundaries, no limits.

Luigi owed his parents everything.

A slim lady came up to him wheeling a mini buffet table, laden with an assortment of beverages and light food. Ornamental cups, glasses and small plates were laid down on an oversized embroidered white cloth that loosely hugged the entire frame of the table. She ensured the mobile table was positioned in front of his seat, within easy reach. Luigi was served strong black coffee, croissants, strained yoghurt, black olives and a tall glass of freshly squeezed orange juice. Luigi thanked Graziella, praising as usual the aromatic smell of her brewed coffee. She flexed her body and bowed before him. She held his hand and tried to kiss it reverently. The Pontiff withdrew his hand and, instead, planted a kiss on her forehead.

He had learned to enjoy his breakfast since he was seven years old. His dad had incessantly stressed on the benefits of a hearty meal in the morning. Luigi had often sat at the breakfast table, next to his father, wondering when he would have his first cup of coffee. His dad would let the hot beverage wash down the strained yoghurt and cheese that he would spread on crunchy baguettes and golden crispy croissants. Once done with his breakfast, Luigi's father would catch a glimpse of the morning papers and share major topics with his wife. Luigi would listen to the conversations with eagerness, but most of the time he couldn't understand what was being said. He tried his best though to participate in few discussions just to please his parents and catch their attention. Luigi had been inquisitive since childhood and Fabriano had treated him like a grown-up since, always willing to answer his son's queries in a simplistic manner, in a way that a child could fathom. Luigi's enthusiasm and incessant yearning for knowledge had encouraged his dad to converse with him like a grown-up. Fabriano had to delve into challenging explanations, while exercising caution not to cloud his kid's innocent thinking. He had to make sure that there was no contradiction between his replies and the school teachings. He succeeded most of the time but not entirely.

Luigi couldn't help recalling a scene that took place in Milan sixty years earlier, just a few days after his father's recovery from a surgical procedure. They were having a relaxed breakfast on a sunny Saturday, filled with hope that his dad would overcome his illness. Paula suddenly raised the topic of fate and religion. Fabriano dismissed the slight tingling pain inflicted by the surgical incision and, with a brief reflection, let out those words that still resonated in Luigi's ears:

"There's no such thing as fate. At least not in a fixed sort of way. Fate, even if it existed, is bound to be altered through our good deeds, redemption and the way we communicate with God."

Luigi had been unable then to grasp his dad's statement. It was beyond his capacity and it deviated from his school learning. It had taken Luigi decades to realise that his dad had nailed the impact of fate on civilisations. According to his father, those who believed in destiny chose the easy way out. They were prone to blame fate for every impediment that might befall them. Why bother if providence decreed and sealed one's life events? If incapable to alter what was written; if incapable to incur any change to a defined course, one would rather surrender to his fate. Throughout history, various civilisations had succumbed to the clemency and wrath of God, believing in a divine intervention in their daily lives. They called it destiny.

They truly believed that their misery and their happiness had been etched since the day they were born. Everything had been pre-determined and sealed. Nobody could change what had been written. Easy explanations were found for murders, thefts, adultery…People, presumably, had no control over their actions. Things were meant to occur as devised by God Almighty. It was an easy explanation and an easy way out. Judicial verdicts were not based on proper trials. The accused was executed regardless of the presence or lack of evidence. It was his destiny to die. God would have otherwise intervened to spare his life. The culprit wouldn't have been caught had it not been for the providence. Had the accused been not guilty, he would have survived the execution: God would have intervened.

Luigi reflected on those moments and praised his father's wisdom. He was ten years old when he had first experienced his dad's views on fate. At the time, they sounded like a discorded account that he couldn't grasp. But as he grew up, over the years and decades that followed, it was ironic how deep his father's reflections had been. Fabriano had never challenged the existence of God. He had understood the greatness of God as a Creator but couldn't accept the idea that God would intervene in people's daily lives. That made his dad special.

Fabriano often said: "A man would only strive to excel and earn credit through his good deeds. Otherwise, God would be responsible for every problem that afflicted people: God would be blamed for social segregation, wealth, poverty, illnesses and wars."

Luigi took in the scenic view stretching in front of him. His wide-angle vision captured the mountains, the lake, the beaming sunlight. His hearing picked up the chirping of starlings, the flutter of wings as birds flew from one tree branch to another. Fishermen were returning to their moorings. Some were already bargaining to sell their catch. Life was resuming its regular beat.

He closed his eyes for a few seconds, enjoying the gentle fresh breeze that blew on his face. The wind carried a hint of cold air, probably emanating from hundreds of miles away; originating from the Lombardy region. That's where he was born and grew up. He could picture his past, with its happy and sad moments. He drifted in his thoughts. Scenes and pictures emerged from various corners of his mind, as if the story of his family generation was being recounted by an observer acquainted with its life chapters.

What a long journey it had been and when it all started, what had he been looking for? To chase the ghosts of his parents? To lay them to rest, or to give their stories freedom to fly alongside his?

**Part One**

# Chapter One

The surgeon who saved countless lives was lying in bed in an awkward posture. Two pillows were stuck behind his weak frame propping him up. His hazy vision barely enabled him to scan the room. He had just been administered a morphine injection by a chubby nurse who had learned to control her emotions: handling numerous patients in their terminal phases. The surgeon was forty-six years of age.

Often referred to as "the handsome doctor" or "the good Samaritan," Dr Fabriano's body was now frail and tired. His face was pale with severe wrinkles under lazy eyes that once sparkled with their piercing gaze and brightness. The thick hair that once covered his scalp was no longer there. He had refused to undertake any further treatment. There was no point elongating the suffering.

Two days earlier, he pleaded with his fellow physicians and family members to be discharged, so that he could depart in peace. He couldn't bear the idea of staying helpless within the cold and unfriendly walls of the medical centre. He wanted to die with dignity within the confinement of his sweet home, as he used to call it. Fabriano could no longer bear the pitiful look and sad expressions displayed by the medical team attending to him. His friends who often visited him, drowned his morale each time they saw him regressing in his illness. He just wanted to be surrounded by his wife Paula and his son Luigi. He no longer cared so much about the presence of Eva, his visiting sister. Once revered by Fabriano, Eva had turned lately into an enigmatic woman with deep secrets and a darn belief that she was right about almost everything that plagued the world. She was a vindictive person, a side that Fabriano didn't acknowledge at first and failed to recognise for decades: a dominating personality with loud accusations. She scared him but he succeeded to conceal the rift between them and kept it away from his immediate family. There was no need for aggravation.

The ambience within the spacious bedroom was strange and heavy, particularly for little Luigi. Sadness loomed heavily on each family member amid soft lighting and Yanni's music playing in the background. Fabriano enjoyed Yanni's rich and eclectic assortment of musical instruments and shared his passion with his son, whose appreciation for music was evident. Luigi had always been very close to his dad and emulated him in every way. Even now while battling the suffering, Fabriano smiled, realising that Luigi was behind the idea of playing music to soothe his anxiety. His son was trying to restore normalcy to a sombre situation, doing his best to assure his father that this particular moment was like any other. That everything was still under control.

Sitting on the bed by his dad's side, Luigi held Fabriano's right hand fearing for it to slip away. He stroked the bony fingers and kissed them. Every now and then, while still holding Fabriano's hand, he would lean over Fabriano's bald head and plant a tender kiss on the shiny skin. Just this once, their roles have been reversed: the son was flooding his dad with tenderness and unconditional love. Tears ran down Luigi's cheeks, landing on his father's bald head. Even in the confusion and anxiety of departing, Fabriano regained his weary senses, looked around while squeezing his son's hand.

Eva whispered an order to the housekeeper to switch off the hi-fi system, plunging the room into a morbid silence that caused Luigi's heart to succumb further into sadness. Feeling his father's grip loosening by the minute, Luigi flinched and yelled aloud: "Please Daddy, don't leave us. My mum and I need you. We cannot live without you."

With difficulty, Fabriano turned his head towards his son and muttered with heavy pauses: "I wish I...could stay, my son. Everything...has an end. I love you, teddy bear. Be strong. I'll always be...with you, watch over you. Grow up...to be a good man. Take care of your...mother and strive to become...a leader in...whatever you do. We'll be...physically apart. That's all. I'll be...checking your school grades, what games...you're playing, your first date."

Those final words bore heavily on all those present. Together, they wept silently, making snivelling sounds that punctuated the dark silence.

Eva's tears, though, were different from the rest. They carried pain and reproach. She was witnessing the exit of a dear brother that she would probably no longer meet, not even in the afterworld. He was destined for hell or the purgatory, should he be on the lucky side.

Soon afterwards, the space around them felt different as if air was stifled. Fabriano tilted his head slightly and exhaled his last breath. His wife, Paula, rose from her armchair and reached her husband's bed. His eyes were closed in a serene sort of way as if he were sleeping. His chest showed no movement. He was gone.

Paula's heart was filled with sadness. She didn't have the chance to talk to him and express, for the nth time, her deep love and gratitude for the lovely years they had spent together. His parting was quicker than expected. It happened so fast. She was grateful however that Luigi had ample time to let out his emotions. Paula bent down and kissed Fabriano's lips and cheeks. She rested her head on his skeletal shoulder and wept. Luigi caressed and sniffed his father's bald head, trying to catch the smell of his dad's preferred Eau de Toilette which he had worn every single day. He used to spray it on his shaved beard, but recently he had been applying it slightly to his neck and forehead.

"Sleep, Daddy. Sleep. I'm here with you. I won't let you go."

Luigi did not let go of his father's hand. Holding on gave him a fake assurance that bodily separation wouldn't take place.

Eva stepped forward and gently detached the son and mother from the deceased. She made the sign of the cross and prayed out loud, asking for redemption and absolution. She could have posed for a female priest.

Lightning followed by thunder startled everyone within the room. That night, torrential rain fell on Milan, accompanied by hail and high wind. The asphalted streets and roof tops were battered by golf size hailstones. Windowpanes rattled as they were hit obliquely by pellets of frozen rain. A drenched old sage owl hooted from afar, uttering unvoiced wisdom to be discovered by those who outlived the dead.

# Chapter Two

Dr Fabriano Khoury was of Lebanese descent, born in the north of the country where snowcapped mountains and deep valleys embraced one another. He had resided in Beirut with his father Michel and his Italian mother, Sophia. His parents met each other in Capri when Michel undertook a leisure trip to abate the work stress he was enduring: a consequence of long hours expanded at construction sites all over the rich Arabian Peninsula.

Having performed well in the Gulf area and having prospered, Michel settled back in Lebanon in the year 1994, ensuring his children Eva and Fabriano had the best secondary education. Michel always discouraged his son to enter the engineering domain, urging him to aim for a medical degree instead and open his own practice.

As a matter of fact, Fabriano excelled in his studies, enabling him to get enrolled at Harvard Medical School. He emerged in 2012 as a coronary surgeon with the highest distinction. Even though not a holder of the green card, Fabriano had been approached by several US medical centres to consider working for their facilities with promise of securing him the residency, based on special credentials, linguistic abilities and diversity: he was fluent in English, Arabic, French and Italian.

Spending more than a decade in Boston, Massachusetts, Dr Fabriano had developed a liking to a nation that made itself through hard work and stiff resolve. Nevertheless, he missed the slower pace of Europe and the Middle East, fearing that he might end up with no personal life at all. Deep down he knew very well that the main reason was his longing to be close to his parents and his native country. Despite his father's plea to remain in the USA and not commit such a grave mistake, Fabriano headed for Beirut on September 29, 2012.

Fabriano was shocked. Watching the news from afar and pursuing Lebanon's daily events did not prepare him for what he was experiencing on the ground.

Nothing made sense. Politicians did not care the least about their nation; news media were always aiming for scoops, rather than sincere and truthful depiction of events; boring and misleading television talk shows were aired regularly, hosted by either biased or illiterate personnel who could not express themselves in a true manner for fear of reprisal. Hence, under the alleged umbrella of free speech. There was only one permitted truth, that mouthed by corrupt politicians. Dismal actors on stage, talking relentlessly with animated gestures, exhibiting impeccable Arabic grammar and vocabulary, yet devoid of logical and humane material.

What disturbed Fabriano the most was the recklessness of the vast majority of people and their blind allegiance to warlords who prevailed through their false accusations of each other. They never ceased claiming that reforms were necessary, vouching to protect their homeland, and yet did nothing to alleviate the situation. Christians and Muslims alike sided with their respective sects and corrupt tyrants, ignoring what patriotism meant. The majority of people abandoned the core essence of nationalistic fervour, which was the key element that would allow an independent and thriving nation to prevail. Rather than assuming a pacifist role, religious leaders fomented disputes by taking sides with sectarian political parties. Chaos ensued with no let-up.

Fabriano came from Hasroun, a Christian enclave in the mountainous north; a village overlooking the famous Valley of the Saints. Throughout history, the nation had been blessed by that valley, roamed by several pious monks who got canonised by the Vatican. It was baffling that from then on, not a single saint was bound to be nominated in the future: as the whole country was being cursed and forsaken by God.

As a matter of fact, Lebanon, a scenically beautiful nation, had been paradise on Earth. It was rightly named the Switzerland of the Middle East. Like Adam and Eve, its rulers had become insatiable. They sacrificed their nation to the greed of neighbouring countries and those beyond, unleashing irrational civil wars. Inhabitants slumbered and blindly followed their leaders. Under misleading pretexts, those wars had sectarian, nationalistic and regional issues for ignitors. Thus, inhabitants had neither experienced proper civic rules nor authentic nationalistic fervour. Succeeding governments failed to set the basis for a sovereign state.

Fabriano resisted various temptations to practice surgery in renowned Beirut hospitals. He received lucrative offers but hesitated to sign any agreement. The traffic jams, the relentless city noise, the smoky haze, the street litter, and confined spaces, all made him curse. The city was a living hell during the day. At night, Beirut brightened up and projected a totally different image, reminiscent of old times. Streets bustled with late shoppers, pub and restaurant goers.

Above all, the greyish colour of concrete buildings was subdued and often concealed, replaced by colourful reflections on their walls and facades caused by artificial lighting.

Fabriano enjoyed the atmosphere of a local Irish pub that served authentic ales and stouts.

Sitting outdoors on a wooden bench with colleagues, he often cherished a few hours spent watching gorgeous ladies pass by, catching a whiff of their scent and eyeing their toned legs and figures. After all, the glamour and charm of Lebanese women could not be ignored. Well-dressed, always projecting the latest fashion trends, Lebanese women were so appealing and sensual.

Flirtatious and charming, it was easy to fall under their spell. His father, Michel, used to warn him: "Be cautious, ladies over here are avid hunters. They could suck your blood and walk away undaunted. Just be sure they really like you for what you are, and not as a provider of wealth and security."

Even though Fabriano dismissed his father's statements as too cautionary, he had to experience for himself the truth and validity of such remarks. He dated two ladies within the course of twelve weeks, just to realise that their interest was more in his financial and social status rather than personality and sincere emotions. Even in bed, they were sort of frigid, unlike the sensuality they had projected when he first made their acquaintance.

Fabriano was not ready to change the world around him, nor was he willing to concede to the surrounding eccentricities of the city, so he took refuge in the red-tiled roof of his parents' house in the village. Perched on top of a rocky mountain, 1600m above sea level, the house overlooked the deep Valley of the Saints. The air was clean and crisp. It was mid-January.

Snowflakes drifted lazily with the wind before settling on the ground and pitched roof tops. Dark green pine trees extended their white capped branches with tiny water droplets dripping slowly at their tips; monasteries at the bottom of the valley reached out to the first snow with their tall spires; the green cascading fields stretched from the mountain top to the bottom of the valley, turning gradually white. It snowed in Boston, but the valley here was awesome and majestic, almost to the point of being surreal.

As Fabriano sat on a couch observing the scenery he couldn't help feeling mystic and dreamy. Catholic by birth, and having attended schools run by religious teaching congregations, Fabriano had been exposed to daily catechesis and mass service attendance. He formed part of the school choir. He had loved all the ritual aspects, finding them essential to reach out to God and be blessed by the Almighty.

In the back of his mind though, his infatuation with God could not appease his concern about the stern and austere measures taken by God in the Old Testament. Was it necessary to slaughter children because of their parents' disobedience and sins? But on second thought, God was merciful, sending his own son to salvage humanity by spreading words of love, forgiveness and charity. The New Testament seemed to negate all violent aspects of the Old Testament.

Religious scholars would tell believers that both Testaments should not be interpreted separately and that their continuity prevailed. Fabriano thought otherwise. He simply could not digest the ruthlessness depicted in the Old Testament. But then again: was he supposed to query that issue or just be contented with the post era? The latter was much easier to grasp. It was the greatest true story ever told, witnessed by thousands of people and twelve disciples and all events accounted for. Above all, the purpose was crystal clear: Jesus defied death and rose to heaven, giving hope to all humans willing to follow his path.

Fabriano, at that time, felt quite content with his belief. The crackling of the logs burning in the fireplace, mixed with the tolling of monasteries' bells jolted Fabriano out of his daze.

It dawned on him that it had been more than twelve years since he purposely attended mass service. His gradual loathing of clergy spiked immediately after high school graduation. Realising how badly Lebanon was fairing in economy, social and political grounds, Fabriano put the blame mainly on religious leaders, Christians and Muslims alike. He couldn't fathom how they could represent two major religions while being incapable to curtail the greed and disloyalty of politicians and party leaders who had sold themselves to foreign influence. In his opinion, their inefficiency and unsuitability to control politicians had indirectly contributed to false misinterpretations among their congregations that fanatism was behind the civil war flare-ups. Thus, religious leaders had contributed inadvertently to the dissection of a fragile so-called pluralism, allowing party and faction leaders to impose their will on masses who felt threatened under the absence of clarity and guidance.

On a separate note, religious court ruling in divorce matters had always been under scrutiny for its transparency and fairness. Verdicts were often whimsical: the product of greed and corruption. Fabriano gradually alienated himself from religion. From a devout Catholic with a simple doubt about God's fairness in the Old Testament, to a believer in God with resentment of clergy. He had become closer to being agnostic at the age of thirty while still at Harvard.

The living room got cold. The fireplace was running out of tree logs. Fabriano got up, stirred the fireplace with the poker and shoved few logs that he took out from a basket. Dusk was spreading its darkness over the scenic view. Snow had stopped falling, replaced by a howling wind that rattled the windowpanes and filtered through the small gaps of the wooden frame, emanating a constant whistle accompanied with a cold spell.

Fabriano put down the poker, approached the bookshelves adorning the stony walls and stared at the dusty old books that were stacked in alphabetical order starting from the top shelf. His eyes wondered from one tier to another, scanning the titles and authors' names. Most books were French literary works depicting the sixteenth century all the way to the twentieth. French literature had a deep influence on Fabriano's upbringing and had captivated his soul with the diversity that each century had brought. He had been fascinated by the nineteenth century in particular: Musset, Baudelaire, Verlaine, Chateaubriand and Lamartine. They wrote poetry and prose that suited his romantic side and scepticism. At that precise moment, he seemed closer to Baudelaire in his quest for symbolism and modernist movement.

Under B, he found what he was looking for. Baudelaire's masterpiece, *Les Fleurs du Mal*.

It had been more than twenty years since he read the lovely poems portraying themes of decadence and erotism. He retrieved the book, wiped the dust off its cover and went back to his seat. He flipped the pages at random, recalling the general content of each poem through its subject title. He was a teenager once again preparing for his baccalaureate. It was gratifying to read a French book after such a long time. He closed the book and reopened it as if his destiny were linked to the page where his thumb would rest. "Invitation to the Voyage" unfolded before his eyes and he pondered over the poem.

Fabriano mulled over one of the verses: "Off in that land made to your measure!"

He closed the book and tried the game once more. This time his finger guided him to a different page that bore the title, Le Voyage. He grinned, amazed by the coincidence of stumbling on two successive poems that addressed voyages. His lips parted and he mumbled in French: "Faut-il partir? Rester? Si tu peux rester, reste. Must one depart? Remain? If you can stay, remain. Pars, s'il le faut. L'un court, et l'autre se tapit. Leave, if you must. One runs, another hides." The mobile phone rang. His mother was calling from her Beirut residence landline.

"Yes, Mum? How are you?" He answered, as soon as he picked up the receiver.

"Fine, dear. I just want to let you know that I'll be leaving this Sunday for Milan. Going there for a few days. Your grandma seems to be missing me." She said that in a kidding tone.

"Is Dad accompanying you?"

"Actually, he's not. Getting lazy I guess."

A brief silence prevailed. A short moment of reflection when someone pondered over a situation and tried to make an evaluation. Finally, Fabriano let out: "It's not a bad idea for me to join you on this trip. It's been a while since I saw grandma. And it wouldn't hurt exploring the possibility of finding a good job over there."

"That comes to me as a surprise. Never thought you would consider working overseas. You were so keen to come over to Beirut and settle down. Anything that matters?"

"Yes. I do have regrets. I shouldn't have come over. Dad was quite right from the outset. The country needs a complete overhaul. The only place where I find peace and get some inspiration is where I'm at, right now. The mountains, the valleys and the winding rivers are still appealing and are luring me to stay."

"Yes. It's a different world up there. Still unspoiled and mystic. Would be nice to have you as a companion. My flight departs on Sunday before noon. I'll send you the travel agency contact details. Call them the soonest and insist on reserving two adjacent seats. Flights are not fully jammed this time of year."

"Sure. Will do, the soonest possible, once I receive your message with all the details."

"Great, honey. I guess until then you'll be staying in the village. Drive down to Beirut early Sunday morning and leave the car in the second parking lot. We'll have coffee with your dad before heading together for the airport."

"Sure thing. I'll see you, Mum. Love you."

"Love you too," she said. That moment drew together the path of all events that took place afterwards.

# Chapter Three

Fabriano's cursory visit to Milan turned out to be a permanent residency. In no time, he had secured a great job at St Raffaele Hospital at Segrate, an eastern suburb of Milan. Two years had elapsed since, and he was performing a minimum of five cardiovascular surgeries a week.

Dr Fabriano was highly respected by his colleagues and patients alike. Always smiling even under extreme duress. He indulged in critical medical procedures without faltering. Surgical instruments took heed of his experienced crafty hands and served him well. He saved so many lives and had total confidence in his skills, which was evidently projected onto his patients and supporting medical teams. In addition to the long hours, put in daily, his contribution to research and training was relentless. A constant communication link was established with Harvard Medical Centre, focusing on shared cooperation regarding latest invasive procedures that would minimise risks and shorten surgical time intervention.

Fabriano believed that success relied mainly on the assured confidence a physician could provide to his patients. Clearly explaining the pros and cons of surgical procedures, stopping at every detail, describing risk, convalescence period and required follow-up, appeared to achieve that goal with the patients. They felt secure and attended to. Often, he had to relinquish his operating theatre fees, in order to assist those who had insurance problems and were incapable of remitting their dues. The hospital's administration tried its best to curtail health care charges, based on his insistence to support and aid those concerned.

Few times, Fabriano would laugh at himself. It was somewhat awkward: had he not rejected American employment for the sake of personal salvation and life enjoyment? Well, it seemed it was the same everywhere. He should have realised that medical practice required full availability and attendance, particularly to those who really believed in their oath and dedicated their lives to the safety and well-being of fellow humans.

Fabriano was not however regretting the choices he had made. After all, he was living in northern Italy, in the Lombardy region and precisely in Milan, the city of fashion and architectural wonder. People were cultured, somewhat sophisticated like other northern European nations, good mannered and respectful. The Lombardy region offered furthermore, a nuance of natural beauty, with tolerable weather, that reminded him of his native land.

Still a bachelor, he spent the first two years in a rented one-bedroom apartment in a bourgeois neighbourhood, West of Milan. Wagner Buonarroti neighbourhood was a convenient place, offering green patches, restaurants, supermarkets, bookshops and clothing stores. Fabriano lived in a flat facing Parco Vergani. Strolling within the park eased the tension and stress that he endured during the day. He felt some kind of bond with nature: watching the water features, the tall trimmed trees and the neat alley ways that snaked through the park. The sight of people walking their pets along those alleys, the sneak kisses and embraces exchanged between young lovers, made him feel sometimes envious and lonely. Showing one's emotions was a fascinating display of sharing and belonging. Nature offered the ideal setting for love seekers who sought refuge in its warm and chimerical haven. He wished he had the time to find his match. Spending more than twelve hours a day at St Raffaele Medical Centre had restricted Fabriano's endeavour to build decent and lasting relationships. He left home at 6:30 am, took the suburban line to Segrate railway station and reached his office by 8am. He seldom left the hospital before 7pm. The same scenario repeated itself five days a week, Fabriano had literally no time, let alone the will to venture out of his home. There was simply no time for such indulgence.

The weekend was a reprieve period. Very rarely did they schedule surgical interventions unless they were deemed essential and top urgent. Saturday visits to convalescing patients drained most of the day, but still allowed Fabriano precious free time, to enjoy Saturday evening and whole day Sunday.

On one Saturday night, in April 2013, Fabriano dressed up, putting on an Armani suit made of plain dark blue wool fabric, a light blue shirt and an orange-coloured tie grazed with blue stripes. He admired himself in the mirror and felt quite content with himself. To complement his looks, he picked his favourite Eau de Toilette and sprayed it on the palm of his hands and rubbed it on his shaved face. He was in a good mood. Andrea, a colleague of his was joining him at the best aperitivo on Via Sanzio. He was certainly overdressed for the occasion, but he was planning a long night and had no clue where and how it would end.

Fabriano decided to walk. It was a clear night. The air was crisp with a gentle breeze caressing the aligned trees, rustling the leaves on the outstretched branches, carrying the soothing sound to the opened windows of nearby buildings. Fabriano had his relatively long hair tousled by the light wind and had to adjust the strands in a mechanical manner, whenever they covered his eyes and blurred his vision. It was a nice feeling though: being free. He was blending with passersby and listening to the steady rumble of traffic: common occurrences that he had been missing for quite some time. For the first time in a long while, he was aware of his own existence. Saving lives had made him oblivious to his own self.

After thirty-five minutes, he reached his destination and found Dr Andrea sitting at an outdoor table, waiting for him. They shook hands and exchanged compliments on their outfits with sarcastic but otherwise friendly remarks. The waiter attended to them and they ordered Campari mixed with gin along with salty snacks.

Toasting each other first, they spent half an hour discussing communism and how strong it used to be in Milan, Bologna, Crema and Bergamo. Italy, the cradle of Catholicism had a strong communist influence, particularly among industrial cities and northern regions.

Fabriano couldn't help thinking of Pier Paolo Pasolini and his film "The Gospel according to St Matthew." A respectful austere masterpiece made by a Marxist director. Amid the animated discussion, laying out the pros and cons of communism, the adjoining table was occupied by a gorgeous woman with a tall figure. She sat quietly and crossed her legs. Fabriano couldn't help taking sneaky stares at her white satin thighs. Her wicked smile was a clear indication of her awareness of his furtive gaze. She ordered a glass of white wine with olives and cheese platter on the side.

She was definitely a very attractive and pretty lady. The black dress that she wore revealed a generous bosom; evidently a natural chest, not tampered with. The dark colour of her dress accentuated the whiteness of her skin. Fabriano was fascinated by her high cheek bones, fluffy auburn hair; slightly turned up defiant nose and big green eyes that seemed to pierce through the person facing her. Her sporadic but warm chat with the waiter showed that they were acquainted long since. A frequent customer apparently. She appeared to be assertive and confident; someone with an extended exposure to life.

After the lapse of fifteen minutes, Andrea had to excuse himself. He was invited to dinner and had to head back home to pick up his wife. Fabriano gave him a bear hug while gesturing for the waiter to fetch the bill. His hand gesture was like signing a non-existent document in thin air.

As Carlo the waiter approached his table with the cheque, Fabriano felt his heart squeezing, realising it was time for him to leave. It was a boyish feeling but a genuine one. Once he left the scene, the lady in black would become just a faint memory of the past. He paid the bill but remained seated, pretending that he was checking his mobile phone for incoming messages. Five minutes passed by, during which he caught few more glimpses of the beautiful woman.

Only this time, her smile turned affectionate and warm; the playful mischievous look had vanished. She rose from her chair, extended her arm, and they shook hands. She planted herself in what used to be Andrea's chair and spoke with a melodious voice: "Hi, I'm Paula Bianchi."

"Fabriano," he said, with a hidden shyness showing on his face. His flesh turned red as the blood flow increased in his veins.

"You're not from this area. Are you? Your accent suggests that you're not a native to Milan. And your clumsy approach with women confirms that." She treated him to a coy smile.

"Very observant of you. I'm a mix: Italian mother, Lebanese father," Fabriano replied. "Seriously, were you expecting me to be forceful, like asking you to join me at the table? I couldn't do that. I don't even have the nerve to express myself in such a manner. Couldn't tell if you were married, engaged or waiting for your date to show up—"

"Then you shouldn't have been eying me like that, in the first place," she said with a sudden interjection.

Embarrassed, Fabriano found himself stumbling for words: "I'm really sorry if I offended you in any way. Wasn't my intention. I guess my attitude was simply childish and unjustified." He stared at her gorgeous face, the way her lips parted, the way her gleaming eyes stared at him with an alien intensity that he had never encountered before. He paused and then continued:

"It seems my manners were not at their best. Once again, I'm so sorry." As Fabriano uttered those words, he pulled the chair backwards and rose up to leave.

"So that's it?" Paula cried out. "You gaze at women, get your kicks, and slip away as if nothing happened. The least you could do is ask the lady out for dinner. She might forgive your actions." Fabriano realised at that moment that Paula was indeed flirting with him. His heart resumed its regular beating and he couldn't help smiling at the woman that faced him across the coffee table. Was he hearing correctly? Her enigmatic smile and bright eyes were enough to convince him that the lady was asking him to take her out. After all, he hadn't lost his charm.

Gaining back his self-confidence, Fabriano reached out and held her hand, kissed it respectfully the way courtiers used to in the 17th century and joyfully said: "At your service, Milady. I happen to know the best place in town. Let's hit the city centre."

It would have been more appropriate to hail a taxi, but both decided to take the subway instead, in order to stimulate themselves and embark on a new adventure.

As they headed for Wagner subway station, they walked side by side, not really knowing what to say, interrupting the silence to utter few remarks about the moderate weather and the animated street buzz around them. They spoke little, as if they feared to spoil the achievement they had made so far. Fabriano was hesitating: should he hold her hand? Put his arm around her waist? How would she react to it all? He knew it was too soon for that, but still couldn't help debating what he had to do under the circumstances. There was an air of sophistication about her.

She radiated an aura of respect, while diffusing warmth and gentleness. He wondered what was going on inside her head at that very instant.

His apprehension came to an end once they entered Wagner Station. Seven minutes later they were on their way to Duomo via the M1 underground line. Unable to find available seating, they held on firmly onto the grab handles by the car door, huddled against each other, swinging at every sharp turn and making fun out of it. A couple of times, his face brushed against her soft cascading hair, giving him a tingling sensation that spread over his entire body. The scent of her deodorant was noticeable, particularly when she moved. Her pouting lips were so close, inches away from his own, but then again, he was a perfect gentleman who would try to curb his feelings and control his actions, at least for the time being.

The car doors opened and closed around eight times and there they were at Duomo Station. Coming out of the station was like bursting into a wide spacious world. They were dwarfed by the sheer wideness of the Square. The basilica was standing majestic with its pointed spires, stretching way up high. Artificial lighting caressed the cathedral's marbled façade, making it glow with faith and warmth. Fabriano had always appreciated the scene architecturally rather than religiously. He could not digest the idea that it took six centuries to complete the cathedral. The roof design was awesome and seemed to overshadow the whole structure with its elaborate details. Yet, those details were stuck so high up that few people could notice them.

Regardless of what one thought, the cathedral was still imposing with its capacity to accommodate thousands of worshippers.

As these reflections crossed his mind, Fabriano was pulled back to reality when Paula suggested to go inside the cathedral for few minutes. She was fascinated by the religious chanting and organ music reaching her ears from the blaring speakers. They were spiritually beckoning her to visit the basilica. It felt like a different era altogether, possibly medieval ages. Without realising it, Fabriano took hold of her hand and marched towards the gigantic structure.

Once inside, Paula made the sign of the cross and stood praying silently, while Fabriano wondered lazily from one nave to another. He had been there before, but each time he discovered a certain detail that he had missed. Artificial lighting from the powerful external floodlights seeped through the stained glass of immense windows, underlining the numerous pillars that spread over the 15,000 m2 footprint area. Finally, in his wandering stroll, he found himself facing the renowned statue of Saint Bartholomew, depicting his flayed body with amazing skills. One could easily see the fine skin lines thrown over the saint's shoulders like a stole. A hand rested on Fabriano's left shoulder and startled him. Paula was just behind him.

"Quite a masterpiece by Marco d'Agrate. Isn't it? The agony and pain are clearly depicted. Not on a sheet of paper or canvas but carved out of stone. The marble itself speaks for itself. Fabulous! Having said that, don't take that as an excuse to linger some more around here. I'm starving."

At the main entrance of the basilica, they held hands and crossed the Duomo Square towards BOEUCC restaurant.

Paula had heard about the restaurant, pronounced "Boush" and had walked past it a few times on her way to La Scala Theatre without attempting to try its renowned cuisine. She was struck by the setting, it seemed to capture the essence of late 19th century, with white-washed arches and greyish columns. No wonder the dining place was called La Sala Delle Colonne.

The manager greeted Fabriano with a warm "Dottore" and ushered the young couple to a round table covered in immaculate white cloth. She noticed the glances and nods of well-dressed customers, many of whom had probably met Dr Fabriano previously on the premises or elsewhere.

This time, however, his female companion overshadowed his previous dates; she captured everyone's attention by her charm and regal beauty. The pair exuded a perfect match to the observer. Fabriano couldn't help noticing people whispering and nudging each other as they walked in.

Once seated, Fabriano held and scanned the wine list, ending up proposing a bottle of Barolo La Serra. She concurred and seemed happy to be with a man who appreciated the joy of life. Fabriano asked the waiter to substitute the Burgundy wine glasses for larger Bordeaux bowl crystal glasses. Paula sifted through the extensive menu list and couldn't make up her mind.

Finally, she gave in, deciding to rely on the connoisseur who was facing her with glittering eyes. "I'll settle for whatever you're having," she said, as she set the menu aside, towards the edge of the dining table.

Fabriano ordered one lobster salad and one tuna tartare with mustard for starters and two filet carpaccio with truffle for the main dishes.

The wine breathed for a while and the waiter filled the two glasses, once Fabriano had tasted it and given his consent. They clinked the wineglasses together and took a long sip. Paula appreciated the rich intense ethereal bouquets and ruby-red colour. She followed her companion's recommendation to let the wine linger in her mouth for few seconds before gulping it. She found out he was right about that, and like a child experimenting and discovering the world around her, she giggled.

The waiter returned with the starters and immediately went through the ritual of pouring equal measures of lobster pieces and spoonfuls of tuna tartare in each plate. A sprinkle of freshly ground black pepper ensued. Paula pierced a chunk of lobster with her stainless steel fork and brought it close to her mouth for a tasting bite:

"Interesting dish," she commented. "The taste of ginger is exquisite. Now, tell me: I gather you're a doctor. A physician or a PhD holder?"

"Actually, I'm a cardiovascular surgeon working at San Raffaele Medical Centre. I've been practicing there for two years now."

"You're amazing," she replied, with a wicked wink. "I thought you were a clumsy businessman, playing Casanova or Don Juan without actually filling the role. Somehow I cannot imagine you with a scalpel." She picked up the knife and made a gesture of slashing the air with it. They both laughed. Fabriano liked her sense of humour and enjoyed being toyed with. It was an acknowledgement that Paula was accepting his presence and found him approachable. He appreciated her carefree attitude, which reminded him of his own personality. He was desperate to tease her back, but she seemed impermeable. He knew nothing about her and decided it was time to find out:

"How about you, bella? Spell it out! What do you do in life?"

"I used to be a model until I reached the age of 24. I guess my ample cleavage acted eventually against me. You know how they crave small breasts in that line of business. I guess I shouldn't complain. Over the span of five modelling years, I was able to save enough money to open a cosmetics boutique on Corso Vittorio Emanuele II. Business has been thriving. Four ladies assist me in the shop, and I enjoy spending my time there, giving advice to young and mid-age clientele, helping them select medical creams, suitable perfumes, so on and so forth…"

"Wow! No wonder you smell so nice and you have such a lovely complexion. As to the fashion industry, I pity them for preferring small breasts."

She chuckled and gave a fabulous wink. The main dishes, meanwhile, were being served.

They ravaged the food as soon as the waiter disappeared. The dishes were as exquisite and delicious as the starters. Throughout the meal, they learned more about each other. Paula had one sister and two brothers; Fabriano had a sister named Eva. Unlike Paula's parents, his own were not divorced, for which he was thankful, especially after learning how painful it had been on Paula to live through an indecisive period with dire consequences. Based on Paula's insistence to learn more about his family, he gave a concise description of his parents, praising them for their upbringing and unconditional love. He gave on the other hand, a detailed description of Eva: a tall good-looking brunette with so many admirers and yet she had abstained from marriage, like a priest who had taken a vow of celibacy. Nobody could decipher why. She was a devout Catholic and flaunted it, to the point of getting abrasive and aggressive towards people whom she knew.

Paula couldn't help noticing Fabriano's fondness and brotherly concern. According to him, Eva had no excuse to lead a lonely austere life and confine herself like a nun in a convent.

"What a contrast between the two of you!" exclaimed Paula. "I couldn't help wondering how you strayed through the cathedral without making the sign of the cross or even taking a moment to pray. Do you have an issue with that?"

"Certainly not," he replied. "I was born a Catholic and grew up very fond of my religion. Gradually, I started asking questions regarding certain inconsistencies between the two Testaments, while trying to correlate between science and theology. I guess, seeking such knowledge made me an agnostic. To top that, the various misconducts within the Catholic church, whether in my own country or across most continents, pulled me further away from clergy men, subsequently keeping me away from religious practices. The core of my resentment though, is the total silence of God vis-à-vis of miseries and wars."

"Few people consider me as an atheist but I'm not. It hurts me when Eva accuses me of straying from the herd. Whereas, being a medical surgeon has instilled in me a formidable admiration regarding the complexity of the human body, that no machine or invention can ever emulate. The laws of Physics, whether optical, acoustical, static, dynamic or otherwise, are all represented in one coherent entity communicating with a complex nervous system with the brain at its centre. As far as I'm concerned, DNA could be the universal language of God, bestowed on us to comprehend life mysteries as we evolve. As a knowledge seeker, I guess I'm an agnostic on the surface. I believe in the tremendous energy that the universe exudes, and I cannot deny the existence of God. I wish He could guide me. In the meantime, I try my best to be as moral as I can be. I decided therefore to lead a good and honourable life inasmuch possible. That's the purpose of Christianity and all religions, isn't it? Just being a good person is what counts."

Paula had been focusing intently on Fabriano's measured words. She had listened carefully and weighed each syllable. She was sympathetic to his concerns but viewed religion a bit differently. She was not after knowledge. She was content with what she had learned since childhood. She had to concur however with Fabriano that the church had been badly battered by many mishaps caused by its clergymen along with its dogma. Paula had also felt abandonment by God. Earth needed certainly more Godly intervention.

After finishing her dessert of lemon and green apple sorbets, Paula held Fabriano's hand while scanning his eyes. They were big brown expressive eyes denoting intelligence, passion and honesty. She had never faced a similar situation with any other man before. Four hours ago, Dr Fabriano did not exist and was not even a shred of her life. Why was she discussing personal matters with him? Why was she staring at his eyes, his handsome face? She had picked on him. Something she usually did with her ex-lovers: men she had dated for quite a long time. Paula suddenly realised that her left hand was gently caressing Fabriano's right thumb. She had to withdraw it before her date became aware that her hand had engulfed his for a few seconds. Her blushing betrayed her and her heartbeats were increasing in an ascending manner. She knew they had to leave the restaurant soon, but she wished she could linger some more and order a cappuccino perhaps. Her strayed mind lost its concentration until she felt a tingle spreading all over her left arm. Fabriano was gently rubbing her wrist while staring in admiration at the blue veins underneath her smooth skin. Only this time, the touching lingered and no one made any attempt to interrupt their first physical contact.

Ten minutes later, they rose to leave. It was the moment of truth for both of them. Was it the end or the beginning? They stood outside the restaurant waiting for the cab to pick Paula up and drive her back to her place. Fabriano had decided to take the underground as he craved some fresh air.

As he opened the car door for her, Fabriano held Paula by the waist and said: "I hate to say goodbye. I could have travelled with you, but I don't want to invade your space and embarrass you. I don't even know for certain how to behave. Thanks for a lovely evening. Hope we'll see each other again."

Afterwards, he drew his lips close to hers, but instead, aimed for her cheek, her chin, and her neck, planting emotional and compassionate kisses. He was basically tasting more than pecking her white perfumed skin. He wanted her, he craved for her, but it was too soon for that. Paula lifted his face and met him with her luscious pouting lips. The moistness and the softness were unimaginable. There was a tinge of strawberry lipstick scent, with a lingering red wine taste. A long embrace ensued, interrupted by an impatient taxi driver.

"Ciao," Paula said. "I enjoyed the night as well. By the way, I have plans to meet a recent acquaintance of mine tomorrow evening at the Aperitivo. He's a surgeon. You look like his twin. Would love seeing you there at seven?" She exclaimed, giggling, as she climbed into the cab.

Once settled, she rolled down the rear window on her side of the car, and hastily blurted out before the taxi sped off:

"I cannot resist a man wearing Creed Aventus. I have a weakness for the pineapple hint in its fragrance. Ciao!" She waved, then threw him a kiss. He responded by running two fingers on his lips and then tossing her back a kiss through the cool night air. Fabriano didn't move a bit until the taxi disappeared around the corner.

He had normally complained about the exorbitant price of his most favourite fragrance.

That night he was so grateful to Oliver Creed. He felt he should thank him.

# Chapter Four

The newly acquainted couple met each other on Sunday, the next day. It happened before evening time. Neither could wait for the concurred seven PM encounter at the Aperitivo. Fabriano did not hesitate to call Paula the moment he woke up. They had exchanged their mobile numbers the night before, prior to hailing a cab. To his delight, Paula sounded eager and happy to hear from him so soon.

Life continued and they saw each other every single weekday night and spent the weekends roaming through interesting parts of Milan. She had been to his place and he had visited hers. Four weeks had passed by, and their emotional relationship was gradually building up. They flirted, kissed and hugged, rubbed against each other, shared their daily burdens and feats, but sexual indulgence was not there yet. Despite her openness, Paula was a somewhat reserved and conservative person. Fabriano appreciated that, being of Middle Eastern extraction. He could understand the situation, but he was getting on the verge of insanity. He was desperate. He needed to feel her through and through.

It even crossed his mind to contact a female escort agency and satisfy his physical needs. After all, it had been more than six weeks since he had sex with a biomedical female engineer that he encountered at a medical equipment seminar. All his previous relationships were casual and short-lived, but he curbed his feelings and refrained establishing any rapport.

On the 36$^{th}$ day of their acquaintance, on a Sunday afternoon, Paula came over to Fabriano's residence after finishing a meal with her sister at a nearby bistro. Fabriano had just showered and just had time to put on his white bath robe to let her in. She stood by the door, staring at him with her green eyes. He checked whether his robe was decent and tightened the belt further. She crossed the threshold and closed the door behind her. She headed towards him, grabbed his belt and loosened it. The robe flew open revealing Fabriano's hairy chest and his semi-erect penis poking out of the garment. While kissing him avidly with her tongue probing his inner mouth, she took off his robe and threw it on the nearby couch. There he was stark naked in front of her. She touched and kissed reverently his abdomen, his biceps, his neck and stroked his male organ.

It was his turn to undress her. Her jacket, blouse, shoes and pants were hastily dispensed of. He admired her shapely body still clad in black bra and matching string panties. Paula removed her bra releasing nicely rounded tits with big pert inviting nipples sticking out of their sizeable areolas. That's how he fancied women: big nipples and natural breasts. He came closer and cupped her breasts, sensing their warmth and softness. He kissed them with tender emotion. Paula's nipples got harder. She flexed her body with every flick of his tongue and whenever his teeth got hold of her tingling nipples. Excitation was mounting and her tits developed goose bumps. She gave low appreciative moans.

Fabriano pulled down her string panties, released them from her ankles and knelt down, admiring her trimmed pubes that formed a triangular patch above her genitals. That's how he liked a woman: with trimmed light pubic hair and a barely noticeable fine hairline stretching to the navel. He rose, took Paula's hand and led her to the bedroom. He was in some sort of reverie. Was that really happening? Indeed, it was!

Before lying in bed, he realised what made Paula such a beautiful and sensual lady: her body frame was tall, more on the skinny than plump side, which highlighted and enhanced her prominent sexy features. He particularly liked her toned thighs, her firm round bottom, her slightly curved abdomen and voluptuous bosom. And her face was angelic with a hint of naughtiness. Her eyes were capable of speaking. Her brows were indicators for happiness or sadness. Her earlobes weren't in need of ornaments, and her hair: it was a soft cascaded crown of undulating strands.

Without uttering a word, as if in harmony, they lay down and explored each other with all their senses. Oral sex was not necessary for them to feel aroused. It was performed in a casual affectionate way with each partner discovering the private parts of the other; communicating with them rather than performing sex. An observer would have sworn they were worshipping each other.

The warmth of Paula's mouth around his glans was sensational. She was telling him in her own sensual way: your member belongs to me and none other. The foreskin stretching inwards and outwards, amused her. Most her ex-partners had been circumcised.

Fabriano probed her entire pubic region with passion and avidity. He tasted the nectar of her femininity. She flexed her body and pulled away few times when her excitement rose to the maximum and reached its climax. Her wetness became evident. She lay on her back and he penetrated her. He experienced an enjoyable sensation of heat and friction. Paula moaned and moved her body harmoniously to encounter every single stroke.

They made love for hours, tackling every imaginable position. It was not just sex though. For the first time in her life, Paula understood the meaning of making love. She gave herself totally to a man she had started to love. She meant every single sigh. There was no pretention, no egoistical pleasure. Fabriano realised too that the usual anxiety of pleasing his partner did not occur to him this time. He was acting on impulse and out of love and affection. They both knew that once those two elements were present, there was no need to prove anything or to fake one's performance.

They rolled over, quite content with their love session. Fabriano lifted himself slightly to his right side and stared at Paula for few seconds. Then he kissed her forehead while caressing her tousled hair. Their eyes locked for a moment. They parted their lips and simultaneously let out: "I love you."

Their relationship continued for six consecutive months. Love grew further and they were fond of each other; convinced that they were a match. They decided to get married.

Even though civil marriage was still denied and couldn't be performed in Lebanon, the authorities still recognised it. Marriage certificates issued abroad were accepted as legal documents. For convenience sake and to eradicate travel burden on elderly people on both sides of their families, they opted and planned for a civil marriage in Larnaca, Cyprus, which would be followed by a wedding reception at the groom's native village in the North of Lebanon.

The stone and red brick villa belonging to the Khoury family was constructed on a huge field overlooking the Valley of the Saints. Apple, cherries and hazelnut trees grew wildly all across the land. Fabriano requested and relied on his father to organise the ceremony in the man-made garden that surrounded the house.

According to their plans, the civil marriage was held on a Friday in Cyprus, and then the newlyweds flew to Lebanon on the same night, allowing them enough time to rest and attend the wedding ceremony scheduled for the next day.

Paula's parents had arrived in Lebanon 3 days earlier. Fabriano's father Michel acted as their tour guide, whisking them from one historic place to another. Being Italians, they were astonished by the Roman ruins and were further enchanted by the important role Berytus (Beirut) played within the Roman Empire, specifically in the domain of jurisprudence. With its law school, Berytus became known as the Mother of Laws. They were also impressed by the ancient ruins of Baalbeck, Sidon, Tyre and Byblos which reflected various civilisations, namely: Roman, Phoenician, Ottoman and European (of the Crusaders era). It was early November 2013 and the weather was mild and a gentle wind blew most of the time reminding everyone that cold weather was expected soon. That was a great opportunity for Michel to drive his visitors across the country, from the sandy seashores to the mountain ridges, North and East. Visitors were not embroiled in Lebanon's politics and civil strife. Touring Lebanon was a total bliss for them.

The wedding reception was properly organised by Michel, precisely as expected. Being a thorough person, he went through and addressed all the details, no matter how minute they might be. Two hundred guests spread across the huge garden, seated at round tables facing a makeshift stage, heavily lit with floodlights whose glare was only noticeable at certain awkward angles. Live music was performed by two bands, one playing western songs and the other specialising in oriental style music. Alcohol flowed like mad and cold dishes were set on each table, laid out by bow-tied waiters. Hot plates were to follow upon specific orders. The newlyweds spent much of their time chatting with the guests and taking pictures with the imposing mountains in the background. It was just after dusk and little bright dots started appearing haphazardly across the mountain range and deep down across the valley limits: scattered villages were greeting the sprawling night.

Paula was exceptionally happy. She liked what she had seen so far of Lebanon and local customs. She wondered where she was! There was a certain similarity with southern Italy. The country could pass for Greece as well. Villagers surprised the attendees with an unrehearsed folk dance "Dabkeh" reminding Paula of native Greek dancing witnessed on her latest trip to the Hellenic islands. The villagers and other invitees from far away regions were kind people, enthusiastic and dignified. Fabriano's parents were as expected, warm and easy to get along with. Despite their social and professional exposure, they were modest and down to earth. They accepted her the moment they laid eyes on her, and it was obvious that Fabriano meant a lot to them. They simply loved whomever he loved.

Michel snatched her from her groom and led her to the dancing floor. The band intoned Matt Monro's romantic song "The Music Played" which was appropriate for the moment. Michel was a good dancer, gracious in his moves. She only had to follow his steps. Michel could understand his son's infatuation with that woman.

Once they retracted, Paula caught a glimpse of Eva standing at the edge of the fenced cliff. She seemed to be peering at the void underneath her: the Valley of the Saints.

Paula watched and contemplated Eva thoroughly. She was baffled that such a gorgeous lady wasn't escorted by a male companion: one to dance with, someone to toast champagne with. She had gathered earlier from Fabriano that he had doubts whether she ever had sex with anyone. Something very difficult to believe, realising how gorgeous the lady was. Awkward situation for a woman in her late twenties. Paula hesitated to interrupt Eva's privacy, but decided to approach her and uttered:

"Fabulous valley. So mystic and enigmatic. No wonder monks who walked the rocky paths beneath, felt close to God and Heaven." Without glancing at Paula, Fabriano's sister murmured: "I wish Fabriano shared your view."

"He does in his own particular way. I'm sure. He never stops talking about the valley. It's inside his heart."

"How could it be? My brother is an atheist. He's a lost soul."

Paula trembled. She didn't quite expect such a response from a sister who was supposedly fond of her brother. "I believe you're being too harsh on him," retorted Paula with a high tone. "You're being too vindictive on a person who has devoted his life helping others while searching for God. He's not an atheist. He's looking at life in a grand scale. He accepts and respects one's belief, while conceding that he's confused himself: not knowing whether there will ever be a shred of hope that he might one day get an answer to his queries."

"I love my brother so much. I can see him drifting away and I'm scared for him. How can your marriage be blessed in the absence of a religious ceremony?"

Paula, who was becoming annoyed with her sister-in-law's misconstrued fanatism, responded back with bitterness: "Are you telling me that a soldier who got shot and buried in a desolate area without religious rites is bound to be doomed? You can't be serious! That's atrocious."

"That's the problem with you people. You always find answers and excuses for your religious drift. I fear for Fabriano."

"Well. Don't be."

With that said, Paula joined her husband and tried her best to forget about the incident altogether. After all, it was their night and they were going to enjoy it.

In the distance, the faint sound of church bells echoed through the foggy valley, carried by the light southern wind that made window curtains ruffle and tree leaves rustle. Despite the wonderful occasion, Paula was sleepless that night, unable to toss aside the unusual conversation that she held with Eva. The woman was sheer trouble. Paula loathed her unpredictable character, but her love for her husband prevailed: she had to yield and give Eva a break.

The newlyweds spent four days in Lebanon, huddled in a spacious suite at a renowned mountain resort within half hour reach from Beirut. They seldom slept, trying to make the most out of this special time. For a visitor, unaware of local political disputes, Lebanon was a piece of heaven: the ever-changing sceneries with their diversified nuance of colours, the great food, the top-notch nightclubbing and above all, the sociable people with good hearts doing their best to please.

Early morning on the fifth day, a taxi picked them up and gave them a ride to the airport. They flew to the United Kingdom for the remaining seven days of their honeymoon.

They arrived at London Heathrow around eleven-thirty AM local time and by one-thirty pm they reached their hotel which faced Hyde Park. It was the groom's first trip to Great Britain. Paula had frantically been there few times before, on assignment during her modelling career.

There were many things to see and do. Fabriano was a theatre lover, he was looking forward to the plays he had booked for in advance. Late dinners afterwards complemented the fun. London lived up to its reputation of having the best Chinese and Italian restaurants. Paula was captivated by the narrow streets and mews that harboured small but elegant retail shops. Those alleys seemed to extend in a star formation, emanating from roundabouts and squares that formed the nucleus of the whole ensemble.

One could not miss the traditional pubs, serving ales, stouts and English bitter. Those were spread all over, sprawling across every neighbourhood. Paula and Fabriano learned for the first time that regular beer was called "Lager," while the word "Beer" was reserved for English brew.

To their astonishment, the quality of pub food was noticeable. The best fish and chips, shepherd's pies and sausages were available and couldn't be missed. The ambience was laid back and social. Patrons mingled mainly by the counter, discussing abusive managers at work, economy, movies or just exchanged tips to solve their crosswords. Fabriano thanked Paula for being Italian through and through. After all, the Romans were the pioneers who introduced taverns during their reign over Great Britain.

Two days were dedicated to roam the southern areas of England: Cornwall, Devon, Bournemouth and Brighton. Fabriano couldn't help admiring the lush greenery mixing with the blue colour of the English Channel. Occasionally, flocks of sheep were seen grazing in the slightly hilly meadows where oak and hazel trees grew.

The trip was drawing to its end and the loving couple wished they could stay longer. They would have liked to visit Stonehenge and Edinburgh but that required at least three to four days extension. Fabriano had to be back in Milan. Duty called.

A brief celebration was planned by Andrea and his wife Carla on the next day of their arrival. A bistro was reserved to accommodate their close colleagues from work along with Fabriano's grandma, who had been unable to attend the wedding ceremony in Lebanon. Fabriano appreciated Andrea's genuine friendship. Since acquaintance, they had become buddies, sharing their worries and medical opinions. They ended up being like brothers.

Life resumed as usual. The same work routine with a quicker pace this time. Over the span of almost two weeks, a lot needed to be done. Absorbed heavily in his medical career, Fabriano counted on Paula to search for a larger apartment, relying on her better grasp of Milan's geography and real estate affairs. Above all, she was a sturdy businesslike woman who could bargain her way through a world filled with sharks.

Paula tried her best to secure a suitable three-bedroom flat in the Moscova Corso Como neighbourhood just before Christmas and struck a good deal with the agency. The premises were large and exposed to direct sunlight. Parco Sempione was close by and could be seen from the living room side. According to the real estate agency and as per the list of the building residents displayed on the intercom panel, they should get along fine with their neighbours.

Assisted by her mother and sister, Paula handled the furnishing and decoration in all its aspects, placing orders, deciding what to retrieve from her existing studio and Fabriano's one-bedroom apartment. She would show her selection to her husband, who seemed to acquiesce without even listening to the details. The moment he returned home, his whole interest and obsession had been to be with her: to order take away and dine together in front of the television set, kiss her, smell her and make love to her. He kept saying, "I trust your choice. You're crafty with a good taste. Don't forget you chose me as your husband!"

She would reply back in an amused way, "True. You got me drunk and stole my heart. I married a crazy person."

Finally, by the end of January 2014, they moved into the new apartment over a sunny weekend and settled happily. Fabriano held his breath once he set eyes on the furniture, the living and dining rooms wallpaper, the contrast paint of the bedrooms, luxury sanitary fittings, parquet flooring, kitchen counters and fitted-in equipment, paintings. He was full of joy and he loved the place. He expressed his thanks to Paula and embraced her.

"Wait until the bank statement reaches you, honey," she said coyly. And they laughed. Three weeks later, Paula found out she was pregnant. Fabriano was in seventh heaven. And so was she.

# Chapter Five

Luigi was born in November 2014. A healthy baby who made his parents treasure the meaning of life. His presence added happiness to their household. There was a vivid purpose to come back home to: a thrill to watch the little creature growing beautiful by the day. He took after both parents, but more so on his mother's side. Fabriano feared for his fragility. He would ask Paula to heave Luigi off his crib and deposit him gently in his own arms. He would lift him up and watch his relatively big head swaying and then resting on his shoulder. What a sensation! Fabriano would either plant an affectionate kiss on the top of the little head or the tender tiny arms. He always tried to avoid having contact with the baby's cheeks, fearing to graze the soft skin with his shadowy one-day old beard.

Fabriano went mad with excitement whenever he watched Luigi staring at him with his big coloured eyes while emitting gurgling sounds. "Look at him talking to me!" He would exclaim to his wife.

As if to drive his father's exaltation to the extreme, the little baby would probe Fabriano's face with his tiny fingers, using them as pincers, clawing Dad's cheeks harmlessly, trying to attract further attention from an elated man.

Despite few sleepless nights, both parents never complained about their son's cries and periodic uneasiness. They took turn helping each other out, attending to Luigi's needs without a complaint. It was total bliss. Genuine family love reigned everywhere.

In the fourth month, Luigi started babbling and his parents went ecstatic. "He'll be talking soon," they would say to each other.

It was on an exceptionally rainy winter day that an international call from Eva transformed the happy mood into a perturbed ambience. Unlike her previous bi-weekly courtesy calls, in which she enquired mainly about the infant, she brought up this time the subject of baptism and its importance as a Christian rite. The fact she was interfering in their lives was annoying. Fabriano could read well through his sister's mind: she certainly considered him as an obstacle and a dormant threat to Luigi's upbringing. Eva had no more faith in him; she judged that he was out of the Christian league. Paula was dismayed by her sister-in-law's effort to impinge on their private life, but tried her best to conceal it from her husband. She didn't want to incite feud and misunderstanding between family members. Paula was longing for Luigi to get baptized the soonest possible, but she couldn't tolerate being pushed and told what to do. So, she waited for few weeks before she brought the subject up with her husband. As she had expected, Fabriano gave his immediate consent, wholeheartedly, without flinching.

"Sure, honey," he told her. "Baptism symbolises purification and admission to the Christian faith. My sister thinks I'm an atheist. No matter what she thinks of me, who am I to deny baptism to my child and why would I do that? As parents, our role is to lay forth the right path for our children. I have no doubt that the Christian faith, regardless whether few issues require addressing and clarification, or are misunderstood by us humans because of our limited capacity to grasp something beyond our comprehension, remains the right course to follow."

"Parents are not supposed to impose on their children their own views. Our role is to guide. So far humanity hasn't found a replacement to heavenly religions. Our duty therefore is to instil faith in our children until they grow up and reach adulthood. Only then would they be able to make up their own minds and raise their own queries."

Paula fought a few tears in her eyes. In front of her stood, a husband, a friend, a father, an honest man devoid of hatred and deviousness. Just a sophisticated person with a heart of gold.

An individual in search of sincere replies to his worldly observations on poverty, looming injustice, and heedless human annihilation waged in the name of winning wars. Atrocities such as nuclear bombs dropped on Hiroshima and Nagasaki. And yet, God remained silent, even when the Nagasaki device was detonated 600m above the Catholic sector of the city, which was the heart of Catholicism in Japan since the 16th century. Whether by mere coincidence or otherwise, a once devout Christian wondered about the reasons that caused the Americans to carry out such a specific strike. Did they deliberately hit the Christian sector so that it wouldn't be called a discriminate act? Were they seeking a mitigated rebuke? Making it look as if their deed were directed at a foe, regardless whether he belonged to Shintoism, Buddhism or Christianity? By whose right could they act in such a ruthless way?

A planned attack on civilians with pre-knowledge of damage extent should not be condoned or allowed, neither by God nor by the concerned governments. Fabriano was convinced that it was the greatest criminal act in recorded history, perpetrated by a big Christian power determined to decide the fate of other fellow humans. It seemed that the killing of a believer by the hands of another believer had a lesser moral impact that found acceptance in the human mind. Worldwide events clearly demonstrated that the worst atrocities ever committed were the result of conflicts among identical religious sects.

Luigi was baptized few days later, Back in Lebanon, Eva combed through the various pics and watched the short video that was sent to her by Fabriano. She felt proud of herself. None of that would have happened were it not because of her persistence and intervention. There was a hidden bitterness though inside her being. Her brother should have invited her to attend the baptism. Most probably he had wanted to, but his wife must have resisted the idea. *Foreign wives were unpredictable and bossy,* she thought.

Luigi grew up in the love and care of his diligent parents. At home, besides the Italian language, the Khoury family uttered few Arabic and English words. The parents realised the importance of languages in their child's formation, particularly at the early stages when his vivid imagination and learning curve were at their highest. Finishing two years in preschool activities, Luigi was admitted to a renowned Jesuit-Catholic school at the age of five.

Paula had picked that institution based on its discipline, the credibility of its educational staff, the teaching of foreign languages and its relative proximity to home. Luigi resented waking up early with dawn barely breaking in, but he showed contentment once he was all dressed up, rearing to board the school bus at eight in the morning. Paula would accompany him downstairs ensuring he wouldn't be late. He looked cute in his school uniform. It gave him a certain grace. By four-thirty pm, he would return home, to be greeted by his mum and the Spanish au-pair Julia who had joined them recently. Both attended to him, ensuring his homework was completed and his dinner taken. He was allowed one hour to watch television or just lie about on the thick beige carpet fiddling with his toys. Luigi would wait for his dad to get home between seven and eight, wrestle with him on the Persian rug by the fireplace and pin him down for a victorious submission.

Just before going to bed and being tucked in by Paula, Luigi would call upon his father to lie down with him on the bed and read him a story. Few times, he would enquire about God. He was full of questions. How did he look? Like a huge white bearded old man floating on a white cloud surrounded by winged angels? Luigi asked questions about Jesus and the Virgin Mary.

Fabriano was reliving a phase of his earlier life and saw himself in his kid. Only this time, he had to be careful. He had to ensure his son was getting the same replies as those given to him by his mentors at school. Hence, Fabriano would first, sift through Luigi's junior religious illustration books, refraining to release any answer that might contradict his son's preconceived faith and confuse his perception or even his prejudices. *Too young, too early,* he thought.

The new family made it a point to visit Lebanon once a year. It was a relaxing retreat to detach oneself from work stress and spend some time with the parents whose age had started to impede and restrict their mobility.

Eva looked fabulous, as usual. She devoted most of her time driving Luigi from one convent to another, crossing the Lebanese mountains and valleys from the North to the South. Eventually, those convents were in beautiful areas with breathtaking panoramic views stretching as far as the eye could see. Luigi enjoyed those trips tremendously.

"Aunt Eva is wonderful!" He would exclaim once they were back.

Luigi's excitement grew when Eva suggested that they should all get down the steep footpaths leading to the monasteries lying at the bottom of the Valley of the Saints. Paula and Fabriano put on their sports shoes and joined the party. It had been ages, probably three decades since Fabriano last scoured the valley. So, the four of them carefully marched down the rocky and shrubby cliffs, admiring the caves and waterfalls, until they reached low grounds where trees grew dense and herds consisting of white and black goats feasted on weeds and tree leaves. Old monasteries were built amid the fields. Knots of visitors could be seen in their vicinities. They were successful taking few pictures with a Polish monk who inhabited the valley several decades earlier, secluding himself from the world, dedicating his time to prayers and feeding himself from whatever vegetables and fruits that he cultivated.

That visit had a great impact on Luigi. Whenever he felt tired, someone would attempt to lift him up to shoulder level and let him rest each knee on the blade, while clasping hands for support. He enjoyed the attention he was getting and the extended field of view that he could muster from the elevated position.

Fabriano felt rejuvenated, recalling the old days and the time she had spent with his schoolmates in that mountainous region. He wondered what has become of them. Paula was fascinated by the unfolding scenery. The mystic sensation she was getting surpassed her expectations. And Eva was pleased with herself. She was asserting herself, becoming the good aunt that all kids would like to have and depend on. She had forged her way into her nephew's life and succeeded in making an impact.

On that particular evening, once they were back in the village house and resting after hot showers, Eva crammed herself beside Luigi as he lay in bed and asked him to pray loudly with her. He emulated the signs and the syllables she articulated, uttering Arabic words that he didn't comprehend but knew for certain that he was reciting prayers. Few words were familiar to him and he understood their meaning. He had heard them spoken by his father. Time to prove to his dad that he was worthy of his merit. Again and again he recited the prayers with his aunt. Eva stroked his face as he memorised the words. Her eyes gleamed with the reflected light inside the bedroom. She had registered another success.

The vacation days wore off. It was time to return to Milan.

Luigi waved his hand outside the cab window before they departed.

"Promise to come and see me!" He shouted at his aunt.

Eva threw him a kiss and said in a loud voice: "I promise I'll be there soon."

# Chapter Six

Fabriano was doing extremely well and prospering rapidly. After nine years of relentless work, he oversaw the cardiovascular department at the medical centre. Over the weekends, he would book a suite and bring along his family for a two-day stay at Lake Como. For an extended stay of one week or more, Fabriano would rent lavish short term villas with panoramic views.

They would drive on Friday evening to the resort town of Bellagio and reach the place by eight pm. Early enough to enjoy the dusky breathtaking views from the patios: a nuance of fading warm colours embracing the sunset and the rising heavenly stars.

In daytime, one could trace the three slender branches of the lake merging into Bellagio. Incredible scenic views of the Alps' foothills that flanked the lake, with a blend of 18th century structures and modern villas that were strewn across the green mounds of surrounding hills.

The family found peace and serenity at Bellagio. Fabriano could spend his lifetime admiring those majestic perspectives unfolding in front of him. He would reminisce about his native mountains and seashore. At night, he would gaze at the clear dark skies with their twinkling faint stars beckoning to the observer. He took heed of the expanding vast universe that had no limits and no defined boundaries. Back home in his own village, he used to be able to discern constellations with his naked eyes: municipality lighting was non-existent in those days: it did not spoil the glittered domed dark canvas up above. Luigi would sit next to his parents or rest himself on their laps, asking while pointing at a relatively shiny celestial body: "Look Mummy, look Daddy! That's a big star!" Fabriano would laugh and patiently describe in details, the difference between a star's inherent visible light emanating from within, and a planet's surface reflecting the sun's light. Gradually, Luigi grasped the concept and with the assistance from illustrated astronomy magazines, became more knowledgeable and certainly more inquisitive. The boy was fascinated by the planets and their orbiting moons. Were those planets inhabited? Had Jesus been there? Why so many galaxies and stars? Paula seldom replied, relying on her well educated and cultured husband to reply back. He had been there before and had raised similar queries during his childhood. His concerns however, remained unanswered still.

Fabriano's issue with God was never raised in front of his son. On the contrary, he assumed the role of a staunch clergyman with a slight scientific twitch. Careful not to bias his son's thinking, he would leave tricky questions to the catechism teacher, encouraging Luigi to seek such information from people who oversaw his upbringing at school. His kid should discover the world far from any imposition. The latter is much more tolerated if inflicted by a Jesuit school rather than a parent.

Luigi was eight years old when he convinced his parents to get him a pet. He was yearning for a gold retriever. His parents fought the idea for a few weeks but then concurred. The Khoury family grew fond of the pet, arguing who would walk the dog, what sort of food it should eat. On the other hand, the confined and restricted space within the apartment curtailed the pet's activity. It dawned on them that it was time to move out of the city and acquire a house in the countryside. Paula proposed to maintain the Milan apartment for the weekdays and encouraged Fabriano to purchase a detached villa in Bellagio. Doing so, they would spare the excruciating rental expenses that they incurred during the weekends and holiday seasons. Milou, the golden retriever, would also have ample space and enough time to play outdoors in the private garden.

Fabriano gave his consent. Assisted by real estate agents, he searched high and low for the ideal residence. He narrowed down the search, focusing on Villa Melzi Gardens area. Paula took over the final hunt and soon afterwards, they bought the house of their dreams.

They would often take the ferry and enjoy the scenery around the 146 km2 lake, stopping at small towns and villages. On a few occasions, trips to Lugano, Switzerland were undertaken. On long holidays, the Khoury family would drive all the way to Geneva, passing by Montreux, Lausanne and the Diablerets ski resort.

All were happy and satisfied. Fabriano found his own self amid nature: a landscape somewhat similar to his native Lebanon. Paula was enjoying her life with a devoted husband and an eager little boy who brought a different meaning to their lives. Luigi was content and undemanding. He was grateful to have such loving and caring parents.

In the meantime, back in Lebanon, Eva was furious. She thought her brother was wasting his wealth on trivial matters, spending money left, right and centre, while he could be contributing in the financing of local church renovation works. He shouldn't have married a liberal and self-centred foreign woman. Fabriano was losing it; he was slipping further away.

In line with Jesuit school teachings, Luigi would insist that his parents took him to church every Sunday. Far from depriving him of such a wish, they made it a point to attend mass at the Basilica di San Giacomo. They were always there at ten am sharp. They would sit at the back pews in order to catch the panoramic view of the altar with the curved apse, the arches, mosaics and artful high ceiling.

Paula and Luigi prayed silently and every now and then, joined the rest of the worshippers, chanting hymns whose lyrics were printed within thin booklets deposited on the long bench seats.

Fabriano never sat or stood. Instead he would get down on the kneelers and raise his head towards the ornated ceiling and become transfixed as if in a trance. His lips would move silently as if he were whispering. Had someone heard him, they would have picked up the following words:

"Jesus! I'm really torn apart. Here I am kneeling before you out of love and respect. I have never ceased to believe in you. My faith in you is still running through my veins, through the marrow of my bones. I admit, my faith wavers at times, but it does so because of my endless search for you. It's about time you came back to salvage what we humans have inflicted upon each other since your coming 2,000 years ago. My problem is with your silence. You've been silent for too long. The world needs you. Please come back. Like me, millions of people have reached a deadlock. Faith requires continuity to become more assertive. I do realise that faith ought to be unconditional and undisputable, but after all, you know quite well that we are mere weaklings who need periodic pampering. We need to gain assurance that we're being taken good care of."

"Forgive me, Jesus, for my bluntness, but I take you as a brother and as a friend. There are no frontiers, no boundaries between us. It is true that I don't pray often, and I don't fast anymore. It is true that my belief is wavering, but nevertheless, my daily life is spent according to your teachings and principles. Do you find me really straying? Believe me, I don't mean to, but you've got to help me and to help many of us, who are caught in the middle of uncertainty. We are incapable of tallying between religion and science, unable to pretend life is moving along smoothly. Everything around us is full of misery, deviousness and atrocities."

"I beg your pardon for being so direct. The fact that I'm here talking to you makes me feel happy. I find myself relaxed and close to a great Father. I'm not an atheist. I'm an abandoned human searching for knowledge and compassion."

"I wish I had lived in your era. I would have asked you to take me on board and have me as one of your disciples. I could have touched you. I would have listened to your sermons and watched the miracles unfolding in front of my eyes. The fact you were the Son of God in a human form made you tangible and vulnerable. People loved you. They valued your deity, compassion, wisdom and fairness. No wonder you captured the hearts of friends and foes alike. Your resurrection was the culmination of it all. What happened during the past 2,000 years?"

"Have you changed your mind about us? Do you find us appalling and unworthy of your unconditional love? Are you no longer willing to listen to our pleas? All I'm asking you, Jesus, is to return to us and save our souls. You did it 2,000 years ago while prevailing conditions on Earth were much better than the current ones. Is that too much to ask for? Should you want to, you could prevent atrocities by direct heavenly intervention."

Fabriano would only come out of his trance after receiving a nudge on the shoulder by his wife. One hour would elapse. Paula had always been keen on knowing what her husband uttered while in church, but he would never say. She would smile though, realising that beyond the surgeon was a mystic guy in search of answers. Even though mysticism could be attained through blind self-surrender or contemplation, her husband had chosen the second path.

Paula appreciated Fabriano's non-interference with his son's conception of religion as taught to him at school. Luigi had no knowledge whatsoever that his dad was in constant search for a permissive and ever omnipresent God.

# Chapter Seven

Few months later, Milou had to be put down by the veterinarian. Pancreatic cancer was the cause. Luigi and his parents were saddened. He was missed heavily. The event reminded them how fragile living creatures were. Luigi was concerned about the whereabouts of Milou. It was his first immediate encounter with death and the loss of a dear presence. Where do all creatures go after they die?

Fabriano found it difficult to explain and had to improvise somewhat. He told his kid that God's heaven was reserved for humans as they were created in his image; however God was merciful and made exemptions for good behaving pets. Thus, Luigi's anxiety appeased a little. It was not a solemn assurance that he would reunite with Milou one day. But the fact that there was a possibility to see him again, no matter how slim that chance might be, provided him with the needed satisfaction to continue further on.

One spring evening, Fabriano came home from an exhausting day at work, and found his wife dismayed, brandishing a letter in her hands: a brief note from Luigi's school requesting their presence. The meeting was set for nine AM the next day, in the principal's office. Nothing else was stated. No reason was given for the summon. Both parents refrained to open the subject with their son even though he was the bearer of the letter. As if to soothe their worry, Luigi assured them he was doing well in all his studies and that he had no row or dispute with any other pupil.

Instead of easing the tension, the ambience became more dramatic as the parents braced themselves for a major breach of conduct.

The next morning, Luigi accompanied his parents to school, riding in his dad's car. He was excited taking a different and faster route than the usual bus ride routine. They arrived in Father Giovanni's office five minutes earlier than scheduled. They were greeted with a smile by the assistant and with a stiff officious handshake by the principal. Luigi's audience was not apparently necessary, as he was dismissed and sent to his classroom. They were ushered in and shown a leather couch facing the principal's oak desk. He sat in his opulent swivelling chair, trying to appear majestic and domineering. In fact, as if contrived, the couch was much lower than the principal's elevated desk, giving the impression that one was sunken and being looked down at.

Despite his weight, Father Giovanni assumed a straight posture and spoke with a high tone: "You might be wondering why you're here, but I can assure you that had it not been for a serious matter, we wouldn't have bothered you and taken any of your time." With that, he ceased talking as if assessing the impact of his words on those present.

Paula shrank further in the already low couch. Fabriano could feel his heart pounding heavily, almost trying to exit his chest.

"Can you tell us please what it's all about?" Paula exclaimed.

"Your son has shown, since joining our school, an inquisitive streak regarding religion. He would interrupt his catechism teacher, asking for clarifications, picking on certain ambiguities in the texts. The situation was controllable to a certain extent, until yesterday."

Fabriano was getting more and more irritated by the moment. "Can you tell us what happened yesterday?"

"During the teaching session, a bee infiltrated the room through the open window and was humming noisily on the glass pane. Annoyed, the teacher Juliano smashed it against the glass with a book that he was holding. Your son stood up and shouted at him, asking him how he could do that? Killing a harmless insect. The teacher compared that to the killing of animals for food. Your son complained that nobody was going to eat the bee. Hence, it died for no reason."

"Far from reproaching Luigi for raising his voice and objecting, the teacher controlled himself and was patient enough to explain the difference between humans and other living creatures. The teacher made it clear that humans had supremacy and that animals and insects do not have souls like us. Luigi went totally mad and retorted back at his teacher. Your son went even further, mentioning in front of other pupils that his dog Milou was in heaven and that God had mercy for all living creatures."

"That was inexcusable and unacceptable. We strongly recommend that Luigi refrains from such outbursts and stick to what we teach him, unconditionally. He's a bright kid, but he has to understand there's a limit to everything."

Fabriano felt his earlobes pulsating. He stood up and offered his hand to Paula as a support to lift herself up from the sunken sofa. He said in a clear voice: "Father Giovanni. I believe this meeting is over. Thanks for confirming my previous and present worries. Rather than saving souls and encouraging people to understand what they read and hear, you of all people should show flexibility and tolerance. Would Jesus Christ tell a young boy what you have just said? Can you support your claim that living creatures are banned from eternity? All you have to back your statement is that humans were created in God's image and have souls."

"Animals have no souls—" Father Giovanni retorted, before getting interrupted by Mr Khoury.

"But how could you be so emphatic when no specific reference has ever been made regarding the eternal whereabouts of non-human living creatures? A veterinarian attends to animals in order to save their lives so they do not perish. Why do we bother to treat them and cure their illnesses? We might as well forfeit the whole thing and do nothing about it. Don't they merit to survive death? Shouldn't there be another level of afterlife for other living creatures?"

"What is Heaven without the roar of a river, the sight of birds flapping their wings while soaring through its blue skies? It's about time people's apprehension is attended to. Your role is to explain, clarify and dwell on vague issues, by assisting people to digest and grasp Bible verses rather than just reciting them."

"The Bible is our reference and has to be adhered to, without questioning," the principal said.

"Expressing doubt and raising objections are true assets, when they are put forth in a decent manner," Fabriano continued. "When their purpose is to serve the comprehension of certain matters, then they should be accepted as tools for better learning. There's a big difference when objections have for essence the aim of criticising or refuting ideologies for the sake of deviousness. Being inquisitive must be a gift from God. Supposedly our skills emanate from Him. Our brain cells function because He endowed us with their complexity. Had we refrained from seeking answers to specific scientific queries we wouldn't have achieved the current technological advancement. So please spare us from such lectures."

"Our son will leave your school when this term ends. Meanwhile, I expect that those incidents will be forgotten altogether and that we'll proceed on new footings. Luigi will be asked to restrain and hold back his inquisitive streak.

From your side, I beg for your patience for another two months, until the term is over."

Father Giovanni looked stupefied and concentrated on the lulling soft patter of the raindrops squashing against the glass windows. Words escaped him. A nervous twitch spasmed his left cheek. In a thin reedy voice, he said: "I'm sorry you feel this way. I'm sure this misunderstanding will heal with time. Luigi is welcome in our school."

Paula interjected: "Don't count on it."

Back in Lebanon, Eva cursed under her breath. She called her brother several times, urging him to go back on his decision, but he paid no attention to her pleas, stating at each occasion that his decision was irreversible; that he couldn't bear double standards. Eva turned to Paula to convince him otherwise, but even that approach failed. Eva couldn't recognise her brother. He had changed a lot since he got married to that witch. It was up to her to salvage the situation. She would go to the village church and pray for Fabriano's salvation. She would light a candle, kneel on the cold marble floor, make the sign of the cross in a frenzy rhythmic manner.

The religious ritual would be followed by another recreational ritual. Evening time, she would drive down to the coastline, straight to the nearest sea resort where her parents had rented a 2-bedroom chalet. Not that she cared about the seashore. Eva needed to forget the worries that she was immersed in. Few cocktail drinks at the bar would cheer her up. She would recall her latest encounter with a married man in his early forties. It turned out to be a wild sexual experience. It was a thrill dating married men. The mere idea that they might abandon their wives for her sake was so gratifying. She would feel like a conqueror. Eva loved to inflict collateral damage in her brief but intense relationships. She mastered the art of intentionally leaving love bites on a man's neck and shoulders. Those bites were not just the reflection of her prowess and torrent love affairs; they offered enough vivid evidence that led to marriage annulment. It wasn't a big deal for her. One Our Father Who Art In Heaven and one Hail Mary would suffice to cleanse her sins. She prayed a lot and that mattered to the Almighty. God would forgive her naughty behaviour.

That was the essence of Christianity: repent for your sins!

In September on that same year, Luigi was transferred to the British School of Milan. His parents tried their best to compensate for their son's detachment from his old schoolmates, ensuring they met each other over weekends and whenever possible. Both parents succeeded in ensuring Luigi a smooth transition. With no time, he overcame his apprehension and ended up having new acquaintances, in addition to his previous buddies. Though still very young, Luigi did notice a tangible difference between his old and new mates. While the former were reserved, respectful and mundane, the latter displayed more self-confidence and asserted themselves as being more liberal in expressing their views. He was caught in the middle of two separate worlds, each with its own goodness and drawbacks.

As months passed by, Luigi had established his own old buddies proved to be more disciplined, but kind of boring to hang around with. They had a serious approach towards everything. New mates on the other hand, were more fun to be with. In their company, time elapsed discussing light topics and playing games that had more variety and spice. Despite his youth, Luigi understood that he had to extract the best attributes out of each clan, mix them together and face the world accordingly.

He maintained his exposure to religion therefore, through his old buddies and the parental tutoring at home. Paula purchased most available DVD's at electronic stores and bookshops, depicting Old and New Testaments. Luigi wanted to know the exact time Adam and Eve were created. Was the flood necessary? What if Abraham had slaughtered his son Isaac just seconds before the ram appeared before him? Replies to his numerous queries were often made furtively by Paula who often saw her son as a vivid replica of his father. There had to be an explanation to everything: failing that, her son would bring back the same subject again and again relentlessly. Often Paula would resort to Fabriano for support. Using his intellect and crafty argumentative approach, he would answer the question with another question: "Would you or wouldn't you punish someone for challenging and disobeying you? Would you or wouldn't you test someone's allegiance to you?"

Such an approach worked most of the time, but marginally failed to convince Luigi on few occasions. Nevertheless, his respect and reverence for his dad, made him rest the matter, skipping to another subject that might be thoroughly and easily explained. Wishing his son wouldn't get entrapped in unexplained anomalies, Fabriano urged his wife to focus on the New Testament, where the reader felt much more at ease comprehending the Christian values and the meaning of salvation. Luigi was content with that. Evidently, he was able to grasp the love and warmth as depicted in the Holy Book. He could imagine the handsome face of Jesus Christ, his soft smile and clever eyes. How He performed miracles and raised the dead. He could picture the beautiful features of the Virgin Mary, her purity and kindness. Jesus was a hero. A strong man who could have fought back if he had wanted to. The Son of God who could annihilate all foes with his gaze, without even resorting to physical force. Luigi also liked the twelve disciples. He wished he had lived in that era. He would have become one. Maybe he could have used his sword to save Jesus.

# Chapter Eight

Days and weeks passed by. Observing blood traces in his stool and an unusual severe constipation, Fabriano subjected himself to medical tests and colonoscopy, which confirmed his suspicion of colon cancer. Under normal circumstances, the news would have been annoying but nobody envisaged that they could be so disturbing. Finding out that one had terminal cancer at an advanced stage was debilitating. It was sudden, without any warning signs. The cancer had been spreading asymptomatically, revealing itself at a very critical and advanced state.

Being a pragmatic person, and believing in grabbing any proffered opportunity that might extend his survival rate, Fabriano gave his immediate consent to a surgical intervention. It was followed by sessions of adjuvant chemotherapy. Unfortunately, during a brief period of few months, the malignancy proved to be of the galloping type, spreading fast to other tissues and the rest of the body.

The family was distraught. Paula lived in total denial, expecting some form of gradual recovery. Luigi prayed for his dad, begging Jesus for a miracle. The latter never occurred.

Dr Andrea stood by his friend and his family. He went as far as researching what could be done under the circumstances: seek medical advice elsewhere? Try unconventional methods of treatment? Ironically, it was Fabriano who calmed down everyone's anxiety, accepting his fate as it unfolded.

In the end, loathing a senseless life in a clinical environment, Fabriano convinced his colleagues and principally Paula, that he had to die at home. He uttered those words: "Paula, my love. I do understand your concern and how much you care for me, but I'd rather be home with you and Luigi. I want my dignity back. I want you guys to remember me as I used to be, not as a rotten vegetable. I prefer lying in my bed, staring through the windows at the night stars, at the moon and the distant mountains. I want to say: I love you, in a romantic way, not amid the beeping of electronic gadgets that monitor my heart and respiration rates. I need to feel the pillow that you rest your head on, kiss it and smell your hair shampoo. Who knows? Maybe I'll be able to make love to you, although that would be a miracle. It's funny Paula. I'm not afraid at all. I'm just pissed off that I wouldn't be spending more time with you and the little inquisitive bear. By the way, I have asked Eva to come over and assist you."

Fabriano passed away in December 2024, just one month after leaving hospital and saying those final words.

# Part Two

# Chapter One

Fulfilling Fabriano's wishes, Paula arranged that his burial took place in his native village. It was a nippy breezy afternoon with snowfall expected at late hours. A heavy storm was building up. Weather conditions accentuated the sombreness of the situation. One would have expected a shy turn up. The scene contradicted all expectations. The village, the surrounding hamlets, towns and cities were represented by hundreds of people, swarming in from all directions, to pay respect to the good Samaritan. Also attending, were friends and fellow physicians who crossed the oceans just to be there and pay their respect, regardless the enormous travel distances. Apart from Andrea and a handful of doctors, Paula couldn't recognise a familiar face among so many.

Mourners filled the church, its square and all roads that led to it. The traffic police force had to deploy its units at all bifurcations and intersections. Still, roads were blocked most of the time because of the narrow streets and alleys. Yet, nobody complained, resigning themselves to the seriousness of the occasion.

Michel and his wife Sophia were devastated. It was so difficult for them to outlive their beloved son. There was a certain unfairness in all that. There they were inside the church, hearing but not listening to a knot of bishops delivering sermons and praising the deceased for his great achievements in the medical field, not to mention being a good husband and caring father.

Paula could grasp few words of the sermons. Having attended few masses in local churches and considering the repetitive contents of religious discourses, she was capable of partially deducing what was being said. Luigi sat next to her with watery eyes and traces of dried and wet tears on his cheeks. She held his hand and refrained from sobbing for fear of further aggravating her son's grief. She had to support her son by showing him how to be strong. It was her role to do that. Collapsing and surrendering to grief wouldn't bring Fabriano back, nor would he condone it. She felt so sad and devastated inside. Her stomach burned, her heart palpitated and missed few beats; her right eye twitched and her hands were dead cold. How could she continue without him and beat that hollow emptiness? She had to fight back just for the sake of Luigi. He was such a little copy of Fabriano.

Eva flanked Luigi on the other side. She wept quietly while praying fervently, asking God to forgive her strayed brother and grant him, through purification in the purgatory, the chance to redeem his sins. Could he be in hell? Hell was too much for her to contemplate. In any case, God was the judge for that. Where Fabriano might end up, would be God's will.

Condolences were held for three consecutive days. People offered their sympathies to the Khoury families who were stupefied to learn from a great number of villagers the generosity and the financial assistance that Fabriano used to provide. As it seemed, he had been secretly extending his support for the past five years, to those in need. He had never revealed his good deeds to anyone, not even to his wife. But she recalled the numerous times in which he had stated: "A good deed should never be mentioned or talked about. It would lose its essence and what it symbolised."

"Amazing!" That's all that came to Paula's mind. She loved him more by the minute. A great person with a golden heart. She missed him already. His parents were not astonished to learn about their son's assistance to needy villagers, recalling past incidents, whereby as a kid, he used to distribute his pocket money to the poor. He was caught red handed due to his constant shortage of money; subsequently he was obliged to give an explanation and admit it.

As far as Eva was concerned, providing financial support to other fellowmen was a good but dismal thing, compared to substantial contributions to renovate or build new churches. Her brother should have done that instead. May God consider Fabriano's actions in the afterlife and mitigate His verdict.

Paula took no heed of the various interpretations and accusations brought forward by her sister-in-law. She was a real pain in the neck and seemed incapable of assessing any situation in a proper impartial manner. She was nonetheless, a member of the Khoury family, and Luigi seemed to be mesmerised in her presence and got along fine with her. After all, he had seen a lot of her in recent months, which ultimately culminated into a bond with a lady supposedly close to his dad.

Paula couldn't help noticing that Andrea was showing a keen interest in Eva. Paula had started noticing that infatuation upon Eva's latest visit to Milan, when

Fabriano got diagnosed with a terminal illness. One could obviously see the reason behind such a fascination. Eva embodied what a man sought in a woman: wild sensuality and enigma. She was difficult to understand, with a hint of hidden history that no one could infiltrate. Her olive complexion and voluptuous features made her stunning, to say the least. Her long black hair adorned a gorgeous face with hazelnut eyes, perfect nose and luscious lips. Her body was curved where curves ought to be and she dressed well, bolstering her body features in a fatal sort of way. Nobody could comprehend why she was unattached and still a celibate. The absence of a steady man in her life, let alone a casual boyfriend was evident. Time was running fast. But despite being thirty-six years old, she was still capable of attracting men and inflict damage to her female counterparts.

It was evident during their recent trip to Lebanon, that Andrea took any available opportunity to spend time with Eva. He could be seen in the evenings chatting with her by the fireplace; going with her for short errands on behalf of the family and toasting her during and after dinners. Everyone noticed, but nobody commented. Was he establishing a friendly rapport with a close member of his departing friend? It didn't really matter. Dwelling on the issue wouldn't serve any purpose. All that, was sort of a temporary occurrence that would soon fade away, once he returned to Italy. There was no need for Paula or anyone else to dwell on the subject.

Any further suspicion of a friendly or romantic relationship between Eva and Andrea was erased from the minds of all those who speculated on the subject. On the 5th of January 2025, Paula, Luigi and Andrea took the same flight back to Milan. Eva stayed in Lebanon.

# Chapter Two

Two weeks later, and after an emotional telephone conversation with Luigi, in which she expressed her desire to see him, Eva advised Paula of her intention to visit Milan for few weeks and sought the latter's permission to do so. Unquestionably, Paula thought, *Eva's presence would alleviate her low morale, and give her some free time to attend to her cosmetic shop. Luigi would also benefit from the change.* Weighing the pros and cons, Paula gave her consent. Eva arrived eventually on the 26th of January dragging behind her two large suitcases and one carry-on bag. As she unpacked her heavy luggage in her assigned bedroom, Eva wore a grin on her face. She was basically moving in. She had rehearsed how to achieve that goal with subtlety; without drawing any attention to her goal and without causing any clash with her sister-in-law. Eva would spend a great deal of her time with Luigi, helping him out with his homework and accompanying him to movie theatres and playgrounds. With time, her visits increased in frequency and each duration period got extended.

Paula attempted to block Eva's visits but couldn't find a valid reason to do so. Luigi wouldn't fathom the idea that his aunt wasn't welcome in their midst. Eva had few escapades and stayed late at times, but that was her right and Paula couldn't intervene. Most of her absences from home were clandestine, but she was a grown-up and it was her prerogative to do so. Paula gave up monitoring Eva's moves. She couldn't accuse her of any misconduct, particularly any attributed to Andrea.

As was their habit, Paula and Luigi maintained their ritual of spending the weekends at Lake Como. Eva would accompany them whenever she visited the country; which was like six times a year, with an escalating duration of one month or more, at each go.

At least twice a week, Eva would vanish for several hours, returning home long after the Khoury family had fallen asleep. No matter how sneaky she had tried to be and unaware of Paula's latest insomnia issues, she could often be heard inserting and turning the keys to unlock the door. Once she had entered the premises, she would try her best to tiptoe, avoiding her high heels to pound systematically on the marbled floor. She wasn't aware of Paula's insomnia problem and thought her movements had gone unnoticed. Paula never bothered to pry into her personal life. Nevertheless, the whiff of alcohol breath was regularly detected while they shared cups of cappuccino in the breakfast room, on the next morning. Eva would furthermore project the demeanour of sexual satisfaction: faint bruises could be seen on her toned thighs and love bites on her neck. *What a shift,* Paula thought, *from one extreme to another.* A virgin turning into an insatiable woman. That certainly was a great leap.

Intrigued, Paula decided on that particular morning to try to talk to Eva, to reach out to her: "How was it yesterday? Did you go anywhere in particular?"

"Went to the movies and on the way back, stopped for a couple of drinks."

Yeah for sure. The bartender got rough and bit your neck. You got so excited you stayed there for four hours, Paula would say to herself.

As if reading Paula's mind, Eva hastily added: "Then, I walked around the park, sat on the benches and went into a reverie. I thought of dear Fabriano, Luigi and yourself. Wondering how I could help you guys and be useful to you, during this sad phase."

Soon after, their conversation got interrupted by a mysterious call. Eva walked out of the kitchen with her cellular phone, obviously not wanting to be heard, and started chatting animatedly. Paula picked up a few words and was convinced more than ever that Eva was seeing Andrea. Far from being vindictive, Paula couldn't care less what her sister-in-law did with her life on the whole, but she had a dread about that particular relationship. She cared deeply about Carla and couldn't fathom a possible split between her and Andrea. They formed a loving married couple. The couple had also two children, which made the whole thing more critical than it simply appeared to be.

But what was most baffling and intriguing was Eva's metamorphosis. No transition period had been noticed, linking her past and recent life. That indicated perhaps that she had been dating men in a clandestine way since her early youth. She must have been so elusive that she had fooled everybody, including her own brother Fabriano. She had lured everyone into believing in her chastity. But still, there was no tangible explanation as to why she avoided marriage and dating steady boyfriends. It just didn't make sense.

Paula was determined to find out the truth behind her theory that Eva was establishing a serious affair with Andrea. She thought it would be best to address the issue directly with him, whenever the time was ripe. Putting the matter temporarily aside, Paula entered her observations in the diary book that she kept. The latter was never intended to account for daily events. It was rather a combination of general outlines which included few daily records. Something she initiated since her husband passed away. It represented a fictitious bridge that allowed her to communicate with Fabriano. Every sentence and every word she wrote down were meant for him. That was her way of saying Hi and staying connected to her loved one. It made her feel better to express her feelings to an absent person who played a big role in her own existence.

Each day, she would almost write the same thing all over, repeating what she expressed on the previous day with slight enhancement of certain events:

*Dear Fabriano*

*I keep thinking about you. I'm not getting used to your absence. Every corner reminds me of you. I still spread my arm while lying in bed, reaching for your chest next to me. It offered me warmth, assurance and dependence beyond imagination. I miss your brief snoring, your handsome face beside mine, our noses almost touching. Going to our Bellagio home over the weekend saddens me a lot. I dare not look at the couch you lay on. Luigi and I still laze by the terrace but believe me, the stars that twinkle above the lake and the mountains have lost their brilliance. I think they miss your interpretation of the universe.*

*Honey: thanks for the loveliest years in my life. Each second was worthwhile living and fighting for. I'm glad I met you at the Aperitivo. I'm sure you're in a better place watching over us. You were, I mean you're a good person who deserves all the best. I guess God reached for you this time. Instead of searching for Him He was the One who picked you up so early in your life. Maybe He did that to appease your apprehension and concerns. But here I am, suffering from the consequences. I can't live without you. My heart has a cavernous nauseating emptiness that's killing me.*

*Luigi is my only reason for living. I still consider myself very beautiful; but I'm sure you can see that from where you are. I need to feel you. I crave to touch you. Few men have made passes at me but I ignored them.*

*Today I'm going to fix a big bowl of Tabbouleh for Luigi. He takes after you. Lebanese food comes first, then Italian cuisine.*

*Eva is here on visit basis. When she's around, she spends almost as much time as I do with Luigi. Sometimes, teaching him French and English. Her favourite topic though, is religion. I overheard her this morning telling him, as he was preparing to leave for school: "You should refrain asking too many questions. Religious teaching has to be accepted unconditionally and taken for granted." I had to step in and ask her not to influence him and that you and I encouraged him to express himself. He was grateful but at the same time didn't want to offend his aunt. So he promised to curb down on his queries.*
*Your loving wife, Paula.*

# Chapter Three

Eva and Luigi had their own secret. Luigi had made a pledge not to reveal it, even to his own mother. Ever since his dad exited this world, the thought of getting reunited with his father haunted him dearly. Luigi was still a child, easily influenced. As far as he was concerned, his dad was a normal Christian, a good person and a wonderful surgeon. He gathered all that from his own exposure to family life and the way his father had been perceived by his colleagues and social circles. His aunt's concern for his daddy's soul worried him.

"Your dad was not a believer!" She would say to him with a hissing voice that added guilt and condemnation to the rough accusation. "I can picture your dad writhing from the extortionate heat of the flames of hell. He did that to himself! On the lucky side, he might be stranded in the purgatory, watching the heels of Heaven above him. He would scream with pain and anger, surrounded by remorse. A heavy price to pay for not believing in God Almighty." Eva would let her rage subside. Her reddish angry face would regain its normal colour. She would wear a half-smile while gently cupping Luigi's face. She would stroke the soft wet skin and wipe the tears with her long-nailed fingers.

Luigi would tremble uncontrollably and sniff. "Don't be afraid, my dear!" She would utter with a confident tone. "Your daddy's soul might be salvaged in case he is stranded between heaven and the purgatory. And you are the only person who might achieve that. God listens to the constant prayers of an innocent child."

Luigi would rub his red eyes and utter: "What should I do, Aunty?"

"Pray incessantly, whenever you can," she would say, while thrusting a string of rosary beads in Luigi's tiny palm. The boy would kneel, make the sign of the cross and start praying aloud, accounting for every bead on the string.

Shutting himself off inside his bedroom became a daily ritual. Luigi pretended that he was studying. He concentrated less and less on his homework. He would leave his school books open on his tiny desk, as a precautionary measure, just in case his mum walked in unannounced. He dreaded the thought that she might find out about the sworn pact that bound him to his aunt.

He no longer could focus on his studies and his recent grades were vivid proof of that. He was regressing in most courses to the amazement of his teachers and Paula alike. Luigi managed however to earn first ranking at catechism. His aunt rejoiced to that and rewarded him with gifts and special outings. But Luigi was forlorn and unhappy. Unaware that his aunt had impeded his innocent pure life; oblivious that she had murdered the child in him; that she had ripped his wonderful perception of an ideal father and shrouded his mind with grey disturbing thoughts.

Luigi had been assigned with a serious task: redeem the soul of a very dear father.

Eva, on the other hand, had for quite some time considered her brother as being an atheist. He was a condemned soul destined for either hell or purgatory. She prayed God to salvage him through purification. However, the graveness of the matter necessitated further interventions. Being a pure child with innate innocence, Luigi was the right choice. He would act like a catalyst. His daily prayers to God, Jesus and the Virgin Mary might redeem her brother's soul.

Luigi had shown resistance to Eva's claims that his dad was doomed, but her influence and strong character were too much for a nine-year-old. So, he succumbed to the pressure, eradicating any possibility to let her down and consequently abandon his father. Luigi was therefore assigned an officious role with a serious responsibility to save a person he had loved and cherished. His prayers were necessary to ensure the father and son reunion in the afterworld.

So many times, Paula found her son kneeling devotedly by his bed praying intently, shifting from one rosary bead to another while staring upwards at a framed picture of the Virgin Mary draped in blue, holding baby Jesus in her pure arms. Deep down, Paula knew the depth of his devotion but ignored the cause of that newly acquired obsession. Somehow, she found solace watching him praying and a few times, came inside his room and kissed him on the top of his head. He wouldn't flinch. He was in an entirely different world.

Nobody knew what pain and suffering the little kid was enduring. His eyes held constant tears associated with a boy's fear for his father's whereabouts. He loved him so much to lose him eternally. He would pray endlessly if need be, to salvage his dad's soul. His aunt made it clear to him that his prayers were essential to get his father to heaven; but Luigi never comprehended why would a great person like his dad require such a humongous support to enter paradise? His mind couldn't fathom where his dad had gone wrong. As far as he was concerned, there couldn't be a better human being. So, he prayed and prayed. There was no room for faltering.

# Chapter Four

Paula didn't have to wait long to confirm her suspicions about Eva's relationship with Andrea. Her fears materialised on a spring Saturday night, when an abrupt change of plans took her to Bellagio: Luigi's best friend birthday party in Milan had been cancelled due to the sudden illness of the kid's mum.

The Khoury villa was dimly lit but the external floodlights around the swimming pool area were shedding immense lighting on the water surface. Loud music blared from powerful outdoor speakers. Whenever the beat subsided, wild female shrieks could be heard over the background. Paula instinctively asked the housekeeper who accompanied her, to lead her son upstairs to his room and ordered her to remain there and not budge unless called upon.

Paula entered the living room whose sliding glass doors stood wide open. The commotion grew bigger as she moved closer towards the back garden that adjoined the large seating room. Right there in front of her, Eva was stark naked, riding a man whose face couldn't be seen. He was lying on one of the fibreglass deck chairs, moaning and thrusting himself upwards to meet his partner's downwards movement. Eva was in a frenzy, roaring like a wild tigress, offering her mouth and tits to the passionate care of a svelte blonde by her side.

Paula shook badly all over. The man's features were hidden by Eva's big round ass, wobbling madly in all directions. But the sporadic moans and sensual words that the man emitted gave him away. Paula retreated to the living room and climbed up the stairs to her room. There was no point confronting the others. She waited for almost an hour until the noises had ceased. Then, she dropped at Luigi's room, asked him and the nanny to come down after thirty minutes. She went straight to the living room and startled the threesome. Paula found them lying nude on the parquet flooring, flirting with each other, getting aroused, preparing themselves for another round. With an open gaping mouth, Andrea attempted to cover his genitals with one of the cushions adorning a nearby couch.

Eva rose defiantly and shamelessly. The blonde retrieved her clothes from the outdoor garden and simply vanished, closing the wooden exit door behind her.

"I'm so sorry!" murmured Andrea. "I shouldn't be here. I was assured that your home was going to be vacant. But still, I should have abstained. How despicable of me."

"I put the blame on your lover. She breached the code of ethics. How long has this been going on? I mean, between you two?" Paula asked.

Eva remained silent, her eyes gleaming with rage and anticipation. "Since Eva's first visit to Milan," Andrea replied.

"Great! And Carla? Is she aware of your fling?" asked Paula.

"She suspects I am having an affair. She has brought up the subject few times but gave up afterwards. I believe she is living in total denial, dealing with the matter as a casual and temporary fling. There have been few times when she made poignant complaints that I was coming home at late hours; she would murmur for a while, raise and wave her hand, trying to hush me and stop me from uttering a lie."

"You have a beautiful family. Don't ruin it. That's my advice to you," Paula said and turned to Eva who was still standing nude: "You have twenty minutes to pack and leave. On Monday morning, you can come over to our Milan apartment and collect all your belongings. Your actions are perverse. You are full of shit. You're so full of contradictions that you scare the hell out of me. Why can't you live with what you preach? Your brother was worried about you all the time, wondering whether you had any sexual and emotional rapport at all. It turns out you're a real expert, indulging yourself in threesomes, enjoying yourself bisexually, and taking no heed dating a married man: Fabriano's best friend, as a matter of fact. Just get out, both of you!" She yelled, pointing her index finger at the front door entrance.

Eva and Andrea grabbed their clothes off the pool's deck chairs and put them on. Andrea finished first and in five minutes joined Paula in the living room.

"Paula. I'm very sorry for what happened here tonight. I also value your stance regarding Carla, but I want to be honest and level with you. Eva has taken me to places I never thought existed. Her physical attraction is beyond me. Nothing will stop me seeing her. Where and how it might end, I have no clue. I have to take it one step at a time."

He ceased talking when Eva stepped back into the living room. He encircled her waist with his arm and led her towards the main entrance door.

"Nothing can obstruct my relationship with Andrea. Take heed of that. Once settled in an hotel, you'll be given the necessary details. I just wish you would allow me and Luigi to see each other whenever possible," Eva said with panache.

"I will consider that out of respect for your brother Fabriano."

With that, the door was shut behind them. Luigi and the housekeeper rushed down, enquiring about the events that had taken place that night. Paula was careful to say the bare minimum, enough to let her son understand that his aunt was moving out in order to be on her own, embarking in whatever she might be contemplating to do.

# Chapter Five

Eva stayed at a hotel for few weeks until eventually moved into a one-bedroom apartment in the Navigli neighbourhood. The inconvenience of vacating Paula's flat worked out in her favour. Eva now had ample time and total freedom to entertain her once clandestine sexual desire. Andrea frequented her apartment at least twice a week, spending prime time discovering wild sex and realising the beast in him. She had conquered his body while smashing his soul. He couldn't think straight anymore. At work, he was lately distracted and felt out of focus. Sensual thoughts often crossed his mind. He would imagine Eva in his arms, writhing like a wounded snake, wrapping her plump thighs around his waist, extracting his energy in a stifling yet enjoyable manner.

Andrea was pleased with himself. He felt he was a real pro, satisfying an insatiable woman. Carla, his wife, was on the other hand neglected. Her sex life was inexistent and she had recently complained about it. She had started to trust her female intuition and faced the bitter reality: her husband was having a serious and permanent affair. She was scared and resented the thought that her marriage was under a looming threat. She wept silently, sensing danger hovering over her head. Their marital bond was doubtlessly flailing and she was unsure what to do about it.

Andrea was totally careless and paid no attention to his wife's suffering. His strong infatuation with Eva made him too blind to realise that lust and promiscuity were uncontainable. He was unaware of Eva's peripheral affairs with young studs in their early twenties and her great penchant for lesbianism.

In the midst of all this, Eva often dedicated Friday evenings to her nephew Luigi. She would call Paula asking for her permission to pick him up upon his return from school. In remembrance of Fabriano, Paula acquiesced. Regardless how she felt about her sister-in-law, Paula thought it would be wise to keep Luigi within the family loop. It would give him an assurance that his father's kin were there for him, ready to provide needed assistance and comfort should he ever require it. She and Eva spoke with each other once a week for a few minutes; a courtesy call ensuring that everyone was doing fine and kept abreast of family matters.

Faithful to her late husband's Middle Eastern customs, Paula was incited to invite Eva over on holiday seasons. A move highly appreciated by Luigi. His aunt demanded a lot from him and had rebuked him for not praying enough lately. He couldn't lie to her when she enquired about the intensity of his prayers. To everybody's surprise, his grades had improved marginally since she moved out of the apartment. Despite her austere attitude and imposing presence, she was a special person to him. He saw in her a guru who had laid the rules and drawn the path that would secure his father's spiritual well-being. As a loving son, he had a big role to play. No one else could act as a catalyst between his dad's earthly deeds and God's judgement. Luigi couldn't contemplate being in paradise one day, unable to find his father amid that infinite heaven. He had to work hard, pray most of the time, ask for clemency and pave the way for his dad's smooth transition.

Life went on. Paula hardly recovered from the hollowness that Fabriano's loss had inflicted. She refrained dating other men, no matter how hard they tried to win her heart. She thought that dating was inappropriate and that it would be a breach of her love for her husband. Fabriano's dying wish however, was a candid encouragement for her to go on with her life. He always made it a point to highlight the big difference between indispensable and irreplaceable. "Nobody is indispensable, including myself," he would say to her. "However, you might find me irreplaceable." He would smile as he said that to her and give a wink. According to Fabriano, life continued with different players. Life needed to be lived.

Paula experienced therefore periodic frustration. Her physical needs were at times at their saturation point, but she couldn't bear the idea of being touched by men just for the sake of having sex. Countering that, she had the alternative of developing serious relationships. But she lacked the will to enter into a frenzy of uncertain relationships. She presently had neither the emotions nor the courage to test the grounds.

Her frustration subsided whenever she was in the company of her son. Luigi spiced up her life and gave it an ever escalating momentum. Her first priority was to be a successful mum. All the rest seemed peripheral. Far from being an alcoholic, Paula enjoyed her evenings, consuming half a bottle of wine per session, enough to soften her anxiety.

# Chapter Six

Meanwhile and after few years of acquaintance, Andrea and Eva got married. Had it not been for Eva's pregnancy, Andrea wouldn't have taken such a big leap. Spending a few years dating a sensual lady, it wasn't so difficult for him to realise in the end that the woman was just satisfying his libido. Their relationship lacked sincere emotions. It relied heavily on physical attraction and lust. Those gratifying assets outweighed noble emotions: pleasure and excitement versus true spiritual love. Andrea had also realised that other men and women formed a major part of Eva's life. He indulged nevertheless in his adventure because he couldn't resist the sexual pleasure on offer, and mainly because of Carla's indifference towards him lately. He was convinced that she didn't care anymore what he did outside her home, as long as he returned to his den. Her family mattered the most and she was prepared to sacrifice her happiness for the sake of maintaining their shattered unity. After all, her best friend was a vivid proof: Paula had managed so far to survive her ordeal, relying on herself and putting aside her personal feelings and desires.

But Eva got pregnant and Andrea had to do something about it and react. Being promiscuous and all, he couldn't fathom how she got impregnated in the first place. Was it intentional and did he fall for it? There was no way of knowing. Somehow he was certain that he had been misled. He begged Eva to have an abortion. But being a devout Catholic she wouldn't even contemplate such thing. So, there he was torn between his family ties and a newly formed bond enforced on him by a manipulative woman who outmanoeuvred him, he who thought being clever and impermeable. He had no choice but to deceive and inflict pain on the weaker tie, which at that moment had been Carla. He filed for divorce and broke her heart. His children were devastated. Paula was shocked by the news. She severed all communication links with Eva and wrote in her diary:

*Dearest Fabriano,*

*Eva has turned out to be full of deceit. Because of her, Andrea and Carla are divorcing.*

*Your friend is marrying your sister who's pregnant. Yes! Eva is not the innocent woman you thought you had for a sister. Your parents were astonished as well. Michel had to be admitted to the hospital due to high blood pressure issues and heart palpitations. I learned from Andrea that the foetal ultrasound scan revealed it's a boy. Eva is insisting to name him after you. I'm sipping a glass of white wine; nibbling on goat cheese. Feel I need a bottle of scotch to calm me down.*

*Love you loads. I can't live without you.*

*Your wife, Paula.*

Luigi was sixteen at the time. He was baffled to learn about his aunt's intention to marry Dr Andrea. He understood they were getting married because of his aunt's conception. How careless could adults be? They were supposed to take necessary precautions to prevent pregnancy.

Eva took her time defending her actions before Luigi. He mattered to her and couldn't foresee him being vindictive. She couldn't allow that to happen. Andrea was depicted as the culprit, responsible for seducing her and abusing her weakness. She had offered herself to him because of his repeated and relentless advances. She had to smother her burning emotions, as she was getting so fond of him lately. Luigi was not naïve and she knew it. But she had to abuse his reverence for her and rely on his goodness.

Fabriano Junior was born in February 2032. It was a difficult delivery caused by the tightening of the umbilical cord. A caesarean section had to be performed to save the baby's life.

Luigi urged his mother to accompany him to the hospital to bid his aunt their best wishes.

Paula conceded reluctantly and went ahead with his proposal. The name of the new-born alleviated her grudge towards her sister-in-law. It would be unethical to let a baby pay the price of sour rifts between adults.

They stopped on their way at a flower shop and bought a bouquet of white tulips. Luigi carried the flowers into his aunt's room, entering first, followed by his mum. Eva was sitting upright in her bed, holding little Fabriano in her arms.

They all exchanged kisses as if yester differences were tossed behind them. The visit went well, much better than expected. Paula stared at Fabriano Junior. A cuddly little baby with nice features. He looked so innocent and fragile. That made her heart soften and she relived past feelings. She was ecstatic holding him in her arms. He flashed a furtive smile while his eyes were closed and tried liberating his tiny hands from the tight clothing that wrapped his little body. Her heart melted and she swayed him while singing nursery rhymes. She kissed affectionately the top of his head, catching that peculiar lovely smell, so common with babies.

Little Fabriano restored the ruptured bond between Eva and Paula. Regular visits ensued with Paula helping out with the baby; providing her sister-in-law with advice whenever necessary. Those frequent encounters were made easy due to the relatively proximity of both residences. Andrea had purchased a flat within a walking distance from the Khoury's. Paula cherished and welcomed the re-established ties. She felt rejuvenated and fresh. Her husband would certainly be in accord with the outcome. He wouldn't want it any other way.

# Chapter Seven

Luigi reverted to his strong attachment to his aunt. He spent at least an hour per day listening to her sermons and religious guiding; his father being the main focus of her discussion. By now, Luigi had grown up and was blessed with high intelligence, enabling him to grasp logic and make up his own mind. However, religious topics sounded far more serious than worldly subjects. With the former, logic and rational thinking required a supplement; and that addition was embedded in faith. Eva's sermons were thus not foolproof anymore and didn't carry the same weight as previously felt by Luigi the kid. He was afraid however that any slight truth behind his aunt's advice, no matter how small, could tip the balance between his father's salvation and doom. So, he listened carefully and paid attention to what she said.

Luigi grew up to be a young adolescent, tall and handsome, witty and caring. He was now preparing for his international baccalaureate. He would study with his girlfriend Gina. She was one year older and steered him into his first sexual encounter a few weeks back. Gina was good-looking and considerate. Her liking for Luigi was sincere. She guided him into love making in a gentle way. Paula liked her a lot and found in her an honest person aspiring for a steady relationship.

Luigi had already received acceptances from the Massachusetts Institute of Technology in Boston and the University of Cambridge in the United Kingdom. He got enrolled in their respective mechanical engineering department. He had always been interested in gas dynamics and fascinated by aircrafts and rockets. He just needed to obtain his baccalaureate certificate and it would pave the way for his future. Paula was proud of her son. She wished he would opt for the United Kingdom, as it was closer to home, but then again, she knew that his selection of MIT had to do with his father's past academic life in Boston. That was another way for her son to reach out to his dad.

# Chapter Eight

Luigi excelled in his exams and the family decided to celebrate at their Bellagio home.

Gina was asked to join him and Paula at their Milan address, so that they would leave off together. She had passed her exams as well. They drove to Lake Como with Andrea pursuing them in his Alpha Romeo. Once there, the two families relaxed for a while and changed their clothes. They headed for the garden afterwards and sat next to the pool. Champagne bottles were intentionally jerked wildly and opened, releasing jets of foaming liquid through the air, which then fell on the deck with a fizzy sound. Everyone stepped closer and extended his or her glass for a quick filling, before the champagne, under pressure, poured out of the bottle neck. There was a merry happy atmosphere. Gina and Luigi exchanged tender kisses, with an applaud from all those present except Eva who looked the other way, feigning she hadn't noticed. Suddenly, she got up and raised a toast:

"To my dear nephew and his success."

"And Gina's success too," exclaimed Paula.

"Sorry Gina, for missing you out. Cheers to you as well," said Eva. "I believe Luigi has an announcement to make," she continued.

Startled and caught by surprise, Luigi looked like someone in search for words. He stared at his aunt in a way that suggested it wasn't the right moment for such an announcement, but her gaze prompted him to utter through quivering lips: "I have decided to join priesthood."

"What? What are you talking about?" said Paula. "I should have been the first person to know. Whatever happened to your college acceptances? Is this a joke?"

"No Mother. It's not a joke. I took my decision two months ago. I avoided discussing the matter with you because I knew you'd be pissed off. So I informed my aunt about it."

Bewildered, pale and feeling feeble, Paula turned to Andrea and Gina, throwing an astonished gaze, as if enquiring whether they had known about it.

"Believe me, this is the first time. I'm as surprised as you," said Andrea.

Gina shook her head to emphasise her unawareness of her boyfriend's decision, while simultaneously expressing her astonishment and disbelief: "What about us? Have you thought of that? How can you do this to me?"

Luigi stood silent with his head down. One could swear he had aged at that very moment.

His shoulders were stiff, his back arched and his face flushed.

"That's you, Eva. Is it not? You have poisoned my son's brain with your weird interpretations. The fact you held the info from your husband is proof enough that you concocted the whole thing in a clandestine way."

Eva's face radiated with the aura of a glorious winner. She was capable of stirring fights and initiating hurdles whenever she wanted. She had the determination and the will; she had picked the right tools to make them work to her advantage.

"Luigi came to me few weeks ago and informed me about his intentions. He believed God was calling upon him and that he had the vocation for priesthood. I did not exert any influence on him. I was pleased to hear what he had to say. I won't deny it."

Paula was bitterly furious. Word after word flowing from her sister-in-law angered her more by the second. She thrust herself towards Eva and slapped her face with all her might. Pain vibrated through her palm and fingertips. The sound was muffled by the huge garden space, but Eva's stupefied look and dizziness were witnesses to the strength of the slap. She touched her sore cheek. It felt hot and a throbbing pain extended all the way to her left ear. She had the urge to hit back, especially as her physique was stronger than Paula's. As if reading her thoughts, Andrea stepped forward and stood between the two women, keeping a separation distance.

"Do whatever you want to do with your own son in the future. Leave Luigi alone. You hear?" shouted Paula uncontrollably. "Get out of our lives. Stop lying through your teeth. Don't pretend to be a saint. Your presence is ever annoying. You've caused enough damage already. Problems surround you wherever you go. You inflict misery onto people around you. I am certain that your pregnancy was deliberate to force Andrea into marrying you; but that's not the main reason for your conniving behaviour. The target had always been Luigi and his indoctrination."

"Giving birth to a baby child would restore back the severed ties between our families and open a new communication link. You were always betting on our good hearts and apparently, you've succeeded. It was a clever thing naming your son Fabriano Junior. You won our affection through an innocent baby and a name that was dear and precious to us."

At that moment in time, Andrea's mobile phone started ringing. He picked up the call and froze stiff. He turned pale and could be heard exclaiming the words: "What? When? How?"

His grip loosened and he dropped the phone down on the grass. He struggled to move his body and sit on the nearest deck chair, holding his face in both hands, bursting into tears. All those present were taken aback as if time had stopped and all their disputes had suddenly vanished. They cried out, "What's wrong?"

"It's…Carla," replied Andrea. "She's gone. She's committed…suicide by taking a whole pack…of sleeping pills. They found a note on her…bedside table. Oh God! What have I done?"

The night that was meant for celebration turned out to be one of the worst nights ever: Paula had lost her best friend Carla and was uncertain about her son's future. Luigi realised his weakness in the presence of his domineering aunt. Andrea had experienced the result of his deeds in a very detrimental way. Gina found herself dating a boyfriend with whom eternal love and marital expectations had suddenly ceased. Eva had been hit for the first time in her life by a woman who accused her of double standards. Her husband Andrea seemed regretful and resentful that he had abandoned his first spouse. What disturbed her the most was Paula's ability to grasp her manipulation.

It was true what Paula deduced from her pregnancy and marriage to Andrea. She had stopped taking her pills and hid the whole matter from her partner. What a fool! So infatuated with her beauty, he never took any precautions. He knew the whole truth but never queried how she became pregnant, fearing he might lose her and consequently the wild sex she was giving him. How weak could a man be? No wonder wars were launched in the name of love. Contrary to what Paula saw in her sister-in-law's actions, Eva considered her moves necessary to save her brother's soul. She had achieved a lot so far and nothing could stop her.

# Chapter Nine

On their way home, back to Milan, silence dominated the scene. Paula was driving absent-mindedly, grieving over the loss of a friend who had taken her own life. How sad she must had been to commit such an act? Luigi avoided opening any subject fearing rebuke by either his mum or Gina. It was a lesson for him not to have shared his thoughts with the closest people around him. He had resided daily with his mum; studied daily with his schoolmate and somehow his intentions had been only revealed to his aunt.

Did he really possess the vocation or was he merely acquiescing to his aunt's constant battering and wishes? She made a fool out of him back there. She had taken control over all events. She had spoiled a night meant for celebration and succeeded in making it an outright disaster for everyone. Then came the sad news of Carla's demise to crown the burden already inflicted. He couldn't refrain thinking of Gina and how badly he must have hurt her feelings. Far from being committed for life, as they were still very young, their relationship had moulded an honest perfect bond based on true emotions and compatibility. Gina wouldn't have offered herself to him if not because of her sincere love and her true belief that he shared the same feeling.

His reverie got interrupted when he heard the car door opening and shutting. Gina was already on the pavement, in front of her parents' home, waving goodbye to Paula, her lips uttering: "Thank you," behind the closed windows. He was completely ignored. Still, he waved his wrist in a funny mechanical motion, expecting nothing.

Once they were within the comfort of their sweet home, Paula broke the silence and bid Luigi goodnight as she pecked a tender kiss on his forehead:

"All I'm asking of you is to reconsider your decision. Take a few days and reflect on what you really want to become. I'm all ears for you. You're my everything. I love you so much son. Just beware of your aunt Eva. Make your own choice. Your future should not be affected and guided by others, including me, your own mother. Had your father been alive, he would have told you the same thing. Don't let anyone stand in your way. Please promise me to rethink the whole situation."

"I promise," Luigi said. He hugged his mum and both remained motionless for a minute.

Quietly, they retreated into their respective bedrooms, feeling lonely and dejected.

Paula was unable to sleep. Carla and the night's events haunted her. Luigi was tossing in bed, struggling to get a decent sleep. He would doze off, dive into weird dreams that didn't make sense or coherence, then suddenly wake up bewildered. As dawn was breaking, he surrendered to a deep sleep.

He was drifting aimlessly in space. A dark void so vast and shapeless, lit by uncountable galaxies in elliptical and spiral formations. They appeared like shiny clusters deriving their sheen from the billions of stars that shaped them. The black emptiness seemed to exchange its coldness with the warmth of their glow.

As he floated, his fear of the unknown subsided and he could swear he was hearing a pleasing universal symphony. He observed numerous planets moving close by, displaying a fantastic show of different colours, while emitting revolving musical sounds as they orbited their relative stars and turned around their axes. He could discern high and low frequency notes, varying according to the spherical size of each individual planet. A marvellous sight enhanced by magical music unknown to mankind.

The more he drifted, the more he felt at ease. He navigated himself confidently through celestial bodies with no concern whatsoever that he might collide with any. A mysterious force was beaconing him. He thought he might be able to steer but the pulling force was certainly overpowering and beyond his control. It dawned on him that regardless how he navigated, the path course had already been set for him in advance. It wasn't meant to be altered.

Suddenly he was not floating anymore. A sucking force was drawing him downwards and yet nothing could be seen below. There was total darkness beneath him. Could it be a black hole? He shuddered and got scared at the thought, but as he was pulled down further, the darkness got lighter and gave way to a hidden world unfolding underneath him. Luigi's feet didn't touch the ground; they just hovered slightly above the surface. The view was three-dimensional and his eyes could zoom in and out. His vision spread broadly, covering panoramic wide angles that neither human eyes nor optical equipment were capable of.

He was in a world of unimaginable peaked mountain ranges with varied colours. They extended way far into the infinite horizon with their flanks embracing large bodies of clear blue water stretching as far as the eye could see. The landscape filling the wide gaps between the seas and the lakes consisted of a combination of dense forests and lush green meadows with sprawling tall trees and vegetation, bordering rivers with cascading water. The blue sky above had white fluffy clouds sailing through its canvas, seemingly carried by a light wind that Luigi couldn't feel on his face. He also noticed that the tree leaves were motionless; there were no rustle, no flutter, no breeze. He realised too, that he wasn't able to hear the flowing sound of the rushing water. No chirping sound of birds reached his ears from the nearby dense trees. More importantly, there were no humans to be seen anywhere.

The sensation was that of awe and bewilderment. And yet, Luigi felt content and immersed in unexplained serenity: one that couldn't be found in the physical world.

As he roamed that strange place, still without touching its soil, something within him and something beyond him were instigating him to search for the first cedar tree that he could find. Suddenly a forest laid before him in a scene so familiar that it made him gasp. It was reminiscent of the Cedars of God, a vestige still thriving since ancient biblical times. His dad used to stress on visiting that sacred place whenever they were vacationing in Lebanon. His father's native village lay few kilometres away, overlooking the Valley of the Saints. Luigi snapped back as he spotted the silhouette of a man standing next to a giant cedar tree. He felt drawn to the human form as he got nearer. Joy swept across his limbs as his expectations materialised.

Suddenly, he was facing a smiling dad with unsurpassable charm. His father was at his best. Exactly the way he looked when he was still healthy. He wore a chequered woollen jacket with matching trousers, and a grey shirt, clothes that Luigi liked on his dad. He tried to leap the remaining metre that separated them and hug him; but he couldn't. His feet were still not in contact with the ground below him, although his dad's rested weightlessly on the thick grass beneath, without flexing it. He tried extending his arms to embrace or at least touch his father's face, but his fingers failed to reach.

"It's fine, my son." Those words were heard without being spoken. Luigi realised his father was speaking to him mentally through the ether. Lips didn't move a bit. "We're not in a physical world. We communicate through telepathy. It's our universal language."

"Where are we, Father?" asked Luigi inquisitively.

"We're in paradise," injected Fabriano into Luigi's mind.

"This is Heaven? But where's everybody? Why is it so beautiful and yet so still?" Luigi barely finished his sentence when his dad replied, obviously having read his mind.

"Luigi, my son. You're seeing me because you were searching for me and none other. Your mind is communicating with me from the Beyond because the influence of your physical body has drastically diminished while sleeping. Somehow, your soul has exited and escaped its entrapment, but you are still alive. That's the reason you couldn't set your feet on the ground. You don't belong here yet. The drifting clouds above would seem to you as the only moving entity. That's because you're watching the portal through which you've penetrated our eternal world. Heaven my son is a fascinating world where time has no measure; where boundaries have no limits; where occupants picture one another the way they want to."

"Contrary to what you're perceiving, this amazing universe is crawling with people. We all recognise each other even if we hadn't been acquainted. You make your own world over here. If you fancied watching a bird flying overhead, flitting through foliage, then perching on a tree branch and swaying it under its weight, you could achieve it, because it was your wish to see just that. If you longed for a gentle breeze to sweep across the lakes and fields; watch the water ripple and the grass lean over, then your wish would come true."

"Heaven is a vivid place tailored so that each soul experiences what it likes the most. I can't tell how I'm appearing before you, but I'm certain I look impeccably dressed, as you'd like to perceive me."

"You must have turned into a handsome young man. Tall with broad shoulders. However, I'm looking at you wearing the school uniform which looked so well on you. You see, my perception of you covers the era we shared together on Earth. My soul longs for your mum. We had a happy life together. Paradise is a world where only pleasant memories prevail. Sad earthly moments are not remembered at all. That's what renders the place so special. Do not stay any longer! I believe it's time for you to leave now. Go back my son. I love you. Recall our conversation and may God bless you."

Luigi tried once again to hug his father. He couldn't. But the intensity of love around him surpassed the physical display of earthly emotions. He was engulfed in pure heavenly love that so appeasing. The silhouette disappeared as did the large cedar tree.

Luigi woke up, breathing heavily and sweating. He lay in bed for ten minutes staring at the ceiling, not knowing if his metaphysical travel was real or just a super dream. Finally, he got up, put on his slippers and followed the coffee maker gurgling noise and the aroma that emanated from the kitchen. He found Paula sitting at the breakfast table, waiting for the coffee to brew.

"I saw him, Mother! I saw my dad! He's in Heaven." And he revealed the contents of his strange encounter, avoiding all along to refer to it as a dream.

While hugging each other, tears of joy streamed down from their eyes and Paula could be heard murmuring, "I never had a doubt."

# Chapter Ten

It took Luigi one week to get in touch with his aunt, requesting of her a visit. He opted to keep his mum out of the loop in order not to offend her and clash with her. Eva invited him over for lunch, fixing him traditional vegetarian dishes that she knew he fancied. He arrived a bit earlier than expected. He avoided disturbing Eva and her arduous kitchen preparation, spending emotional prime time with little Fabriano, wondering about the splendour of birth and Creation. The way the baby got agitated at his sight, instilled in Luigi's heart indescribable emotions; those of recognition, kinship and dependence. The baby was flashing joyful smiles that would melt one's heart due to their sincerity, innocence and spontaneity. Luigi would pull him up from the crib, hold him gently in his arms, kissing the little fingers and tiny wrists that were reaching out to poke his eyes.

Then came lunchtime. They savoured the tasty dishes while downing Puligny Montrachet wine. Luigi was usually allowed one glass per day. He consumed two glasses, leaving his aunt to finish the rest of the bottle. Until then, their conversation focused on mundane issues. As they sat next to each other on the sofa drinking black tea and munching homemade cheesecake, Luigi recited to his aunt the accounts of his strange dream. He avoided mentioning the word "encounter" in front of her.

"So, you really believe he's in Heaven. Maybe he is, even though it's doubtful. Luigi: that was just a dream. A deep dream directed and produced by your sub-conscience. I won't try to influence your judgement any longer. Do what you must do. Already I'm having numerous problems with my husband, his children, your mother and even my parents. It's obvious you've come over because of your intention to breach our covenant. But do remember that you're under the influence of a dream that you're so desperate to believe in. After all, you created that dream and you wish it were true. It's your choice, Luigi. I promise that from now on, I won't raise the issue of priesthood. The matter is entirely in your hands."

Luigi returned home, more confused than when he had left to visit his aunt. She made sense. After all, it was a dream, not a reality, regardless how true it had seemed. Yet, he resented seeking her advice. His entire spirit took a leap from contentment to dissatisfaction. That mysterious looming doubt that bore heavily on him came back to haunt him. The dismal possibility that his father might require his support engulfed him in a sombre mood. His mum noticed his dejection and remoteness. She tried her utmost to gather the fact behind her son's melancholy and apparent hesitation but failed. Her morning cheerful state of mind vanished as the night closed. She noted that down in her diary, in total contradiction with what she had written earlier during the day. Paula had used her diary literally to converse with Fabriano and express her eagerness to join him in Heaven; telling him she wasn't scared of death anymore.

Luigi's account had breathed faith into her and boosted her son's tenfold. With the night creeping in, it seemed the word "dream" prevailed over the reality and potency of Luigi's account, washing away the encounter theory.

## Chapter Eleven

The christening of Fabriano Junior three weeks later, restored family ties between Eva and Paula. The latter was asked to be the Godmother for the child. A hesitant Paula succumbed to Andrea and Luigi's pleas and finally accepted. She felt happy after the ceremony and enjoyed watching the little darling wearing the gold chain and icon she had bought for the occasion. The icon depicted Virgin Mary holding baby Jesus in her arms.

The event brought Paula's parents in law to Milan. The occasion brightened up the lives of all gathered families. It was so good seeing Fabriano's parents. They had aged and their mobility had been affected, but they still maintained their mental faculties while showing faint signs of hearing problems. They stayed over at Paula's for ten consecutive days before returning to their homeland.

Weekly visits became somewhat regular between the late antagonists. Luigi liked the setup. Holding grudges led nowhere. The two women often went to the movies together, frequented bistros and cafes. They would occasionally raise with him, in an individual manner, the issue of college education and his final verdict. Aiming to please both women while giving himself the edge to satisfy his own craving and appease his apprehension, Luigi decided to opt for priesthood, giving himself a one-year trial run. The first year would therefore be a self-searching sort of journey, paving the path for ultimate priesthood. Failing that, he could always revert to his most favourite major, mechanical engineering. His decision was put to all family members over a dinner hosted by Paula in their Bellagio home.

To render it official and somewhat seal the subject, Luigi made it clear that he had approached the parish priest, who in turn set up an interview with the Diocese Bishop. Luigi declared his vocation to become a priest, and expressed his intention to join the Rome Diocese. A psychological assessment ensued, along with a medical check-up. The Diocese Bishop in Milan consequently issued a letter to the Pontiff allowing the transfer of Luigi from the local diocese to Rome's. He was ready to leave in one month's time. Paula frowned but showed no signs of disappointment. Eva bore a wide smile. Andrea enquired about the time it took to become a priest.

"There'll be one year of discernment, which is an introductory year dedicated to spirituality. Once that training is completed, seven more years will be required to become ordained. The first two years will be devoted to philosophy, then three years of theology, followed by another two years for the licence."

"That long? I didn't know that," exclaimed Andrea.

"But why Rome?" asked Paula. "Can't you conduct your studies in Milan?"

"Sure I can. But Rome Diocese offers a great opportunity to co-share mass with the Pope, seeing him at Wednesday Audience and Sunday Angelus. It's vibrant and its members are diversified, coming from various Catholic countries."

That night, Luigi felt like a man for the first time in his life. He was eighteen years of age, going on nineteen. His decision to enter priesthood was neither debated nor opposed. Had his mum finally resigned to the idea or was she betting he would eventually opt out after the first year of discernment?

# Chapter Twelve

Luigi's most difficult task was to say goodbye to Gina. He called on to her over one weekend and convinced her to accompany him. They strolled lazily along the busy streets, holding hands, talking little. They stopped at shop windows and watched the displayed articles. It was striking how the prices had drastically gone up in 2032. He ended up buying her a false jewellery necklace of crafty design. He made her wear it immediately upon purchase and it looked elegant on her long neck.

They kept walking until they reached a pizzeria. The weather was slightly nippy, and they sat inside. The place had the peculiar smell of wood-fired oven, basil and garlic. They placed their order for a large pepperoni pizza and two glasses of local red wine, punching a small keyboard mounted at the side of the table. A tiny red light, the size of a dot, flashed against the electronic menu, ensuring the right selection had been made. Then the amber light came on, indicating the order was being processed in the kitchen.

Fifteen minutes elapsed and the waiter laid the large sizzling dough in front of them. The smell of cheese and tomato tickled the nostrils of the young couple. By the time the wine glasses were served, the green light turned on. They clinked the glasses together, took a sip and dived into the crisp pizza. Gina used the knife and fork on her slice, while Luigi held and plied the triangular slice in his hand and bit through it, starting at the pointed edge.

"My dad used to say: pizza is meant to be eaten by hand. It's tastier that way. It ensures none of the toppings is left out on the plate," said Luigi.

"My dad says: using a fork and a knife on a pizza slice ensures that none of the toppings is going to fall over on your clothes," retorted Gina.

Both laughed at that. *It was amazing how joy fitted her,* thought Luigi. He knew she was beautiful but tonight she looked more ladylike and gorgeous. He had to tell her, otherwise he wouldn't be fair.

"Gina! You look wonderful tonight. I also appreciate your company. You make me happy. Under different circumstances, I would have clung to you forever. I shall love you in my own spiritual way until eternity."

"But you have until the end of the month to love me physically. I don't mind feeling you for some moments even though that our physical love is going to wane soon, very soon. No matter the distance, no matter the reasons, I'll be there for you. I love you, Luigi. That training year, the discernment, once it's finished, you'll find me waiting. If your decision were to continue with the priesthood, then I'd step aside, leaving you to your spiritual world, but I'd be loving you my own way. Should you abandon your vocation you'll find me there for you. The moment we made love, we've become one soul in two bodies."

"Gina! I need you tonight. Please stay with me."

That night they lay side by side in Luigi's bed. In the adjacent room, Paula got agitated under the bed sheets; a crazy fantasy seizing her. The closer the young couple could get, the better it was. Contrary to what she believed, the young couple were in bed with their clothes on, embracing each other in the purest form ever, as if they were preparing themselves for the aftermath of the days ahead.

Daylight seeped through the thin curtains, engulfing the room with filtered beams of light that tickled Luigi's eyelids, bidding him to wake up. He rubbed his eyes and gradually opened them. His body felt relaxed but his mind seemed distorted. Slowly, last night's events crept in and he realised he had slept with his clothes on. He swept his right arm across the bed space adjoining him but there was no sign of Gina. A quick glance at his watch revealed it was ten fifteen AM. Emptiness got hold of him. Sadness filled his heart. He got up, guided by a glimmer of hope that he would find her in the bathroom but he was deceived. His heart contracted even harder. He chased a phantom down the corridor, ended up in the living room with his eyes searching wildly for Gina's presence. The only occupant was his mother watching TV with the sound turned down so low that it wasn't perceivable. Lately, the television set had been a companion, a silent one, an entity that could be conveniently switched on and off, with topics changed whimsically at the touch of a button. What a wonderful feeling to be in full control.

Seeing her in such a state rendered his case trivial and of lesser importance. He politely kissed her hand and followed it with a kiss on her forehead. He stared at her in admiration. Fifty years old and still immaculate. Her natural beauty didn't require any enhancement. She barely used cosmetics and unlike his aunt Eva, no attempt had been made to resort to plastic surgery.

Her asymmetrical features were vivid example of that. She was so beautiful because she looked different from most women whose bodies and facial features had been tempered with. His drifting thoughts were disrupted when Paula uttered: "I saw Gina this morning. We had coffee together at 8 am. She had to leave early and didn't want to disturb you. She asked me for an envelope and has left you a note in the breakfast room."

Luigi dashed towards the kitchen and found a white envelope resting on the toaster. It was not sealed. He took out the note, unfolded it and read its contents:

*Dear Luigi*

*By the time you read this letter, I'll be gone. Last night was a new experience. For the first time in my life, I learned that true love could be obtained without any physical supplement. My whole body shivered as our hands got entwined. Your soft lips on my ear lobes made me shudder with pleasure and excitement. You were loving me in a way I never got accustomed to. You were loving my soul, you were communicating with it. The glow in your eyes when you told me how much you loved me outweighed any sexual fulfilment. It was rather strange; that secure feeling I had while you held me in your arms.*

*Oddly enough, it seems I engaged you in physical sexual pleasure while you taught me the purity of love. I could live with the second option, but with the path you're pursuing, I'm not sure whether we're going to end up experiencing either one.*

*I wish you all the best. As we had previously agreed, I shall wait for you, just in case you decided to opt out from priesthood. Don't give it a long time though. One year is fair on both of us.*

*Good luck. Don't worry about your mum. I'll be dropping by to check on her. She's a lovely person.*
*With love, Gina*

# Chapter Thirteen

Rome proved to be a vibrating city. Luigi was overwhelmed by its size and diversity. Life differed tremendously from that of Milan's. Even the dialect seemed like a foreign language.

People were warm and jovial. Things were not, however, as well-organised as in Milan. Train stations lacked maintenance and were no match to the clean ones found in Milan. Luigi was an alien, similar to the rest of the men enrolled in the discernment year. The Rome Diocese was a smaller version of the United Nations.

Luigi combined formal study with pastoral guidance. He was assigned a supportive mentor. He recorded his thoughts and reflections and shared them periodically, as they formed the basis for discussions. He went deeply into the history and policy of the Catholic church, He found adequate time for reflection and soul searching. Each passing day brought him closer to God. He knew his vocation was genuine, regardless what had instigated it, but he needed to test it further. Not a single day elapsed without Gina crossing his mind. That was the primary source of concern. He truly missed her: her laugh, demeanour, wit.

A few times, he couldn't avoid fantasising that she was lying next to him. He had to ask his mentor whether it was normal for him to picture her naked and to have naughty dreams, over which he had no control whatsoever. His mentor would smile and appease his concern, telling him that it was perfectly alright to encounter such feelings, particularly during the first year. He was urged not to succumb to physical needs and just let go. No matter how hard he tried, Gina haunted his subconscious. To ease the pain and relieve himself from the caving emptiness, he found solace in phoning her or chatting with her at least twice a day. He would enquire about her whereabouts, happiness and well-being. Hearing her voice gave him a push, a kind of momentum that would launch him through the day's activities and studies.

What hurt him, though, was his inability to express his true inner feelings, especially when he intentionally refrained from reciprocating her love expressions. He couldn't bear the idea of replying: "Yes I know" to a dear person telling him that he was loved and missed a lot. His whole being suffered a silent pain. He could neither admit nor chuck away his emotions.

That suffering would eventually wane. Six more months to go and the discernment year would be over. At the end of that phase, he would be able to either regain his love or just walk away for good. That second alternative, though disturbing, carried one minor consolation prize, which would be the reliance of an ex-lover's friendship. Thus, Luigi was convincing himself that ultimately Gina would always be there for him, at least as a friend. That deduction soothed his soul momentarily until a dream or a wicked thought eradicated it. Why does it have to be like that? Why can't a priest just lead a normal life like everyone else? But then again, Jesus had a celibate life. The purpose is to be the father of a flock, the father of Christians; with sole mission: to spread equal and unconditional love to all humans.

Paula's heart would jump at the ringing tone of her phone even when the call had been timely and expected. Luigi communicated regularly with his mum, abiding by her wish to reach her at two pm each day. He perfectly understood her insistence on the timing: the only way to find out what he had eaten for lunch. Was the food nutritious? Well-balanced? Was it tasty? Deep down, even though she truly cared about the food quality and intake he was having, she was desperate like most mothers, to hear her son praising her cooking and telling her that no kitchen can surpass her gourmet skills. So, he delved into the game and boosted her morale, omitting to mention that the lasagna he had for lunch was exquisite and at par with her cooking. Calling her daily was not a kind of homework or ritual. He cherished that moment.

He loved his mother so much and cared a lot about her. A woman who raised him and devoted most of her time to bridge the gap caused by the early death of his father. A woman whose presence was so essential in his life. A person who had appreciated and loved her husband dearly.

Their daily conversation would last for 10 minutes or so. Her inquisitive nature, particularly regarding his feelings towards Gina and his personal contentment with his studies, prompted him to reiterate his conviction that he was indeed answering God's calling. Describing his emotions was out of question. She was too smart to be allowed such info. He could picture her reproaching him relentlessly, begging him to listen to his heart. Loving someone was after all one of God's commandments. Her husband's resentment of the clergy played another suffocating role. Her own son was seeking priesthood. Had Fabriano been alive, would he have condoned it? Would his objection have led to a dispute with his own son? So many questions and yet no answers. Discarding the issue until the end of the discernment year might prove detrimental. It was much better to tackle the matter from the outset, before it was too late.

Talking to his mum provided him with the assurance that Gina was fulfilling her promise to check upon her on a regular basis. He avoided mentioning his aunt's name in any of the telephone conversations.

## Chapter Fourteen

As far as Eva was concerned, it wasn't necessary to await her nephew's calls, even though they occurred on a weekly basis. She took over the whole situation, placing regular calls, asking Luigi questions that she answered herself. Most of the time, she would put words into his mouth, relying on his respectful mannered nature of not offending people and especially her.

"I'm certain you are happy with what you're doing. You're finally finding yourself and are convinced you're taking the right path for inner salvation and beyond that." Her allusion to his father's redemption was starting to bother him. He was not a kid anymore. Enough being told what to do. Her influence on him had prevailed and took him to the place he was in right now.

He wanted to make it his new home, his haven.

Luigi found it odd that his aunt always refrained from mentioning Andrea and little Fabriano. He had to enquire about them and request the most recent pics of the child. On one occasion, he had a brief chat with Uncle Andrea, as he used to call him. To his surprise, he denoted a certain ennui, if not despondency in his tone. Not a happy man for sure.

Luigi missed home, but distances were tolerated by Paula's frequent visits to Rome and his picking every opportunity to visit Milan, with periodic drops at Bellagio, his most favourite place.

# Chapter Fifteen

It was Easter 2033. Luigi returned to Milan on a Thursday afternoon, aiming to spend four days altogether. As customary, he was met at the airport by Gina and his mother. They drove straight away to Lake Como as per their scheduled agreement.

Upon arrival, Luigi changed into more comfortable clothes and joined the two women at the terrace. It was dusk already with the dark part of twilight at its maximum. The sky overhead was overcast, forecasting a sombre mood for Good Friday. Paula served refreshments and light strawberry cheese cake, the way her son liked. She was so happy in his presence and noticed he had gained maybe two kilos. He needed that supplement to match his tall figure. It suited him well. He was definitely a handsome man. She felt proud. Her infatuation was nonetheless countered by the nagging thought that he might not exercise his charm on women. It saddened her to consider such possibility and fought the idea through a tall glass of single malt Japanese whiskey. Gina shared the same concern but refrained sharing alcohol due to her stomach upset.

Amid the dark cloudy sky above, a small clearing opened, revealing a slender crescent moon snuggled up by planet Venus whose light reflection shone like a beautiful jewel. The scene insinuated that a glimmer of hope was always possible. Luigi couldn't help reminiscing of the old days when his father made him sit on his lap and taught him his first astronomy lessons. He missed him so much. Nine years had elapsed since he lost his dad and time didn't heal the wound. There was always something looming in the back of his mind, there was always a Deja-vu unfolding before him. There was no escape from it all. Good people could not just be forgotten. Luigi realised just then that he was resting in the bamboo chair that his father used to sit on. And yet, he wondered if he would ever experience the same sensation as his father did. To whom was he going to have the opportunity to describe one day the differences between stars and planets? Obviously, he was not going to be part of the league. Unless, unless…

"It's your aunt on the phone. Are you with us?" said Paula.

"Sure. Sure I am," he muttered as he clumsily picked up the phone.

"Hi! I miss you too. How is everybody? I can hear little Fabriano in the background. I saw pictures of him taking the first steps. It's so funny when he stumbles, especially when he tries to adjust his balance. Can't wait to see him. Nice talking to you Auntie. I'll be seeing you around. Let me say hello to Uncle Andrea. He is what? When? I see. Bye."

"What's that all about?" asked Paula.

"Did you know Uncle Andrea moved out a couple of days ago?"

"What are you saying? No, I didn't. But why? Did she provide any reason?"

"She said it wasn't the first time. She's accustomed to it. And that he always comes back."

Luigi, with a worried look, heard his mother murmuring: "Poor Andrea."

At precisely twelve o'clock, the group of three retired to their individual bedrooms. Gina didn't even try to suggest sharing the same bedroom as Luigi's. Neither did he.

He shut the bedroom door and for the first time in his life, he locked it. Was he scared of himself? Was he afraid for himself? It was amazing how a locked door could put someone in total denial.

He was tired after his long journey. The problems that plagued his aunt were becoming numerous and unpredictable. It seemed she had the knack for ruining lives, spoiling pleasant events and most importantly, skip over them as if they were trivial. Bottom line: she wanted to prevail. Nothing could stop her single mindedness. Together with his mum, they would try to mediate and persuade Andrea to mend fences with his aunt.

Luigi undressed, wore his pyjamas and stretched himself on the soft bed. The few glasses of red wine that he had over dinner were numbing his nervous system. He was a bit flustered.

He pulled on the bed sheets, exposing his ankles; he wiggled his toes; fetched the second pillow next to him and hugged it. He felt secure and thought of his father. Gradually he succumbed to a deep sleep.

# Chapter Sixteen

He was diving into a dark space filled with comets that trailed gaseous light behind them. A magnificent display of thick and thin lines, tracing bright and faint lines across a vast universe that had no limits. As the glowing masses swooped across the blackness, their previous trails traded their positions with faint wavering dots of light which were unperceivable amid the comets' brightness. Billions of stars appeared before him. He took heed of the Creator who devised this infinite expanse with such marvellous and mysterious beauty.

One star outshone the rest and Luigi was drawn to it. As he got nearer, the light subsided, and total darkness engulfed him. He couldn't tell where he was. Did he miss the beaconing star? His confusion faded away the moment he got pulled downwards. It was an already experienced sensation, yet Luigi could not ignore the chill along his spine. Then the light came back in a gradual manner, intensifying as he penetrated the portal and saw paradise unfolding before him. The scenic beauty and inner satisfaction surpassed the previous observations and feelings he had encountered before. This time he felt more at ease. His feet were almost grazing but not in contact with the lush green grass beneath. In the far distance, he glimpsed a figure standing by the edge of a scintillating lake. The nearer he got, the more familiar the figure became.

"Dad!" He cried out.

His father turned and addressed his son's mind, "Luigi! What are you doing here?"

Luigi didn't have to reply. Already his mind had been scanned and read. Fabriano understood the reason behind his son's second leap into Heaven. He asked him telepathically to approach him and once the distance shrank, Luigi was able to observe the calm and satiated features of his dad. This time he could notice a visible aura radiating from his father's silhouette. The smile on his face was so welcoming and charming, it took Luigi into a comfort zone unlike any other he had experienced. Fabriano's eyes gleamed with heavenly intelligence.

Without emitting any sound, the surface of the lake undulated, and waves of scintillating ripples spread towards the shore.

Luigi was dumbfounded. Nothing could cause the water to displace except matter. His first visit had revealed that Heaven was a spiritual place where physical laws did not apply. His dad had made it clear that outsiders were not capable of seeing any movement, to the exception of the portal through which they got transported. So, what was happening this time around?

Fabriano understood the confusion that lingered in his son's mind. It was too much for Luigi to digest the rules and conditions that prevailed in paradise. As a father, he had to inform his son of the pure basic laws that governed the metaphysical universe he had been drawn to.

"Don't be alarmed, my son. You remember our first encounter: you were hovering above the ground, seeing trees without birds, still motionless water filling lakes and rivers, feeling no wind, seeing no people, just me and you communicating through our minds, no sound at all. The only movement you noticed was that of moving clouds at the heavenly portal."

"This time, on your second visit, your feet are almost touching the soil but not resting on it yet. That's because you are alive. You're having sneak previews of Heaven; a luxury denied to most living creatures. Make it your last encounter, for your search and your relentless craving to learn and gain knowledge would lead you here by default. Next time, your feet will establish contact with the ground, and you'll become one of us. Unlike what many people believe, God is not clocking humans, setting their departure time from the living world, but our quest to explore and search for the afterworld might hasten our exit."

"God has given us freedom to lead our lives the way we want, abiding by the teachings of Jesus and the Prophets. I was searching for God for decades, asking and praying for His daily intervention to stop wars, famine, miseries and illnesses. Yet the answer was there in front of me and I never grasped it. Humans always try to shove responsibilities on the Creator, but that's a simplistic and childish approach not to admit our wrongdoing."

"Any Godly intervention would disturb the balance between good and evil. One must be philosophical about it: without sadness there's no happiness; nothing can be evaluated without a benchmark."

"Humans would have no value whatsoever, if daily interventions by God were to take place. Preventing wars should be the responsibility of world leaders. God would and should not step in. If He were to rectify our mishaps and alter the course of events, then we wouldn't be worthy of his trust and love. We wouldn't be worthy of being called humans. Yes, His love is unconditional. He laid the truth in front of us, but unfortunately, we try to evade it by elaborating and turning simple facts into complex issues that our mind cannot fathom."

"You see, there are several kinds of people: those who believe in God without questioning and lead a pure perfect life: those who think they believe in God and lead an immoral life; those who do not believe in God but are good natured and well behaved; those who don't believe in God and subsequently follow a totally misleading life, devoid of any goodness; those who believe in God but keep searching for Him, trying to find logical patterns in whatever they do while seeking His compassion."

"I belonged to that last category. Contrary to how I was perceived, I had always been a firm believer in a Creator and thus God. Few people would resort to fancy scientific words labelling the Creator various names: atom, hydrogen, particle, Bing Bang…but, ironically, no one could ever dispute the existence of life itself. Could it be triggered from nothing? If not, then we have to believe in a Creator. If yes, then that "nothing" is everything and it makes it more impelling to believe further in the greatness of Creation. We learned from the beginning that for every stimulus there's a reaction. The universe is a reaction. It's the consequence of an event that took place. The stimulus will always remain vague and intangible no matter how advanced humans can get. Being simple at times is far more difficult than being complex."

Luigi tried to interrupt the flow of information reaching him through the mind but was blocked. His father continued:

"All your queries will be replied to, as they are all transparent and known to me the moment you entered the portal. God welcome any soul that is pure and sincere. Questioning God's existence is not a sin in itself. It is part of a continuous search to further grasp matters, particularly spiritual issues that cannot be explained through science. Nonetheless, doubting His presence while planting bad seeds to undermine His teachings is a different matter. Those who tread on that course will be denied eternity and Heaven's doors will be shut in their faces."

"There's no such thing as hell. It's either Heaven or nothing at all. Since our childhood, we were instilled with the belief that good people end up in Heaven, while bad people will burn in hell. Such depictions are metaphors. Heaven is knowledge; hell is ignorance. That's the importance of unconditional belief. It spares one the effort of searching for the Truth, accepting written scriptures without casting a doubt on anything. However, that's not enough on its own; the faithful has to merit eternity by leading a life full of love, charity and good deeds. Those who think or pretend to believe and fail to fulfil God's teachings have no merit whatsoever and will be denied his Love. Those who have no faith at all but offer support to those in need and refrain from hurting anyone, might be considered as potential candidates for eternal life."

"You see, religion is a threshold, a gangplank that assists a person to leap from one world to another. No need for one to indulge in explanations or philosophise about anything. The Old and New Testaments laid out the path; all one needs is to come on board the ship that will sail him to eternity."

"What we never understood were the few contradictions encountered while reading the Testaments. Those contradictions alienated us from the Books and forced us to query their validity or question God's wrath and infliction of severe punishment on his people."

"The failure of clergy to reply to such queries and provide proper explanations had led to self-inflicted exodus from religious matters. And yet, the answers were right there in front of us, but nobody had the simplicity to understand why the Old Testament depicted a vindictive God."

"We tend to forget that transmitted words end up losing their meaning by the time they reached us. Few thousand years ago, there were no written official documents, no photographs, no voice recording…Hence, the word was conveyed from generation to generation, described in such rudimentary ways that a modern reader would find incoherent and inconsistent. Any description therefore of natural disasters was attributed to God's wrath. I reiterate: God would not intervene in changing the course of events. Human anxiety and desperation craved for heavenly interventions. It suited them to rely on God to resolve their problems; to forgive them because He created them. Therefore, responsibility was all His. The only intervention He could make was a combined Godly and earthly embodiment, but unfortunately people at that time were not ready yet for such an event. Jesus enacted that embodiment thousands of years later because the time was ripe for the intervention."

"One might ask why such an intervention is not occurring nowadays. The answer is simple and straightforward. The world has changed a lot and has become so advanced that a second return will give us no merit if we were to turn into better human beings. Imagine all sermons and teachings recorded and archived. Jesus will be on all networks; tangible evidence of miracles and resurrection will be recorded as solid proof that Jesus and consequently God do exist and have super powers. But the issue will always be: do we really deserve eternity because we saw it all on video and social media? Was it not more suitable to have faith when disciples were the only available media?"

"The problem lies in our failure to think spiritually; in our attempt to understand what we could only see. No effort seems to be undertaken. We don't want to search for the Truth although it is looming around us."

"The moment I joined this heavenly spiritual world, the truth revealed itself to me. It's like massive data being fed into one's soul to keep it abreast of real and true knowledge. That's the real purpose of being here: to grasp what we missed in our physical life and to understand what we couldn't comprehend. God want us to share His wisdom within His kingdom. Our thoughts are scanned and answers waved back at us, shedding light on many issues we deemed unexplainable, unfeasible. I'm getting educated on various surgical procedures in a way that outperforms what I used to practice in a grotesque sort of way. I was a layman."

Luigi tried to speak, but his father continued:

"You are right to question the value and importance of our ever-continuing search for knowledge, here in Heaven. But that is God's mysterious way of intervening and providing assistance to the whole of humanity. Often there are encounters like ours taking place between the two worlds. Call them: information exchanges; communication with the afterworld…it doesn't matter. Such encounters occur during deep sleep. The information seeker must be at the peak of his search for knowledge to the point of desperation; he lacks one piece of the puzzle and requires support to find a solution to a medical procedure, a scientific discovery…"

"During his strongest spiritual state and lowest bodily entrapment, the fusion of his physical world and that of the Beyond might become possible, depending on the strength of his spiritual level. Ideas never before thought of, will be transmitted and received during that out-of-body experience. The next day, upon waking up, the doctor or scientist won't be aware of what had exactly transpired but they would have gained knowledge, oblivious of the source behind their enlightenment."

"In your case, there's a certain awareness that you had either a dream or an out-of-body experience. That's due to the specific search you're conducting to seek a dear person and ensure that his soul is indeed in Heaven. You have thus, the added advantage of having previews of what it's like. Such encounters are very rare and could become luring to the person who is experiencing them. That's the danger. It's such a strong attraction. The more you get immersed in it the more you want out of it."

"Just to make you aware of what's happening with you, the ripples you saw in the water materialised before you because your second encounter has brought you closer and closer to heavenly conditions. That was Carla taking a dip in the lake. She communicated with me after crossing the portal. Over here, newcomers fetch those who preceded them. She's happy. You were able to see the ripple effect but not her. You're not there yet because you don't belong here."

"You crave to dive into this limpid transparent water, feel its crisp freshness cooling your body. I usually immerse myself in the lake and while totally covered by the clear transparent water, I watch the deer and flamingos lapping water at the edges. But you cannot see and do that yet. Go back, my son! Make good use of our discussions and remember that God is Merciful and Loving. He is everywhere; in your world, the whole universe and Heaven. Before you leave through the portal, I want to reveal to you that the Beginning and the End are analogous."

"The Big Bang, as it is called, was the beginning. An explosion that culminated into an expanding universe whose far edges receded away from the centre, picking hydrogen atoms along the way and creating star systems, constellations and galaxies. Earth is among trillions of planets that are suitable for life formation."

"Eventually, all living creatures return to the centre of that phenomenal blast once their lives are exhausted. It's quite simple to grasp. The origin of the Big Bang is Heaven. The ultimate eternal trip we make from our respective worlds is also back to Heaven. All galaxies and spatial objects relate therefore to Heaven as their focal point. What we called "aliens" also roam the infinite boundaries of Heaven, the same way we do. I communicated with few of them and it was fascinating. Paradise is basically a black hole where all deserving souls linger to praise God and thrive to assist physical worlds, through telepathic encounters, releasing info of their ever-continuing learning process."

"It's holistically too difficult to digest what I'm conveying to you. However, anything you might remember is over and above the grasp of most people. Make it useful and benefit from those valuable tips. May God be with you. I always pray for you and your mum. I have no means to watch over you. That conception proved to be erroneous. I can only ask God to guide you and watch over you. Take care, my son. I love you loads."

Luigi tried to get closer to his dad and hug him. He just couldn't. But his father's immaculate smile was enough to radiate love and happiness. An incredible world where peace and tranquillity prevailed.

# Chapter Seventeen

Luigi moved in his bed, his heart racing. How could he explain what he had experienced to anyone? Would they take it as a hallucination? A mere dream? Or a real spiritual encounter?

Whatever the verdict, he wasn't sure himself of the credibility of what he was dealing with. He knew deep down that such deep thoughts and revelations couldn't be attributed to earthly and mundane events. Regardless the truthfulness in his dream/encounter, the knowledge he was obtaining surpassed by far anything he had ever learned. It opened up his eyes and mind to a different approach of evaluating existence. Few seconds made all the difference. There was logic and philosophy in what his father had revealed to him. Knowledge is everything. The road towards Heaven.

He wished he could share his encounters with his mentor, with the Pope. But how would he be perceived? As a lunatic or a clairvoyant? Back to its normal beat, his heart felt light. The serenity that engulfed him, was far more intense than the previous one he experienced during his first encounter. He felt special: a person who knew too much, beyond anyone's comprehension. He stretched his limbs, yawned couple of times and rose. He brushed his teeth and washed his face, unlocked the door and went down to the kitchen. He had to switch the lights on along the way. No wonder Gina and his mum were not awake yet. The wall clock read five fourteen am.

Through the windows, he could faintly make out the outline of the mountain ranges beyond, swept by the faint light of dawn that percolated through dark clouds. The mixture of dim natural lighting and the dispersed artificial lights of Lake Como villages presented a breathtaking view. Luigi could picture early risers like him, putting on their kitchen lights and fixing coffee for themselves.

He extracted the orange juice bottle from the fridge and poured a long glass. As he gulped the contents, his free hand was busy inserting the coffee filter and filling up the percolator with water and ground coffee.

Five minutes later, he was drinking his hot coffee out of a special mug that his dad brought back from Lugano following their first family visit to Switzerland. Among all mugs and cups, he wondered at the first sip how oddly he selected that particular one. Was it by chance? Or was it meant to be? He preferred the second speculation. As far as he was concerned, it was some form of continuity; a link between his recent encounter and the physical world he was living in. It was a sign that the deep and intense dream he had was more of an encounter rather than a mere weird dream.

Luigi reflected on the persuasive contents of his dream and winced at the recollection of their details. The information he had amassed was substantial; it exceeded common knowledge and overshadowed scientific advancement by its philosophical potency. The value of the contents couldn't be presented to any scientific institution, let alone religious. Even if his claims were to be sustained with tangible evidence, he had no right to intervene and impact common belief. He could nevertheless indirectly use his acquired knowledge to improve certain things, and above all, spread and reinstate faith. No one would ever find out the source behind his intricate ideas and principles. He would have to liaise with the Catholic church on any unorthodox method of explaining or clarifying religious matters. He should not deviate from the rules set by the church unless the latter could be convinced that certain modifications were necessary to simplify and expand religious explanations. The essence of it all was the credibility of those spiritual dreams.

There was no way to prove the truth behind those revelations. But on the other hand, those visions were not in contradiction with the Christian faith. Contrary to all expectations, they promoted the greatness of God and valued the importance of human goodness as an essential tool to earn eternal life.

Luigi prepared breakfast for Gina and his mum: omelette with mushroom, cheese and hot spices; fried bacon and toasted bread. He didn't have to wake them up. The inviting odoriferous smell reached their bedrooms, itched their noses and were the sweetest wake-up call they could get. In no time, they were sitting around the oak breakfast table, eating greedily while listening to Luigi's detailed account of the strange dream.

Both women listened in bewilderment. Luigi's vivid description carried an undisputable mental stamina, clearly showing a genuine recitation of what happened during that strange dream. Paula enquired a lot about Fabriano. "How did he look like; did he appear happy…?"

Gina focused mainly on the spiritual aspect of the dream. She stared at Luigi in an inquisitive way, as if she wanted to hear more accounts, but refrained asking. Luigi's enthusiasm and excitement were at their saturation point. No need to extract from him any further information. He said it all. What she had to digest was already beyond her. Even as a mere dream, one had to admire its deep meaning. In his torment and concern about his father, topped by his inner self-searching, Luigi had attained a high-level state of mind where physical and spiritual elements got fused together. The outcome, be it true or just fiction, yielded metaphysical explanations that held logical patterns. An invention had always been after all the product of reverie. Luigi's experience was most certainly awesome and worthy of consideration. Together they agreed to keep the whole account for themselves.

Paula interrupted the looming silence and addressed Luigi, "I'm going to meet Andrea in Milan at the hotel where he's staying. He'll be down at the reception lobby at eleven. Would you care to join me or do you have other plans?"

"Sure. I'll accompany you. That will be my only chance to see him. Gina will ride with us. Lunch is on me. We'll attend Good Friday mass afterwards at the basilica."

# Chapter Eighteen

Andrea had been waiting in the coffee shop, adjoining the hotel lobby, since 10:50 am.

He had killed the time sifting through the newspapers and ordering a foaming cup of cappuccino. He could hear the clopping noise of high heels growing louder by the second. He caught the scent of woman's fragrance and instinctively rose from his armchair. Paula was in front of him, graceful and pretty as usual. Behind her stood Luigi, looking like a bodyguard watching her back. It was so good to see them, particularly Paula. Memories from the past stirred in his mind, heightening his emotional state. He moved one step closer and hugged her dearly. Andrea appeared to be sniffing her, trying to catch her smell and that of the past.

The intensity of the situation brought back fond memories of his beloved friend Fabriano. Andrea let go of Paula and turned to Luigi hugging him as well while patting his shoulders. Once the greeting was over, he ushered them to sit down. Twenty metres away, Gina sat in the lobby browsing the fashion magazines that were laid out on the table beside her seat.

The first few minutes were spent enquiring about each other's whereabouts and what each had been up to lately, focusing mainly on Luigi's discernment year and life in Rome.

Andrea purposely avoided the main topic of discussion: the specific one that had prompted Paula to call him and ask for the present gathering. He would wind himself up after each pause giving the impression that he was going to commence discussing his present issue with Eva. But Andrea would take instead an evasive action, opening a different topic altogether without indulging himself.

Paula realised that she had to take the initiative, so she interjected: "Andrea! What's going on? Moving out and staying at hotels and serviced apartments isn't going to solve anything. On the contrary, it would make things worse. You and Eva have to seriously talk it out and mend fences. I don't know the details behind the rift between you two, but Luigi understood that there were previous occasions in which you had fallen out with each other."

"She scares me," Andrea blurted out, "my life with her since we got married has been an undeclared nightmare. I did most of the compromising to save our marriage. As you know, her pregnancy and her insistence on not having an abortion forced me to marry her and leave Carla. What a fool I've been. The misery I had caused to Carla and my family, let alone myself is irreversible. All that for the sake of a miscalculated step driven by physical attraction. What bothers me the most is my weakness and failure to control my desires. I was not a teenager to commit such drastic mistakes."

"Hell, I was in my forties, married, with a loving family. I hated myself for abandoning Carla and her recent suicide has jolted me. Imagine living my life with a constant reminder that I caused the death of a dear person. A woman who devoted her time to her family, playing two roles, that of a mother and a father. Most of the time I wasn't there for her. I was either working long hours or spending my remaining spare time in the arms of an insatiable woman, who happened to be my best friend's sister."

"I wish I had told Fabriano of our affair, but how could I? He was ill and suffering, with constant worries that his sister was a virgin, a lonely person devoid of male companionship…What a shock I had when I dated Eva. She was the perfect female partner a man could have. She knew how to please a man, even a woman, I should add. She introduced me to threesomes and I got carried away with my carnal wants. Sorry Luigi, for my bluntness. I realise she's your aunt. I've said enough. Maybe I shouldn't talk any further."

"Uncle Andrea. Please continue. I'm not a kid anymore. We are here to help. We care about you both. No solution to your conjugal problem can be found if the causes were not outwardly divulged."

"Well, you know what transpired later," continued Andrea. "She got pregnant, we got married and were blessed with little Fabriano. His birth put our marital life on the right track. Suddenly, there was a reason for us to be there for him, to raise him together. There was a new meaning to our life."

"But Carla's suicide reminded me that I had another family to attend to. I tried my best to spend some time with my children, aiding them to recover from the pain that besieged them day and night. I even urged Eva to show them some affection; at least to let them feel their dad had not forgotten them, that he was indeed their security…I was asking her to condone my spending time with them,

I begged her to invite them, at her convenience, over for lunch or dinner, especially on holidays…"

"She got infuriated and asked me to rejoin them. That's when she began mentioning that I was no longer needed. I ignored her and kept seeing my kids every now and then, ensuring they were doing well in school…"

"One night I came home very late. It was past midnight. I caught her having sex with her fitness trainer. They were at it in our bed while little Fabriano was crying at the top of his lungs in the adjoining room. I turned away, picked my son up and comforted him. Once he fell asleep, I lay on the couch in the living room in order to relieve my exhaustion, hoping to doze off. But I could hear her ecstatic moaning. I wondered right then, how many competitors I must have and quietly laughed at my naivety. I recalled an anecdote Fabriano used to recite jokingly: a man has two heads but only one of them will prevail."

"In my case, it was obvious I had screwed it up completely. I had relied on the wrong head. The nagging part of it all was the indifference Eva displayed the next morning when she and her new lover found me asleep in the living room. She shouted like a mad woman, asking me how long I had been in the apartment…"

"Since then, Eva has been living her life the way she had always wanted. Male and female lovers come and go as they please, unhindered by my presence, as if I were not there. I frequently escaped from her hell, but had to return back for the sake of little Fabriano. I had to be sure he wasn't neglected. But at present, I can no longer continue with this farce. It's wearing me out. I don't want to lose my children from either marriage. Those are innocent bystanders in a cruel world directed by weaklings like us."

"Paula! I can't go back to her. I guess I have woken up to a cruel reality. Eva has twisted the knife inside my wound and I'm bleeding heavily. My whole life is screwed. I've become a miserable person. I won't file for divorce; at least not now. I've got plenty on my hands. All I ask of you is to persuade her that I pick little Fabriano up either on Saturdays or Sundays."

All the while, Andrea made snivelling sounds, commensurate with the sad state he was in.

Paula felt sorry for him, whatever happened to that strong and jolly fellow she once knew? He was obviously cracking under the weight of the burden inflicted on him.

"I'll speak to Eva this afternoon. She's meeting us at Duomo Cathedral," she said in a comforting way.

"Thanks, Paula for your time and patience. You're my last and only resort. And once again, sorry Luigi, for spoiling your vacation with my personal problems. Tell me about yourself."

# Chapter Nineteen

Good Friday mass was attended by hundreds of people. The Archbishop delivered a sermon describing the sufferings of Jesus Christ while picking on the debauchery of the society. Most worshippers nodded in agreement although they seemed to be hearing rather than listening. Only a few reflected on the oration and the message his Excellency was trying to convey. Luigi wished the speech had a simplistic spiritual tang, one that would somehow grab the attention of listeners and seep through their minds.

Once the mass had finished, Eva and Paula first came out of the basilica and were joined at the main entrance few minutes later by Gina and Luigi. Soon afterwards, they were chatting animatedly at a nearby Starbucks coffee shop.

Luigi recounted several times what he'd been up to in Rome. Eva's inquisitive style extracted all the details from him in a crafty manner. She was joyful and enthusiastic. Contrary to Andrea's depiction of her, one would have fallen for her charm and joyfulness. However, her past incidents and Andrea's credible account would pull off the mask she was putting on. Either she was a great actress or she was in total denial. Most probably a combination of both: thought Paula.

As time slipped by, Luigi had to struggle maintaining his respect for her. He noticed that she was deliberately ignoring Gina as if she weren't part of the group. Her previous laid back and cajoling attitude gave way to a demanding and assertive one. She reverted to her previous ways of enforcing her views and principles onto him. That he shouldn't be in female company; that God's calling must be taken seriously.

Luigi was appalled by her double standards and was on the verge of showing his disdain, when his mother cut the conversation and blurted out: "All that is trivial. The important issue worth discussing is your family. Andrea didn't tell us what caused him to move out (she lied because she had to), but he seemed willing to open a new chapter. He would like to have a one-day access to Fabriano on a weekly basis until both of you decided what course of action to take."

"No way!" Eva shouted. "I'm going to make him pay for his sins."

"What sins?" Luigi asked.

"He comes home late, claiming he had been spending time with Clara's children. He has no right to integrate his previous family within mine. That's not fair. Plus I have no time for such indulgence."

"But their mother died because of you two," retorted Paula. "For God's sake, do you expect him to abandon his children? A little affection from your side would resolve the whole issue. Is it a lot to ask for? Marriage is a compromise. Each one of you has to make concessions."

"Certainly not me," Eva blurted out. She got up and hurriedly walked away bumping into a waiter who was taken off-guard.

Luigi ran after his aunt and pleaded with her to reconsider at least Andrea's request to see his son once a week. Eva didn't bother to look back at him and kept rushing towards the underground station. She went down the stairs and vanished. He rejoined Gina and his mum.

They stared at him inquisitively but his frustration said it all. No need to explain what had happened. Paula tried to conceal her dismay, conversing in various irrelevant topics that had no interest to the listeners, including herself. She realised the fruitless effort she was trying to exert and pointed out it was time to leave.

By seven o'clock, the three of them were back at the Bellagio home, where they took refuge in the peaceful setting of their garden. Assisted by Ella the housekeeper, Paula fixed a big bowl of tabbouleh salad and served fried eggplants and zucchini dipped in a sauce consisting of olive oil, garlic, red pepper and lemon juice. She opened a Frascati white wine bottle and shared it with Gina. Luigi had always refrained on Good Fridays to drink alcohol or consume meat and dairy products.

Gina held her glass and took a sip. She appreciated the wine quality and its crispness. She felt a bit naughty, as if she were teasing Luigi with her indulgence. The weather was slightly cold but bearable. It didn't rain all day despite the immense grey clouds that drifted in the sky. She put down her glass, nibbled on salty roasted cashew nuts and addressed Luigi directly: "I've been thinking of the recent dreams you were having. They carry lots of meaning regardless how one looks at them. It doesn't really matter whether they carried truthful elements or not, but there's logic somehow behind their contents. The troubled state you were in when both dreams materialised, topped by your continuous search for your father, have rendered you susceptible and extremely sensitive to pick up waves that a normal person wouldn't perceive."

"You are therefore privileged but at the same time plagued with a burden you'll have to carry for the rest of your lifetime. It's a pity you'll never be able to prove the accuracy of what you have experienced. I'm scared for you, Luigi. Any further encounter is going to affect you bigtime."

"Please, let go. Relax and lead a life, far from the influence of other people. Your aunt has been running your life for you. What I gathered from you in the past and based on today's turnout, is enough to condemn her ethics and her insistent call for religious adherence. She is a devious woman. Sorry for my harsh appraisal but obviously she only cares about herself. Her religious conception is based on erroneous comprehension of faith and teachings. Far from abiding by the rules, she throws all the blame onto others. She believes that salvaging all those around her, is her duty and that she will be subsequently rewarded for her guidance. She messes therefore everyone's life for her personal goals and wild goose chases."

"That's your friend saying it. Not me," said Paula, while gazing at her son.

"My aunt had a big influence on me," retorted Luigi. "That's true, but she no longer has a grip on me. I'm where I am because of her. Omitting the causes and reasons behind my current choices I'm finding myself in the right place. I wouldn't say that I'm grateful to her, but priesthood suits my expectations. It is rather a complicated course, but it has spiritual rewards. The fact that worshippers will turn to me for advice and consolation gives me encouragement to continue."

Gina took a big wine gulp and wished she hadn't raised the issue at all. "Are you insinuating that the discernment year is not a testing period anymore? Have you sealed your future already?"

Luigi realised the big mistake he had just committed. There he was demolishing Gina's hopes that they might have a chance to reunite physically. Although there had never been a real vocation in the first place and neither was it God's calling in the real sense of the word, somehow, the latest dreams or encounters had sealed his fate. He had enough knowledge to persist and prevail as a modern priest who would instil faith in the heart of believers and the doubtful. He could no longer back down. It would be unfair.

"It seems like it. But no one can be so certain. I care for you, Gina," Luigi cried out. "I think of you each day, sometimes platonically, sometimes with lust. But I need to proceed undaunted with my choice. I beg of you, don't let me be an obstacle in your life."

"Speaking for myself, I won't be a hindrance either," replied Gina. She thanked Paula for the dinner, kissed him on the cheek and headed outside and drove off hurriedly, tyres emitting screeching sound as they rubbed against the asphalted pavement.

"I hope you know what you're doing, Luigi," said Paula after a short while. "Have you noticed your failure to kiss her back even on the cheek? Wow! That's too much. Soon you might find it awkward to kiss your own mother. Does it have to be so strict? Compassion shouldn't be torn out of your heart; at least not so swiftly."

Luigi approached his mum quietly and kissed her face, laying a few teardrops on her smooth skin. He snivelled for a few seconds, collected himself, bid his mum goodnight and went to his room upstairs. Tonight, he was not going to lock the door. Tonight, he wasn't going to dream about his father and heaven. Tonight was reserved for him and him alone.

# Part Three

# Chapter One

One year later, on the 27th of April 2034, Paula received a call informing her that Michel, her father-in-law, had passed away peacefully at home. She was saddened by the news. He had celebrated his eighty second birthday a couple of months earlier. He had sent her a video showing him dancing artfully with his wife, oozing eagerness for life. Michel had always been a solid link in Paula's life. He was always there for her, pushing her expectations high and comforting her whenever she sought refuge in him. He reminded her of Fabriano. Being able to communicate with him audibly and visually on almost a daily basis, had provided her with a sense of security. He cared for her and cherished her. She had been the true love that his son had wished for. Michel never failed to remind her of that whenever she succumbed to her loneliness.

She made airline reservations and called Luigi. He would fly out of Rome and join her in Beirut. Together they would ride the two-hour drive to the Valley of the Saints.

In the morning that followed, they were in a rented car driving along the coastal highway that led to the north of the country. The Mediterranean Sea on the left-hand side was relatively calm, with little white crests forming on its surface: result of the slight breeze that blew intermittently. The tiny waves gently slashed the seashore rocks spraying water upwards. The gentle swooshing sound of withdrawing water could be heard, though faintly. The windows were rolled down, allowing the cool air to sweep across the internal space of the vehicle and bring along the fresh stale, sulphury scent of the deep sea.

Far from being a sombre day, it turned out that the drive was indeed pleasant and heart lightening. The riders were returning to the native land of their respective husband and father. They felt closer to Fabriano as they got nearer to their destination.

A huge road sign had an arrow pointing to the right with bold giant letters reading: VALLEY OF THE SAINTS. Paula turned right and remembered the twenty-kilometre steep climb that separated them from Fabriano's village. The nearer they got, the more the scenery varied. Deep valleys laid in a venerable manner at the base of high mountain ranges, where dozens of caves could be seen carved out of the rocks. The riders were fascinated by the wild and raw natural beauty that captivated the heart and mind of the observer.

On previous occasions, they had admired those mountains but hadn't appreciated them the way they deserved. One could feel God's impending presence. Luigi wore a smile while recalling his dad's advice that everything was there for us to see but somehow went ignored. How was it possible for his aunt, let alone himself to contemplate redeeming his dad? His father found God since he had access to the Valley of the Saints. He had further searched for Him to widen his knowledge. His dad talked to God whenever he found refuge in those mountains. An advantage that most believers didn't have. Hence, his father got acquainted with God in a natural way: through religious teachings and mysticism. Most humans had only the former for guidance. His dad had acquired both. But he wanted much more. He kept searching not just for his own sake but rather for the sake of all those who couldn't fathom the silence of God; why He deserted them? His father's quest had been pure and sincere. God knew that and rewarded him with eternal life.

Michel was buried next to his son. Eva who had travelled for the purpose of attending her father's funeral, barely spoke to Paula and Luigi. It had been quite a long time since they had socialised, particularly after their infamous encounter one year earlier at Duomo. Paula and Luigi spent three days in the village doing their best to comfort Sophia for the loss of her husband and showed sincere emotions that touched the old lady's heart. Paula went as far as suggesting the relocation of her mother-in-law to her home in Milan, explaining all the while that Sophia needed good care. No promises were made, except that Sophia would consider the proposal in due time.

Deep down, Sophia wished such a gesture had come from her own daughter. But it came as no surprise to her: Eva had changed a lot. She possessed a heart of stone that nothing mollified. Her split with Andrea had hardened her even further. Eva had turned possessive and demanding soon after her high school graduation. Her university friends had been just a handful and seemed to change every three months or so. She wouldn't tolerate being asked about it.

Often, she would fall out with her parents accusing them of interfering with her life. Fabriano acted as a catalyst, whose subtle intervention always led to reconciliation. He had to protect his sister from any harm and never refrained to bring the smile back to her face. He was worried about her lack of emotional stability, normally acquired through steady relationships. He wished she had a boyfriend. He would attribute that failure to Eva's misconception of Catholic teachings. He had genuinely thought she was too conservative and died believing she truly was. His love and affection for her blinded his judgement and he couldn't see the mysterious bad side of her character.

Luigi and Paula stayed in Beirut for a couple of days before departing to their destinations. It was a good opportunity for them to travel South, towards the village of Qana where Jesus performed his first miracle. On their way, they visited the city of Tyre and admired its fishing port and Phoenician ruins.

It was wonderful to stroll along the southern coast mixing with Muslims and Christians alike; chatting with shop owners and getting good bargains on local artifacts.

It was an enjoyable day, casual and carefree. They reached Beirut around seven in the evening and had ample time to shower and dress up for their planned dinner at a renowned Lebanese restaurant in the Downtown area. Sophia joined them there and reiterated her promise to consider Paula's proposal to leave for Italy soon enough. During the meal, they learned Eva had already returned to Milan the day before.

# Chapter Two

Andrea visited Paula few days later to pay his respect. It turned out he was the one who needed consolation. He had grown a beard mostly dominated by white hair. He looked older: obviously due to heavy smoking and alcohol consumption. Sitting close to her on the couch, he looked dejected, with his neck tie twisted to one side with wrinkles running through the length of the silk fabric. Involuntarily, Paula adjusted the tie knot and straightened it. And instantly, in a split second, Andrea pecked her lips. Dazed and caught off-guard, Paula slung herself to the far side of the sofa avoiding further advance from Andrea's side.

"I'm so sorry, Paula. I don't know what got over me. But I guess it was a reflection of my desperate need for consolation rather than lust. You know my sincere admiration for you. You combine most qualities a man could find in a woman: goodness, compassion and friendship."

"Knowing you for several years fomented emotions based on admiration and appreciation. I'm certain it would apply to all those who got acquainted with you and Fabriano. Both of you idealised the perfect couple, the pair that all pairs should emulate."

"It's OK. Maybe I exaggerated my reaction. But I must admit it took me by surprise. I wasn't expecting a kiss, even a dry one."

She had lived the past ten years of her life driven by the momentum gained by the strong love she had for her late husband. She often longed for sexual pleasure but denied herself this physical necessity even though Fabriano had persuaded her to continue with her life. At times, she just needed the presence of a man beside her, embracing her and comforting her. She was lonely and nothing in her life filled the big gap caused by Fabriano's departure. She put her thoughts aside and her face drew her usual dashing smile. That encouraged Andrea to discuss his personal life with her.

"As you know, I'm presently staying with my children in Carla's home. They have recuperated from the aftermath of their mother's suicide and are doing well in college. They still blame me partially for the incident, but I don't mind anymore. Getting used to it, I guess. Time would heal the wound." Andrea said that with a shrug. "My problem is little Fabriano. I rarely see him. I need to concoct special scenarios to get close to him. At times, I call Eva pretending that I'm worried about her welfare and whether she needed any financial supplement. Being greedy and all, she would affirm her need for money and consequently I seize such opportunities to see my son. I love to hold him and make funny faces that make him laugh. I desperately need to see him more often, but unfortunately, she's not willing to cooperate. She is torturing me."

"Why don't you file for divorce?" asked Paula inquisitively. "Would you call that a married life? Eva is lusting over men and women, while extorting you financially. What's the point of being married when you don't play any part in her life?"

Andrea sighed and shook his head. "She has vowed to inflict harm on little Fabriano in return for any divorce proceeding. She's frightening and I can't put her to the test. She's liable to carry out her threats. I'm living a nightmare," he exclaimed.

"She's crazy. The selfish bitch might do anything," Paula concurred. "Maybe you should find a way that would compel her to file for divorce herself."

"I don't know," Andrea said, as he thought the matter over. "Eventually, it might be the right course of action."

Wielding his tweed jacket, Andrea rose up and excused himself: he had late consultations at the medical centre. Paula stood up and accompanied him to the door, bidding him goodbye.

Andrea suddenly froze and remained idle, his right hand holding down the cold metallic doorknob. He stood there by the entrance door, hesitated for a while, then turned and walked the few steps that separated him from Paula. He stared at her bewildered eyes and drowned in their gaze. Without spoken words, he lifted his right hand and caressed the outlines of her moist lips with his index, marvelling at their smoothness. He slightly bent his head and found her reciprocating his move. Their lips touched and parted. He squeezed his chest against her heaving breasts and grabbed her slim waist holding her in captivity.

Andrea was savouring these strawberry-scented kisses previously unknown to him. The femininity that Paula exuded surpassed his expectations. His mouth lingered on her long neck, his tongue probed her earlobes. She emitted a stifled moan and retreated backwards, adjusting her top and jeans.

"Andrea, you're going to be late for your consultations. Let us forget what has transpired between us. I guess we were both vulnerable due to our obvious frustration and emotional instability."

"Paula! We need to talk next time we meet. I can speak for myself and I know damn well that I'm infatuated by your warmth. You're a charming woman. Kissing you and touching you are enough to drive me crazy. Now I understand perfectly well Fabriano's fondness of you."

"Please Andrea, just leave. I cannot think straight at the moment."

He shut the door behind him, feeling very unsure of this new venture and Paula's perception of him.

Paula was relieved that he was finally gone. The whole thing was a mistake. Closing the door behind him was comparable to waking up after a weird nightmare. Andrea had stirred wild feelings in her that she had almost forgotten. She couldn't ignore neither her sensuality nor the pleasure she felt during those few minutes. His arousal when their bodies pressed against each other, made her feel wanted. It asserted that she was still very attractive. Her nipples were still hurting with pulsating soreness spreading from the base to the tip.

She didn't write anything down in her diary book that day. Paula thought that doing so would conceal her betrayal. But was it really a betrayal? Was a widow supposed to alienate herself from romantic relationships? Fabriano certainly saw it differently. He spent his last days encouraging her to proceed with her own life after he was gone. He wouldn't want it otherwise. Her happiness meant a lot to him. She was certain of that; yet would he condone an affair with his best friend who also happened to be a widower and his brother-in-law?

# Chapter Three

Paula switched on the television set. News flashed on every channel: NASA, in conjunction with the Russian Federal Space Agency, the Beijing Aerospace Command and the European Space Operations Centre were preparing for a manned space journey to Planet Proxima B on the 25th of June 2034. The exoplanet orbited the Alpha Centauri star system, the nearest 3-star system to our world, 4.24 light years away.

The preparation had been under way for the past three years and concerned governments had pledged total secrecy about the space program and its intention. Scientists and technicians were forced to sign special contracts denying them to divulge any form of info even to their family members. Failing that, they were liable for severe prosecution and job loss.

President Thomas Walker of the United States of America revealed on live televised broadcast from the White House that recent technological advancements, particularly the development of spaceships capable of travelling at the speed of light, had provided the big powers with a great leap to scour the deep space and search for civilisations beyond our solar system.

Even though few planets within our own star system were still relatively unexplored, the likelihood of finding evidence of life had seemed remote. The big decision to probe another star system had therefore become justified. Collected data from Proxima B in the Alpha Centauri star system revealed contrary to previous belief that intelligent life did exist on that exoplanet. It was therefore found empirical to rely on a manned mission.

Twelve astronauts had been carefully chosen from different nations and were subjected to rigorous training. The one-way four-year trip duration would be mostly spent in hibernation pods with environmental controls that put the astronauts in suspended animation.

Paula was enthused and confused at the same time. There she was questioning the ethics of her fling with Andrea while the world was busying itself with space travel. Amazing how everything was so relative. She picked up her cell phone and called Luigi. He quickly answered the call and sounded agitated. He had also watched the news flash and was on the verge of calling his mum but she had been faster.

"Fascinating news, Mum! Who would have thought we could travel at the speed of light? Those who were chosen for the interspatial travel are so lucky."

"No one expected that," Paula agreed. "But remember that your mind has also taken you much farther at greater speeds: you've been floating in space next to comets, star constellations, galaxies, and beyond. They are trying to compete with you," she said in a cajoling way.

Luigi mulled over her words and twitched. It was true what she had mentioned. His dreams regardless the realistic value they held, surpassed technological feats by far. Mental power versus man-made probes. Spending a total of 8.5 years on space travel to explore the nearest star system was difficult to grasp. One had to admire the greatness of the universe.

"From launching date, it's going to take 8.5 years to receive the first live coverage of the spacecraft landing and planet exploration. That's the drawback of such missions. But it's a scientific challenge."

Paula could picture the excitement in her son's eyes. She agreed: "So true. Communication signals transmitted from the surface of the planet will take 4.24 years to reach Earth. It's going to be interesting to learn about another solar system. Your father would have been jumping with enthusiasm. But I guess it doesn't matter anymore. The knowledge acquired in the afterworld surpasses by far the nitty gritty facts we amass and gather through space exploration. Anyway, reverting to mundane issues: plan to come over soon. Otherwise you're going to find me looking for you in Rome." She giggled.

"That's a great idea. Try to get out of Milan and spend few days over here? The change will do you some good. Think about it! Expecting you soon. Bye. Love you."

"Love you too," she replied. "I'll do my best." The call ended and Paula returned to her reverie.

# Chapter Four

Andrea woke up the next day, hearing the tweeting of birds reaching him from the garden that adjoined his bedroom. The oak tree that grew few metres away from his open windows, must have been a nesting place for dozens of birds greeting the first sun rays with their chirp. A beautiful pleasing symphony that spread waves of comfort, emphasising that life was continuing. He listened to that music and was encouraged to move and lift his eye lids, unveiling streams of sunlight that poured in at various angles.

He felt energetic and joyful; sensations he had missed for so long. He lifted himself up and tucked the pillow tightly behind his back. He sat lazily in bed enjoying the light breeze that caressed his face. Andrea turned his head towards the stretch of blue sky captured within the window frame and saw scattered white fluffy clouds hovering over the city skyline at the far distance. A view he had probably seen numerous times but never treasured. Funny how people missed and skipped such moments in life.

He found the answer. Living was all that mattered. He still had his children from his previous marriage; he still had his thriving career and he, and he…had a tender woman in his life. He fancied Paula and longed for a relationship, but she needed to reciprocate. He had to remain positive for that dream to materialise. Maybe that beautiful morning was an indication, a sign that things were bound to change.

Andrea got out of bed, went straight to the bathroom. He stared in the mirror and saw the reflection of a haggard person; an image conflicting with his spirit that morning. His beard had grown uneven with a greyish hint to it; maybe he should dye it to match the auburn hair on his head. Deep down he blamed his genes for the weak melanin production which was betraying the colour of his hair follicles. Ironically he had to admit that the wise and intellectual look that he had acquired lately were due to the greyish beard that he wore.

Without hesitation, he used scissors to trim the thick bush; lathered his beard and passed the razor blade on the remaining hair for a complete clean shave. He washed his face with warm water, dried it with a towel and glanced at the mirror that faced him. A different man appeared within the chromed frame; a younger person with fresh aspiration for hope and willingness to live. He touched the contours of his face and smiled. A quick shower boosted his rejuvenating sensation. He took his time selecting a blue shirt, a navy-blue tie and a grey suit. He polished his shoes while whistling a soft tune. A splash of Armani fragrance on his cheeks made his skin tingle slightly. He was now ready to face the world.

Andrea brewed coffee in the kitchen, filled his mug with the hot liquid and headed for the sitting area. His son Alphonso and daughter Maria aged twenty and eighteen respectively were wearing their satin robes and were kneeling on the rug, glued to the television set. News about the space mission to Planet Proxima B was making the headlines everywhere in the world.

Andrea planted kisses on his children's heads and they reciprocated without turning, sending kisses in mid-air. He sat on an arm chair and was immediately mesmerised by the news. He had a late night yesterday and apparently missed the excitement. It took a while to absorb what was being said in the aired interviews with scientists, astronauts and heads of states.

The three of them remained silent for an hour until the news flashes became sort of routine and repetitive. Alphonso and Maria moved away from the TV set and dumped their weight on the couch near their father. Maria noticed first her dad's metamorphosis. Her reaction was spontaneous. She got up and held his face in her two hands, stroked it in disbelief and with an angelic smile bent down and kissed him. Her brother followed suit.

The family was back, even though Carla was not in their midst. The gloom that loomed over them was being eradicated. Just a simple deviation from the sore past had brought them faith that a new life was still possible. It had been a while since they saw him as they had perceived him: a dashing man with stylish demeanour; a dad who could smile; who could cheer them up and try his best to compensate for their big loss; a dad who wouldn't abandon them.

Andrea was happy after years of atrocious struggle with himself. The last eight months were particularly difficult. He didn't know how he managed to survive those dreadful moments, but Eva had that domineering effect on those around her. One had to resist her and prove to her that her influence could waver and eventually plummet. Finally, he decided to do so. No more yielding, no more acquiescing.

# Chapter Five

Paula had a nice dream. It was interrupted by a phone call from her cosmetics shop. It came through at 10: 15 am. She answered reluctantly and gave her instructions in a slumbering way that made her assistant regret calling her at such time. It was amazing how dreams could not be recalled in their entirety. She could only remember sketchy parts. Her thighs were being stroked by a man whose face she couldn't make out. His touch sent streams of exciting waves through her nude body. That night she had slept completely naked. She didn't know why. Was it due to her reinstated sensuality? She had forgotten how it felt like to kiss a man, to be caressed and to be held in strong arms. Yesterday afternoon shuffled all the cards. What she had been ignoring for years proved to be a hoax; a farce far from reality. She had loved Fabriano with all her senses, but since he'd been gone, she was fooling herself, believing that she could survive without the company of a man; without the physical need of a man. But Andrea in a clumsy way had reactivated her inner longings. How silly a human could be! She resented Luigi's choice for celibacy while denying herself the chance to lead a new life. Ten years had elapsed since Fabriano's departure and she had been living like a nun, secluded in her home, barely going out. At fifty-two years of age, she was still in her prime, looking gorgeous with a physique of a forty-year-old woman. She craved attention yet lived in total denial. The love and affection she once sought after, were not on top of her priority list. They were still plausible but her immediate goal as of yesterday was to fulfil her sexual desire. Was she turning into another Eva? Was it possible that Eva belonged to the avant-garde group of people who knew sensuality played a big role and placed it at the top of their agenda? She hoped not. Nonetheless, she conceded that emotions and intertwined feelings no longer played a major role in her life. Probably her priorities were being reversed. At a young age, emotions often led to physical acts. It seemed in her present case that the physical acts would lead to emotions. She most certainly belonged to that category. What a transformation!

Two hours later Paula was at the shop doing an inventory of recently delivered cosmetic products. Sylvia, the shop assistant couldn't help noticing a change in her attitude. She was as composed and collected as she had been long time ago. She was radiating inner peace and contentment. She wore a smile that had faded away for years. Her cheerfulness reflected on all those who worked in the shop.

Sylvia fixed two double espressos and walked into Paula's office. They chatted for a while and sipped coffee; discussing work issues and latest news: the manned space mission.

Regular customers were delighted by Paula's presence and few had long chats with her.

Sales soared on that day as if buyers were reaffirming their loyalty towards the shop owner.

On her way home that evening, Paula had a call from Andrea. She was surprised to watch his altered look when video mode was switched on. She also noticed the allure he exuded.

"Hi. Is that really you?" she exclaimed.

"I guess," he replied sarcastically. "Do you like my new image?"

"Actually, I do. That's the joyful man I had known."

"How about handsome and dashing?"

"That too," she blurted. There she was being vulnerable.

"I've been promising myself a big juicy grilled burger. I'll pick you up at nine tonight and we'll dine at Tizzy's NY Bar and Grill. Are you in?"

Paula's reply came in an instant: "I'll be waiting." Her heart was racing. What was happening to her?

She spent half an hour on her make-up; not because she needed it, but for self-assurance that she looked her best. She put on tight black jeans, a white top with black stripes and a white leather jacket. She sprayed perfume on her neck and cheeks, checked her watch and went down to the building entrance. The concierge stared at her appreciatively. It had been a long time since he saw her so bubbly and beautiful. He gave her a thumbs-up and she nodded.

Andrea had already parked in front of the building's entrance. He got out of the car, kissed her hand, opened the door for her and ushered her in. He looked like a desperate butler who didn't want to spoil or miss any detail. He was casually but fashionably dressed. His newly acquired appearance surpassed the video display Paula had watched earlier on her mobile.

Andrea was his usual self: elegant, handsome and polite.

Andrea drove his Audi through wide and narrow streets, guided by the GPS navigation system. Traffic wasn't that bad and they reached their destination in thirty-five minutes.

Dinner reservation was made at ten. As they arrived few minutes earlier than scheduled, Andrea suggested that they strolled along the canal. The night was lit up by a full moon shedding white glow on the undulating water surface that ruffled under a moderate breeze. Boats bopped up and down at every wave crest that hit them. Hundreds of people walked along the length of the canal admiring the residential buildings and the variety of shops and restaurants. The place was heavily frequented by late shoppers and diners.

They spent their remaining twenty-five minutes pacing the same stretch of pavement, pointing at few structures that attracted their attention; listening to the metallic squealing noise of the tram; watching foreign visitors posing for pictures. They avoided gazing at scattered couples embracing in few dark areas, leaving those lovers to their private secluded world.

The burgers with chili con carne for topping were messy but exquisite. Chin dripping juice oozed out of the bun following each bite. The beef was still moist despite the thorough charcoal grilling and had a smoky taste. In between bites, they downed cold beer straight from the bottle. It cooled down the effect of the hot sauce. The sweet bitter taste of the beer blended well with the thickly cut French fries that were served.

The couple reminisced about the past, recalling good times they shared together with Carla and Fabriano and often laughed wholeheartedly. The kids within them got loose and manifested their excitement in a carefree way.

Once the burger plates were consumed, Andrea ordered a pitcher of draft beer. Two refrigerated Dartington stemmed beer glasses were brought in and Andrea filled them up, allowing the white foam to settle evenly at the top without spilling.

"Cheers to a charming lady," he cried out.

"Cheers to a mad man," she replied teasingly. They giggled, bonked the glasses together and chugged on the beer. It had been a while since any of them felt at ease.

"Because of you, I'm going to end up with a big belly," Paula blurted out.

"Still, you would look great. Some deformities are tolerable when a person is extremely beautiful. Maybe you need a slight ugliness to render you manageable and approachable. Otherwise you're too much to handle. Too good to be true," replied Andrea jokingly. It was obvious however that he was trying to conceal in a shy way, the sincerity behind his statement.

Paula blushed and fluttered her eyelashes. She was astonished by what she heard although she was expecting it.

"You're not so bad yourself but I've been around better-looking men," she said that with a facetious tone and a wink.

Andrea enjoyed her playful approach. Fabriano had told him of Paula's spontaneity and wit. He found himself seduced simultaneously by her charm and sharpness. The man inside him was stimulated.

Paula pulled him back from his momentary distraction: "Yesterday evening you looked like crap and you smelled of cigarette smoke; your beard was awful and your clothes were disgusting. You were a miserable wreck but a lucky one. You seemed so vulnerable you got away with few kisses out of compassion."

"Aha," he retorted. "That was thirty hours ago. Now that I'm in my prime: well-dressed, smelling nice and clean shaved, can I be eligible for few kisses out of passion?" He said those words with a hidden fright. Their impact could take him into a make or break situation. He had no indication where that would lead him.

Time got suspended and Paula interrupted the silence: "You don't need compassion, that's for sure. On the other hand, I guess one needs to find out your suitability for passion." She cracked that in a coy way that melted his heart.

Five minutes later, they joined the scattered couples by the canal and indulged in a long embrace. Andrea dropped Paula at her home around one am. They stayed in the car for several minutes, kissing and fondling. They agreed to see each other soon and Andrea drove off.

Paula wanted a reprieve. She needed time to consider the impact of any serious relationship with Andrea. She couldn't take risks, particularly escalating the feud between Eva and Andrea, or even between her sister-in-law and herself. The situation was very tricky and required an impartial judgement. Andrea on the other hand, didn't share her view. He was willing to gamble, even though his previous decisions and actions had led him to catastrophic falls that devastated him. Yet, he seemed to be an emotional person who couldn't be driven by lessons learned.

Paula couldn't deny her liking towards Andrea. If she were to have a sexual relationship, she wouldn't want a man other than him. He had been her husband's best friend and she was familiar with his mentality. He was predictable but rather impulsive. He was handsome, educated and cultured. He had a family and a child from a second failed marriage. Their relationship would not culminate into a marriage proposal. At least, that's what she thought. She could speak for herself. Their infatuation with each other was based on liking, lust and friendship. Their relationship shouldn't cross the boundaries set by those factors.

She owed it to herself to be happy and satisfied, no matter what it took to achieve that.

She had confined herself to a prison since Fabriano's departure; a physical and emotional captivity that deprived her of sheer basic pleasures. She had lived in total denial; something that Fabriano would have loathed. Her late husband cared for her and would have condoned any action taken by his beloved wife to live happily after he was gone. Paula undressed. She took off her bra and panties and once again slipped under the bed sheets completely naked. She caressed her breasts, touched her vagina; but mentally those imaginary hands belonged to Andrea.

# Chapter Six

On Saturday that same week, Sophia placed a call to her daughter-in-law. She had considered her proposal to relocate and decided to remain in Lebanon; the only place that connected her to her late husband Michel. Paula knew quite well that the main reason was Eva's presence in Milan. The mother in Sofia didn't fancy any confrontation with her untamed daughter. Recent rows and problems were clear indicators that any form of remedy was non-existent. It was rather difficult for a mum to stay at her daughter-in-law's when her own daughter lived just few minutes away in a spacious apartment. Paula would have acted the same way.

Sophia's decision was conveyed to Luigi who expressed his regret. His grandmother's decision heightened his insistence to invite his mum over to Rome. Paula promised to undertake the trip the soonest possible. She was also contemplating the idea to spend a few days in Capri.

Andrea had been constantly in touch, at least twice a day. The weekend was nearing and he couldn't bear the idea of not seeing Paula. Paula had so far faked excuses to restrain him but couldn't keep up that stance. After all, resisting him for too long, would blow her chances to keep him interested. She didn't want to lose him and particularly his friendship.

Andrea was in seventh heaven when he finally had the clearance from Paula to drop by at her place, on a Saturday night, for a light dinner. He was right on time, ringing the bell at eight pm. Paula opened the door for him and was handed a big bouquet of multicoloured flowers. That was a nice gesture long forsaken. She used both hands to hold the bouquet, handling it as if it were a fragile item. She brought it close to her nose and inhaled deeply. The smell of wild roses and tulips filled the air with a sweet and unique fragrance that only nature could produce.

They pecked each other on the cheeks and settled immediately afterwards in the living room. Paula had set a long narrow table by one of the leather couches.

A variety of cold dishes, salads and dips were laid on it: an assortment of Italian, Mexican and Lebanese dishes. An opened bottle of Tacama Seleccion Especial 2012, a Peruvian red wine was laid next to small porcelain bowls containing a mixture of roasted pistachios and cashew nuts.

Andrea sat as closely possible next to Paula, seized the bottle and poured wine into the two Bordeaux crystal glasses in front of them. They swirled the wine a couple of times moving the glasses in a circular motion; then placed their noses right over the rim and breathed in. They made a toast for good health and happiness, clinked their glasses and took a sip of the wine. It was well balanced with a violet purple colour, a characteristic typical of a mix of Petit Verdot and Tannat grapes.

Brie and cheddar cheese on salty crackers accompanied the first glass. The couple conversed about their whereabouts during the day and the unusual pleasant weather that had reigned in the past few days. As they talked, Paula would glance at Andrea's high bridged nose which made him manly and attractive. In a similar way, he would gaze at her moist lips, drop his eyes furtively towards her tight skirt which exposed her white thighs through the open side slit of the fabric.

In two-hour time, they had ravaged most dishes and commenced drinking their second bottle of wine. Paula was on her fourth glass and Andrea his fifth. They felt slightly tipsy, but their faculties were still alert. Their alcohol consumption had been gradual and composed, allowing them to remain calm and collected. Their spirits though had reached the saturation point where audacity and shyness converged. Andrea found himself shrouded by a shield of boldness and self-confidence.

He slid closer to Paula, ran his fingers along her nape. He held her head, tilted it towards him and started kissing her passionately. She responded with intense reciprocation. The moment was ripe and right. She gave in to his daring moves to stroke her legs and thighs, to pass his hands over her blouse feeling her heaving breasts. She was in the mood for sex. Her body needed attention and she was at the height of her excitement.

Paula stood up, grabbed Andrea's hand and led him to the bedroom. He undressed hastily, revealing a well-preserved toned body with a massive erection. Paula was pleased with herself.

She had already aroused him. She came forward and pushed him towards the bed, letting him fall on his back with his penis swaying and setting on his flat abdomen, its glans rubbing against his navel.

She teasingly took off her blouse and skirt; then her sandals. Slowly she removed her bra exposing her marvellous tits and slipped out of her panties. Andrea's heart was pounding with irregular beats. A wonderful naked sculpture was standing two metres away from him. A perfect woman that words couldn't describe. She joined him in bed and surrendered her body to his wishes.

Not a single surface of Paula's magnificent body had been spared. Intercourse started as a pleasurable pain and culminated into a euphoria. Paula was amazed by her ability to accommodate Andrea's manhood, especially after a long period of sexual deprivation. His performance was also super great. As of her own prowess, his multiple ejaculations were proof enough of her worthiness.

Catching few hours of needed sleep until sunrise, Andrea woke up exhausted and spent. He stared at Paula's sensuous body beside him, admiring the fleshy curves of a fantastic woman. He bent down and kissed her, awakening her gently.

They had an early breakfast and bid each other goodbye with a promise to meet the week after. Andrea had planned to spend Sunday in its entirety with his children. Paula could hear Andrea's car engine roaring as he drove off the wide street below. Sitting in the living room kept her in close contact with the outside world. That was achieved through the drawn curtains and open windows that allowed natural lighting, wind and noises to fill the space around her with life and animation. She pondered the recent developments as she drank her green tea.

Her body felt satiated. Flashes of her sexual session with Andrea reminded her of the intense physical prowess each one of them had exhibited. They had indulged in few awkward positions that only athletes could perform. Having sex with Andrea had been awesome. Her body couldn't wait to repeat that experience.

Paula's mind nonetheless was perturbed by the eventual consequences of such a relationship. Was there any purpose to build on it beyond the physical aspect? Andrea was plagued with unresolved issues that he seemed to ignore and toss aside. She was neither prepared nor willing to entertain marriage or any other formal association with anyone. She was in it just for sex and companionship. Why not? It wasn't as if she was hurting anyone. On the contrary, she was helping Andrea out emotionally while diminishing her own frustration which had lasted for ten years. On second thoughts, would Andrea use their relationship to antagonise Eva to get even? Paula dreaded any confrontation with her mean sister-in-law. She had to discuss the matter with him; to keep Eva totally out of the picture.

Amid a chaotic diffusion of various thoughts, Paula went inside her bedroom, opened the top drawer of her bedside cabinet and took out her diary book and a blue ball pen. She returned to the sitting room, sat on an antique chair by the sash window, gazed at the street below, took a deep breath and wrote:

*Dear Fabriano,*

*I'm used to being sincere and honest. My love for you does not allow me to hide anything from you. After so long, I submitted myself to mundane desires. I guess I was in a vulnerable state and so was your best friend Andrea. Yes: Andrea. One thing has led to another. We had sex this morning; wild sex in all its forms. Pardon me if I've gone astray. But you had encouraged me to carry on with my life after you were gone. I held out as much as I could. Believe me it was and still is very difficult to live without you. Being lonely had softened my resolve but I'm certain that I haven't breached our vow; that I haven't upset you in any way. You're my everything.*

*Pardon the pun. Sex with you Fabriano was an expression of love, a natural performance where biological parts were just obedient tools for our souls. With Andrea, the physical aspect prevails. It's wonderful while it happens. It makes one look forward to it, but at the same time there's a lack of that peculiar spiritual bond that accompanied our love making.*

*Miss you loads! Can't wait to see you in Heaven. On account of that, Luigi's dreams have boosted my morale and given me a great sense of relief. His dreams are so vivid; I'm certain they are much more than just dreams. There's truth and wisdom behind them. I'm not afraid to die anymore. You have given us assurance that the afterworld existed in the form of a wonderful spiritual world where good people are admitted based on their values.*

*Love you so much!*

*Your wife, Paula*

# Chapter Seven

Sunday the 25th of June 2034. People were indoors huddled around their television sets, or watching any smart screen in their possession. The launch from Kennedy Space Centre was scheduled at 10 am, Florida time.

Paula, Luigi and Andrea sat mesmerised, listening to the feedback provided by multinational media. Five minutes were left for lift off; it was 3:55 pm Milan time. Excitement got hold of every single person. It felt as if destiny was tied to the success and findings of that manned mission.

In a hurried manner, Paula fixed cold lemonade for the three of them and served it just in time as the thirty-five second countdown began....nine...four...one, we have lift off. White smoke engulfed the launching platform. The whole combination of rocket, spaceship and external fuel tanks looked huge and massive. One would have found it inconceivable for such a huge mass to fly. And yet, with a slow motion, the rocket assembly lifted off in a sluggish manner: thrust versus mass and gravity. An incredible captivating sight that an observer would never forsake. The higher it got, the more speed it gained. The rotation around its axis as it shot through the blue sky gave the viewer ample time to gaze at the bulky external fuel tanks and the shiny surface of the spaceship.

"Well done," exclaimed Luigi. "That's a real challenge."

"Amazing what the human brain can achieve," said Andrea.

"May God protect the crew and render this space mission a successful one," said Paula.

"Very true," replied Luigi. "Oh, by the way. I had the chance to meet the Pope last Sunday."

"Really?" Paula looked at him. "How did you miss telling me about it?"

"I actually tried to communicate with you at ten-thirty that morning but your cell phone was shut. Realising I was coming home in a few days, I thought leaving you voice and text messages on your mobile phone and other devices was not important."

Paula recalled that Sunday morning. She had been in bed with Andrea. "So, how did it feel meeting the Pope in person?"

"He's superb, Mum. In his presence, I found peace and comfort. He's got modern views on many issues. Dad would have liked him. He has genuine concerns towards poverty, miseries…According to him, this unified manned trip to Proxima B is an expensive lavish exploration that will lead nowhere. He considered the data received from the Alpha Centauri system not enough to justify such a space venture. As far as he was concerned, mankind had better things to cater for. My fifteen minutes in his audience went fast. He was pleased that I'm in my second-year preparation for priesthood. We agreed to meet for half an hour, a week this Wednesday. He asked me to get in touch with his personal assistant and sort out the details."

"Wow," exclaimed both Andrea and Paula. "Maybe I can join you if you deem it fine to do so?" the latter continued: "As I had told you before, I was leaving soon for Rome and Capri. It would be a pleasure to meet the Pontiff face to face. I always admired his simplicity, his pure sincerity and above all his charisma."

As she said that, the space rocket was soaring through the sky, trailing a thick blanket of white smoke.

# Chapter Eight

Eva had her TV screen on but was paying no attention to the aired events. Her mind was astray. Andrea had been keeping quiet for the past few weeks. Not a single attempt had been made to bridge fences with her; to discuss little Fabriano; to beg her to see his son. None of that occurred and it bothered her. Was she losing her grip on him? Something mysterious was happening and for the first time in her life, she felt useless and scared. She had been accustomed being in full control, directing people and enforcing her views. Was all that slipping away from her? Her rejection of Andrea's recent proposals: his right to see little Fabriano; asking for divorce…had been based on basic cruel principles: to tame him and infuriate him. She had pictured him crawling on his knees, begging for her mercy, telling her he couldn't live without her; that he condoned her bizarre fornication; her lousy tantrums…

She had placed her bet on his fear of retribution; on his concern for his son. Seeking divorce had always been his most powerful weapon. He had an advantage over her: being a renowned surgeon; being Italian by birth; let alone her undisputed promiscuity that would jeopardise her legal fight against him. She was left with the threat to harm little Fabriano if he ever contemplated filing for divorce. Andrea had seemed to take heed of that and refrained taking any action to that effect. He had been calling her, every now and then, enquiring about her financial means; whether his son needed anything and was doing well. He would beg her to hear his son uttering the words: "Love you, Daddy!"

What bothered her now was the sudden silence. Eva couldn't comprehend Andrea's newly acquired attitude. He didn't seem to bother anymore. Something was going on. Oh! How she resented being cast aside and ignored. There must be a reason for that change.

She picked up her cell phone and composed Andrea's number. It rang and rang and rang.

There was no answer. Was he intentionally avoiding her call? She had cramps in her lower abdomen. What the hell was happening? He should be running after her; not the other way around.

She got up, paced the length of her apartment, entered and exited the kitchen and yet fetched nothing. She was moving about aimlessly, talking and answering herself with stifled anger. After a while, the stifled anger turned into a rage. Eva took it on her house helper, yelling and shouting orders which forced little Fabriano to hang on to the helper's apron and cry fearfully.

Half an hour later, Eva came out of her bedroom, all dressed up, looking calm and collected. She pecked her son and blurted out: "I'll be back in three hours." Those words were meant for the house helper whose eyes were reddened by sore tears.

Eva regained her confidence as she drove her BMW through the suburban area of Milan.

She was headed for San Donato where Andrea lived with his children. She reached her destination around six, parked her car in front of the detached villa, next to a Honda Civic. The absence of Andrea's car was noticeable, but someone was inside the residence. She rang the doorbell and waited for a few seconds before hearing the door unlocking. The door swung open and an inquisitive blonde girl in her late teens appeared behind it. Once her blue eyes settled on the woman standing outside the threshold, a sense of annoyance engulfed her.

"Yes! How can I help you?"

"Hi. You must be Maria. I'm Eva, your—"

"I know who you are!" said Andrea's daughter. "We have nothing to say to each other. If you want my dad, well, he's not here."

"It's only that I'm worried about him and he hasn't returned my calls," replied Eva defensively.

"Well, I'm afraid I can't help you. He left home before noon," said Maria.

The muffled sound of a car engine grew louder as it neared and stopped abruptly in front of the residence entrance. Had it not been for the make of the car, Eva wouldn't have been able to associate the driver to the car itself. Andrea shocked her by his younger looks and shaved beard. Even his clothes were trendy and what mostly pissed her off was his apparent goodnature.

"What are you doing here?" He yelled out.

"Got worried about you. It had been a while." Eva looked furious. "I called you earlier, but you didn't answer your phone."

"I was busy," Andrea retorted. "Plus, I don't recall we have anything to say to each other," Andrea continued, as he gently pushed her aside, crossed the threshold and joined his daughter as she swung the front door closed behind them.

Eva stood baffled in front of a solid oak door that symbolised a barrier between her and the rest of the world. Fury was building up inside her chest. She had never been so degraded and humiliated. What prompted that sudden change? Andrea appeared totally relaxed and confident, unlike the sensitive character she had been acquainted with. Someone was certainly behind that conversion. His family couldn't possibly be the culprit; a woman would most likely fit in as the main reason behind that shift. His new elegant looks were the evidence he was having an affair. It was obvious to her that Andrea was discarding his past, dismantling every single link that tied him to her. For the first time ever, he had scored. She had to concede her defeat. This time round, Andrea had the upper hand.

Eva lurched backwards, turned, walked few paces and got inside her car. She rested her head on the steering wheel trying to exchange the heat inside her forehead with the coolness of the wheel. She kept at it for a couple of minutes, raised her head and writhed in her seat. Driving back to the city centre was not a joyful ride. She was cursing and swearing under her teeth; her lips quivering from apparent nervousness. She banged her hands on the wheel; turned off the radio for the third consecutive time. Worse than that, she violated the traffic signal at an intersection; her face and licence plate were captured by the CCTV camera which flashed an accusing light. She wished she could vanish from the face of the world. Everything was crumbling around her. But Why? What had she done to deserve such demeaning treatment? Why her? Was that the reward, worthy of a devout Catholic and a firm believer?

By the time she arrived home, little Fabriano was already tucked in bed. Lucky for him, as the house helper was not so fortunate. She had to cope with Eva's tantrums for the entire night. She cursed the day the agency introduced her to that household. She wept until early morning hours; got up; packed her suitcase; fixed breakfast for little Fabriano; kissed him affectionately and to his childish bewilderment, left without uttering a single word. She didn't bother waiting for Eva to wake up.

Soon afterwards, Fabriano Junior entered his mum's bedroom, reached her bedside and shook her broad shoulders. She woke up and it took her a few seconds to realise where she was.

She adjusted herself and sat in her bed, listening to her two-and-a-half-year-old son describing to her what had just happened:

"Nina has gone out," he cried out.

The moment she heard that, Eva's jugular veins started to throb. She rose like an insane woman, dashed towards Nina's bedroom, opened the closet and found it empty. All clothes, shoes and suitcase were gone. Eva was on the verge of total collapse. Then she heard her mobile phone ringing in her bedroom, ten metres away from where she stood. She hurried back, fearing the caller would lose patience. It was the domestic helper agency informing her that Nina was at their offices and that she had officially resigned from her current duties. The agent asked Eva in a polite reconciliatory way if she needed a replacement.

Her answer came swiftly: "Go to hell with your lousy domestic help…!" He hung up, leaving her in an unfinished state of fury. She hated that. She wanted everyone to be under her control, but somehow she had lost her knack recently. She was a loner; fighting a war of attrition on several fronts. She had enemies everywhere and friends nowhere.

As if to make matters worse, little Fabriano was snivelling out of fear, having heard his mother shouting over the phone and witnessing her rage. More aggravating was his running search around the flat, shouting Nina's name and calling out for his father. Eva cracked under the pressure and for the first time in her life yielded to a crying fit.

# Chapter Nine

Each day was an ordeal. Eva no longer had time for herself; for her lovers. No time to exercise in the gym. No more pedicure and manicure. No time for laser hair removal. Taking care of Fabriano Junior had proven to be a tedious task. So demanding of her. She had contacted several agencies seeking a nanny, a housekeeper, any help at all. Her records and previous rows with various staff household agencies stood as a hindrance to any engagement. It seemed they all shared a common data base that no longer in her favour. Eva couldn't breathe easily. She was suffocating. Life had turned against her in a big one hundred and eighty-degree sweep.

A dreadful week followed and Eva caved into the mounting pressure. She phoned Andrea several times but to no avail. He wouldn't answer her calls. She had to reach his soft heart somehow. She decided to leave him a written message cautioning him that he was terribly missed by little Fabriano. Andrea was on the phone the moment he read her message. "I'll pass by, once my consultations are over," he said cryptically, allowing no conversation to take place.

The short distance that separated him from Fabriano Junior seemed infinite. Andrea wished there were no traffic signals; no vehicles on the road; nothing that would stand in his way to see his son. Finally, he was there. He drove his car down the ramp and through the first basement parking where he found a vacant place. He shut the engine, got out, locked the doors pressing the remote-control key in a backward motion as he headed towards the lift. Five minutes later he was bending and kneeling in front of his son, holding him in his arms, kissing every skin surface that Fabriano Junior proffered. He missed his son tremendously. His heart jumped inside his chest, missing few beats. The excitement was high. Little Fabriano kept repeating the word: "Daddy" while glancing at his mother. It seemed to her as if he were taking sides with his dad; threatening her to treat him nicely: otherwise…

Andrea stretched himself on the carpeted floor allowing Fabriano Junior to throw his weight upon him and wrestle until his father was seemingly pinned down and subdued.

"I can't cope on my own," Eva blurted out; spoiling the fun and happiness that rarely filled her home.

"What the hell you mean by that?" exclaimed Andrea. But by the time he spoke, he could notice the untidy state of the apartment and, above all, the absence of a domestic helper. He could have sworn he had never seen Eva looking so haggard and distraught.

"Can you tell me what's going on?" Andrea enquired. Eva gave a full account of the recent events, downplaying her role as the main culprit; putting the blame on the insolence of the domestic helper and the agency's backing and support of the "maid." Eva had never called Nina by her name, even after more than twenty months of continuous service.

Andrea listened intently, convinced more than ever that the woman he married three years ago would never change. She was a manipulative person who would only acquiesce for a selfish purpose. She was apparently requesting his support, while offering Fabriano Junior as a collateral. What a clever scheme!

"Eva, let's level with each other," he said calmly but decisively. "Don't expect me to move in. I'm not prepared to revert to the dreadful life I have experienced; thanks to you! You denied me of my own son and you objected to my plea for personal deliverance. Look where your stubborn and domineering attitude has gotten you. You're a loner who surrounds herself with muppets rather than normal human beings. That's due to your continuous endeavour to control people rather than hearing them out. You're full of contradictions. Nothing will ever work for you. You set rules for others under different pretexts and yet you don't abide by them. You proclaim Catholicism and yet you're so far away from its teachings. The whole thing is absurd."

"You need my support? Let's agree first on getting a divorce. Bearing in mind your previous threats to harm our son, little Fabriano will stay with me. You'll be welcome to see him any time as long as you're watched. Together we'll take him out but under no circumstances will you be allowed being with him on your own. Once the divorce is settled, Fabriano Junior's custodial arrangement will be determined. I'm going to fight for him with all my might."

"How can you deprive me of him?" She cried out.

"You're the one who made threats," Andrea retorted. "How could you mention that when your own child is involved?"

"I didn't mean it," she blurted out. "I love Fabriano Junior."

"Well! You should have controlled your emotions then. I cannot risk anything." Andrea was clearly decisive.

Eva's guts were boiling, emitting gurgling sounds. How could she lose the battle? A war consisted of several battles. Maybe she failed in one of them but it was not over yet.

"OK! You have my consent," she muttered in a low voice. "Proceed with the papers and I'll sign them, but I need just one favour from you. Can we pretend being one united family and spend some time together? We can do it here, somewhere else; any place of your choosing."

"Let me think about it," replied Andrea. "I'll do anything that makes little Fabriano happy."

Eva came forward and kissed Andrea on the cheeks. Somehow, he felt like Jesus, betrayed by Judas' kiss. He did not reciprocate the kiss and this made Eva angrier. She was making successive concessions and she couldn't recognise herself anymore. The beautiful, sexy and strong woman was crumbling under the enormous unrelenting stress that she was experiencing. Her strain wasn't adequate for the occasion. She had been stronger in the past.

She was eager to ask him an obvious question: "Are you in love with someone else?" But she refrained. The circumstances were not appropriate for such a trivial question. That could wait. The imminent problem was her son and her private life. She needed help to proceed with her own life and above all, someone's unlimited attention for Fabriano Junior. Andrea gave his son a bear hug and promised he'll be back soon. Little Fabriano looked satisfied.

## Part Four

# Chapter One

Paula had travelled to Rome the night before. Staying at the Palazzo Manfredi near the Colosseum. She was in her suite sharing the plush three-seater couch with Luigi. She was anxious and full of anticipation. Tomorrow was going to be an historical day for her and Luigi. Rarely did people meet the Pontiff; at least not based on fixed schedules. The meeting was set for nine am. She felt privileged and proud of her son who had been behind this forthcoming event.

She rose up, paced the room and stopped at the mini bar. She picked a crisp Frascati white wine bottle, fetched two glasses from a bottom shelf and rejoined Luigi.

While sipping wine, Paula went over the recent events as conveyed to her by Andrea.

Luigi listened intently and nodded most of the time without uttering a word. Deep down he still felt sorry for his aunt. He would describe her actions as "unfortunate" but never criticised her beyond that. Filing for a divorce might salvage whatever sane relationship had remained after such a hectic marriage.

"Do you really believe she might harm her own son?" Luigi asked.

"Knowing how possessive she can be, I would say yes," Paula said.

"I can picture her getting even and hurting people her own age," Luigi said without noticing the impact of his words on his mum, whose body flinched. Eva's wrath couldn't be taken lightly.

Paula changed the subject, emphasising how thrilled she was to see the Pope in person. "I can't wait to meet him! Everyone I talked to envied me for such an audience. You'll find me in the hotel lobby waiting as of seven-thirty am."

"Great. Better being at the Vatican early rather than late," said Luigi. "I'll fetch you early morning. Sleep well and don't finish the whole bottle." He gave his mother a wink. Then he added before leaving: "By the way, when are you intending to leave for Capri?"

"This Thursday we'll ride together, you and I, to Naples. Once we're there, my intention is to proceed towards Pompeii, spend the whole afternoon touring the place and then returning back to Naples to board an evening ferry to Capri. Andrea is flying and joining us there with his family over the weekend. I mean, both families. He's trying to grant Eva her wish of getting together before the divorce proceedings. I have already reserved two rooms for us at the Punta Tragara Hotel. Magnificent scenic views. Your dad used to like it."

"Great." Luigi kissed her goodnight and walked out into the wide long corridor. Paula stood by the door watching his tall figure disappearing at the curved lift lobby. She closed the door behind her once she heard the audible tone of the hall's lantern.

She had another glass of wine. A quick glance at the TV screen revealed all was going well with the manned space mission with long signalling delays reaching the space control centres. Such delays annoyed her. There was some futility in such missions. It was such a drawback to listen and watch the past rather than the present. With a slight frustration, she undressed and went to bed, sinking into a deep comforting sleep.

The next day, Paula and Luigi were subjected to rigorous security checks. The car licence plate number and personal Identification documents had been previously submitted to the Vatican Security by the Rome Diocese. The visitors were accompanied by two Swiss guards who silently guided them through horizontal vestibules and onwards vertically through a medium size lift. The Papal apartments represented a collection of state, religious and residential apartments that wrapped around the Courtyard of Sixtus V, on two sides of the top third floor of the Apostolic Palace. Paula and Luigi were fascinated by the plush interior decorations and particularly the frescoes and wall paintings.

The Papal apartments were relatively small and it was kind of easy noticing the Library, the Medical Suite and the bedrooms section. Paula and Luigi were led into a small living room next to a chapel where they were received by a cheerful clergyman in his late fifties. He introduced himself as Archbishop Gambino, the Pontiff's secretary.

"Welcome! Welcome!" He exclaimed. "His Holiness will join you in few minutes. He is preparing himself for the usual Wednesday 10 AM audience." The Archbishop grabbed the opportunity to provide them with few historical details regarding the Papal Suite; the various successions; the various artists who renovated the quarters; the valuable books displayed on the Library shelves; and the marbled floors and wallpapered rooms.

As the visitors listened intently to the vivid description, an old man wearing a gleaming white robe and a small white skullcap, silently came in. They all got startled at his sight, including the Archbishop Gambino. The latter knelt and kissed the ring that the Pope wore on one of his right-hand fingers. Paula and Luigi followed suit, emulating the Archbishop's gestures. The Archbishop excused himself and quietly exited amid an eerie silence.

There they were in the presence of Pope John Paul the Third. Paula found herself staring at his serene face whose features projected tranquillity and comfort. He looked fit and younger than his real age of sixty-two.

"I'm delighted to see you again," he said, looking at Luigi. "Please be seated." He sat comfortably on one of the armchairs. "I'm glad you came along, Madam…?"

"Paula Khoury, your Holiness," she muttered in a subdued tone.

"Ah! Your surname sounds foreign. Your husband's, I presume?"

"Yes," she replied. "My husband was of Lebanese origin. He held two nationalities. Unfortunately, he passed away ten years ago."

"I love your late husband's country," said the Pope. "I've been to Lebanon on two different occasions and each time I had to go on pilgrimage to the Valley of the Saints and Annaya Monastery. Breathtaking sceneries in a land filled with spirituality and mysticism. No wonder the Catholic church has canonised many saints that hailed from that land. Shame about the political strife and foreign intervention though. They never seem to cease."

"My husband's village overlooks the Valley of the Saints," Paula said enthusiastically.

"Then he must be in Heaven," retorted the Pope in a cajoling way.

"Actually, I believe so!" Luigi added earnestly. "Your Holiness! I would like to share with you peculiar events that I have recently experienced. Your wisdom and interpretation of those events would prove essential to soothe my apprehension and strengthen my understanding."

"Sure, my son! Go ahead! I'm listening," said the Pope.

Luigi related the contents of his dreams, making sure to include every single detail, avoiding to use the word "encounters." John Paul the Third was listening with keen interest, nodding few times. Luigi felt encouraged enough to proceed with his recitation, baffled by the depth of his dreams as he was reliving the events once again. Once his monologue had finished, a heavy silence engulfed the space around them. Luigi felt relieved to have unleashed the burden that burned through his chest. Yet the unpredictable reaction of the Pontiff weighed heavily on him. Anticipation took hold of Paula as well. Were they going to be dismissed as lunatics? As psychopaths? The Pope stared at Luigi for some time, then took his gaze towards Paula as if he were assessing their credibility, and then returned his gaze back to Luigi for few seconds more.

"I envy you, my son!" The Pope said. "Your dreams carry a revelation. One has to respect their meaning regardless the virtual impossibility of proving their authenticity and worthiness. Whether labelled dreams, visions or encounters, they seem to carry a logical pattern that physical life can neither reveal nor sustain. I wouldn't mind having dreams that open up my wisdom and increase my capacity to grasp matters, which I have already accepted for granted."

"Few such incidents, even though considered minor in their nature, have been reported to the Vatican. A special team carried out investigations, which have shown that most reports were hoaxes or figments of imagination. Your experience is different though. Your second dream tallies with the contents of the first and there's a solid continuity. Your description of outer space, paradise and your father's dialogue put your experience in a different category altogether."

"There are though, few issues that contradict our Catholic teachings, such as the non-existence of hell or even purgatory. But I guess one needs to have a large mind and handle the situation in a manner that respects religion as we've known it, while introducing in parallel, a modern understanding. If you don't mind, I'll make sure your recitation is conveyed to our specialised team. They will eventually seek your presence for a thorough evaluation. They have strict instructions from my side to listen carefully to the contents of such dreams/encounters, analyse logical patterns based on religious benchmarks; similarly, they are not allowed to impose their analysis or views onto those who are being debriefed."

"I don't mind, your Holiness. I'm seeking the truth as well. I'm preparing for my priesthood and anything that might shed light on the credibility of my dreams would be welcome." Luigi's voice grew in confidence.

"Very well then! I have to go now for my Wednesday audience," exclaimed the Pope. "Glad you came over for this chat. I'll be including you in my prayers. Take care, my son. You know now how to get in touch in case there's any further development. I'll be leaving tomorrow for Castel Gandolfo. I'm always reachable. Have a good day. Nice to meet you, Mrs Paula. You are a wonderful family. May God bless you all!"

Paula wished to take few pictures with the Pope, but her cell phone had been taken away from her by the security guards. As if reading her mind, John Paul the Third fetched his mobile phone from a side pocket and handed it to her. "Use this!" He said. "The pictures will be forwarded to your son."

The Pontiff rose from his chair, posed with the Khoury family for few selfie shots, bid them goodbye and left the room as silently as he entered it.

Archbishop Gambino was there in a jiffy. He accompanied the couple to the security gate where they retrieved their phones and picked their car from the parking lot.

Luigi felt light-hearted. A heavy load had been lifted off his shoulders. He had shared his dreams with the Pontiff and had been taken seriously. It was becoming very clear that his recent experience with the afterworld fell under the realm of logic. To classify it under the realm of reality would require certainty and flawless deduction that those dreams were indeed encounters. It was almost certain that any further meeting with the specialised committee would neither resolve nor seal the issue. Luigi nonetheless, needed the guidance of the religious team, as its members would bring out the philosophical aspect of that logic and use it to bolster the understanding of religion.

Paula was dazed. She wanted to tell the whole world that she had met the Pope. What a wonderful person! So modest and amiable. He dedicated his time for the poor, the wretched; speaking out on behalf of oppressed nations, defying the Big Powers whenever the need arose. He curbed down infringements within the Catholic church, restoring discipline in all dioceses, spreading modesty throughout the Catholic World. The Pontiff's modern approach, particularly his openness to hear out people and accept them for what they were, had won him unanimous respect and encouraged non-believers to regain faith.

"I still can't believe what happened," Paula said, looking at Luigi.

"Yeah. Me too," replied Luigi as he steered the vehicle through narrow busy streets. "He's a fabulous person. So content and calm. It's going to be a pleasure serving under Him. Did you notice his interest while I spoke? He is a good listener. I also learned from my mentor that he is well versed in the Quran. Apparently, he discusses it with Islamic leaders and religious figures when they visit him. He has won the hearts of most humans regardless of their religion."

Luigi dropped his mum at the hotel, promising to take her out for dinner. Once in her room, Paula sank in the sofa after pouring herself a glass of mineral water. She checked her smart phone for new messages. Andrea had tried to place two video calls and ended up sending her a written text that said: "Can't stop thinking about you! I miss you loads. Can't wait to see you in Capri."

Paula hesitated before responding. She took instead a sip of Pellegrino, savouring the lemon slices she had thrown in. She liked Andrea, but not to the point of loving him. At least not yet. The fact he had fallen for her disturbed her somehow. She was not ready for any commitment. Andrea was way ahead in his feelings. She would hate herself misleading him in any way. There was a wide difference between liking and loving someone. Sex between them had been great but only physical as far as she was concerned. Her body needed a man, but her soul was already satiated with her deep and sincere love for her late husband. Intruders were not allowed in. Somehow it was a private world that no one was supposed to trespass. She held her phone and typed: "Nice to hear from you. See you soon."

The reply came almost immediately: "I was expecting some emotional declaration."

This time, she did not answer. Deception was not on her agenda and she couldn't lie about her feelings. The phone vibrated and startled her. Gina was on the line enquiring about her meeting with the Pontiff. Paula regained her good mood and like a child who had seen his first toy, described her audience with the most powerful man in the world. Yes. He was powerful because of his faith and his domination of human hearts. Gina listened and uttered exclamation words. She enquired afterwards about Luigi, and wondered if he had been mentioning her by name. Paula replied diplomatically, as anticipated by Gina, stressing that her son was recently absorbed with the latest events; that he had alienated himself from the rest of the world.

Before ending her call, Gina surprised Paula, declaring her planned engagement to a university colleague in mid-July. Paula was simultaneously happy and saddened by the news. Gina deserved all the best. Yet, Paula wished she could be her mother-in-law.

A quick hot shower relaxed Paula's muscles and the spray of high-pressure water on her stiff back made the tension ease away. Her spine seemed more flexible by the minute. She dried her hair, put on the bath robe and stretched herself on the sofa facing the TV screen. She turned it on and flipped through the channels. Most stations were displaying images from space that were three days old. The mission was on its sixth day. The delay between transmission and reception was getting annoying by the minute. The impact was going to get worse as the spaceship ventured farther into the dark universe. Videos depicted total darkness outside the craft and instruments activity inside it. Huge and small control and monitoring panels were lit up with hundreds of tiny flickering lights with analogue and digital displays of external temperature, ambient temperature, pump status, solar panel power generation, backup battery status, heat exchangers input and output readings.

Four robots were either sitting or standing in front of those display panels, focusing mainly on a massive digital map that showed the relative position of the craft along a preset trajectory. They appeared to assimilate data and act accordingly; activating switches, typing instructions on fixed keyboards. They also appeared to be communicating with three astronauts who were in active duty. There were also internal scenes of the hibernation plexiglass cubicles stacked in rows. Human figures could be seen lying inside them with processing panels continuously analysing the ambient conditions within each capsule while capturing biological readout from the hibernated bodies.

*Amazing what a man could achieve with science*, Paula thought. His creativity had contributed to magnificent technological advancements and yet, people remained ignorant of their past, their origin. The future seemed much simpler to grasp and deal with than the past.

# Chapter Two

Paula smiled at the ideas haunting her mind and resigned to think about the present. She was hungry and needed to get out of her hotel room; feel free, as light as a gentle breeze. She put on a dress and stood facing the air conditioning diffuser, enjoying the cool air ruffling her hair and pressing the dress fabric to the soft curves of her body. Rome was hot that time of year.

Paula was storing as much coolness as she could possibly harvest.

The moment she exited the revolving door, a stifling heat engulfed her. It felt more than 32 C. The doorman hailed a taxi for her and Paula commanded the driver to take her to Piazza di Spagna. Had the weather been cooler she would have walked the distance. Paula got out of the cab at Via di S. Sebastianello and went straight into Gina's restaurant. It was two-thirty in the afternoon. The place had four empty tables while the rest were taken up by mostly foreign visitors. Paula was relieved when cool air blew against her face. The slight hum of the air conditioning units was a welcome sign, along with the nice smell of food. The cream-coloured modern tables with their white chairs were still looking the same, even after eleven years. Wall paintings had been added with few decorative lighting fixtures.

Paula was ushered to a corner table that had a street view. She ordered a glass of dry white wine and took hold of the menu.

She recalled the exquisite taste of Quiche Lorraine and eggplant panini with pesto. She placed her order as if she had made it in the presence of Fabriano. She didn't contemplate any change. She lived through her love for her late husband and couldn't deviate from the path they had set together. She downed her first glass of wine before the waiter served the food. A second glass paired with the ordered dishes and she enjoyed the crispness and softness of the dough.

There was no need for a salad to wash the food down. The Quiche and panini were juicy enough and succulent.

A cup of well-made cappuccino, rich in flavour and texture, brought out the bold coffee taste and the smoothness of steamed milk. Paula enjoyed every single gulp. She paid the bill, thanked the waiter and went out into the sizzling heat. She climbed up the Spanish steps and reached Villa Borghese park in seven minutes.

Paula strolled along the landscaped and hardscaped pathways of the gardens, admiring the erected monuments and variety of trees that sprawled across the eighty-hectare park. The nuance of different shades of green was striking, particularly near water patches. The ambient temperature felt bearable, obviously cooled by the wind that swayed the extended leafy branches.

Like tourists around her, she bought a ticket and went inside the Galleria, relishing on the collection of paintings, sculptures and antiquities dating from the early seventeenth century. Even though she had already seen those artifacts before, she was scrutinising every single piece, enjoying the moment; anxious to report to Fabriano in her diary, her pilgrimage to Rome. As a matter of fact, she wanted to express to him how things remained the same, unvaried, unchanged; to the exception of those who saw them and exited this world. It was funny how matter survived humans. There must be a reward somehow, somewhere, for humans. How could it be possible that the maker of a porcelain vase would simply vanish while the vase that he had created would last for centuries unless it was mishandled?

Paula was thankful to Luigi. He had brought hope that the afterworld might actually be true, where eternal life prevailed in a spiritual sense. Even though it had been mentioned in scriptures, it would be an enhancement to have vivid description and ascertainment that Heaven indeed existed.

Yearning to feel like a foreign tourist, Paula took the public transport from Villa Borghese station back to the hotel. She was there by five-thirty pm. First thing she did was to scribble down her observations in the diary book. It was a good way to express herself and yell out: life can never be the same without you.

Paula spent the remaining two hours communicating with her shop assistant, listening to pop music and watching distractingly a movie. Her cell phone vibrated. A missed call from Luigi. He had arrived to pick her up.

They had a lovely night out, dining at a Chinese restaurant renowned for its spicy seafood dishes. That didn't prevent Paula from trying their crispy duck.

On their way back, she informed Luigi of Gina's engagement plans and watched her son sinking in his car seat with an expressionless face. Not a single word was uttered. Paula realised that her son still had strong emotions for Gina. She refrained commenting or prompting him to take any action, fearing that it would further aggravate the situation. She kept silent and heard him murmuring to himself: "Wish you all the best, Gina. You're a good lady." While dropping his mum at the hotel, and as she tried to kiss his cheek, Paula could swear she saw a trickle of tears. No wonder his face tasted salty when her lips brushed his cheeks. She felt sorry for him, but she knew he had made his choices and wouldn't back off.

# Chapter Three

Eva was preparing herself for the forthcoming weekend when she learned a while ago that Andrea's kids were not joining them in their combined trip to Capri. That made her plans to soften her rapport with Andrea's family an impossible task to achieve. She could picture their enthusiasm dying away the moment they found out that she was among the group. Andrea had apparently refrained from telling them from the outset, fearing their reaction. Eva had been rehearsing a new reconciliatory role that would enable her to win their hearts and subsequently their father's. She couldn't picture herself divorced and most of all abandoned. Andrea's kids would have been her catalyst to enhance and regain his affection. She had to work on him instead.

All that was annoying. Recent events had obliterated her life; dissected it into shreds of nothingness. Eva couldn't grasp Andrea's firmness. She couldn't comprehend the reason behind his happiness and physiological change. She wished she had access to his mobile phone.

Her mind was not used to processing so many thoughts simultaneously. She had a headache and she was scared too. Was Capri her last official trip as a wife? How would she be perceived by Paula and Luigi? Her current weakness shouldn't be noticed; it had to be concealed. A show of strength and self-control was required. Had Andrea revealed his intention to get a divorce to all his acquaintances? If news had already spread, any false pretence from her side would be futile. She had to convey therefore, a self-confident image as if nothing mattered to her. She only had to overplay her affection towards Fabriano Junior. That would influence all those present and Andrea alike. It might lead to a re-evaluation of the strained relationship between the married couple. Children were the essence of family bonds. Depriving a child from either parent might prove detrimental to his mental and emotional stability. At least, that was the opinion of psychologists. She was supposed to fight back, using any means to salvage her marriage; not for the sake of keeping her family together, but for the sole purpose of reaping the advantages of such a rapport: benefiting from the security and the convenience it offered to raise a kid and be able to watch him grow on a daily basis. She never doubted Andrea's pledge that she could visit her son at her convenience, any time she wished. Waking up early to dress her son up, to fix him breakfast, all that would fade away. She wouldn't be able to tuck him in bed and read him a bedtime story. It dawned on her that she never did read Fabriano Junior a tale. Nina used to.

Eva had failed to comply with those duties, relying on nannies, housekeepers and to a certain extent on her husband. She loved Fabriano Junior but showing him love had always been her weakness. She simply was incapable of carrying heavy loads. She had been a selfish woman pursuing her desires and had forsaken people who were close to her. She was paying a heavy price for her actions. She feared being alone and she feared God's wrath. A divorce was a serious breach of a sacred Christian rite. Would God forgive her? In the event Andrea went all the way with the divorce proceeding and in case of annulment, she would resort to prayers so that God would forgive her. Her sin was a minor one compared to Andrea's. He was the one insisting on having a divorce.

Little Fabriano came inside her bedroom holding a plastic car toy. He got near her and flung the toy into the suitcase that she was packing. Eva sat on her bed, lifted him up, held him in her arms, ruffled his long hair and kissed him tenderly.

"I love you so much," she said in a low sincere voice.

# Chapter Four

Luigi woke up early Thursday morning. He felt tired though he had slept well. It was one of those days when the human mind appeared to be preoccupied with scrambled thoughts that had no cohesion. Picking up his mum from the hotel at 8:30 cheered him up. He loved and respected her. Her charming smile was sufficient to take away all his worries.

Paula dumped her suitcase in the trunk before Luigi had the time to get out of the car to assist her. She occupied the front seat and bent over to plant a kiss on his cheek. "Off we go!" She exclaimed enthusiastically.

Getting out of Rome was a relief. Driving along Autostrada A1 altered Luigi's mood. In just one hour, the Abbey of Monte Cassino could be seen perched 520m on top of the rocky mountain which overlooked the Latin valley, on their left-hand side. The sight of the historic abbey broke the monotony of the scenic views around them. Highway A1 was certainly convenient time wise, saving almost two hours; but it was no match for the scenic beauty of the coastal road. Paula resented her decision to opt for the A1, although Luigi had advised otherwise. The drive however, was still enjoyable and convenient: saving time on the road meant more time could be spent in Pompeii.

They were listening to soundtracks: Luigi's favourite vintage, when Paula's cell phone beeped and vibrated. It was a message from Andrea:

"Hi sweetie! My kids have opted out. They won't be joining us. I guess I should have told them earlier that Eva was joining us on this planned trip. I know Luigi was looking forward to their presence. The moment they learned that she would be accompanying us, their outright refusal hit me. I'm afraid it's going to be just me, Eva and Fabriano Junior. See you soon Friday evening. Bye love."

Paula couldn't tell what made her more furious: Luigi not having company his age or Andrea's cryptic messages that kept insinuating that they were in deep love: infatuated with each other. She hated emotional terms such as sweetie, baby, love. Their relationship had remained purely physical and was not supposed to go beyond that. Paula was getting scared at the thought of Andrea's pursuance of divorce. His deliverance was bound to strangle her freedom. She gasped for air. Luigi took a glimpse of his mother. She was not her usual self since she got her electronic message. "What is it, Mum? Are you alright?"

"I'm fine," she muttered, realising how unconvincing she sounded. "Andrea's kids won't be coming. They couldn't contemplate being with your aunt."

"So what? Why are you overreacting? Fine, I would have enjoyed their presence but it's not the end of the world. We're having this trip to enjoy ourselves and relax. Let's not spoil it because of others."

"You're absolutely right," responded Paula absentmindedly.

An hour later, they were driving through heavy traffic inside Naples' congested streets. Paula had forgotten how bad it could be. They had reached nevertheless their destination in less than three hours, which wasn't bad at all. They headed for Parcheggio Ufficio car park on Viale della Costituzione, where they left the car and walked the short distance to the nearby Gianturco train station.

The thirty-two-minute train ride to Pompeii station went like a blur. Luigi and his mum quenched their thirst with cold beverages while watching tourists chatting enthusiastically in a cheerful atmosphere. How odd it was to forget all worries and put behind daily burdens. The whole thing was an escapade; an effort to revert to childhood; to rediscover oneself and appreciate living.

The guide Emiliano was a joyful man in his forties. Eight Italian-speaking people were in his group, including Paula and Luigi. On their previous visit to Pompeii, the Khoury family had toured the site unaided. Fabriano was an adventurer who disliked being led by a guide and listen to his historical accounts. Paula had attributed that to his impatience and craving to discover things by searching rather than being told.

Emiliano took his time describing the sudden eruption of Mount Vesuvius in the year 79 AD and how Pompeii and Herculaneum were swept by the lava and ashes that spewed and ejected from the 610m wide crater, burying the city in a horrific calamity killing its inhabitants who were caught off guard. By a hand gesture, the guide pointed at Mount Vesuvius, looming majestically few kilometres away, with its two peaks: the old Monte Somma and the much younger Main Cone. The latter was apparently the culprit for the disaster that had taken place. Its crater had released the built-up pressure that mounted inside its vents.

Luigi and Paula gazed at Mount Vesuvius. It looked so peaceful with its two peaks clearly separated by the Atrio de Cavalio valley. The Main Cone stood at 1,281m, exceeding Monte Somma's height by one hundred metres. Pompeii laid buried until the 16th century when serious efforts were made to excavate and expose the ancient ruins.

Emiliano took his group to the House of Faun, the Amphitheatre, the Lupanar, the Forum, the Villa of the Mysteries…The guide's vivid description allowed Luigi and his mum to picture the residents pressing their own wine and olive oil and performing illicit sex with their slaves in secret side rooms inside their villas. It was evident how rich the inhabitants had been: the paintings, frescoes and statues were abundant. It was ironic how the volcanic ashes that destroyed that marvellous civilisation had preserved the ruins and artifacts, as though the eruption of Mount Vesuvius was specifically meant against humans rather than objects. It was a Deja-vu experience. Paula recalled her impressions when she visited Villa Borghese in Rome. People come and go, but artifacts live on, unless they got burned or broken. Yet, few of them survive for centuries and for thousands of years. Absurd but true. Maybe that was the price humans had to pay for gaining eternity: a short physical life for an eternal spiritual one.

The tour was informative and pleasing. Luigi and his mum were detached from the present world and dived into a past full of mysteries and passion for pleasure. It was sinister and yet the ruins were speaking out loud to the visitors; telling them that: "We the ill-fated Pompeiians enjoyed our lives until death took hold of us. We would do the same thing all over if we ever had another chance."

Awaiting their bus ride to Mount Vesuvius, Luigi fetched two eggplant paninis and cold beers. The fact he was going to climb the Main Cone excited him. His mum was also eager to undertake the climb for she had never done it before.

The bus left the Archaeological Park and reached its destination in 50 minutes. They were dropped at the car park which was at the flank of Mount Vesuvius, at an altitude of 1,000 metres.

The climb took 22 minutes. It wasn't arduous by any means. They were astonished by the relatively easy ascent to the crater whose rim was about 300 metres higher than the car park elevation. The trail was wide enough with fencing all around it for protection. The path consisted of volcanic stone pocked with large rocks.

The view from the top was amazing. The bay of Naples and Herculaneum could be seen underneath. Visibility was clear as the sky was cloudless; its clear blue colour blended well with the dark blue colour of the sea. Standing at the rim of the crater provided a surreal view of the 600m wide and 300m deep crater. One could smell Sulphur in the air. A steady stream of steam could be seen around the rim, reminding the observer that Mount Vesuvius was far from being extinct. Its wrath might one day bury nearby towns, unleashing viscous lava running down its flanks and catapulting hot ashes onto the land beneath it. Warning means were available those days to evacuate living creatures prior to any eruption, but nothing could prevent the impact on stone and properties. There remained still a dormant vengeance beneath the volcano that humans couldn't deal with. Hence the quest to shift human attention to space exploration and other ventures where failure could be attributed to unknown factors: the vastness of the universe, equipment malfunctions due to solar radiation.

Nighttime around 8 PM, Paula and Luigi were at the port of Molo Beverello in Naples, boarding the high-speed ferry bound for Capri. The light display of the mainland as the ferry receded was awesome. The moon shone behind a veil of thin clouds giving the impression the scenery was a huge oil painting. The gentle bobbing of the boat reminded the observer that the scene was real indeed. Fifty minutes later, the ferry moored at the Marina di Capri.

Luigi was thankful for his mother's advice not to bring his car along. The best way to enjoy a trip was to act like a foreign tourist, relying on trains, buses and taxis. He had left his car back in Naples and was enjoying the satisfaction of letting others handle the driving especially in congested areas and narrow streets.

Paula hailed a cab. The fat driver helped them shove their suitcases inside the trunk of his car and had a problem getting in the driver's seat as his belly touched and squeezed the steering wheel. They arrived at the Punta Tragara Hotel after 12 minutes. Paula glanced at her watch: it was 9: 15 PM. Perfect timing.

It was a nice feeling to be back in that hotel. The arched reception area with its lavishly elegant decoration matched the warm welcome of the front desk staff. Luigi turned to his mother and simply exclaimed, "It must cost a fortune! But it's definitely worth every penny."

"Wait until you see the suite and the views from the balconies," replied Paula. She was very pleased to be with her son, exploring things together.

# Chapter Five

The view from the suite was spectacular. Luigi noticed it the moment he walked in. The arched balcony and bay windows could be spotted from any angle, yielding a magnificent night scene where the lit coastline and the twinkling lights of residential villas merged, creating one sloping entity that stretched from the seashore to the adjoining hills. The sitting-corner by the arched balcony was beaconing him to sit down, relax and enjoy the endless view. Far in the distance, tiny dots of light could be seen sailing slowly in the Gulf of Naples. Larger ships displayed shiny horizontal strips combing the sea.

Luigi hurriedly unpacked and darted out onto the wide balcony where he sat on a comfortable padded white armchair, closed his eyes and reopened them, as if to make sure he wasn't dreaming. He thought about his father; wished he could be with them, but what for? His dad was in a much better place where agony and sorrow did not exist. Gina crossed his mind and he wondered what life would have been with her around. There she was planning her engagement and there he was preparing for priesthood. How silly they had been, believing they could be friends forever. What was friendship after all? How could it last when one barely sees, speaks to, or touches another person? God knew how much he craved to be with her. She could have been sitting right here next to him on the balcony. They could have felt and kissed each other. How he missed letting go of his emotions, releasing the tenderness and compassion he was trying to curtail.

Luigi took his gaze upwards. No stars were visible in the moonlit sky. The moon dominated the night sky with its brightness and shed its reflection on the surface of the sea creating a lateral corridor of light that split the water into two halves. It was baffling how a satellite orbiting our planet could play such a big role in our daily lives: affecting the tide; dwarfing stars and eclipsing the sun. God's creation had given each element a role to play, no matter how infinitesimal it might be. A universal gravitational pull held things together emphasising the importance of every single entity and its contribution to the holistic bond.

Luigi's intertwined neurons conveyed to him scenes from space: a manned spaceship hurtling towards a planet outside the solar system, coasting in solemn silence out of respect for the musical symphony of the expanding universe. The incredible thrill he had experienced when he dreamed his close encounters with his dad in Heaven. Not being certain for sure of the credibility and reality of those dreams, their impact though had influenced his life in a grand way. There was a sincere message in their revelation: those dreams laid grounds for eternity and immortality; stressing on the need to believe unconditionally; search for the Truth in a genuine sort of way; being a good person.

As he mulled over those issues, Luigi's telephone set gave out several beeps. He picked up the handset off the square-shaped table near him and heard his mother's enthused voice: "Hello there! Care to join me for a drink? Waiting for you."

Luigi smiled without uttering a word. He scrambled out of the room and walked down the corridor, past three doors and found himself in front of room 334. He pressed the bell button and almost immediately his mum opened the door with a welcoming heartening smile.

She had ordered a chilled bottle of Dom Perignon which sat cradled in a huge bucket filled with crushed ice. They grabbed the bucket and moved to the balcony where an assortment of cheese, black olives and caviar awaited them.

"I thought a light snack with champagne would be appropriate for the occasion. Didn't fancy a heavy dinner this late," said Paula.

"Wise thinking," replied Luigi. "To be honest, I wasn't planning to nibble on anything, but now you're enticing me."

"I can't tell you how happy I am," Paula said. "We both needed this time out. Your father used to say: What's the point in saving money if you don't spend it? He was absolutely right."

"Life is a gift from God and we should do our utmost to live it sanely and happily. That's my motto these days. Did you know that on our previous visit to Capri, your father and I stayed in this same room? I stressed on booking it. I miss him loads but somehow your dreams have provided me with self-assurance and strength which render his absence bearable. If he's happy, I'm happy. I'm not scared anymore of what lies beyond. I feel grateful that you shared your experience with me. Making the Pope aware of it as well has lifted the weight off our shoulders. These days I'm not resenting your pursuit to become ordained. I have accepted it because you are convinced of what you're doing and your latest experience with the afterworld gives it more potency. You have a good heart like your dad. You've been extremely close since the day you were born. No wonder you've been seeing and talking to each other in your dreams/encounters, whatever you want to call them."

"Mum! You're great as well," exclaimed Luigi. "You complemented my dad and made him joyful throughout the years you've known each other. Even when you argued, each one of you made a keen effort to mend fences. Your beautiful smile was enough for him to cool down."

"His hug was good enough to melt you down. You were a perfect match together. Midway through my discernment year I started believing in my call. Prior to that, my aunt's influence and persistence in redeeming my dad's soul had put a great burden upon me. I felt responsible for his salvation. According to her, I had to pray consistently and had to become a priest and pray even further. Her concern emanated from her firm belief that Dad was an atheist. Her best scenario had placed him, on the lucky side, in the purgatory. Hence the need for my prayers to allow his transition to Heaven."

"I was a kid and a teenager then, wanting desperately the best for my father. I knew he was a good person and that he was an agnostic rather than an atheist, but the slightest possibility that I could be wrong in my assessment loomed heavily on me. My first dream relieved me from that pain and released me from those frightening thoughts. It was just a dream nonetheless. A wonderful dream that took me to my father and to the afterworld. Was it reality or mere fantasy concocted by my brain? No one could ever tell."

"No need to scrutinise the past," Paula said. "Your aunt had an influence on you, on all of us! She manipulated us because of her selfishness and misconception of religious teachings. I should have been more assertive with her, but I was vulnerable at the time and wasn't made aware of her strong influence on you. I blame you for hiding that from me, but I comprehend your desire to bring peace between us. Again, what counts now is your conviction to become a priest and I respect you for that. Meanwhile let's feast on these snacks. Try those sliced baguettes: so crisp and tasty."

By midnight, the last champagne sip was taken. Paula felt tipsy and Luigi enjoyed watching her rising from her seat, holding the empty bottle, pretending it was a microphone and singing: *O sole mio*.

# Chapter Six

Paula had a nice sleep and was awakened by a stream of daylight infiltrating her eye lids. She opened her eyes and surrendered to the warm rays that sieved through the windows and the ajar balcony door. A gentle wind blew from the sea side, carrying with it the earthy herb-like odour of heather shrubs and the distinct sage-woodsy smell of cypress trees. She called room service and ordered breakfast.

Paula avoided calling Luigi, fearing he would still be asleep. By the time she had a quick shower and put on casual wear, her breakfast was delivered and set on the balcony. The aroma of freshly baked croissants and roasted black coffee filled the air. She poured herself a cup of black coffee and enjoyed holding the steaming cup in both hands, enough for her to take a sip and then placing it back on the saucer. In front of her, the Tyrrhenian sea was calm; its blue colour streaked with white foam trailing behind motor boats whose wake gently battered the Faraglioni rocks as they passed near them.

One of the rocks reminded Paula of the Pigeon Grotto off the coast of Beirut. Fabriano had always made an analogy between them. Almost the same shape, height and colour. She wished he could be with her, right then, sharing those incredible moments. Life had been a bliss with him around.

Paula had almost forgotten that Andrea, Eva and their son would be soon joining them around evening time. It had been a while since she saw Eva. Occasional frigid phone calls had been exchanged between the two, restricted in nature, not exceeding courtesy discussions. Paula was not really looking forward to seeing her, but it would be wonderful to have Fabriano Junior in their midst.

Paula finished her breakfast and called Luigi. He had been awake for two hours and was awaiting her call, believing last night's booze had made her plunge into a deep sleep.

They agreed to meet at the reception in half an hour. They had already decided to explore Capri on that sunny day as they still had the freedom to do so, without being hindered by the presence of others.

They headed for the Marina Grande port and boarded a boat for a guided sea tour. They sailed along the southern shore of the island, past Faraglioni rock formations, round Punta Carena with its picturesque lighthouse. The brick tower with its lantern and gallery stood twenty-eight metres high above a two-storey building perched on top of a rocky hill covered with wild green landscape. The keeper's house neighboured the lighthouse structure, matching its brick colour.

After a while, at a relatively short distance, Paula and Luigi could see the Blue Grotto with several row boats either entering or exiting the cavern, laden with tourists that were expressing their excitement through high shrieks. On board their craft, passengers were given the choice to either remain on the boat or transfer to the row boats for a quick visit to the grotto.

Most passengers opted for the second choice, including Paula and Luigi. Getting through the narrow opening with a slightly choppy water was manageable. People had to duck their heads a little more than usual. The time spent inside the cavern lasted only five minutes. Watching the blue reflection caused by the sun rays was nevertheless sufficient to counter the waiting time the visitors had to endure before entering the grotto. Luigi had a flashback of the limpid water he had observed in his dreams. He even flinched when he experienced the serenity inside the cave.

Back to the mainland, Paula and Luigi had a quick bite at a bistro in the Main Square.

They took a cab and spent the rest of the day in Anacapri, wandering the village's lanes lined by artisan workshops and the tiny squares with their majolica benches. Paula purchased few hand-painted ceramics and encouraged her son to do the same. "As a present for Gina's forthcoming engagement," she said that and regretted it immediately afterwards. She didn't have the right to remind him of an event that obviously hurt him. He nonetheless acquiesced and bought some artifacts, requesting the saleswoman to put them inside one box and wrap them up in fancy paper and ribbons.

Luigi had heard of Mount Solero and the hermits who lived in Cetrella hermitage. Asking around, they aimed for Piazza Vittoria and took the chairlift up to the 600m high peak. The view was superb. Capri spread underneath with a nuance of colours proffered by the sky, the sea, the rocks and the green vegetation.

They walked down the mountain slope, side by side, until they reached the hermitage. They visited the church and the cramped cells where Franciscans and Dominicans dwelt to find peace and serenity. They looked at each other as if bonded by a universal harmony, and understood what crossed each other's mind: it was a deja-vu situation. The place was analogous with the monasteries found in the Valley of the Saints and Annaya, back in Lebanon.

The similarity was undisputable. Finding peace and quiet, tranquillity and self-searching were only possible in secluded places like that. Deity and humanity seemed to merge together as a holistic entity whose purity could only be attained through seclusion and meditation.

Luigi was assessing his future life and comparing it with that of monks and hermits. He came to realise that each category had its benefit and had a particular role to play. A monk reached out to God and communicated with Him through continuous prayers and complete alienation from the material world; while a priest liaised with God to promote and proliferate His teachings. Luigi's contribution to Christianity wouldn't therefore be of a lesser importance. He was further convinced that priesthood was the right thing for him and that it suited his expectations. No more the slightest remorse or regret about the path he had undertaken.

He felt relieved and content. Paula could see it in his sparkling eyes; in his demeanour. She sensed it as well. The mysterious world of seclusion and physically abandoning oneself looked tempting, even for her. How often had she begged to be away from the maddening crowd? How often had she wished to talk to God without being interrupted by mundane issues that appeared peripheral and meaningless, most of the time?

They descended back to Piazza Vittoria and got in the taxi that had waited for them. It was five o'clock already and it seemed a good idea to return back to their hotel for a quick rest before the arrival of Andrea, Eva and little Fabriano.

Paula lay on her bed with her clothes on, reflecting on the past, the present and the future. The past had been wonderful, filled with memorable events, even though it was fraught with sad moments; the present was manageable but lacked the virtues of the past; and the future appeared bleak and frightening. Loneliness was a dreadful thing and aging was an enemy that kept creeping in, reminding oneself how vulnerable one could be. Any irreversible process was worrying on its own. Not being in control of things, of events, was scary enough. She had lost the stubbornness and resolve she once had. She knew she was giving in rather than holding and fighting back. She used to be stronger and thought the whole world revolved around her and Fabriano…until she lost him…her real and true love.

# Chapter Seven

Andrea and his party arrived at seven in the evening; one hour later than scheduled. They were met by Paula and Luigi at the front desk where real and fake emotions fused together. There was that overreaction looming over the scene. Paula was sincere about her feelings for little Fabriano, honest and neutral about Andrea's and certainly exaggerated when it came to Eva's.

Luigi was genuinely happy to see Andrea and his little son; neutral to slightly enthusiastic to see his aunt after a relatively long time.

Andrea was extremely enthused over the sight of Paula and Luigi. His face brightened up whenever he laid eyes on Paula, oblivious to the presence of Eva next to him. Eva on the other hand tried her best to display emotions towards her sister-in-law and her nephew when in reality her feelings were neutral and sincere towards the former and the latter respectively.

It took a while to check in. Both parties agreed to meet at the reception in an hour before hitting the Piazzetta for a night out. Andrea and Luigi decided to loosen up in their rooms: they had a long tiring day, each in a different manner. They couldn't comprehend why women were more fit and had more endurance than men.

Paula fancied a stroll through the hotel premises and requested to take Fabriano Junior along with her. Meanwhile, Eva stayed behind, working with the hotel manager on the selection of a babysitter to watch over her son once they got out. Paula held little Fabriano's hand and walked with him to the canopied terrace where she found a table with two chairs. She eased herself down on one of the chairs then lifted the child up, amazed how heavy he had become. She made him sit on her lap and stroked his chestnut hair. She missed that basic and motherly bond with a child, realising very well that she would never have the opportunity to raise a nephew or a niece herself. She had been denied even that. She wasn't going to be called grandma and that saddened her.

Paula kissed Fabriano Junior on his plump cheeks and he reciprocated by throwing kisses at her. She muttered: "I love you, little one," and he replied, "love you too." That broke her heart. She couldn't bear thinking what Eva might go through, were she to lose custody of her son. Somehow it was unfair to take a kid away from his mother, whatever the reasons. Eva did not deserve any compassion but one had to be realistic and fully understand what it really meant to be alienated from loved ones, no matter what the reasons and conditions were. There was a definite difference between loving and showing love. Eva was incapable of fulfilling the second role, but that wasn't enough to overshadow the first category. Andrea could file for divorce but there was no need to deprive either parent from their child. They had to work it out together, at least for the sake of little Fabriano.

Paula ordered strawberry ice cream for little Fabriano and fizzy water for herself. She enjoyed feeding him, asking him to open his mouth wide enough to slip a partially filled spoonful of ice cream, begging him in a cajoling way to swallow the stuff afterwards. Time went by so quickly. Fabriano Junior was happy to stay awake that late, enjoying the dessert and the sea view. He would yell in excitement whenever a sprinkle of water hit his face while people swam in the nearby floodlit pool splashing water whenever they dived. His joy made her happy. She had an internal peace, long forsaken.

Just before nine o'clock they were seated around a table in a traditional restaurant where the peculiar combined smell of garlic, onion, tomato sauce and oven baked dough welcomed the guest. The four of them opted for a variety of dishes which included mushroom bruschetta, mushroom risotto, Fettuccine Alfredo and Linguini with clam sauce. Andrea ordered a bottle of Castello Monsanto Chardonnay white wine and a bottle of Nastro Azzurro beer for Eva. As they waited for dinner to be served, Andrea presided over the conversation, revealing to those present his latest intention to file for divorce. Even though his decision was somewhat expected, his statement rendered it official and irrevocable. Eva felt embarrassed and fragile. Paula was on the verge of expressing her own opinion regarding little Fabriano, but held it back. Luigi played the role of a mediator, acting as if he were already ordained. Eva was listening and managed to remain silent. In order to make an impact, she decided to interject towards the end, when all ideas had been exhausted and cross-examined. Andrea appeared to be decisive about his rupture with his wife but seemed on the hesitant side where it concerned his son. Rightly so. Allowing a mother to see her child, had the same equivalency as having him in her custody. It didn't make sense at all. Luigi and Paula recalled Andrea's concern about the child's safety, but harm could come at anytime, anywhere, if the intention were nasty indeed. Any threat to hurt the little boy could therefore be carried out regardless who the custodian was. The whole thing was a hoax.

Eva would never harm her own son. She had been making threats in order to play on her husband's nerves. All for the sake of preventing him from divorcing her. That was all there was to it.

The food was excellent. Everyone indulged in heavy eating to the exception of Eva. She was into her second beer bottle. That was her chance. A short reprieve period reigned at the dinner table, allowing her to interject by saying, "I know I've done awkward things lately but they were not intentional. I love my family; it's the only thing left for me. I need you Andrea and most of all I need my son. I want to hold him and read him a bed time story. I want him in my home, in our home, where we all belong together. After all, I'm a mother who dreads the thought of not being able to say goodnight to her child and fix breakfast for him in the morning; dressing him up for school; waiting for the bus to bring him home in the afternoon and helping him out with his homework…Please don't deny me that satisfaction."

"You're forgetting that you're the one who caused the rift between us," replied Andrea. "Fabriano Junior was neglected in the past few months. No nanny, no housekeeper, no genuine effort from your part to handle the situation except lately. Your ego has destroyed everything. The culmination point peaked out when your continuous threat to take it out on him. I cannot gamble with the life of my child. I find it paramount that he'd be raised with Carla's children. They'd take good care of him and take him on board as their kid brother."

"I believe I have the right to raise him more than anybody else," muttered Eva in a low voice. "Actually, I want you both. I promise I will change. Just give me one more chance and I'll prove it to you."

Never had Paula imagined that her sister-in-law could be so distraught and broken. She felt pity for her and believed that her willingness to mend fences with Andrea and above all become a good mother, was genuine.

"Eva! We have already discussed the issue and we both concurred that a divorce was necessary. Fabriano Junior has to be under my protection. You scared the shit out of me with your crazy threats and I'm quite familiar with your tantrums. Believe me, I've witnessed a few." He paused for a while, assessed the impact on Eva and continued, "I have also found the love of my life. So the divorce matter is irrevocable and cannot be contemplated."

This time he was simultaneously evaluating the whack of his words on Eva and Paula.

The former was struck in the heart, her suspicions confirmed; the latter was dumbfounded realising the insinuation Andrea had just made. She disliked being torn in between two sides, particularly when one of them had taken her for granted. It was true they had sex together but as far as she was concerned that was it. She had made no promises. She had never mentioned the word "love" under any circumstance. She found a hint of naivety in Andrea's approach to matters. He had just thrown a grenade whose blast could have massive repercussions on all those present, and she wasn't prepared to defend herself or take the offensive. She decided instead to calm down and absorb the situation as if nothing had happened. There was also that slim chance that Andrea had indeed found the love of his life and that it could be someone else. His staring eyes however revealed otherwise.

"How long have you known her?" Eva demanded.

Paula bit her lips and frowned while staring at Andrea. She tried using telepathy, any communication method she could muster just to warn him not to utter senseless words that would backfire on all of them.

"Long enough," he replied.

"We need to talk. You know that," Eva exclaimed.

A long heavy pause ensued. Paula cleared her throat and said, "I don't know about you guys, but let us order some dessert. I crave a torta caprese."

The night continued without an incident, though Paula was disturbed by Andrea's periodic gazes. He didn't seem aware that he was jeopardising the situation and exposing her to undue problems. She had to talk to him the soonest possible and clear all those issues.

Eva spent most of her time, either reflecting or chatting with Luigi. Her reflections were combing the past and sifting through it, digging out Andrea's acquaintances, trying to remember any name he might have mentioned, any place he had frequented. A complete blank filled her database. Who might the mysterious lady be?

Upon Paula's insistence, the group of four headed for the Taverna night club. The place was crowded but the music was fantastic combining Tarantella rhythm with Neapolitan classics. A classy businessman kept staring at Paula, raising his glass often and saluting her. She reciprocated with her killing smile, which was enough for him to come forth and ask her politely for a dance. Andrea was cursing under his lips. But under the circumstances he couldn't do anything or react. Eva was jealous of her. Luigi was proud of his mum. She was still devastating and appealing.

One hour later, they were retiring in their hotel rooms. Paula sat on the balcony and read the business card that her recent admirer had given her. His name was Matthew Anderson: an American film producer. She recalled one of his movies. It had become a big hit in the box office and made quite a big impact on her. A film based on a novel she had once read. The script had followed the story line of the original book almost to the letter, resulting in a fabulous success.

He had asked her permission to call her. She coyly refrained giving him any hint whether it would be fine to do so or not. Giving her his business card was a wise move, leaving the matter entirely up to her. He was staying in Capri for the next three days and would love to invite her for lunch or dinner at her convenience. She placed the card on the table and was excited at the thought men still found her attractive. But where would she go from there? That was the ultimate question.

# Chapter Eight

Eva stirred in the King-size bed for most of the night. She intentionally slept with no clothes on, except for her panties. Andrea avoided any bodily contact, lying at the edge on the opposite side, risking to fall off at the slightest movement. His reluctance to establish any bodily contact with her was clearly obvious: not even toes touching.

She thought she had performed well over dinner: displaying remorse and begging for another chance. It had certainly made an impact on her sister-in-law and her nephew, but what disturbed her the most was the new love in Andrea's life. Who was that mysterious woman? Probably a nurse or a female physician. She must be an attractive woman to inflict such influence over him. Andrea had turned into a womaniser: Eva had also noticed the way he gazed at Paula with a hidden lust in his eyes, let alone his daring glances at dancing females swaying their bodies and writhing to the beat of the music. What an embarrassment to her? He was acting as if she never existed in his life anymore. He was simply on the loose.

Eva dozed off in the early morning hours, waking up around eight-twenty to the scent and swishing sound of Andrea's deodorant spray. He had already showered and was preparing himself to go down for breakfast. "Wait for me," she said in a somnolent way.

"Join me when you're ready. I need to find a good seating on the terrace. Don't be late! We're all going to the beach later," he blurted out.

Andrea picked a table with a scenic view. He ordered black coffee and messaged Paula, giving her his coordinates. Five minutes later, there she was approaching his table striding along with her hair blown by the wind and her blouse glued to her figure. He rose from his chair and embraced her affectionately. Paula stood there like a statue, unable to back away or reciprocate. She heard herself uttering: "Please! Hold on! Not here! Andrea, we have to talk." He withdrew and quietly sat back on the chair looking appalled and bewildered.

Paula wanted to confront him right there and then, desperate to explain her point of view. He was making her feel like an inert object; taking her for granted as if she were already his prize. She resented the fact her opinion wasn't even taken into consideration.

"Andrea, please hear me out!" Paula said. "What happened between us had been spontaneous and I admit it was quite enjoyable. But it is still early to declare that our relationship is founded on love. Our recent encounters were bound to occur due to our mutual frustration and impending stress. I like you so much but I'm not sure that I'm ready for love. You see, I'm not prepared for serious relationships. Promise me you'll forgive me for any misconstruction I might have induced. It has never been my intention to lure you into anything. Similarly, I cannot accept being coerced into an affair that has interrogation marks associated with it. Your life is already too complicated; mine as well, though to a lesser degree."

"But I love you so much. I thought you shared the same feeling," cried out Andrea. "Eva has been a hindrance; soon she'll be out of my life."

"It has nothing to do with Eva," retorted Paula. "I like you so much but not to the extent of falling in love. I'm not yet ready for relationships and particularly serious ones. I hope your determination to get a divorce was not a direct consequence of what happened between us. It would make me feel awkward. Watching Eva last night made my heart ache. She appeared sincere in her remorse. Can't you both give it a try?"

"I cannot believe what I'm hearing," replied Andrea. "Don't you have any feelings for me?" He said that in an agitated way with a hoarse upset voice. His words echoed loudly and lingered long enough to reach Eva's ears as she neared their table with little Fabriano by her side.

"What are you talking about? What feelings?" Eva was shouting, her jugular veins bulging on the sides of her neck. "What's going on? Am I missing something?"

"Eva. Take it easy," replied Paula in a low but firm intonation. "I was asking Andrea to reconsider his decision to seek a divorce. I shouldn't have requested that. Apparently, he feels I'm not sympathising with him," Paula uttered those words while lying through her teeth. The stakes were high. She knew Andrea couldn't salvage the situation. Maybe he even fancied aggravating the situation so that it blew up in the face of everyone, once and for all, revealing all the cards. It would suit him to do just that. She shouldn't give him the upper hand and hence her spontaneous response to Eva's inquisition was the perfect thing to do, the perfect lie to concoct.

Eva quieted down and seemed to have taken the bait. "I'm sorry, Paula. But my mind has been so blurred recently that I've become suspicious of everyone." She turned to Andrea. "Sorry. Forgive me for my blunt behaviour."

Andrea nodded. His calm reaction was extraordinary. Paula however did notice the nervous twitch that took hold of his right cheek. He kept pouring coffee in his cup. He looked straight down at the cold cuts laid on a plate just in front of him without touching them. Luigi showed up, bid them good morning and sat facing Eva. It took Andrea some time to realise his presence. There was no need for Luigi to enquire about the dull silence that hovered over them. Hotel guests occupying the adjacent tables were roaring with laughter and talking animatedly. It seemed Eva and Andrea had an innate skill to dynamite happiness and nurture gloom around those who sought normal living. Fabriano Junior had been also affected. He was fidgety most of the time, begging for attention amid a heavy parental silence.

"So where are we going?" asked Luigi, even though he knew their destination.

"Fabriano Junior will tell you," Eva said.

"Bagni di Tiberio," yelled the little kid.

Andrea spoke for the first time since Eva joined for breakfast. "Well! At this rate, we won't be going anywhere. Let's move on. The beach will be too crowded as it gets late. We'll meet at the hotel entrance in half an hour."

With that, the whole group stood up almost in unison, attracting the attention of occupied tables nearby. The tiny figure of little Fabriano was the centre of attraction. Few people patted him on the head, ruffling his long hair as he passed by them.

Once the party separated, Luigi asked his mother what lay behind Andrea's diverted spirit. Paula stuck to the story she had invented to appease Eva's concern and hated herself for lying to her own son. It was impossible for her to tell the truth; at least not now. Her brief affair with Andrea had been a terrible mistake. She had been relying on his discretion but his infatuation with her had proven to be beyond his capacity to cope with the situation.

As Luigi reached his room and before swiping his card, he called out his mum as she receded down the corridor and said playfully: "I cannot blame my aunt for being suspicious that Andrea has straying eyes for women. I was watching his furtive gazes directed at you during yesterday's dinner. He was literally fixated on you," he said that with a smile accompanied by a wink.

Paula's heart sank inside her chest. She flashed a fake smile and dreaded herself for concealing the truth from her own son.

# Chapter Nine

Small waves with tiny breakers splashed against the rocks, sprinkling swimmers and sun bathers alike, with refreshing water droplets that lasted few seconds before evaporating under the stifling heat. Paula lay on a thick blanket spread over shiny wet pebbles, wearing a two-piece swimsuit, dark sunglasses and headphones. The volume was set high enough but not too loud to harm her eardrums. Luigi could pick the muffled irregular thump of the musical notes at two-metre distance. He occupied a spot midway between Andrea and his mum. The three of them were sunbathing. Eva, on the other hand was at sea, immersed one metre in the cool water. She held the swim ring that wrapped little Fabriano's body with one hand, and used the other to splash him with the thick salty water. The child was super hyped and extremely happy. He constantly beat the sea water with his tiny hands and kicked his feet in an up and down motion, trying to swim and move along the water surface. His movements splattered the face of his mum who tried her best to shield the salty water from her eyes. She would laugh and cheer, encouraging her son to maintain his playful streak.

Luigi was admiring that scene and felt compassion for his aunt. She didn't deserve being confronted with a divorce and a separation from her son. He turned towards Andrea, "I've never seen Luigi that happy. Look at him!" But the moment he spoke he realised he didn't need to.

Andrea had a concentrated gaze at what was going on. Luigi detected however an unusual glassy stare. Andrea's eyes had no emotions; his lips were glued, unable to display an upward line for a faint smile or sign of shallow satisfaction.

Luigi closed his eyes and shifted his body slightly to expose his skin to the warm sun rays. His face was protected from the burning rays by the canvas of the beach umbrella that fluttered with the gentle wind, right above him. He loved kids but he had chosen a life course that prevented him from raising a family.

The only way to console himself was through the belief that all children were his. One day, they would all need his love and guidance.

Andrea had ordered fresh orange juice and failed to notice that it had been deposited a while ago on the blanket next to him. He propped himself up and grabbed the glass in his hand and took a big gulp. He could feel his fingers trembling around the glass. How weird life could be. There had been times when he felt on top of the world, with everything working smoothly for him. He had the impression that all hurdles had been eradicated and foregone. That gave him the boost and courage to entertain new ideas and plan a different life full of expectations. But all of a sudden, everything seemed to falter, leaving him with nothing, except wishful dreams and fantasies. He was angry with Paula but maybe she was right in her assessment of recent events.

He had come to fast conclusions unsure of the solidity of the parameters that formed the basis of his evaluation. Literally speaking he had got carried away. But he knew that he loved her and that she definitely liked him; she had told him so. His assumptions were therefore not farfetched. She had admitted that she wasn't ready yet for commitments: meaning that there was still some hope that he might gain her heart.

One hundred metres away, the silhouettes of Eva and Fabriano Junior receded farther into the sea. They had reached an isolated zone, away from any batch of swimmers. He could tell just watching Eva's head poking out of the surface of the water that her feet were no longer touching the sea bed underneath her. Little Fabriano appeared like a tiny dot encircled by a white elliptical ring, bobbing up and down with each wave break. Andrea rose up and walked on the roasting pebbles. He headed for the shoreline, towards the invading water. He strode like a zombie, fixated on something. At that very moment, the stern warning of the lifesaver came blaring through a hand-held speaker: "The lady with the little boy, get back, don't drift any farther! I'm coming for you!"

Andrea's feet touched the foamy water for the first time and he had a chill travelling along his spine. He continued forwards sinking his ankles into the water and then his knees. Thirty metres away from him, Eva's hands could be seen waving in a desperate motion. Her head was semi-immersed and her mouth spouted seawater each time she tried to reach for the surface.

Fabriano Junior's stifled cries could be heard. The ring was still wrapped around him but at any moment Eva might let go and he would drift away. The lifesaver swam like a dart past Andrea, aiming for the kid. Andrea's feet were now barely touching the seabed. He was scared; he was a lousy swimmer, but he couldn't lose his son. Was Eva carrying out her threat or was it just a coincidence? Which way he had to go? He had lost his bearings but kept proceeding forwards. He could taste the sea water at each gasp that he was taking. Then he tried to float but couldn't. A shortness of breath seized him and a numb sensation grabbed him. He didn't feel like struggling anymore. He was literally surrendering to the deep waters. He had never anticipated such a senseless death. His past haunted his mind as scenes reeled in a non-cohesive sequence. Then, a silent confusing blur engulfed him.

Luigi had heard the loudspeaker, the shouting and the commotion. He was awakened from his trance. He threw himself into the water and swam for the rescue of his aunt, realising the attempt of the lifesaver to retrieve the boy first, as a priority.

Luigi reached for his gasping aunt, swam up from behind and slid his arms under hers. He grabbed her by the shoulders and swam back in a straight line towards the shore, towing her behind him. All along she was screaming out: "Fabriano! Fabriano! Where is my boy?" Luigi had never imagined that towing someone could be that arduous. It was a real hardship that required patience and fitness. The whole thing took less than a minute to reach shallow waters where both could rest their weight on the floor bed. Only then did they glimpse, twenty metres away, the lifesaver delivering the boy to Paula who stood by the seashore, looking distraught.

"There was a man in the water," cried the lifeguard. "Have you seen him?" He was directing his question at Luigi, who panicked realising the absence of Andrea. Without any further delay, a professional rescue was under way, carried out by a team of four lifesavers who dissected the shoreline into segmented zones. Andrea was found with no pulse. Immediate CPR was performed on him after being pulled to the surface. Water drained abundantly from his mouth and nose. His pulse kicked back faintly. His chest heaved slowly but he did not regain consciousness.

# Chapter Ten

An ambulance with an ear-shattering siren drove Andrea to a nearby hospital. Just behind the ambulance a taxi followed, carrying three adults and a child. Nothing could be said under the circumstances. A complete silence loomed over; a heavy calmness consistent with the state of being astonished, baffled and worried.

Various equipment, electrodes, probes and IV's were hooked to Andrea's body, giving digital readouts of physiological functions and injecting medicine intravenously. Eva was allowed inside the Intensive Care Unit. She sat by her husband's side watching the respiration rate, the blood pressure, the heartbeat and the oxygen rate being displayed on monitors. As time progressed, his bodily functions were getting back to normal. The EEG reading showed nonetheless a slight deficiency in the brain wave pattern.

Andrea kept his eyes shut, responding initially to stimulus by contracting his body and squeezing the examiner's hands. Little by little, his response diminished, and he showed no tangible reaction to the world around him. Further tests were required to determine his condition. The physicians suspected brain damage caused by the lack of oxygen during drowning. They termed it: anoxic brain injury. In other words, Andrea was in a comatose state.

Andrea was transported one week later to one of Milan's Medical Centres. His condition remained unchanged. Eva paid him regular visits and so did his children. Yet they never spoke to each other even under such dramatic circumstances. They made her feel responsible for what happened and Paula had to plead with them to stop such accusations, as they led nowhere and wouldn't resolve anything. Their frequent rows took place in Andrea's room and it was difficult to ascertain or refute whether in his condition he was able to depict what was going on around him. Few times he emitted a groan which would force them to stop. Eva had been unfairly battered for venturing deeper into the water than conceivable. But enough was enough. Paula was the oldest among them and it was her duty to control the situation. Luigi was relying on her to do so. He would communicate with her whenever time allowed, enquiring about Andrea's health and how everyone was coping.

Paula was still under severe shock. She wished she had acted in more leniency with Andrea. Her aim had never been to hurt his feelings. How odd it was for a couple to be discussing the continuation or rupture of a relationship, when suddenly circumstances sneak in, sealing their fate and closing the argument. It was painful to watch Andrea, her husband's best friend, her friend and temporary Romeo being reduced to a breathing vegetable. Her subconscious registered relief from the pending pressure of a romantic and serious relationship but her conscience weighed the drastic effect and prompted her to be sad. She had planned to discuss candidly with Andrea, in full details, how she felt about him and how they should perceive their priorities. After all, the individual window of perception was the core of every misunderstanding and misconception. Often people tended to skip over it as a hurdle, not grasping that their goal might just be the same, but with a different road map.

Sophia was perturbed by the news. The past ten years had been painful: succeeding suffering. She had to be supportive of her daughter and took no time flying out to Milan. Eva found solace in her mum's presence and so did Paula. The old lady somehow diffused comfort and good vibes wherever she went. The rift however, that existed between her daughter and Andrea had never been revealed to her. Little Fabriano became close to her, finding in her a means to sneak a chocolate bar from the kitchen cabinet behind his mother's back. He noticed in his own childish way that his mum's tantrums and yelling had subsided since his grandma came and stayed with them. He wanted her to stay with them forever. Fabriano Junior couldn't comprehend the seriousness of his dad's condition. "Why is he sleeping all the time?" He would ask. "When is he coming home?" He missed his dad and felt so special when Andrea was able to squeeze his tiny hand a few times during hospital visits.

On one Saturday evening, Sophia came to visit her daughter-in-law. Paula was so happy to host her, especially that she really liked and respected the old woman. Not once had she interfered in her marital life or choices. On the contrary, she acted as a mother and an elderly sister to her. Sophia had grace and charm; able to cope with most people regardless of their age.

"What a dreadful situation," Sophia said after laying the coffee cup and saucer on the small table beside her. "Who would imagine a bubbly man being rendered inert by a lousy unpredictable incident? Poor guy! He couldn't swim and yet he acted bravely, trying to rescue his family. Under such drastic circumstances, no wonder that my daughter got panicky as well. She had been seized apparently with terror fearing for her son. She could have drowned too. Eva had won medals in her university years in freestyle swimming competitions. That proves real-life experience is so different from institutional expertise."

"Are you saying Eva is a good swimmer?" Paula's voice was wavering.

"One of the best. She frequented most sea resorts all over Lebanon, indulging herself in swimming activities including deep sea diving. Unlike Fabriano who loved hiking and climbing the mountain slopes, Eva was a sea-goer, spending most of her time in the water; rarely sunbathing."

Sophia's affirmations poured icy water on Paula's neck and shoulders. Her knees trembled involuntary and her teeth crashed into each other. Luckily, she wasn't holding her coffee cup.

"What's wrong?" Exclaimed Sophia.

"Nothing," replied Paula. "It just disturbs me that she got mesmerised and her whole swimming experience hadn't come in handy. What a shame!"

It was not until Sophia left that Paula cradled herself in her seat and pondered over the events. Fear engulfed her; adrenaline ran high. Maybe she was overreacting. But something was bothering her deep inside, and she couldn't place her finger on it. Once again, her mind was creating a complex network of sketchy incoherent hypothesis. That had always been the issue with Eva. She had the knack of causing incessant trouble. Her sister-in-law was shrouded with mystery and any tendency to know her better seemed to stumble and fall. She was full of surprises.

# Chapter Eleven

Paula missed Gina's engagement ceremony due to her preoccupation with Andrea and the need to comfort his children by being there for them. Their mother had committed suicide and now they were on the verge of losing their father. Watching him bed ridden, unable to speak, to eat, to open his eyes and respond to the world around him, filled their heart with pain and sorrow. Alphonso and Maria had that sickening sensation that in his deep sleep, he might never be aware of their great love for him. They would express their love loudly to him, close to his ears, so that he could hear them, but no response had been observed. Just once a slight groan had been detected. It was a heavy price to pay for presuming that love for one's parents could wait, as if they were going to live eternally. Maria often cried, hating herself for missing that chance. If only her dad could recover! She would do things with him she thought they had missed altogether. He was the person supposed to lead her to the altar once she got married.

Luigi tried his best to visit Milan over the weekends, providing support to his aunt, his grandmother, Andrea's children and paying particular attention to little Fabriano, taking him for strolls through the parks, playing video games with him, wrestling with him, the same way his father used to do when he himself was a kid.

Luigi reminisced about his dad and missed him more than ever. He had a smouldering longing for his dad whenever situations were not under control and he found himself feeble. His father's existence had offered a buffer that shielded them from harm and granted the family security and strength. His mother coped very well with the situation once he was gone, but the three of them had been a well-knit entity, capable of warding off obstacles unperturbed.

Two events had recently contributed to his anxiety. One of them had been the attendance of Gina's engagement. His emotions instructed him to decline but social ethics dictated otherwise. So, there he was watching another guy harvesting the love he could have had. It was painful, especially when hiding one's feelings turned into an acting role of someone not concerned. The second disturbing event was the call he had received from the Vatican.

Archbishop Gambino informed him that the Vatican's specialised team that he was supposed to meet, had been briefed by the Pontiff about his recent dreams. The majority of its members had found no tangible reason to classify those visions under paranormal accounts. As far as they were concerned, those were regular dreams perpetrated by intense subconscious activity, not worthy of serious consideration. According to the Archbishop, the Pope had encouraged them nevertheless to reconsider their verdict and hear Luigi out. Should there be any change in their resolution, Luigi were to be contacted. No communication however was expected before the Pontiff's return to the Vatican City from his summer retreat.

Luigi was dismayed. He had never anticipated an outright rejection from the outset. They denied him the prospect of describing the contents of his dreams. Were they right about their assessment? Maybe they were. He wasn't sure himself whether his dreams were the concoction of a tormented subconscious. They might be the consequence of his quest and constant strive to salvage his father's soul, wishing he were indeed in Heaven.

Luigi didn't know what to believe anymore. Conceding that his intense dreams were a figment of either his imagination or subconscious was a painful thing to assume. It meant that the joy he had experienced seeing his father in paradise had been a hoax. It meant his dad wasn't necessarily in Heaven. It meant the whole matter was simply not a vision, not an encounter; just a fabrication of a distressed mind.

There vanished his earlier happiness and near certainty that his dear father had made it to Heaven. A phone call brought him back to square one; just like that! In a flash of a second. His aunt had warned him that his alleged encounters were mere dreams. She had been apparently right. His only consolation prize were his prayers and pursuit of priesthood. Those were essential tools to salvage his father's soul if it were errant. The life course that he had chosen might still work in a positive way.

Luigi preferred not to mention the Vatican issue to his mother. At least for the time being.

She had enough headaches and worries to deal with already. No need to stress her out.

# Chapter Twelve

Days and weeks passed by. Andrea's state remained unchanged. Visits became less frequent even by family standards. The medical team that took care of him often reported his condition to those who called enquiring about his health, repeating the same expression: "still the same, no change."

Sophia stayed with her daughter Eva and proved to be of great assistance. She was successful in re-engaging the services of Nina, dealing with her directly, warding Eva off. Her daughter was calculating, measuring her words whenever she addressed the house helper. No more tantrums, no more shouting. Things went smoothly. Eva appeared to have learned her lesson well. Raising Fabriano Junior was turning into a bearable task.

Paula paid regular visits to Eva's apartment and was astonished by her sister-in-law's friendliness and good reception. For the first time in twenty years of acquaintance, she felt related to her. They spoke with passion about almost everything except Andrea. Past tense was used if and whenever his name was mentioned. The incident itself was no longer referred to. The whole thing was attributed to destiny. The causes that led to the incident and the individual behaviour of each one of them, were never brought up in their conversation. Sophia tried a couple of times to raise the issue in a peripheral sort of way, but it was obvious though that neither her daughter nor Paula were eager to discuss the matter. Paula still had the shiver whenever she recalled Sophia's account that Eva was a professional swimmer. But everyone avoided the issue.

"I would love to have you over at Bellagio this weekend," Paula said, looking firstly at her mother-in-law and then Eva. "It would be a getaway for all of us. Luigi will be there too."

"Oh! It's a wonderful idea," Sophia replied. "I guess little Fabriano would enjoy the change. What do you think, Eva?"

"I'm on," she replied.

The weekend restored everyone's appreciation of being alive. Paula was happy hosting her mother-in-law. She loved her because she reminded her of Fabriano. She would do anything for her. Sophia enjoyed the warmth she was getting from Paula and realised more than ever why her son had fallen madly in love with her. They had left for Lake Como on a Friday evening.

Saturday afternoon, they had Chinese food delivered to the premises. Soon afterwards, they relaxed for more than an hour, drinking coffee and jasmine tea, while Sophia dozed off on the couch. Luigi put on his trunks, went out to the garden, headed for the swimming pool, situated towards the edge of the large green lawn, with the bluish colour of its water contrasting with its surroundings. He swam the length of the pool few times in one stretch, took a deep breath and resumed his combined diving and surface swimming. With each stroke, he remembered how few weeks ago he had to swim and rescue his aunt from a definite drowning.

They all sat near the pool watching Luigi closing in and then receding, splashing chlorine smelling water onto them. Sophia stared at her daughter and remarked: "Aren't you tempted to dive right in and show us your swimming skills. We used to love watching you during competi—"

Eva interrupted her mother in an abrupt way, blurting, "That was a long time ago. Haven't been practicing since. Anyway, just the thought of being in water disturbs me." Eva glanced at Paula, as if trying to assess how attentive she had been to the conversation.

Paula instinctively feigned checking her mobile phone for messages, pretending the whole matter was of no interest to her. A drop of sweat trickled down her back. "Ah! Got a message from Gina," she exclaimed, killing the subject that had been annoying her for weeks.

Luigi's workout took its toll. Just before dinner, his limbs started getting numb with a slight muscular pain, commensurate with over-exercising after a reprieve period. He longed to lie in bed and surrender to a long sleep. He excused himself before eleven and went upstairs to his bedroom.

# Chapter Thirteen

Removing his shoes and socks, Luigi slid in the comfort of his queen-size bed with his clothes on. Tranquillity prevailed. The window was open, letting in a gentle breeze that tickled his exposed toes and invited the whitish glow of the moon to filter in. His mind was overwhelmed by recent incidents and emotional stress. The strain was not at par with the exerted stress. He tried to shrug it all off, but tossed in bed instead. In such moments, Luigi prayed to God and sought out his dad for assistance. Gradually his bodily functions and brain waves slowed down as he dived into the realm of deep sleep, where the physical world got reduced to the bare minimum, overpowered by the influence of spirituality. Luigi was becoming vulnerable to mental ascendancy by the minute.

He was in a convent somewhere up in the mountains. Religious chanting could be heard from within the thick irregular stone walls: a mix of Aramaic and Latin hymns. The smoky scent of burned incense filled the vast corridors and escaped through large semi-circular arched windows that overlooked a familiar valley. Luigi was sitting behind a big grey/ brown oak desk scribbling notes and instructions. He would hand them over to a female secretary who either filed them or entered them electronically on her computer. A knock on the door startled him. His secretary didn't seem to have heard anything. At the threshold stood his father looking great as ever, wearing a loving smile.

"Hi Dad! Please come in," cried out Luigi with happiness. Fabriano entered the office, pulled a chair and sat down. Luigi noticed that his secretary continued her work, oblivious that he had company.

"Would you like anything to drink? Hot or cold?" Luigi asked, while eyeing his secretary who still hadn't registered there was someone else in the room. Only then did he realise he was dreaming and recalled that his father had passed away. It seemed he had the lucidity to be aware that he was indeed dreaming. Luigi stirred in his bed as if regaining consciousness and then fell back into the realm of dreams and visions.

"It was my turn to come and see you," his father said. "You're not allowed to cross over anymore. This time it's a vision you're having and I'm allowed to enter your mind and discuss whatever is bothering you. Beckoning me to be here suggests that you're experiencing a lot of stress. Had it not been for your high anxiety and willingness to share your burden with me, I couldn't and wouldn't be here."

Luigi nodded. "I understand," he replied. "Please Dad, tell me: did I really cross over to Heaven and are you truly there? Other than Mum, I don't seem able to convince anyone about our previous encounters. They have considered them as mere dreams, not factual. What concerns me the most is your well-being. Are you in Heaven or is it a wild fantasy and a trick of my subconscious?"

"I am, Luigi. I truly am!" Fabriano said. "You will never be able to sustain your claim. No evidence can ever be provided. I guess you have to believe it yourself and build on it. The knowledge you have acquired can make tangible changes to the world around you. Try to utilise the info to enhance faith. Nothing comes easily. With all the magnificent, noble and Godly deeds performed on Earth, Jesus had to cope with the scepticism and intransigence of non-believers. Yet, he persisted unabated with his struggle to spread faith and goodness to mankind."

"I know," exclaimed Luigi. "But it's rather difficult to digest and put in good use the knowledge you've conveyed to me in the absence of solid proof. I need to be convinced that my visions reflect the Truth. Each time we established contact I had felt strong, unharmed; on top of the world. I had become ecstatic by the realisation there's an afterworld filled with happiness and beauty. A spiritual universe that I would access one day and inhabit with you by my side. The fact you're in Heaven had given me great comfort and relief. It seems you didn't need my prayers after all. You earned it yourself. That marvellous sensation nonetheless and the acquired confidence got dissipated with time and ended up short-lived. The burden of the physical world with its varied and numerous problems seem to outweigh that infatuation. I therefore find myself controlled by the physical events that plague me, knowing quite well that they exist and therefore are real. Countering those, are spiritual dreams/ visions that my mind perceives but can neither define nor defend…"

"Problems will never fade or cease," Fabriano replied. "Your world is purely physical and it's perfectly normal that you succumb under its weight. Had it not been for the immense pressure exerted on you by mundane matters, your out-of-body experience wouldn't have been possible. Consider yourself fortunate."

Luigi stirred once more. His dream seemed fractionally interrupted but then resumed. He watched his secretary turning up the volume of the TV set. "Transmission from the spaceship Explorer orbiting Proxima B," she said enthusiastically. Two astronauts appeared on the screen, wearing their white space suits. Behind them the scene was that of dark space with a round planet half lit by its star with the other half totally shaded. "By the time you watch this video," one of the astronauts said, "4.2 years of space travel would have been exhausted and 4.2 further years would have been required for the signal to reach you at home. We'd be back to Earth around the same time you'd be seeing this transmission. Four of us were transported onto the planet's surface, precisely to what seemed to be a major city."

"Our first assessment is total annihilation of a once thriving civilisation, supposedly similar if not more sophisticated than our own. Devastation is obvious everywhere. Not a single soul appears to have survived the calamity. Human and animal skeletons are strewn everywhere with evidence of calcined cranial bones indicating exposure to extreme temperatures. The obvious cause is definitely attributed to awesome flare-ups of the red dwarf star which apparently scorched the entire surface of the exposed side of the planet. As far as we know, those flare-ups occurred regularly once every two months, prompting the inhabitants to find ways to shield themselves temporarily from those bursts of radiation. It seems evident a major flare-up of tremendous magnitude had occurred lately, maybe three years ago, for which no protection had been adequate enough to counter its powerful impact contrary to our expectation, no surface water has been found, as if it had been depleted due to the thinning atmosphere. Had it not been for the strong magnetic field, life on this planet wouldn't have been possible. Unlike Earth's axial rotation, Proxima B is devoid of this feature and is tidally tied to its star system. It always has one side facing its sun while the other half remains totally dark and extremely cold."

"We have also observed hundreds of relatively small flying objects that had apparently fallen from the sky and crashed into buildings: sign that the flares had disrupted all equipment working on electromagnetic waves and pulses."

"Our team has no means of assessing if the damage is localised or encompasses the entire habitable portion of the planet. The zooming capability of our powerful onboard cameras tends to confirm our field finding that no city could have been spared. It's a big blow for us. Our space venture has turned into the worst nightmare any scientist or explorer could have. Frustration looms over us. Under the circumstances, Proxima B is considered unsafe, unworthy of any further exploration. Our team will investigate further, conducting field exploration for a limited time. We are unable to move at ease with a gravity surpassing our own. And the incertitude of when the next flare-up is due, force us to abort the mission the soonest possible. Meanwhile we'll be collecting any information that might reveal the secrets of a once intelligent civilisation. Over and out."

Luigi stared at the screen in disbelief while his assistant swiped a bead of sweat from her temple. Luigi turned his head towards his father searching for a comment or an observation. In return, he was met by a knowing smile. His dad stood up and said, "There you go. The evidence could be right there." And he walked out.

"The evidence?" Luigi cried out. He woke bewildered, shaking all over, sweating and panting.

It was dark outside. Dawn had two more hours to break. Luigi propped up the pillow behind his back and gazed at the cloudless night sky. Through the window opening, stars twinkled as their light reached the atmosphere; a light from their mysterious old past. It took fifteen minutes for Luigi's heartbeats to get back to normal. "The evidence could be right there!" That's what his father stated at the end of the dream. He had to call Archbishop Gambino and relay to him what he saw in his dream. But again, his credibility was at stake. Who would believe in his dreams? He tried it before and failed. Only this time, the message carried futuristic events.

He just had to register his warning: the space mission to Planet Proxima B would prove futile and of no value. The planet was no longer habitable. The journey had commenced two months ago, and it would be prudent to abort. His duty anyhow, was to warn the concerned authorities. Their action was entirely in their hands. Should they decide to proceed with the mission, truth would be revealed in almost eight-year time, once actual reporting from the planet had reached Earth. His encounters would be validated based on the outcome. The Vatican committee would then appreciate and accept his previous accounts and more importantly, any partial scepticism he might have, no matter how fractional, would dissipate eternally. The evidence to sustain his claims had been laid out before him in a futuristic dream. Luigi had nothing to lose.

# Chapter Fourteen

Meanwhile in Puerto Rico, Dr Jack Morrison was deciphering interstellar messages at Arecibo Observatory. He was specialised in composing encoded signals and analysing intelligent interstellar signals picked up by the giant radio telescope. His persistent nature and thoroughness had led to the discovery of an intelligent civilisation in the Alpha Centauri star system. In response to 3-minute transmissions from Earth performed daily since 2010, Planet Proxima B responded back to the first signal with an intelligent message that was received in 2019. The flow of outward and inward messages continued since, with one-day interval between each. Both civilisations were ascertaining their existence and intelligence on a regular basis. The encoded signals covered prime numbers, chemistry elements and their atomic numbers, DNA, graphic figures of human beings and animals, composition of corresponding star system…

But since December 2033, almost seven months before launch, signals from Proxima B suddenly stopped. Dr Morrison would wait for the next day and the next, expecting a new radio signal to reach his receivers. Total silence prevailed for two consecutive months until a strange encoded message reached the Observatory, depicting an expanding star whose outer limits extended beyond their original position, almost grazing the tiny dot that encircled it. That was the last intelligent communication emanating from Proxima B.

Jack Morrison shared the abrupt suspension of messages and the latest encoded information with the concerned authorities, expressing his worries that something extraordinary had happened or might still be ongoing. Almost unanimously the panel members blamed the silence on regular solar flares and the non-interest of the exoplanet's officials in further communication due to the dullness of repetitive signals that had no more added value. Dr Dimitri Ivanov sided by his colleague Jack requesting further analysis, suggesting at least a one-year delay for the space mission launch. Following consultation with their respective nations, the panel's verdict came swiftly and explicitly: the manned mission would be launched as per schedule.

Dr Morrison dreaded ambiguities and uncertainties. He was a scientist with an analytical mind. Why would someone breach his usual communication protocol? Why would an intelligent civilisation get dulled by frequent data exchanges and lose interest in an otherwise exciting event that acknowledged life existence in other stellar systems? He was baffled and couldn't fathom the logic behind it. He wished he could just punch a number and discuss the matter with his counterpart at Proxima B. That had always been the frustration that governed the work of astrophysicists and other scientists: the time factor and the limits of the speed of light.

Everything out there represented an image of its past. Its present could never be revealed to humans; its future would remain unknown to both parties. Incredible universe!

# Chapter Fifteen

Paula listened intently to her son's description. She silently admired his ability to experience such intense dreams and understood perfectly well the stress he was enduring as a result. On one hand, those deep sleep visions were gaining him a super knowledge in abstract issues that the human mind couldn't conceive on its own. Regardless the authenticity of those dreams and the common suspicion, that they could be a creation of his subconscious, it was difficult to ignore their logical pattern.

Paula saw in Luigi's latest dream an opportunity to prove the worthiness of her son's visions. The Vatican should be informed. It was a matter of time before the truth unfolded. If Proxima B were to be found intact, then everyone including Luigi would have to concede the whole issue had been a hoax, a figment of subconscious imagination. Nonetheless, a doomed exoplanet would provide solid proof that Luigi's deep sleep visions were indeed some form of supernatural encounters worthy of consideration and study.

Later that morning, and upon her encouragement, Luigi established contact with Archbishop Gambino, laying out a detailed description of his dream. "I'm only trying to register a point. I leave it entirely in the hands of the Vatican to assess the message I'm conveying and decide whether it is necessary to pass it on to the big powers. I know quite well that aborting a manned space mission might be out of question, especially when the warning is based on a dream. But it is my duty to reveal what had been conveyed to me or at least what I have seen."

Once the phone conversation was over, the Archbishop shook his head in disbelief. He liked Luigi and was aware of his sincerity. His previous visions had been spiritual and personal. That dream however had gone beyond the boundary limits of anyone's expectation. It was trespassing into the future. He feared for Luigi's mental state and found himself incapable of informing the Pontiff about the matter. He couldn't drag the Pope into such a mess. There was nothing concrete about the whole story. So, he hesitated for a while. What was he supposed to do? He didn't fancy being reprimanded one day for not reporting it. His duty was to keep the Pope informed about everything, regardless how trivial. Finally, he placed the call to the summer retreat in Castel Gandolfo.

Two weeks later, the Pope was back in Rome. A private audience was held between Him and Archbishop Gambino.

"I have given the issue lots of thinking," said the Pope. "This young man has something peculiar. His previous dreams had affected me greatly and I was dismayed with the committee's decision not to hear him out. That's why I'm working on altering their verdict even if I'm going to end up forcing my opinion on the team. Regarding that latest case, Luigi has an advantage over us. He has warned us and consequently has nothing to lose. He did his job and can now afford sitting and waiting for events to unfold. If the credibility of his vision materialised, he'd be a winner. In case it turned out negative, he could always attribute that to a dream. As far as we are concerned, withholding his vision from the concerned governments could backfire on us in case it proved real. We would be blamed. On the other hand, revealing the contents of his vision might boost our credibility if it were true, or render us a laughingstock in case it turned out to be a hoax."

"I agree, Your Holiness," replied the Archbishop, "maybe we could play it safely by making it sound as if it were our own concern rather than revealing the source of such worries?"

"I thought of that," retorted the Pontiff. "But it would be unfair; as if we were denying Luigi the credit. I guess the best approach would be to take up the subject with the Italian government, expose the source of our worries to the prime minister and reinforce it with our own concern that such missions were a shot in the dark; too risky and fruitless."

"That's a great idea," replied the Archbishop. "I'll personally be in touch with the PM and set up a meeting the soonest possible."

"Call Luigi once the date is fixed," said the Pope. "He has to attend the meeting as well. Make sure he's informed at least 24 hours in advance."

# Chapter Sixteen

One week later, seven people gathered in a spacious room within the Papal residential quarters. Prime Minister Alphonso Ponti was accompanied by two assistants and a bald bearded man who looked like a scientist who needed no introduction. He carried his laptop case as if afraid he might drop it or that someone might snatch it away from him. His life seemed to rely on the encrypted files stored in his computer. The humming of the air conditioning unit accentuated the silence that reigned in the room, making Luigi nervous. Being in the presence of the Pope and the prime minister was enough to make any man edgy and agitated. A friendly chat ensued between the Pontiff and the PM, in which they exchanged greetings and touched on subjects previously discussed, providing each other with updates.

Few minutes later, the atmosphere within the room got less tense. The Pope cleared his voice and said in an officious way: "The reason you were summoned was to inform your Excellency of our dismay regarding the recent space mission to Planet Proxima B. As our nation has contributed to the development of the spaceship and has an Italian astronaut among its crew, The Vatican found it essential to point out to the government that space exploration should not continue unchecked, particularly that high costs were associated with it and crew members ran a great risk venturing out in a universe whose past is the only known entity revealed to us. The present state of the universe will always remain unattainable and therefore unknown. We felt it our responsibility to highlight those factors, and were prompted to act when we found out about Luigi's dream. We'll give the floor to him to describe for you what he saw in his deep sleep. You could, your Excellency, refute what you're going to hear as a plain farce, but it's worthwhile probing and reflecting on it."

His Holiness turned to Luigi and nodded. Luigi briefed the audience with the details and relived each moment. His account was definitely sincere and corresponded with his earlier descriptions; word for word; nothing omitted, nothing added. Once finished, a short silence fell on those present. It was obvious that Luigi's recitation had made an impact on the PM, who sighed and stared inquisitively at Dr Romero who had already switched on his laptop and was opening and closing files as if searching for something in particular.

"As a scientist, I tend to shrug such accounts because I only believe in equations. Human imagination could go wild and impinge on one's subconscious. There had been nonetheless past recommendations from two renowned scientists Dr Morrison and Dr Ivanov to forfeit or delay the launching of Explorer, due to the sudden absence of radio transmission from that planet."

"Reception of intelligent signals had mysteriously stopped six to seven months before launch. The majority of scientists, me included, found no reason for alarm, attributing the radio silence to flare bursts and laziness in forwarding regular messages. Mr Luigi's dream is therefore amazing, for it tallies with their warning. As we all know, Explorer is already 14 weeks into its mission."

"Ordering the crew to abort requires evidence and such proof could only be ascertained through the reception of radio messages from the exoplanet itself. Relying on dreams to forfeit a space mission might prove too expensive to contemplate, let alone detrimental to scientific credibility. Imagine if contact were to be re-established after the termination of the mission, what would the public reaction be? No funds would ever be raised to launch further exploration. On the other hand, proceeding with the mission would tell us for certain if dreams could reveal futuristic visions; the worst scenario being the abortion of the final phase of the mission by the manned crew itself. Certainly, there's a danger that things might go wrong but there's a risk factor in anything we do. Personally, I fear that Luigi's dream might carry a message from the future. Without the knowledge that two renowned scientists had sceptical views about the whole mission, I find it difficult to understand how Luigi's subconscious could concoct such an elaborate and vivid dream. But then again, it's just a dream until proven otherwise."

The Pontiff and the prime minister exchanged glances, each one apparently searching for the other's support. The PM scratched his temple and slumped further in his chair. His assistants were scribbling notes with drawn faces, not comprehending what they were hearing. The Pope stood up, walked few paces across the room, as if trying to reflect on something and then addressed the PM saying:

"The Vatican would appreciate your effort to communicate our concern to all super powers. Each nation has to ask itself a simple question: What's the point of space exploration when we face a universe that only reveals its past? Is it worth it? Is the cost justified when hundreds of millions die each year because of starvation and diseases? Couldn't we explore our own world in a more efficient way?"

"Our government will do its best to convey your message to other nations," replied the PM. "I'll convene our cabinet this week to debate our future involvement in space exploration. It's a waste of time and money. I do concur."

The meeting was over. As they exited the room, Dr Romero patted Luigi on the shoulder and said: "Imagine if your vision came true. Science would have to reconsider its stance regarding the paranormal."

The Pope warmly shook Luigi's hand and thanked him for his diligence. He enquired about the philosophy courses Luigi had taken so far and found him witty and studious. The Pope refrained from telling him anything regarding the Vatican committee but deep inside, Luigi knew that he was going to do his best until they heard him out.

# Part Five

# Chapter One

Two years elapsed, Luigi was waiting in anticipation, hoping to hear from the Vatican, but nothing transpired. A complete silence prevailed. It was too late now to abort the space mission regardless: any instruction to the crew would reach them 2.2 years later at the time of arrival to their destination. So often he had the urge to call Archbishop Gambino, but refrained doing so the moment he started punching the keys on his mobile phone. He didn't fancy being thought of as a bully, as a pushy guy striving for acceptance. He was anguished nevertheless by the lack of feedback from the Vatican. He was expecting more, much more. It seemed to him they had either entirely forgotten the matter or failed drastically in their diplomatic efforts to gain the support of other nations. It was always difficult for officials to admit failure.

Throughout that period, his mother had been his only consolation. She would listen to him complaining, try to calm him down, beg him to proceed with his life, leaving his high expectations aside. According to her, he did what he had to do and wasn't supposed to impose his views onto anyone. What counted the most was his own belief in his dreams. She would also bombard him with several indirect questions trying to figure out his contentment with priesthood and she always got his positive feedback. At least, his frustration was not linked to the choices he had made. Becoming a priest was his goal but he wanted to ascertain what he was experiencing. Knowing the Truth was a necessity. It would boost his comprehension of life, the afterlife and unveil the secrets of the universe and beyond. Knowledge was essential. Certainty was a must. Without certainty knowledge would be uncertain. It was like searching the web for info and picking the most credible and reliable site, ensuring the retrieved material was indeed the correct one.

Luigi's life could be made much easier had he had all the facts. He was scared he would never have the chance to prove the authenticity of his visions. Maybe his mother's advice to lead a normal life without expecting any acknowledgement from others, was rightful.

Far away in Inner Asia, on the lofty Tibetan Plateau, a frail old Buddhist monk was praying and meditating inside a cave carved out of the rocky cliff walls around Rongbuk monastery. Dusk was setting in. Burning torches were shedding light inside the deep cave, flickering vibrantly with variable intensity whenever the cold wind rushed in through the opening. The hermit emitted high- and low-pitched sounds as he chanted, his voice bouncing off the stony walls, mixing with the howling and whistling sound of the wind. Burning incense filled the space with a hazy scented smoke that seemed to seep through the hermit's nostrils right into his brain, putting him in a trance-like state.

The monk's bald head glowed as it reflected the light reaching it from the wall mounted torches. He had stopped chanting and started his usual nightly meditation exercise. His eyelids were closed and yet one could swear he could see through them. He sat cross-legged on a cushion laid on the uneven stony floor wearing a thick brown woollen robe wrapped around his body, leaving his arms exposed to the extreme cold weather that lingered inside the cave. From where he sat facing the relatively wide entrance, he could see the shadowy high peaks of Mount Everest looming in the horizon. The snowcapped mountains appeared menacing, the feeling enhanced by the falling darkness.

Thirty minutes later, Monk Tsomo descended the steeply winding trail, heading for the monastery. He carried a portable lantern holding it by its metallic hook. The kerosene fixture swayed in unison with his hand movement rendering it quite difficult to shed uniform lighting on the frozen ice that covered the surface of the narrow path beneath. The cold air penetrated Tsomo's lungs with every gape of the mouth. In exchange, his hot breath changed into a misty cloud as he exhaled. The sky above him was filled with stars and constellations. Had it not been for the gruesome wind and the very low temperature, one would have thought spring was nearing.

It was almost eight o'clock when he reached the monastery's main entrance which consisted of an old two-leaf huge wooden door decorated with tassels that oscillated with every sweep of the wind. He unlocked the door and stepped in into the warmth of the monastery's walls. Tsomo bowed before a big statue of Buddha and went past the Prayer and Meditation rooms and entered the spacious lounge where other monks and nuns were chatting animatedly, laughing out loud. He had always been baffled by the monks' lifestyle which combined stern and casual rules. There was a sincere camaraderie between all members regardless the gender. They cared for each other when they fell ill, covered for each other, and swapped agricultural assignments. Tsomo joined his colleagues and warmed himself with a cup of concentrated herbal tea with butter.

The room fell silent the moment a shabby old monk came in, greeting all those present. Master Khando had an austere demeanour that imposed respect and awe. He addressed Tsomo with a reverberating voice that bounced off the walls: "A Chinese official wants to see you. He'll be visiting tomorrow morning at nine. He specifically asked for you. Didn't mention the reason behind his quest."

"I'll be available," replied Tsomo with reverence.

The Chinese official was prompt in his arrival. He presented himself as General Wang Wei from the Ministry of State Security. Khando and Tsomo shook hands with him and enquired politely about the purpose of his visit. With a calm voice, devoid of any excitation, he uttered: "Please allow me to get straight to the point. I believe you've been tracking the news about Explorer and its manned mission to Planet Proxima B. Well, there are some speculations that the star that it orbits is unleashing, or should I say: had unleashed massive flare-ups that could be threatening to any life form. As communications with the spaceship Explorer takes ages to reach either side, it might be too late to ward off any danger in case there were any."

He was suddenly interrupted by the master who exclaimed in an indifferent way: "What has that got to do with us?"

"Our scientists are suggesting that we should try telepathy through meditation. They reckon telepathic waves are not speed related. They are quite certain that telepathy is innate with the universal creation. Their perception is that since the Big Bang early start, particles even when they got separated, clung somehow to each other through their origin, no matter the distance. We conducted therefore a thorough research regarding the subject and were informed that your monastery is deeply versed in telepathic meditation. We also learned through recorded archives that Master Tsomo had performed live telepathic communications with people in the USA and Europe, transmitting and receiving messages through the power of the mind."

"So?" Master Khando insisted. "What exactly are you seeking?"

"Explorer has among its team a renowned Chinese astrophysicist, Dr Huang," the general replied. "We need you to communicate with him and find out the situation they are in. Explorer has been coasting through interstellar space for more than two and a half years. On board, sensors and other instruments might have picked abnormal activities. We're also relying on visual observation of the star itself. By now, Alpha Centauri would appear as a very bright star against the dark background."

"But aren't they supposed to be hibernated?" Tsomo said.

"They do alternate, keeping a 3-men crew on the alert. Now Dr Huang is one member of the active team," retorted the General.

The two monks exchanged bewildered glances trying to absorb what they were hearing.

That brief silence revealed even further the graveness of the situation. The rate of telepathic success had been very high lately but this particular case had a big challenge embedded in it. The sender and the receiver didn't know each other, not even their physical appearance. Besides, telepathy worked when the receiver was somewhat relaxed and not preoccupied with mundane or functional matters.

As if reading their minds, the official handed them a picture that showed Dr Huang smiling back at the camera, presumably a photo taken few hours before launch. Tsomo held the picture in his hand and looked at it intently. Fine, at least there's a face to the name but how could the recipient communicate with the sender when the latter was anonymous?

On reflection, Tsomo spoke with an authoritative manner, giving the impression that he ruled over the situation, showing integrity and decisiveness: "General Wang, as the recipient and I ignore each other, I'm afraid we need to involve his wife. I strongly believe in the power of love. Telepathy works when sincere emotions between the sender and the receiver exist. The main issue is to train Mrs Huang and let her perform the messaging. I could also intervene in parallel to enhance the mental communication process, using Dr Huang's photo. But it is almost guaranteed that his wife is the only entity capable of receiving any feedback from him, as he ignores my presence and doesn't know me. Hence, I will teach his spouse the process."

"I prefer that she'd be stationed here with us within the confinement of the monastery for the whole duration. I'm unable to assess the time required for the training, for I'm not certain how capable she might be in mastering telepathy. She'll be exposed to rigorous tutoring. There'll be therefore, a one-way communication channel between me and Dr Huang and a two-way link between him and his spouse. At least, that's how I perceive the scenario at the moment."

"I gather it's going to be a difficult task, but I'm afraid it's our last resort and we have to grab this opportunity," said the General. "The emphasis is to find out what the crew's current situation is. The findings will be conveyed to the Chinese government for evaluation and if found credible enough, they'll try to obtain the approval of other nations to call off the space mission."

"To issue that order, an abort message needs to be transmitted at a later stage to Dr Huang. The problem, of course, is for him to capture that mental signal from his wife and be able to convince the craft's commander that the mission had to be called off. Dr Huang's wife will be notified to relocate in Tibet within a week at the latest."

"Meanwhile, I urge you to consider this matter top secret. Nothing is to be divulged to any party. On behalf of the Chinese government, I thank you in advance for your support and wish you good luck. Feel free to contact me on the numbers shown on the card I've given you. Any logistical assistance falls under my duty. Please let me know if you needed anything."

"I would be grateful if you could provide me with the latest aired video depicting Dr Huang inside the spaceship. It would give me a better prospect to picture him in his working environment. Such things do help while concentrating," Tsomo said.

"Consider it done," replied General Wang.

# Chapter Two

Luigi's heart jumped out of its cavity when he read the caller ID number showing on his mobile screen. Archbishop Gambino wore a comforting smile as he appeared on the video screen. The book shelves of the Papal Library gave an institutional background to the scene.

"Hi Luigi," he started out. "Hope you're doing well. It's been quite a long time since we spoke. But honestly, we had no tangible feedback to convey to you. There had been no developments unfolding. The Italian government had failed to rally other nations to listen to our plea. The Chinese were somewhat sympathetic but not forcefully so. They were overwhelmed by the stiff resilience of the international community, particularly the United States, the United Kingdom and Germany. The Chinese delegation however promised the Italian prime minister to do their utmost to assist inasmuch possible."

Luigi was vexed by what he heard and felt disappointed. Then Archbishop Gambino continued: "Accordingly and after a very long silence, we were informed yesterday of a new initiative undertaken by the Chinese government..." Gambino filled Luigi in on every single detail, emphasising that the next few weeks were crucial and that the Vatican would keep him abreast of any breaking news. Luigi thanked the Archbishop for the information and his continuous support; wished him and the Pontiff the best of health and happiness.

The credibility of his visions depended now on the outcome of the telepathic meditation. He had a few more weeks of waiting and then his consternation would either fade away or stick with him eternally. There were two available options. Success of the telepathic contact: in such instance, it would either reveal the same contents as his latest dream or reject them outright; failure of the telepathic contact: in that case he'd be back to square one. The odds were against him, for only one of those alternatives would authenticate his visions. He was hopeful but scared.

Paula was overwhelmed with joy. She was at work when her son had called her. Finally, some action was being undertaken. Unlike her son's scepticism, she marvelled at the follow-up undertaken by the Vatican. That was good enough for her, regardless how it was going to end. She spent the whole day huddling with her faithful customers and opened a bottle of champagne to celebrate the resumption of normality after such a very long silence.

Ten kilometres away, in a house in San Donato, a thirty-year-old nurse was inserting an intravenous needle through Andrea's skin into a peripheral vein. The patient was breathing on his own but had been in vegetative state for more than two years. Nobody knew whether he was dreaming at all. He had dreams though being with Carla and his friend Fabriano but had no way to tell anyone about it. His spiritual world was a floating dream and his physical world was as inert as death.

Andrea's children kept their distance from Eva and avoided having any rapport with her. As far as they were concerned, she had always been the obstacle and the source of trouble that had plagued their family. Since they had decided to discharge their father from hospital twenty months ago, and have him in their midst, they had refrained from communicating with her, even refusing to take her incoming calls.

Paula tried her best to act as an intermediary between the two parties. She reported to Eva on Andrea's condition and had been astonished at her sister-in-law's consistent concern whether her husband had awakened from his inert state. Eva knew quite well how impossible that would be after such a long time in a vegetative state, but she was definitely concerned and worried that he might regain his lucidity.

Eva had meanwhile reverted to her customary tantrums the moment her mother Sophia returned to Lebanon. Her attitude affected everyone including her own child, who pleaded almost daily with Aunty Paula to either come over or accompany him to the park or playground. Paula was so fond of Fabriano Junior that she didn't turn him down on any occasion, even if that meant to bear Eva's awful conduct. Paula felt somehow responsible for the kid's well-being. He had been deprived of his father's affection and although his mum loved him tremendously, her preoccupation with her mundane affairs had kept her away from him most of the time. Her agenda prevailed over anything else. Nothing could disturb her living pattern and habits, not even her child.

Paula would often bring along Fabriano Junior to Bellagio. They would spend a whole weekend together, getting on board the ferry, sailing across Lake Como, watching the beautiful scattered villages that adorn the green hills. Paula would drive frequently her car through the narrow streets of Bellagio, stopping at outdoor coffee shops, buying ice cream cones and enjoying them the same way little Fabriano did.

Even though cars were self-driven, Paula preferred to be at the controls. Driving was an escapade for her; an emotional release that calmed her down. Processor failure of self-driven vehicles was not uncommon. Relying on full automation had problems of its own. It seemed the solution lay heavily in having multi onboard computers correcting each other's flaws and achieving complete redundancy. Technology would eventually reach its peak, and the fun of manually controlling vehicular functions would soon be eradicated, depriving human beings from their basic pleasures.

Paula's greatest delight was seeing joy and happiness in little Fabriano's eyes. The way he ran towards her and the way he grabbed her skirt, her trousers, melted her heart. He would cling to her for a long moment awaiting that she crouched to reach his own height and plant a kiss on his rosy cheeks. At times, she would hold him tightly, resting his head on her shoulder. He reminded her of Luigi when he was little, and his name was a reminder of her eternal love.

Fabriano Junior would shout in delight, "Paula! You're the best. I love you, Aunty!" And she would pray that her moments with him would stretch and extend. Bringing little Fabriano back on Sunday evening was a difficult undertaking. Paula couldn't bear being separated from the child. She couldn't comprehend her huge affection for him. Was it because she had spoiled his dad's plans? Or was it due to her loneliness?

# Chapter Three

Mrs Yue Huang was in her bedroom packing her suitcase while two uniformed women waited for her in the living room. She was summoned to leave the soonest possible for Lhasa in Tibet. General Wang had already informed her about her mission and she gave her immediate consent once she understood the urgent nature of her task. Her husband's fate depended on her and she would do anything to get reunited with her loved one. As she couldn't disclose the reason behind her sudden travel and destination, Yue had to lie through her teeth and lure her parents into believing she was heading for Shanghai on a training assignment: the company she worked for was keen on standardising the IT procedures for all its branches. Yue had dropped her little girl at her parents' and returned home to pack and leave for the airport. "I would be gone for two weeks at the most," she told them.

The flight from Beijing to Lhasa took four hours and twenty minutes. Yue was met upon arrival by General Wang who introduced himself in a polite and gentle way uncommon with military personnel. He knew he had disrupted her work, her social and above all her parental life, but the situation was an unusual one. Strict orders were issued to expedite the whole matter and his duty was to obey his superiors and let others adhere to his demands. His driver proceeded to the hotel where he had booked two rooms, one for him and one for Mrs Huang. They were to leave early morning for Rongbuk monastery and needed a good rest prior to hitting the road for the 10-hour drive.

The next morning, over breakfast, General Wang reiterated what he had told Yue earlier, posing every now and then to watch the impact of his account on her. She gave him the impression of being a clever person who asked the right question, not for the sake of showing off, but rather to deepen her comprehension and widen her knowledge.

"What certainty is there that this telepathy is going to work? I have never indulged in such activities before and I'm not sure such things really work." She looked at him inquisitively.

"I understand your position," he replied. "I do have my own doubts as well. I'm a practical person who dismisses anything inconceivable. Just because it's not an exact science, one should not nonetheless perceive telepathy as a hoax. Mental power is arguably a potent phenomenon. It had been tested and scored some success; not decisive per se, but definitely it was worth considering. Monk Tsomo, with whom you'll be collaborating had undisputedly demonstrated in few occasions his capability to convey telepathic messages to recipients in faraway places and the results were astounding. Our government is highly interested in people like him. We would be fools to ignore such powers and totally stupid to believe in them. Time will tell."

"I read many articles about telepathic meditation and there were two different schools: one that believed in it and another that shrugged it off completely," retorted Yue. "But I guess that's the case with everything else in this world." She sighed and then continued, "I'll do anything for my husband and I have to abide by his rule."

"Which is?" The General was staring at her intently.

"My husband used to tell me: My dear Yue! Nothing will ever work if you're in doubt; believe and trust what you're doing and it will come true."

"Wise man," replied the General.

The ride in the Haval SUV was comfortable and the party of two sat in the rear of the vehicle separated from the driver's compartment by a sliding hatch made of thick glass. The sky overhead was dark blue with white fluffy clouds strewn haphazardly. A refreshing draft hit the face of Mrs Huang, seeping through the slightly opened window by the general's side. Her hair became a mess of entangled strands. She gazed at him in a charming way, enough to make him understand that he should close it. As if not to concede defeat, he acted five minutes later when the vehicle picked up some speed. Her smile was enough to show him her appreciation and her pre-awareness that he would react as she had expected. General Wang looked at the woman in fascination. *Intelligent,* he thought, *not to mention how beautiful she was.*

The driver, apparently a local, acted as a tourist guide. Through the two-way intercom system, he would describe for them the breathtaking sceneries around them; calling out the names of lakes, peaks, valleys…What was striking was the turquoise colour of lakes blending with their mountainous surrounding. A serene landscape beyond description. He made few stops. They rested, had tea, water and some snacks. Three stops afterwards, Yue's lungs started to seriously experience the lack of oxygen. They had driven for seven hours and reached an altitude of 4,400 metres. The general had previously avoided such quick ascent, and his respiration rate was going overboard. He counted twenty-seven breaths a minute instead of the usual eighteen.

He wasn't going nevertheless to complain unless Yue conceded first. But deep down, he knew that she would never give in. She seemed to be a strong woman and couldn't be underestimated.

As they got closer to Rongbuk monastery, the road winded up and the SUV bounced and slewed on the dirty path.

The general rolled down his window to its full extent, gasping for air. Cold air rushed in, commensurate with an altitude of 5,000 metres. It seemed as if the movement of the wind across the northern flank of Mount Everest had carried with it the low temperature of the white shiny peaks that loomed in the horizon.

Yue shivered and shrivelled in her seat. She buttoned the collar of her coat protecting her neck and throat, realising they had supposedly reached the base camp of Mount Everest. In the distance, Rongbuk temple could be seen growing larger by the minute.

She had never imagined such an immaculate place where snowy mountains, valleys and water sheds blended in a unique panoramic painting, so specific to such a remote region. The sun was setting. Birds were flying over the valley seeking warm shelter for the incoming night. Wild blue sheep could be seen grazing peacefully in the fields, mingling with silhouettes of farmers attending to their crops.

The General seemed glad to watch the excitement in Yue's eyes. He was afraid she might have a grudge on him, dragging her this far from home. But to his bewilderment, she was a factual woman apparently, with a sense for adventure and great devotion for her husband. He fetched his phone pulling it out from his military jacket. He punched seven digits and placed it on his ear. "Few minutes and we'll be there," he called out. Khando and Tsomo put on their thick robes and rushed outside the monastery to greet the two visitors.

# Chapter Four

A cheerful young nun was assigned to show Yue her room. Basic furniture was laid out in a tight space, with a wooden single bed, so narrow that the user had to assume a singular sleeping position. On one side stood a small and short Formica wood chest of drawers. A bamboo chair was positioned across the room, facing the bed, beside a plastic wardrobe. Yue had the impression all furniture had been man-made by the monks. There were no appliances whatsoever, no mirrors, no toilet. The nun had pointed out a shared female bathroom fifteen metres down the wide corridor.

Yue dumped her suitcase on the floor and lay down on her back without turning the sheets and blanket. She was so tired, the hardness of the bed didn't matter. It had apparently a thin mattress that didn't provide the proper cushioning for her back. She had half an hour to rest before joining the others for communal dining. The temperature inside her room was getting lower by the minute. She shivered even with her clothes on. Only then did she realise the absence of any heating means inside the confined space. She hoped the sheets and woollen blanket would suffice to shield her body from the bitter cold.

The dining room was basically a big hall with multiple table benches and a self-service area where big wooden bowls and ladle spoons were laid out. Khando, Tsomo, Yue and the General huddled together in the farthest corner of the spacious hall, away from the service zone and other monks and nuns.

Food consisted mainly of homegrown vegetables cooked with yak butter and fried noodles in sesame oil. Tsomo apologised for the relatively poor accommodation that the monastery offered for its guests, while emphasising the importance of Yue's presence in the temple. The latter had been reconstructed few years back, and efforts were made to render it more comfortable than it had ever been.

According to Monk Tsomo, telepathic meditation required total detachment from a mundane world full of distraction and indiscipline. Tsomo was impressive and exuded self-control like she had never seen before. She trusted him already although his capabilities were yet to be recognised. He requested an early morning start. So many things had to be taught and learned. Time was running out. It suited her to complete her task the soonest possible. She couldn't extend her stay in Tibet; her children and her job dictated that. After dinner, General Wang handed over to Tsomo the latest video transmitted from the spaceship Explorer. It was shot one year earlier. The monk thanked him in return and bid them good night. They were to meet in the monastery's meditation room at 6 am on the next day. They retreated to their quarters immediately afterwards.

Tsomo played the video in Master Khando's office, the only place within the temple's walls equipped with modern electronic equipment. The aired transmission lasted 20 minutes. Dr Huang could be seen facing a cupola window pane, gazing at the stars beyond and entering his observations on a small pad set on his lap. The video depicted him intermittently for a total of four minutes allowing his profile features to appear clearly on the screen. A close-up of his full face was a furtive shot that didn't linger for more than a fraction of a second. The photo Tsomo had been given earlier by the General had therefore more details than the video contents that he had requested. The monk was hoping for more frontal exposure. He needed to study the face in details, to get acquainted with its features. Failing that, his concentration would be compromised. The best approach would be to teach Yue the art of telepathic meditation and let her establish the link directly with her husband. That should achieve the best result. On second thoughts, it wouldn't harm establishing a concurrent communication link from his side too. It might prove to be an efficient tool to ensure flawless mental caption.

Yue had no need to be awakened by the alarm clock. The cold ambient temperature was so low, her teeth rattled, and her limbs got stiff. There was no point turning over and trying a different sleeping position. Her movement was restrained by the narrowness of the bed. She rose at four-thirty am and sat on the bed, covering herself with the blanket and hugging the pillow tightly against her stomach, to protect herself from an impending cold which she couldn't afford to have.

Through the windowpane, Yue could see the Chir Pine trees battling the groaning wind. Branches would sway violently and suddenly rest as the burst subsided. During that pause, Yue could hear the howling of a pack of foxes in the distance. They seemed to celebrate their raid on a local chicken farm. She got up and paced towards the window and stared at the sky. The Milky Way seemed like a colourful river. Stars were within easy reach; she could almost grab one or two. It was striking how bright the stars appeared in the dark indigo sky. She noticed distinct colours of red, gold and even blue.

Her husband was out there, a tiny dot in a massive universe. Had he been at the base of the Himalayas watching the skies above him, he needed not undertake such a crazy mission. It was funny how humans tried to go beyond their boundaries, ignoring the beautiful and meaningful things and places that surround them. One day, she was going to revisit Tibet and bring her husband along with her. They had to go out more often and see new places, new countries…Her husband's infatuation with the special theory of relativity, black holes, supernovas, time dilation and wormholes had secluded him from Earth, from the real world he was living in. He had become imprisoned in a theoretical universe that he'd never fully comprehend; nor would anyone else for that matter.

The closing sound of a nearby door startled her. It would be the General leaving the adjacent room for the Meditation Hall. She inspected her watch. It was fifteen minutes to six. Time had passed quickly while she had been sinking in her thoughts. Yue grabbed a towel from the chest of drawers and headed out for the bathroom. She was the only one there. Scattered water pools indicated everyone had risen before he. She heard the faint sound of people chanting in the distance. The monastery occupants were already praying and greeting a new day. Yue had a problem adjusting the water temperature for a comfortable warm shower. That quickened her exit from the bathroom and was 5 minutes late when she walked into the meditation room.

The General was relaxing on a slim couch, checking his mobile phone for messages. He flinched as he heard her footsteps and saw her entering the room.

"Good morning," she exclaimed. "Sorry for being late."

"It's fine," replied General Wang. "Bhikku Tsomo is still in the adjacent Prayer Room. He'll join us in a minute. Hope you had a good rest?" He sounded genuinely concerned.

"Couldn't sleep well," she retorted. "Too cold in there for someone not moving." She shuddered. "But eventually, I'll manage."

"Good morning!" Tsomo cried out as he came in. He bowed respectfully, folding his hands. The General and Mrs Yuang reciprocated, robotically imitating his gestures.

# Chapter Five

Tsomo turned out to be a great and overly patient teacher. He spent six consecutive days initiating Yue into meditation. For seclusion purposes and swift results, he advised General Wang not to attend the private spiritual lessons, promising a debriefing session before dinner time.

Master Khando ensured the General had settled in his office, which gave the latter the chance to attend to his pending work.

Yue had to wear a sleeved grey inner robe, a sleeved outer robe fastened in the front and a Kashaya wrapped over the outer robe. Her appearance looked like a monastery nun, except her head was not shaved and her eyebrows were left intact. She thanked God for that. According to her guru, the garment was necessary to make her feel like a real nun, to believe in herself and in the internal changes she was bound to encounter.

Tsomo taught her how to focus on her breathing, how to fight off any peripheral thought that might creep in. It was hard to let go and become oblivious of the surroundings. Closing her eyes eliminated most of the physical world around her but the faintest sound made her eyes flutter, her breathing count perturbed; forcing her to repeat the exercise again and again. Yue was frustrated with herself; she had thought she would perform much better. Amazingly, her mentor thought the opposite; he encouraged her and praised her efforts, reaffirming that she was doing well for a beginner. Yue's big challenge was to go beyond her mind and probe her essential nature, searching for peace, tranquillity happiness and bliss. What stood as an obstacle between her and such an awareness was her mind itself.

Meditation sessions intensified on the fourth day and onwards. They became long and intensive. Tsomo was issuing his instructions in bursts of information, divulging only what was necessary at the appropriate time. Yue was deprived of food and water during the daily sessions. She learned how to ignore her hunger and thirst while meditating. She started noticing her complete control over anxiety, fear and sadness. Her world was full of contentment and serenity. Even the supposedly austere General Wang realised the metamorphosis unfolding before him. He was pleased with the result and reported it to Beijing.

Following one day of rest, the second week resumed with more intensity. Tsomo led Yue into the world of telepathic meditation. She had to adhere to a strenuous technique where the most important factor was the alienation of oneself from any form of scepticism. She had to believe in brain power and being able to concentrate on a singular and particular subject. Tsomo reiterated and emphasised the power of love. Communicating with a beloved one was much easier to achieve than with a stranger. He stressed on the visualisation of the recipient in detail; imagining him or her standing or sitting very closely and picturing the actual delivery of the conveyed message.

Tsomo initiated the telepathic process. He would act as the sender of a certain message and wait for Yue's vivid description of what she had perceived. Then he would suggest a role reversal whereby Yue turned into a message sender. Initially the messages were short and concise: a hand wave; a rabbit, escalating to feelings, thoughts, images and desires.

Tsomo defined all the terms associated with telepathic meditation. He explained to her that clairvoyance was related to visual forms; clairaudience was a term used in relation to hearing and inner voices; clairsentience had to do with feelings.

As it turned out, Yue was an excellent recipient but not a good sender. Being relaxed and in an easy state of mind had contributed to the reception of eighty percent of the monk's powerful signals. Tsomo had to work on her ability to focus more on her transmission skills. So far, he was capturing about twenty per cent of her messages and that was not good at all. Sending visual forms appeared to be in her grasp. Nonetheless, transmitting inner voice info had proven virtually impossible to achieve. Something was missing. Her role was to communicate with her husband. The primary interest was in clairaudience and she was failing in it. He had to try something else before passing on his verdict.

"I'm going to ask you to focus on your child in Beijing. I heard you saying she was seven years old. I would like you to visualise a cat while concentrating on an inner sound that tells her it's your intention to get her the pet in return for her good school performance."

Yue delved into a world of love and affection, where nothing mattered except her beautiful darling daughter. It was almost four in the afternoon and she could picture her child returning to her parents' home after school, lounging in the sitting room carrying a bowl of noodles. It was perfect timing as she would be the least distracted. Yue was picturing the sofa, the armchairs, the plant pots, the TV set, her daughter Lynn using her chopsticks clumsily, letting few bean sprouts drop on the thick carpet. Her emotions grew more intense. She was watching herself there in person. Her love was radiating diffusely. She was sitting next to Lynn with her arm around her. A fluffy white kitten was kneading Lynn's legs. The girl put away the food tray on the edge of the table in front of her, picked up the little cat and deposited it on her lap. The furry kitten curled its body, curved up her tail and purred at each caress. Yue extended her head towards her daughter's ears whispering, "Get good grades and the pet is yours."

Tsomo had been watching Yue seated down on a cushion facing him with her eyelids closed. Being an expert in the field, he had felt the intensity of her concentration.

Yue's mobile phone buzzed twenty minutes later. She was drinking herbal tea in the company of Tsomo and General Wang. Her carotid arteries throbbed, and she thought her neck was going to burst. She had a premonition of receiving a call. The ID number that appeared on the screen made her heart flutter and contract in an arrhythmic manner: it was her mother's number.

Yue swiped the acceptance key on her phone and watched Lynn's smiley face materialising on the screen.

"Hi Mummy," Lynn blurted out excitedly. "I miss you loads."

"Me too, honey," said Yue with a tightness in her throat. Two days had gone by since they spoke. "I keep thinking about you all the time. I'm going to fetch few nice things. Promise you won't give your grandparents a hard time."

"For sure I won't. I also promise to get good grades at school. But in return you'll buy me a white kitten. I don't want anything else. Please say yes."

"Yes! Yes!" exclaimed Yue, with tears running down her cheeks. "I love you, rascal. You're the most beautiful thing in my life. Daddy always said the same thing about you. Love you loads."

The conversation ended and the party of three stood up almost simultaneously and hugged each other, fascinated by the amazing success that Yue had achieved. Tsomo silently praised himself for believing in her hidden talents. Yue was an excellent communicator if the recipient was well-known to her and she had strong emotions for him or her.

The General was desperate for celebration. He asked for the monk's permission to down a glass of Japanese whiskey. With Tsomo's acquiescence, he sped to his room, fetched the bottle and paced back hurriedly, filling his empty tea cup and Yue's with the yellowish liquid. Tsomo declined and instinctively covered the upper rim of his cup with his hand as a protective measure. Alcohol was considered as something that shrouded the mind and led to confusion.

General Wang was infatuated. What happened was a breakthrough. No need for anybody's interpretation or input for that matter. There was no foul play. Just plain and simple experimentation. No equipment, no tools had been used. Concentration and extreme love were the essence of that success. Wow. He couldn't wait to report it to the command centre. But meanwhile, he wanted to enjoy the smooth taste of the whiskey infiltrating his throat, tickling his nostrils, burning his oesophagus and warming his stomach lining. The General fancied seeing Yue in a social gathering and the current occasion was the closest it would ever get to that. The woman had a nice slim body, wide inquisitive eyes and nice soft hair. He was not married and wondered at times if he lacked charm and tact. His relationships never lasted long enough to lead to marriage. He had always been torn between his emotional and officious states.

Tsomo didn't want to spoil the moment. An achievement had been made. They had to move for the big one. He was certain now of Yue's ability to reach out to her husband, but he feared the latter's inability to convey messages telepathically. Then their whole combined effort would be gone down the drain. The monk reflected for a long time, as the General and Mrs Huang were conversing and toasting each other. Tsomo was completely detached; absorbed in his thinking. He was the teacher, the guru, supposed to find the solutions and means to render the whole thing a complete success.

The sun had set and dusk settled over the plateau. Nuns roamed the monastery premises lighting candles and torches in small and large spaces respectively. One of them entered the semi-dark room where the party of three lounged, excused herself for interrupting them and attended to the wall mounted torches. The light cast wavering shadows within the space giving it a mystic appearance. As if honouring his guests, Tsomo rose and switched on the ceiling lighting fixtures saying jokingly: "I'm sure you appreciate modern artificial lighting." Both guests nodded in agreement. They were relieved by the supplementary illuminance level.

The monk urged them to listen intently to him, "Mrs Huang, what's vital now is the method we need to employ to render your husband a good sender. In order to do that, your message to him should contain the mechanism that would allow him to harness his concentration."

"What do you suggest?" enquired the General.

Tsomo sighed and spoke with decisiveness: "Mrs Huang message should hold two pieces of information. The first should focus on entering his mind through word whispers: asking him what he's actually seeing or reading out of instruments; the second wave of info should also rely on clairaudience, whereby Yue would set the rules that he should use as a sender. I believe he's got Yue's picture on him or on any electronic gadget he might have taken. Yue's second message ought to guide him into fetching her pic or watch her on any screen; focus on her; picture her inside the spaceship, positioned near him; get close to her ears and utter words, clearly emphasising their syllables. In addition, he ought to visualise anything that he deems important."

"That's expecting a lot of him and Yue," stated the General. "Seems a big deal."

Yue adjusted her posture and turned to General Wang: "I can do it. My husband is very perceptive by nature. I concur that his transmission might turn out to be rudimentary and out of focus. I might not be able to perceive his message unless I'm in a very relaxed state of consciousness. Maybe I should be asleep when that happens? I shouldn't be distracted a single bit."

Tsomo admired her self-confidence. He rested his arm on her shoulder and said in a soft voice: "You and I will leave early morning for a cave four kilometres away. It's up in the mountains, not that difficult to reach but the trail is winding and steep. It would be the best place for telepathic meditation. You'll need to put on heavy warm clothing, bring your husband's picture along and I'll carry the thick blankets; I'm afraid we're going to spend the whole day and night over there. You'll start with the first message on your own. Once finished, you'll commence the second message which is very vital for your husband's comprehension on how to act as a sender. That phase would be supported by my intervention as well. We'll act together as if we were synchronised. Our concentration has to be in unison; otherwise Dr Huang may get diverted and confused by the signals. We'll coordinate on every detail as we climb the path tomorrow. Let's have a light meal before we retire. You need a good night's sleep."

As soon as they finished their dinner, the relatively bearable cold of the day was replaced by a bitter one. The wind sweeping the plateau accentuated in its rhythmic howling and snowflakes drifted in a horizontal and downward motion, depositing themselves on windowpanes and the dark looking grass outside the monastery. Yue was watching the whole scenery lying on her side, being careful not to fall off the bed. She recapitulated meditation rules: think about your toes, your ankles, your legs.

She woke up at five in the morning feeling peaceful and refreshed. The skies were somewhat clear; the snow had ceased and the wind had subsided. She peered out and for the first time since she'd come to the monastery, a thick blanket of white snow covered the ground and tree branches appeared majestic.

Yue visited the shower room and got back inside her room, preparing herself for the mountain climb. She was looking forward to it in the sense of adventure. But there was another aspect that haunted her thoughts: what if she failed?

Yue and Tsomo grabbed some dark bread, turnips and dried meat for the journey. Meat could be eaten on special occasions and that was one of them.

# Chapter Six

Dr Huang was verifying the figures flashing on a video screen in front of him and comparing them to previous readings picked up by onboard X-Ray detectors. The panel facing him was a small part of a long stretch of electronic display panels mounted around the spaceship perimeter walls. Individual monitors with different functions and purposes stacked vertically and horizontally within a holistic video wall that appeared more alive than the individuals staring at them.

X-Ray detectors were essential tools to determine normal and abnormal activities. Since Explorer had ventured out into the dark space, X-Ray energy levels expressed in keV (kilo electron volts) were gradually rising as expected within their normal range. The obtained figures however, were escalating. The energy levels had increased drastically and at times surpassed the X-Ray energy level of 100 keV, turning into gamma radiation with long bursts exceeding 5 MeV (mega electron volts). That was worrisome as the frequency of such readings was alarmingly increasing. It was evident: Alpha Centauri star system was experiencing humongous flare-ups.

Recent radiation figures tallied with the naked eye visual observation of the star system. Dr Huang could easily notice the gaseous expansion of the star Proxima Centauri, augmenting its brightness as flares extended to the outer boundaries of its corona.

He had shared the worrying data with Commander Richardson, reminding him that the readings were one and a half year old and that the actual situation could be much worse than that. He sympathised nevertheless with the commander who had the ultimate authority to continue or abort the mission. But at what cost? He'd rather proceed if the journey was still possible and defer his decisions until later.

A cold chill of fear swept through him. He wondered why he was getting that nagging feeling at that particular moment. It wasn't as if it were the first time he had run through the data, but presently he was thinking of himself; his own safety; his worry that the mission might fail; and what challenges lay ahead.

Subsequently, he thought of Yue and Lynn. He was reminiscing of old days. How he missed his wife, her laugh, her warmth, her lips. He wished he had devoted more time to his daughter, playing with her, reading her various tales of princesses and kings. What was happening to him suddenly? His mind was disturbed by images and whispers, attacking his brain from all angles. He wanted to share his observations with his loving wife, describe to her the current situation, his concerns. He was resenting being part of the space mission. How futile was space exploration when one embarked on it? It was an excitement turned into anxiety and boredom. He was living in a world of beeps and buzzers; a digital environment of control and monitoring panels. He was on board a ship sailing through a deep silent ocean where none other than electromagnetic waves subsisted; a universe whose void weighed much more than its stars and planets. Almost twenty times as much. A heavy emptiness of dark matter and dark energy that explained the universe expansion and infinite stretch.

As far as he knew as an astrophysicist, Planet Proxima B orbited its sun in just eleven days, exposing only one of its sides to the heat of the star, keeping the other side in total darkness and freezing low temperatures. Hence, there were no seasons as such. The weather on the sunny side was somewhat constant. The star itself was a red dwarf, smaller than the sun. Periodic flares were common but not so frequent as to cause a total depletion of the planet's atmosphere and evaporation of its seas and oceans. But now, the indicators were scary. Under such conditions, any life form would be eliminated by the scorching heat waves. Dr Huang shuddered at the thought: "What the hell are we doing?" He kept asking himself since he had started comparing the emission data few hours ago.

He felt unusually nostalgic. How did he accept to be part of a space mission that would deprive him of his family for so long? Eight and a half years of one's lifetime was a heck of a lot. For the first time ever, he realised the selfishness of his deed. Was it worthwhile abandoning one's wife and child for the sake of a wild discovery whose sheen lingered on the outer layer rather than the core? He took away his gaze from the control panel and caught a glimpse of Commander Richardson and Navigator Shastri examining astral video charts. In the other bay section of the spacecraft, nine astronauts were in hibernation, lying in capsules awaiting to be awakened. It was lonely up there. The glamour of the launch had gradually subsided the minute delays in communication with and from Earth Control Centre became more and more noticeable.

Dr Huang had the sudden urge to extract Yue's picture by peeling off the transparent tape that fixed it onto the panel in front of him. He drew it close to his lips and simulated a tender and long kiss. He held the picture close to his heart and then stared at the beautiful smiling woman, admiring her eyes, her nose, her pout lips, her ear lobes that he often had bitten teasingly and playfully. His emotions grew by the second. How could he do that? Leaving such a lady for almost a decade was not only unacceptable but illogical and inconceivable. His mind was in a zooming-in and zooming-out state. Something was impinging on his grey cells. He could sense a weird activity he had never faced before. He could swear her lips were moving, trying to tell him something. The picture was more than a picture; it was alive. Yue's forehead was pulsing with energy. His wife sounded concerned, trying to seek information, querying his current state; wondering if he were happy, doing well.

Then a strong field of visual and aural thoughts hit him simultaneously. Its strength was overwhelming and imposing. He felt like a pupil at school being taught what to do, what was expected of him. Voices were asking him to report his condition. Someone out there cared for him or rather relied on him to communicate. He was imagining Yue with him, within the confinement of the spaceship. He could smell her perfume, he could stare at her bewildered eyes. She was imploring him to share his feelings, his fears with her. His mind was being requested to concentrate on his recent observations and reveal information. Something was telling him to be specific and direct in his account. He was being requested to relax and focus on his current situation; to assume his dear wife was sitting next to him, hearing him out. A mysterious instruction was asking him to be brief and precise; to convey his thoughts in a simple manner. He was fully aware that his wife was reaching out to him but he couldn't grasp the weaker bursts of similar transmissions his mind was picking up almost simultaneously. The latter appeared to be like carrier waves that supported the signal itself.

Dr Huang pretended being in the presence of his wife. He talked aloud as if he had been conversing with her and created concentrated images in his mind which he impregnated through the skin of Yue's forehead as he pictured her face right beside him. Yue had replaced the command centre as a communicator. Commander Richardson observed the scene in bewilderment. Dr Huang had certainly flipped.

Back inside the Tibetan cave, Yue was drifting between consciousness and a dreaming state. One hour earlier she had knelt on a soft cushion and did her utmost to transmit her thoughts to her dear husband. Monk Tsomo had advised her to lie down immediately afterwards and surrender to her acute senses, trying to capture the telepathic signal from her husband, hoping that he would be able to capture her thoughts and consequently communicate with her.

The hardness of the cave's rocky floor was not noticeable anymore, neither was the chilly breeze that blew inside the void, spiralling through the hollow space, emitting a whistling sound with varying intensity. Tsomo was assuming an upright sitting posture few feet away from her, acting like a vigil. Yue was twisting her slim body underneath the blanket that covered her. She looked like a woman in torment. The monk kept watching her eyelids fluttering, moving from complete closure to a semi-open position. She was murmuring few incomprehensible words with no coherence whatsoever. He was only capable of pinching the last words that she uttered: "zhuyi anquan," which translated into "keep safe."

Yue opened her eyes and stared at Tsomo in a dazed manner. It took her a while to adjust to her surroundings after her brief escape from the real world. "His message was disturbing. We were able to communicate," she said calmly.

"Yes, I know," retorted Tsomo. "I could tell from the way you moved your head with every wave of messages that swept your mind. You're a natural. Don't reveal anything to me just yet. Let us first return to the monastery and then you can brief us all on your experience."

As they exited the cave, Yue halted for few seconds and stared with admiration and awe at Mount Everest peaks. A wonderful scenic view that she would soon miss. Would she ever return one day with her husband to this mystic world? She sighed and went down the trail catching up with the monk who looked satisfied and content.

"Thanks for everything," she said in a sincere tone. "You were a wonderful teacher. I will never forget you."

"It was my pleasure to train a person of your calibre," Tsomo replied without turning his head. He knew the wind would carry his words to Yue's listening ears.

As they neared the monastery, a human silhouette could be seen standing by the entrance.

It was not difficult to discern the military green uniform of General Wang. The distance grew shorter by the minute; the General recognised the party of two and hurried in their direction, panting and gasping for oxygen until he surrendered to fatigue and decided to await them.

Inside Master Khando's office, they sat quietly, attempting to digest Yue's debriefing.

General Wang was gently rubbing his hands with a sense of achievement. He succeeded in what he had been assigned to do and had to report his findings the quickest possible. His government would be amazed by the details amassed from the telepathic meditation that he had supervised. Yue had given a vivid description of the appalling state of Alpha Centauri star system. She had mentioned keV, MeV and erg energy measurements; the flare-ups, the likelihood of water depletion, scorching and above all Dr Huang frustration and deep concerns about the mission. It would have been inconceivable for Yue to come up with such tangible feedback on her own. It was obvious that telepathy between the Huang members did indeed take place.

Master Khando congratulated all those present and particularly Yue for having such a broad and receptive open mind. Had it not been for her true belief in her trainer and mind power capabilities the whole thing would have been a complete fiasco. The matter now rested with the Chinese government and consequently other major contributors to the Explorer mission.

General Wang spoke with the defence minister, conveying whatever he had perceived from Yue's account. Fearing any misconception or error in the reporting, the minister requested the presence of Mrs Huang in person. The General informed her that they were both summoned to attend a meeting on Tuesday, the coming week. The venue: Defence Ministry in Beijing.

"I will pass and pick you up at 9am," he told her. "It's just formality. There will be a panel consisting of military chiefs of staff, top scientists from the Chinese space program and, of course, the minister himself."

Yue squinted. "I just hope they have open minds to digest all this." She excused herself and headed straight to her room. She was exhausted, feeling drained. She also needed her own time and space to mull over the latest events. Her husband had returned to settle deeply in her mind. He had assumed back his role of lover. The fact that he might be at risk upset her. Her tiredness overcame her thoughts and she slept for eight consecutive hours.

## Part Six

# Chapter One

Three months later, Archbishop Gambino picked a folder off the top of his office credenza and headed for the Seminary Institution. Luigi was in his mentor's office pondering over conflicting interpretations of Greek Philosophy when the Archbishop was announced. As if in a barrack, both men rose in unison and paced their way towards the room's entrance, almost crashing into Archbishop Gambino who had already crossed the threshold. He would usually wear a big smile but not at that instant. He looked grim and reflected disappointment. Luigi didn't need to ask anything. The answer was already known to him.

The three of them hugged and patted each other. They occupied their seats relinquishing the swivel chair behind the desk to the Archbishop. Luigi scanned the ceiling as if looking for heavenly support and mumbled in a quivering voice: "Your Eminence: where do we go from here? Every door we knock on ends up shutting right in our faces. It seems I have to live through that certain uncertainty, and it troubles me. Life should be simpler than that. Maybe I'm the one who's wrong. Perhaps I'm hallucinating, being so anxious to believe in my visions? I'm therefore presuming that anything contrary to that is unacceptable and unfair."

Archbishop Gambino adjusted the height of his chair and said calmly: "The Chinese government is on our side. Through their own experimentation using telepathic meditation they have reached undisputed results that tally with your description of the fate of Planet Proxima B."

"The wife of astrophysicist Huang was trained by a Tibetan monk to send and receive messages to and fro. The outcome was amazingly successful and matched your account that the space mission was fraught with danger."

"What's the problem then?" Luigi asked with agitation.

"The Americans rejected the proposition drawn by the Chinese and Italian governments, which recommended the abortion of the space mission. They considered Mrs Huang's feedback on energy units of measurement and other description as the culmination of pre-knowledge: relayed to her by her husband at some stage, right before the launch. They also believed that her mind was biased by whatever she had been hearing on the news or through the browsing on the Internet. Based on those factors, the Americans did not support the credibility of her revelations. The majority of participating and contributing nations rallied behind the USA, not out of conviction I may say, but out of vested interests and hidden agendas."

The Archbishop paused for a minute, and continued: "I'm as dismayed as you are! Believe me. I have brought you the account of Mrs Huang's revelations. She testified and got interrogated two and a half months ago by an official Chinese governmental committee. Read through the report. It's interesting. Her trainer was Monk Tsomo, a renowned authority and practitioner of meditative techniques."

"Thank you, Your Eminence," replied Luigi. "I guess life will go on regardless. If there's truth behind my visions and Mrs Huang's revelations, we have to wait for another six years to prove it. That's quite a long time." It was obvious that pain was squashing his heart, rendering his normal breathing a bit difficult. His mentor sympathised with him, realising how important it was for him to rest his case, ascertaining the authenticity of his claims in an emphatic sort of way.

Luigi accompanied the Archbishop to the external courtyard and wished him well. "Give my respect to his Holiness," he said.

Feeling dejected, he went back inside and sifted through the stapled A4 sheets that formed the report of the Chinese government. Individual pictures of General Wang, Dr Huang, Yue, Master Khando and Monk Tsomo were inserted within the fifty-page report. Luigi was captivated by Tsomo's piercing eyes and broad forehead. Yue's face radiated with natural Asian beauty; he stared at her big brown eyes, sculpted nose and parted lips. He tried to curb his furtive emotions and for the first time in quite a while, he grinned. At that very moment, he was getting acquainted with his partisans; colleagues and brothers in arms, suffering from the same tyranny of not being reckoned with. He wondered how they were feeling after all the trouble they had gone through. He was not alone in this crazy mess. But the fight was tough: a handful against political and bureaucratic officials who saw the world as a big cake to be shared, regardless the consequences.

Luigi recalled his mother's warning that he shouldn't build his life on high expectations. He needed to talk to her although it had been less than four hours since they last spoke. Hearing her soothing voice and seeing her comforting face on his mobile screen did calm his nerves. He filled her in and was astonished by her unshaken attitude regarding the matter. "I'm not surprised. Powerful countries are involved and have committed themselves to the brink. Calling off a manned space mission requires guts, resolve and courage, particularly when there's no scientific proof behind those visions and claims. The stakes are high. They would rather go all the way with the mission regardless the risk involved."

Paula made sense and that upset Luigi even further. Logic didn't figure in his book any longer. He couldn't comprehend what was happening to him. What were the visions for? Why carry such a burden? Gina crossed his mind in sensual glimpses. Yue's innocent pure face flashed inside his head. He wanted out. He wanted simplicity and craved for liberty. Those visions had tied him down through their metaphysical clamps and he was incapable of releasing himself from their strong hold. His earthly life was suffering as a consequence. Why did he have to lose his father? That's where it had all started. His aunt's incessant pressure to salvage his dad's tormented soul. And yet, his father didn't seem to require any assistance. On the contrary, his aunt was a total mess of contradiction and he was himself a victim of redemption and salvation. He was the one in need of support and compassion. But who was there to provide that sort of cushion for him? Certainly not his aunt, not the Vatican, nobody in the whole world. Luigi was on his own, battling through life, armed with dreams and abstract visions that no one could fathom, not even himself.

Luigi waited for the weekend to join his mum in Milan. He had the urge to visit Andrea in San Donato. Why was it so important to be with a man oblivious of the world around him? Luigi didn't know. He stayed by Andrea's bedside watching his systematic breathing: diaphragm heaving up and down rhythmically. He stared at Andrea's expressionless face, his closed eyes and wished for an instant he were the one lying there, unaware of his surroundings. It was a funny but scary feeling. Luigi longed to find out in what state Andrea was drifting through?

Could he possibly be in a peculiar dimension, floating between Earth and the Afterworld? Was he capable of communicating with his best friend Fabriano? Was he capable of hearing the sounds emitted by his children? Could he remember what had happened to him?

Nobody had the answer. Andrea's features denoted peace and contentment. He was outlaughing mundane issues. At least, Luigi thought so.

# Chapter Two

Luigi opted for a quiet life, devoid of expectations. He was into his sixth year of priesthood and was singled out as being different from his colleagues. He excelled in his theology studies and was a benchmark for all those who sought explanations. He analysed matters from different angles with a modern touch that nobody fully comprehended but yet accepted and respected. So often his colleagues would call him: the Visionary.

On a Wednesday morning, Luigi was attending a regular classroom session when the clergy mentor received an urgent call. The call was directed to the mentor as none of the students were permitted to switch on his phone. It was against regulations. "Luigi," he called out, "it's for you. It's Archbishop Gambino!"

Luigi took the phone, stared at it for a while and spoke softly into the speaker: "Good day, Your Eminence. How can—"

The Archbishop interrupted him brusquely and blurted: "Luigi! You were right, my son. The prime minister has just informed the Vatican about a video that has been released to individual governments but not to the media. It shows Explorer's active crew of three astronauts in a confused state. The camera zooms in on electronic panels displaying disturbing figures of extreme gamma radiation and other critical measurements. The red dwarf appears visually through the cupola increasing dangerously in brightness. What can be seen inside the craft matches Mrs Huang's revelation."

Luigi was listening intently while his heart beat rapidly. "So how are the governments going to react?"

"That's the problem, Luigi. Nothing can be done. Five years have gone by since the launch. By now, the spaceship would have reached its destination and be on its way back: if they made it through, that is. Just to keep the records straight: this video is two and a half years old."

"I honestly don't know what to say. On one hand, I find it gratifying that the credibility of my visions is mounting but on the other, my compassion for the crew is so intense, I don't feel necessarily happy."

"I understand your concern, but you shouldn't feel responsible for any mishap that might have occurred. You are gifted, Luigi, and don't you forget it." Archbishop Gambino paused for a moment, then continued in a serious voice, "You have visionary capabilities and that's an interesting case and a unique gift that deserves respect. I owe you an apology for having been partly sceptical. The Pontiff believed in you from the very first moment and I should have followed suit."

"I thank you for your call, your Eminence," said Luigi. "Take care and God bless."

For the first time since his first encounter, certainty had imposed itself. No more doubts, no more apprehension, no more anxiety. His dad was eternally safe. The spiritual afterworld was out there for every faithful and decent human being. Regardless the causes that led him to priesthood, he had made the right choice.

That night, he retired to his room, fetched the Chinese report, opened the page where Yue's picture had been glued and stared at her beautiful facial features. He brought two fingers to his lips and kissed them, then he deposited them on her lips, hesitated and moved them across the cheeks, uttering: "Thank you."

Far away in Beijing, it was almost one in the morning when Yue turned in her bed enjoying a gentle hand caressing her face. Had her husband been next to her, he would have heard her muttering the words: "Keep at it! Don't stop!"

Since her return from Tibet, she had tried in vain to communicate with her husband through telepathy. She wasn't sure of the reason behind her failure to do so. Was she in need of Tsomo's presence? Wasn't she isolated enough from the rest of the world? Was her husband fine and well? Was he getting her messages and failing in transmitting his own? Was the whole thing a hoax after all?

General Wang was dying to tell her about the recent video footing. But in her case, any confirmation of the validity of her visions would turn her life upside down. At this critically late stage, the Chinese government saw no point in revealing the contents of the latest video. It wouldn't serve any purpose. On the contrary, it would mess up her life. The general only wished it hadn't taken that long to acknowledge the truth. Mrs Huang had the right to know but he couldn't breach official instructions. He resorted to alcohol for comfort and got embarrassed few times when duty called unexpectedly, and he had to attend unscheduled meetings. He would chew two mint gums in one go to hide his foul breath. Then with a little flip of the tongue, he would conceal the rubbery sphere in the cavity of either jaw, making sure his articulation went unhindered. The bulge however, was noticeable at times, forcing him to claim he was suffering from tooth infections.

When Yue woke up in the morning, she fixed breakfast for her daughter and waited one hour before the school bus picked her up. She recalled a blurry image of a Caucasian male's with nice symmetrical face traits staring at her lips, placing two fingers on her own and thanking her. Thanking her for what? She didn't know. Why a Caucasian male? It had been ages since she had met an American or a European expatriate. Could it be the effect of western movies watched lately? It was funny though that she used to skip over her previous dreams and never bothered to stop and ponder over them. She had realised nonetheless, that since her training in telepathic meditation, details did matter to her. Nowadays, she sought explanations and established links between events and tried to trace any logical pattern she might find.

For unknown reasons, she missed Tsomo and the rudimentary comfort of the Tibetan monastery. She wondered if she could communicate with him. Doing that would appease her apprehension and restore confidence in her acquired skills.

She tried to contact his mind conducting several sessions over the span of the whole week. But to no avail. Yue focused on just one word: greetings. Nothing transpired. Not a sign of a simple "hello." Frustration loomed over her and she regretted even trying to communicate with the monk, but there was a gleam of hope in all that failure. Doubting the efficiency and truthfulness of telepathic meditation meant her husband wasn't in any kind of risk. Maybe the whole meditation issue was a total sham, not worth considering. She had heard how tricky the mind could be. Images might suddenly flash but their real source could be the sub-portion of the cortex triggering stored sketches assimilated through wishful thinking and previous non-sequenced events. What happened with Lynn might have been a mere coincidence. Yue had been accustomed being under control. She dreaded living doubtful moments that instigated more questions than answers. The bright side however was her husband's safety and the ultimate possibility that the space mission was going smoothly as originally planned.

Yue decided to cheer up. She sang in the shower, put on nice clothes and boarded the train to work.

# Chapter Three

Months went by. Nothing much ever happened. Andrea passed away in April 2038. According to his children, he had suddenly opened his eyes, blinked them few times, tried desperately to speak, letting out a cacophony of incomprehensible words that sounded like a prolonged hoarse sound. Those present by his bed side swore they had discerned just one word: Eva.

Everyone else continued with his or her life coping with the daily stress and keeping abreast of technological advancements which demanded full adjustment by the user. Robotic engineering invaded every household, providing help, company and spontaneous informative feedback stored in high capacity data banks.

Automation spread viral, contributing to high unemployment rates. Real estate was hit hard as commercial institutions rented smaller premises: relying on half of their work force to operate from the confinement of their homes. Morning and evening traffic got better: no more congestions. Despite all that, people were missing the spice of old days, along with the basic behavioural normalcy that automation had stolen away. Even armies had been reduced in size. People started complaining: they needed a steady and flowing income to survive. Governments couldn't care less, claiming they were contributing to a stable and uniform employment process, whereby weekly working hours had dropped to a mere 30 hours. Job opportunities had therefore improved to the detriment of lesser working hours, giving a chance to hire more people with lesser pay.

Everybody was somehow affected by that viral automation, including Paula. She dispensed of three employees at the cosmetic shop, spent more time working from home and relied on her robot to set the table, help her out in the kitchen and do vacuum cleaning. She would invite Andrea's children over for dinner at least once a month, corresponding the invitation with Luigi's visit from Rome. She genuinely cared for them and it was her own way to pay respect to a dear person who despite all the odds, had been prepared to enter a serious relationship with her.

Gina got married and moved to Sydney Australia with her groom. Paula and Luigi attended her wedding, feeling disappointed and having remorse respectively. Gina had always been in Luigi's heart and occupied a big chunk of his mind. He had been living through a mental blockade, in complete denial that he still loved her. Luigi nonetheless was a practical person who knew he had chosen a definite course that wasn't in line with his feelings: he had to abide by the rigid rules and concede there were boundaries he couldn't cross.

Eva invested in a health food store and shared its ownership with a male friend. She used her contacts back home to import herbs and grains uncommon in Europe. Business was doing well especially with recent medical reports that encouraged people to revert to old therapeutic recipes that had no contra-indications. Work preoccupied her time, but she made sure she was always back at home before little Fabriano's return from school.

Luigi had a couple of audiences with the Pope; very cordial and informal. The Pontiff genuinely acknowledged Luigi's talent and special spiritual powers but seemed unprepared to go beyond that recognition. The Vatican committee remained silent and never bothered to get in touch with him. Luigi found their behaviour identical to government officials who award medals to deceased artists, rewarding them in their death, though they had been totally ignored while they lived.

In July 2040, Luigi was ordained in a mass celebration in Saint Peter's Basilica. Along with six priests from different countries, they were requested to lie prostrate in front of the Pope. His Holiness urged them to be merciful and emphasised the importance of the penance Sacrament. After mass, the Pontiff appeared at the window of his studio in the Apostolic Palace, blessed the crowd in St Peter's Square and was joined by the seven newly ordained priests.

Paula attended the mass and was proud of her son. He looked immaculate in his white vestment. She was certain people would flock to see him, to confide in him, to pray with him, to listen to his sermons.

Eva had excused herself from attending the ordination as her son had high fever and she was incapable of leaving him. She had congratulated Luigi for his "great achievement" priding herself for being the key and the main driver for his pursuance of priesthood.

Father Luigi was assigned to Saint Anne parish in the Vatican City. He had no doubt the Pope and Archbishop Gambino were behind the appointment. It was a privilege and Luigi was delighted.

At twenty-six years of age, Father Luigi was looked at as the modern young priest who smiled and listened intently to the parishioners, providing them with spiritual comfort.

Churchgoers firmly trusted his sermons. They were certain he believed in what he preached. Describing Heaven to them and its beauty was so vivid and real. God was seen as an Enlightenment; a loving Father whose fairness was beyond the realm of human conception. God represented a non-conditional true love and all He was asking of us is to help one another and cherish each other. A confessional was no longer a church stall inhabited by a clergy man listening to phony confessions of penitents. Sinners confessed because they sincerely believed there was a listener inside the cabinet who was truly close to God. Their admittance of guilt was emanating from the heart, omitting no details whatsoever. Penitents sought forgiveness and left the confessional feeling cleansed and blessed by the priest who represented Jesus Christ in that particular moment. Even infants and children adored the caring modern priest. Baptism became a ritual with a real sense of solemnity, taking people back in time, to the banks of river Jordan.

Communion had a different feel: one could sense the close relationship with Jesus Christ as if truly joining Him for the last supper.

Reports were reaching the Vatican about that unusual priest. Worshippers were growing by the day. The handsome young priest was liked by both genders.

The Pontiff smiled whenever he read the reports. He had an excellent intuition and never ceased to like that young man since the first time he had met him. He expected a great future for Father Luigi.

# Chapter Four

A video clip reached the Space Control Centre on the 27th of December 2042. The contents were horrific and were diffused to all nations that participated in the Explorer mission.

Presidents, ministers, military staff and scientists watched four astronauts in what supposedly used to be an alien city, pacing their way in a slow manner through rubble and debris. Human and animal-like skeletons were strewn all over the shabby streets. The voice of one crewman could be heard saying: "By the time you watch this video, 4.2 years of…space travel would have been exhausted…and 4.2 further years would have been required for…the signal to reach you…at home. Hence God willing…we'd be back to Earth around the…same time you'd be seeing this transmission…Wish us luck."

The audiovisual transmission had been weak and intermittent, indicating electromagnetic interference caused probably by unusual star activity at the time of broadcast. The captured reception required rectification and filtering measures to render it eligible.

On the next day, top officials from various countries convened a meeting in Helsinki. The atmosphere was tense: China and Italy blamed the United States and its allies for their arrogance and their refusal to take any initiative to abort the mission when it was still possible to do so.

Neutral nations acted as mediators to pacify the situation, pleading with all members to focus on the present situation. The outcome of the meeting was unanimous: nothing was to be conveyed to the media. Governments would wait for two more weeks, on the presumption that the spaceship would be back by then.

Ten weeks, twelve weeks…twenty weeks later, there was no sign of Explorer. Presidents and prime ministers started panicking. They withdrew within the confinement of their offices, barely exposing themselves to the press. Their silence said it all. There was no need to call for press conferences. The media was going to be after them. Explorer was supposed to be back in January 2043. It's already four months late.

The grim faces of government spokesmen revealed the truth to the media and subsequently to the public. They even admitted hiding previous information, stating it was all done for the vested interest of participating nations. For the first time ever, there was a sincere apology to all those who tried to warn the officials of the impending problem and particularly to the Vatican, the Italian and Chinese governments for believing and trusting the unexplained capabilities of visions and telepathy.

The Pontiff turned to Archbishop Gambino and said: "He'd been right all along. Ask Father Luigi to come and see me tomorrow."

Yue had tearful eyes and she sobbed quietly. The space mission could have been aborted had the participating nations believed in her and Tsomo. She hoped her husband didn't suffer.

General Wang had called her earlier to express his sympathy and to inform her that the Chinese government would never abandon her, that Dr Huang was a national hero. As if all that consoled her. What was she going to tell Lynn? She longed for the Tibetan cave, for anything that brought her close to her husband. She wished she had been a nun.

Paula was stupefied. She knew her son had powerful visions, but the unfolding news ascertained that power. Luigi was blessed with a special gift. That was awesome but scary in a way. She called him and his voice was subdued with emotions. "I feel sorry for those brave men. I just hope they didn't die in vain," she said with great concern.

The audience with the Pope was private. Even Archbishop Gambino hadn't been asked to join the meeting. The Pontiff welcomed Father Luigi not as a regular clergy, but as a dignitary, worthy of a warm and respectful greeting. His Holiness didn't waste time on peripheral matters and was very direct in his discussion with the modern priest:

"I believed in you from the first instance. Not that your visions were necessarily true, but rather impressive in terms of logic and consistency. You were the only person capable of describing Heaven the way it ought to be perceived. Probably not every single detail was true but your visions came from within and the beyond. They mattered to you as you were searching for your father and finally, they paid off. Reciprocating love is the key to everything. There are apparently no bridges between loved ones. According to the recent

Chinese experience, telepathic meditation was also very likely to succeed when loved ones participated in it. Having said that, I would encourage you to benefit from your encounters and put them to good use."

"Parishioners are amazed by your style and truly believe that you're particular: unlike any other. Keep it up my son and remember I'll be by your side should you require any support. The Vatican is proud to have someone like you in its midst."

"You need to understand the dilemma faced by the Vatican committee. Stating emphatically that your visions were real encounters was and still is virtually impossible. The committee might believe in their authenticity but could never enforce such claims on the public. Doing so, would jeopardise their credibility, for proof would never be tangible. It's analogous to anything else in life. We might believe in something but lack equations and formulae to prove it. What's important is our conviction that you possess special spiritual skills. As such, the Vatican empowers you to use the contents of your visions to stimulate worshippers and strengthen their faith without revealing the sources of your thinking and experience."

"I perfectly understand, Your Holiness," replied Father Luigi. "That's what I've been doing recently."

"God bless you, my son," exclaimed the Pontiff.

Father Luigi was concerned for Yue Huang. He could imagine her suffering and bitterness. Through the Vatican City channels, he was able to contact General Wang and obtain her contact number.

Yue was surprised by the priest's call. She was not fluent in English but managed pretty well to converse with him and thank him for his genuine interest in her well-being. Watching his facial features on her mobile screen made her uneasy. It was a deja-vu situation but she preferred to toss the thought aside, trying not to associate a priest with an affectionate caress she had sensed in a dream.

Father Luigi expressed his fascination with telepathic meditation and thanked her for her contribution in alerting concerned government of the serious plight of Explorer. Even though no action had been taken to abort the mission, Yue's success to communicate with Dr Huang was in itself a great achievement.

"No need to thank me for something I had to do. I believe you already thanked me…" She regretted her words immediately.

"What do you mean by that?" he retorted.

"I...I saw you in a dream a long time ago," she replied shyly. "You were thanking me."

A familiar scene flashed in Father Luigi's mind. Two fingers, lips, fingers stroking a cheek...Was that possible? Did she also feel his caress? He was stunned by that realisation and embarrassed at the same time. Their conversation continued for quite a while and he was fascinated by her clear mind, apparently unperturbed by the recent events. Yue was a clever open-minded person who differentiated between the physical and spiritual states while comprehending the existence of a mysterious bridge that allowed the crossing from one side to another.

Both were so absorbed in their discussion that they resented the idea of disconnecting. Sometime later, they had to say goodbye to each other reluctantly, and promised to remain in constant touch.

# Chapter Five

Father Luigi had just finished celebrating the morning mass. He removed his vestment, wore the purple stole and headed as usual for the confessional wooden structure inside the church. He entered the cabinet through a small door, sat on a wooden stool and waited for penitents. Few minutes later, he heard a shuffle and noticed movement as a believer knelt on the other side of the cubicle. He could detect the warmth of the person's breathing through the latticed opening. He braced himself and made the sign of the cross.

"Forgive me, Father, for I have sinned," a female voice let out. A familiar voice that sent shivers through Father Luigi's spine. "It's been a while since I confessed," the voice continued. "I didn't have the courage to come forth and seek absolution. But the heavy burden I'm carrying is weighing on me."

A dreadful silence loomed over the confessional. Father Luigi peered through the separator, hoping the penitent was someone other than the person he thought it was. The dim lighting and the viewing angle didn't give away the person's features, but the voice was recognisable. Why would Eva pick him up among all priests? Why would she travel all the way to Rome? He resented the fact but his duty obliged him to concede and act like a father to all humans.

"I'm listening," he said in a quivering vocal sound.

Eva cleared her throat and uttered: "Father! Forgive me if I have chosen you in particular for the confession I'm going to make. I truly believe that your personal forgiveness would ultimately lead to God's redemption. I'm therefore seeking dual salvation, for my very existence depends on it."

"I've had a life full of contradictions. I expected a lot of others and yet contributed nothing myself. I was vindictive with my own brother and concealed my bad deeds from all those around me. I preached without practicing. I used religion to facilitate my wrongdoing. Considering myself a faithful subject seemed enough to warrant any deviation from the norm. I imposed myself onto others, to the point of misjudging them. I envied my own brother for being positive and inquisitive. I followed my basic instincts and hid it all. I got married and ended up being a lousy wife and incapable mother."

"Andrea couldn't keep up with my insatiable lust and tantrums. He decided to file for divorce particularly when he seemed to have fallen in love with another woman. The lady was anonymous to me until my suspicions got gradually confirmed during our Capri visit. Following the breakfast incident that took place the morning we had planned our visit to the beach, and prior to leaving, I cornered Andrea in our hotel room and extracted the truth from him: His new love was actually your mother Paula. He admitted sleeping with her but expressed his dismay that his infatuation with her was not reciprocated. He loved her but she had held him at bay."

Eva's account made Father Luigi flinch. His aunt's words sank in. His mother was suddenly a main character in a weird plot. How was the confession going to end?

The penitent sighed and then she continued: "Realising his sincere and deep love for your mum, I threatened him to take it out on little Fabriano: rendering it a win-lose situation. He had no choice: either cancel the divorce proceedings or face my wrath. Instead of yielding to the pressure, Andrea stubbornly opposed me, reiterating his deep emotions for Paula and divulging for the first time his loathing of me."

"I decided to get rid of him in an indirect manner. All I had to do was instil in his mind that Fabriano Junior would eventually pay the price for his selfish actions. Andrea was to be murdered through self-threat induction. The only thing I had to do was create a realistic hostile environment. And I accomplished it with perfection. I faked the whole scene, creating a credible plot, betting on his deep concern for his son, realising in advance that he would take the bait and respond spontaneously to the impending danger. He was not aware that I was a professional swimmer, that I would never harm my child. On the other hand, I knew very well that he couldn't swim."

"Andrea did exactly what I had expected of him. Poor man: instead of drowning and dying instantly, his fate turned out to be far worse than anticipated. He had to live for years like a vegetable, probably suffering without being able to communicate his misery to anyone."

While Eva took some time to recover her breath, Father Luigi was reliving the beach episode. Flashes of disturbing images ravaged his mind: pulling his aunt safely to the shore; the drowning; Andrea's inert body. Anguish took hold of him. It was too much to bear.

Eva cleared her throat and continued: "Father: Please forgive my sins and pray God to help me survive the anxiety I'm being subjected to, every hour, every minute, every second. Had it not been for Fabriano Junior I would have taken my own life, even though it is against my belief to do so. I forgot to mention my contribution to Carla's suicide. Because of me, her life turned into hell. I stole away her husband, destroyed her family and carried on, living out my lust and dragging all those who surrounded me into the abyss. Please forgive me, Father. If you did, God would."

Father Luigi was dumbfounded. Eva's account could have been a horror movie, a tale but not a reality. He pinched his hand to ensure he was living the present. The subsequent pain made him wince, realising the seriousness of the situation. Luigi wanted to get out of the confessional, hit the woman and jolt her head until she repented. He had to let justice prevail. Father Luigi, on the other hand, composed himself, and requested Luigi the man to step aside and leave the woman to face God's judgement. As a priest, he had detected true repent and sincere remorse. His role was to bless and give absolution. Retribution was not one of his features. He was inside the confessional to provide relief to the faithful, not to pass on verdicts.

Father Luigi spoke softly into the latticed opening: "In the power bestowed on me by Jesus Christ my Lord, your sins are therefore forgiven. Make the sign of the cross and repeat after me: 'our Father who art in heaven, blessed…Hail Mary full of grace'…"

Eva said her prayers stopping at every syllable, pondering on their meaning. For the first time in her life, she understood that a prayer was in itself a blessing, a redemption. Tears blinded and itched her eyes. She had found the relief she was seeking and the right person to confess to.

"Thank you, Father," she said, rising to leave.

"Say your prayers on a daily basis. Mean every single word and God will be with you." The woman left the church without seeing her nephew outside the confessional. The Father stayed within the confessional for few minutes, fearing any eye contact with his aunt; making sure he got out when she was definitely gone.

# Part Seven

# Chapter One

Father Luigi became a bishop at the age of 32. Six years later he was appointed Archbishop. Upon his request and the Pontiff's blessing, he was assigned the diplomatic post of Apostolic Nunciature to Lebanon.

Paula was euphoric about her son's position, as it brought him back to his dad's native land, the land that crafted her dear and loving husband. She grabbed that opportunity to visit the country frequently, establishing herself between the city of Jounieh, North of the capital Beirut and Fabriano's village up in the northern mountains.

Sophia had died eight years earlier, ensuring in her will to grant the Beirut apartment to her daughter Eva and the village property to Paula and Luigi.

Archbishop Luigi resided during winter in Harissa, a small town overlooking the bay of Jounieh, shuttling between various cities and towns, visiting clergy from all Christian sects, politicians and government officials. His dynamic personality and charisma were highly praised by all those who met him. His pacifying methods contributed to bring people close to one another. Listening to him making a big effort to utter few Arabic words made everyone appreciate his simplicity, even though he exuded complete awe and respect. His presence was deeply felt because of his decisiveness and persistence to resolve pending issues and pointing out to various religious entities and political factions that their window of perception might differ but that their ultimate goal would always be the same. They were quarrelling about nothing and they all genuinely wanted a big change to happen: no more corruption; no civil wars, not even minor skirmishes. People were striving to fight the bad economy that had plagued the entire Middle East and Europe. People were craving to live decently.

In conjunction with the head of the Catholic church (Maronites), Archbishop Luigi performed mass in Harissa, gave sermons in English and few times in French, but he had to read out his written notes as his French was slightly dodgy. Listening to him delivering his speeches had a magnetic effect on worshippers.

Their faith in God no more carried partial doubts about anything. They firmly believed there was eternal life after death; nobody was scared anymore.

They understood perfectly well that God would never intervene to salvage them, to stop wars, to halt pain and miseries. Prayers were the only tools that brought humans closer to God. True feelings while praying and hailing God were essential to draw his attention towards their problems; only then would He consider altering the course of life. Eventually, humans had to earn God's intervention by standing out and being rather special to Him.

In a personal plea to the Pontiff, and to the Lebanese Maronite Archbishop, Luigi sought permission to reside during summer in a local old monastery built 400 years ago on the rocky terrain of the Valley of the Saints. The Pope gave his consent and the Archbishop moved to the mountains in mid-June of that year.

Archbishop Luigi spent his days at the monastery, working from his office. He had a grey/brown oak desk placed near semi-arched windows in a spacious room protected by thick stone walls offering uneven vertical surface which made hanging paintings and icons a bit difficult to secure. Within the same room, another smaller desk was positioned facing the door. A female secretary occupied the seat behind it and spent her time typing away on her computer handwritten scribbles and notes handed to her by his Eminence. He had a chopper at his service, whisking him away whenever an imminent meeting dictated such luxury.

The whole set up in the monastery was identical to the one he saw in his dream, except his dad never appeared at the door. Archbishop Luigi often strayed his eyes towards the valley stretching beneath the convent's external walls and pictured his father as a young lad running through the fields collecting thyme and oregano, bringing them home as a prize. His mother Sophia would wash the leaves, add chopped onions, fresh lemon, salt and virgin olive oil; mix them together and serve them with leavened bread baked in clay, which her husband Michel would buy early morning from local village bakeries. Luigi knew all that from his dad who never refrained loving his village and its customs. According to his father, Sophia used to dry remaining oregano leaves and use them in Italian dishes, as they brought up the flavour, in a way commercially available spices and herbs wouldn't.

Every evening his Eminence would leave the monastery at six and be at his father's natal village at six forty-five. He loved the partial walk through the rocky wild terrain that connected the valley with the summit. His driver would wait for him and take him to the cosiness of home. It was a regular occurrence. People would venture out of their red-tiled villas just in time to watch him pass by. Sincere salutes and hand waves were exchanged. He was respected and considered one of the locals. His father Fabriano had once belonged to that tightly bonded society. Inhabitants would often stop him and enquire about his mother Paula. When was she intending to come over? How was she doing in Italy? Any news of his aunt Eva? He had forgotten all about her. The only feedback he ever had was from his mother: her liaising with Eva had been intermittent but adequate enough to find out how each one was fairing.

Paula arrived in August and drove straight to the mountain village. Archbishop Luigi was waiting for her at the terrace where her wedding reception had taken place decades ago. Just seeing his seventy-year-old mother brought happiness to his soul. She had few wrinkles here and there but remained elegant and beautiful, retaining her straight posture.

Even in August, the afternoons offered a mystic painting: fog would shroud the entire valley, casting a thick blanket of white-greyish mist that rose and swept across the red-tiled villages that lie scattered around the rim. Fabriano had never failed describing that mystic scenery which brought Heaven and earth so close to each other.

Sitting on the terrace, wearing a light vest or sweater, Paula would watch the fog creeping through the space around her, hiding Luigi and the cherry trees from view. The peculiar distinctive smell of water droplets hung about as the fog engulfed the tables and plastic chairs leaving their surface glistening with humidity. As the night fell and time got late, the mist would dissipate under the cover of darkness, revealing the awesome view of the Valley of the Saints with its sombre landscape silhouette and tiny dots of light, rendering it an inverted image of the night sky above with its shining stars.

Once inside the comfort of their home, the Archbishop and his mother would eat a light dinner and enjoy good quality Lebanese wines. They would talk about Fabriano: the father and the husband, the dear person who after more than three decades was still haunting their minds with his love and affection. They truly missed him.

Every corner of the house reminded them of him. Paula could still hear his laugh when he exchanged dirty jokes with his father Michel. She found it ironic that she would miss him much more while visiting his native country. She never had the same intense feeling back home in Italy. It could be due to the fact she remembered him in his own context; at least that's what she thought.

As one got older, the more emotional one would become. That was Paula's finding lately.

She would sit for hours reminiscing of past events, the rapid technological changes. She was worried about the present and future generations. The human touch was disappearing. She fancied being in Lebanon because it had alienated itself so far from the robotic revolution. In Europe, humans were ending up talking to machines and equipment. People were going out less than before. Movie theatres were no longer lucrative nor practical to operate and maintain. Banks had only a couple of employees supervising the automated transactions. Public transportation had no more drivers. Airplanes were flown relying on their redundant computers and the vigilance of an unassisted captain. Trying to enquire about something over the phone had become strenuous as no humans attended switchboards anymore, or answered calls. Automated messages deferred the caller from one extension to another, leaving him desperate to forsake the purpose of his original query.

Luigi noticed that his mother was drifting away in her thoughts and realised it was occurring more frequently than before and for much longer periods. As they sipped brandy on one cold night, he purposely enquired about his aunt.

"She's fine. Doing well apparently. Always searching for the best organic food sources around the world; placing orders and distributing the goods. She's changed a lot. Not the same pain in the neck woman. Fabriano Junior is fond of her. Since Andrea's unfortunate incident, Eva metamorphosed into a caring mother and succeeded in managing her bad temper."

"How is he? I mean Fabriano," said the Archbishop excitedly. "We speak once a week," His Eminence added.

"He's into his first year at university. Majoring in civil engineering," replied Paula. "He's grown into a handsome man. He takes after both parents. His eyes resemble Andrea's."

"Were you ever fond of him, Mother?" said Luigi.

"Sure. I loved him since he was a little kid," retorted Paula.

"No Mother!" exclaimed Luigi. "I meant Andrea."

It took Paula a few seconds to answer. It seemed her thoughts reeled back and got fixated on an era that one had buried but not deep enough for it not to resurface.

"Andrea was a good man and your dad's best friend. His fling with Eva destroyed his life and his family. He realised his big mistake at a very late stage. He tried his best in the end to recover and readjust but unfortunately, he never had the chance, especially after the Capri incident. It's a shame really. Such a talented and respectful person ending up like a vegetable for several years."

"Did you have any feelings for him?" asked Luigi. "I mean emotional feelings."

Once again, Paula hesitated and couldn't comprehend what brought up that conversation in the first place.

"There was a brief time when I thought I had some feelings for him. I guess it was the culmination of so many events and the human compassion within me that solicited some attention to be given to him."

"How about him?" enquired Luigi. "Did he show any emotions?"

Paula swallowed her saliva and wondered what was going on. She slept on a personal secret for decades and here it is being propped up by a casual conversation.

"He did a few times in a flirtatious sort of way," she uttered that with a trembling voice.

Archbishop Luigi smiled and squinted. Enough was said to sustain Eva's recitation. Not that it mattered anymore, but as Luigi the son, he had to know; to be certain of few things. His mum was not to be blamed for any mishap. She had been at the centre of peripheral disputes and they had all converged on her. Even in her defensive attitude his mum had been gracious. She gave him the answers he was looking for without even describing them in detail. What she said was enough to establish that she and Andrea had a fling and that he took it far more seriously than expected.

He stood up, gulped whatever brandy remained in his glass and paced the living room until he reached the armchair where his mother sat. He grabbed her right hand and kissed it. She lifted herself upwards and kissed his forehead.

From the deep valley, the barely distinct toll of monastery bells could be heard. Once it had stopped, the chirping sound of crickets took over the audible scene.

Both mother and son stood by the windowpane gazing at the surrounding mountains that snoozed under the night sky. They wondered what was going on in those semi-lit houses, what secrets they were holding.

# Chapter Two

Archbishop Luigi became a very well-known figure in Lebanon and the entire Middle East. He was often requested by the Pontiff to handle few missions beyond the Lebanese borders, which involved few travels to Syria, Jordan, Israel, Palestine, Iraq, Iran and the Gulf states. Ten years earlier, a peace treaty had been signed between the Arab League and Israel ending decades of wars, skirmishes and conflicts. The United Nations had also acknowledged the creation of a Palestinian nation that included the West Bank, Gaza and part of Jerusalem. The Middle East was finally enjoying peace and prosperity.

The Archbishop's role was to further nurture religious and political dialogue, bringing countries closer to each other, encouraging dialogue between the three religions that cohabited the region. On a personal level, he studied the Coran extensively and similarly, high ranking mullahs, imams and rabbis indulged in the learning of the Bible.

Regular meetings were held alternatingly in various capitals to share ideas, combat fanaticism and illiteracy. Schools and colleges included special courses within their curriculum and seminars were regularly attended by officials, religious leaders and scholars. Extremist groups and factions had no more room to manoeuvre. Their strength which had been derived from ignorance had waned and had no more seeds to foment hatred and turmoil.

The Middle East was setting out a vivid example of religious and ethnic tolerance unmatched anywhere else in the world. Mosques and cathedrals were constructed next to each other in every major city. Church bells tolled along with adhans (Muslim calls for prayer).

People were praying for God and his Prophets. People understood the fundamental similarity of heavenly religions. It was amazing how the Middle East had always been the cradle of all religions. There must be a common denominator for that. Obviously, it had been the goodness of its inhabitants; their unspoiled purity and mysticism; their quest for the truth and therefore God the

Creator. The region was centrally located allowing proliferation to all corners of Earth.

Astronomy, philosophy, literature, medicine, art…were within the grasp of most citizens. Like any huge success, the difficulty had always been in maintaining that edge over others. It was much easier for great societies to falter while other dormant ones picked up gradually.

The region however had regained itself and realised its vulnerability. Other nations placed their bet on the Middle East plurality, trying to divide and rule in the name of religion and interests. They had succeeded for decades in splitting ethnic groups and sects, believing they had created an irreversible process from which they would gain and profit for centuries to come. The power of divine love and cohabitation had defeated the plans they had intended, and harmony thus prevailed.

The Archbishop enjoyed his debates and gatherings with other religious leaders. They learned from each other and respected one another. Being of Lebanese descent made him acceptable in their midst and altogether couldn't resist cracking jokes about his Arabic accent which denoted an Italian melodious streak to it. He didn't mind that. That made him peculiar and unique.

Mrs Huang had been in constant touch with Archbishop Luigi in whom she found refuge and solace. In their latest conversation, she informed him about her second visit to Tibet a month earlier. Only that time the trip was meant for self-meditation and getting reunited with Monk Tsomo. It was a casual visit, full of spirituality (as she defined it). She was encouraging him to conduct a visit himself whenever he found it suitable to do so. He wished he could, but time was very tight.

Weeks elapsed and the Archbishop learned from Yue that she would be attending a business seminar in the United Arab Emirates, spending two days in Abu Dhabi and three more in Dubai. Archbishop Luigi grabbed this opportunity to invite her over to Lebanon. After all, it was only three hours away. Yue craved the idea and promised to fit few days in her itinerary.

It was late September when Yue landed in Beirut International Airport. An Alpha Romeo bearing the Vatican flag picked her up and drove her to the northern mountain retreat where the Archbishop greeted her with Paula by his side. The housekeeper took care of the luggage while Paula took the lead showing Yue her room. After freshening up, Yue joined the Archbishop and Paula in the living room where a fireplace was blazing with crackling flames that heated up the cold air penetrating through the tiny voids of the wooden window frames. His Holiness poured three glasses of brandy and raised a toast welcoming Mrs Huang. She was supposedly few years older than him but like any most Asian women, she didn't give her age. Her pictures and video frames did not give her justice. She was a beautiful woman indeed. Her big slanting eyes radiated energy and shone like two big marbles. Her body was fit and well proportioned, blending nicely with her grey top, white jacket and black jeans.

It was almost evening time and Yue had been lucky to appreciate the various scenic views seen on her way to the village from Beirut. She was fascinated by the mountain ranges and the valley underneath. Yue had never pictured Lebanon as a country with multiple natural varieties. She would take a sip of the brandy then rush to the windowpane and admire the beauty of the villages perched over the Valley of the Saints, scattered as far as the eye could see around the rim that encircled the valley.

"Awesome," she would say. "Amazing place for meditation. One could find God everywhere around here. No wonder Gibran Khalil Gibran came from this region. I read his book, the Prophet when I was in college. Now I understand the background and the influence of the valley on his upbringing, influencing his thoughts, enabling him to come up with such meaningful writing. What a wonderful nature."

"Yes. I read his books in their entirety," exclaimed Archbishop Luigi. "Definitely his literature bears the seal of the mountains and valleys. You see over there towards the left, that's his hometown with the white cathedral as a famous landmark. There's a museum that displays Gibran's paintings as well. He did quite a few."

"My husband used to love this place," said Paula. "He's buried here, and I'll be one of those days." Paula sighed, "I love Italy, but I can't bear the idea not to be buried alongside my husband."

"We are here to rejoice," said the Archbishop. "Tell me, Yue, about your Tibetan experience."

Mrs Huang described every minute detail while praising Monk Tsomo for his patient and relentless training. She also admitted her failure in communicating further with her husband, attributing the cause probably to his state of mind after realising they were doomed up there.

Nobody knew for certain what had happened. There were many speculations but they remained unsubstantiated. What nagged her the most was the official

American attitude that threw suspicion and scepticism about the whole telepathic meditation issue. Had they believed in its power and credibility, none of that would have happened. She is now dealing with the matter on the presumption that her husband met his destiny searching for a universe that he had craved since childhood. Thus, it was not a total waste. He died for a cause of his own choosing.

Yue lifted her head and turned it towards the Archbishop revealing wet eyes full of tears: "You believed in me although we had never met. You were able to communicate with me and I picked your signal as I was sleeping. Isn't that fantastic?"

Paula was caught unaware by Yue's last statement. She refrained though from interjecting. Few things were better left unquestioned and unanswered.

"Tsomo kept telling me that love was the most powerful tool humans possess. Nothing would ever work for us if we were devoid of love and emotions. No wonder you had amazing encounters with your deceased father. General Wang informed me about your visions and dreams. You're kind of special. Your family is special too. I can see that already. Your dad's native village is special indeed. The Valley of the Saints is behind your sensitivity and peculiar capacity to listen to your vibes and those of your loved ones. You are simply blessed your Eminence."

"You are also special Mrs Huang," exclaimed the Archbishop. "You have the Tibet region in lieu of our valley and your family is overwhelmed by genuine emotions too."

"Yes. I guess I'm kind of blessed. But the difference between you and I your Holiness is so wide. As a Christian, you have the doors of Heaven awaiting you. While all I've got is reincarnation. I might transcend or regress in my new life."

"Leading a life full of good deeds would make you transcend until you purify your soul and then Heaven would be open for you," replied the Archbishop. "Regardless how you perceive life, religion and the afterworld, the key to the final trip would always be one's good performance on Earth. So, there are no differences in the ultimate goal. The variance is in the steps we take. God judges us based on our knowledge of what is good and bad; on how we perceive things. Eventually it's all the same. Always remember that."

Shortly afterwards, dinner was served. It was a mix of Italian and Lebanese cuisine. Exquisite food, mostly organic with garden grown vegetables that tasted so fresh as if eaten straight from their picking time. Yue enjoyed her food and was surprised by the amount she had. His Holiness recommended a glass of homemade Arak to accompany Lebanese dishes and suggested local red wine to down Italian food. In order to prepare themselves for an early start on the next day, the party of three withdrew to their chambers by ten-thirty.

# Chapter Three

Walking down the trail leading to the Valley of the Saints reminded Yue of her descent from the Tibetan cave to the Rongbuk Monastery. The mystic feeling was intense. Tranquillity and peace reigned in the area. Yue had never seen that many caves carved into the surrounding mountains. She gathered from his Eminence that few of them were used as burial places rather than for hiding purposes. It was interesting to know that mummified bodies had been found inside those deep mysterious caverns.

Monasteries and churches spread across the valley keeping their secrets and historical events hidden behind their closed massive doors. Few waterfalls could be seen depositing their transparent liquid into small pools of rocky terrain tens of metres beneath. One could picture the abundant flow expected two months later when fresh snow would melt and nourish those cascades.

The Archbishop had the clout to get inside those monasteries, as most of them were closed to the public. Wandering inside, Yue noticed the austere living conditions within the rocky walls and recalled those she had experienced at Rongbuk monastery. The latter nevertheless, had more lenient rules. For the first time in her life, she was looking at primitive cooking utensils, tools and thick bearded monks who only spoke words during prayers. She envied their life. So harsh and yet so harmonious. They definitely had God to themselves. No mundane events could disturb their minds; no noise; no communication devices; no politics; just a huge aspiration for physical nothingness in their continual efforts to reach better understanding of the spiritual world.

The views were breathtaking. The valley's past seemed to fade gradually as one climbed the path back to the modern world where red-tiled villas were built, hanging over the sharp edges of the outer rim. The group of three along with their driver had lunch in a nearby village, on the terrace of a restaurant offering a magnificent view of the Cedars. Below them, the afternoon fog had just started to form, covering the Valley of the Saints with a white-greyish veil that spread upwards, giving the observer a chill, a feeling of reverence and awe. Yue expressed her joy like a kid having his first ice cream. Paula combed the mountain range and gorges with her gaze, revelling at the awesome sight, so captivating and imposing. A scenery she had watched before on several occasions. A setting that she would never get tired of. Meanwhile, Archbishop Luigi was preoccupied shaking hands and chatting with local customers who recognised him because of his frequent appearances on television. They were bewildered by his modesty and simplicity.

After lunch, they drove up to the Cedars; bought few handmade cedar wood artifacts and walked through the forest, admiring the large ancient trees and took photos. The Archbishop was caught wiping his watery eyes. Paula made the right guess: her son was remembering his first encounter with his father. That was precisely the forest where they had made contact in paradise. She extended her arm and placed her hand on his shoulder. That's when he wept like a kid. Yue looked strangely at them, not comprehending what was going on. Paula had to explain the situation, which made both of them desolate.

"That's precisely where I saw him," he cried out. "Now that I'm observing the trees with their flat crowns and thick horizontal branches, their greyish-brown bark and short dark green needles and the way the trees are positioned, the scene couldn't be more elaborate and realistic. Actually, that cedar tree over there is where we met and talked."

Luigi pointed at a huge cedar tree that must have exceeded twenty metres in height. "This is overwhelming. I can feel his presence with us."

The Archbishop walked towards the huge tree and once he got near it, stopped and rested his head against its bark, closed his eyes and listened to his heart beating awkwardly. As far as he was concerned, he was leaning on his dad's shoulders, feeling the protection and warmth of unconditional love.

"I love you, Father," he said aloud. "I am what I am because of you. My life is wonderful because of you. I learned a lot through you and I owe you everything. My mission will be fulfilled to the best of my ability. I thank you for everything and above all I would like to convey through your pure soul, my deepest and sincere thanks to the Virgin Mary, Jesus Christ and God Almighty for judging you the way compassionate parents would have done: they looked inside your inner core and found its unblemished beauty."

Luigi spoke in Italian. Paula had tears in her eyes while Yue was stupefied by the intensity of the moment; she didn't comprehend a single word but understood quite well the emotional side of the situation.

They proceeded towards the highest peak reaching an altitude of 3400 metres. When the passengers got out of the car, a cold wind made them shiver. The temperature read 4C. They should have worn heavier clothing. The chilly sensation nonetheless around them vanished gradually as the lovely scenery from up there unfolded: beneath the mountain flanks, the fertile Bekaa valley was in full view with its segmented fields of varying greenish colours depending on vegetation type. The valley stretched in between two mountain ranges with an approximate area of 2000 km2 almost one fifth of Lebanon's expanse.

"We're going there tomorrow. You've got to visit wine distilleries," pointed out the Archbishop.

"I'm really baffled," replied Yue. "I never imagined such a small nation could have this kind of diversity."

And so, the next two days were devoted to the Bekaa valley and to the ancient Phoenician, Roman and Crusader ruins scattered all across the country. Mrs Huang had little time left to spare. Her flight back to Dubai was scheduled on Monday morning. Sunday was intended for relaxation. On Saturday night, Archbishop Luigi proposed they all head for Jounieh early Sunday morning. His Eminence thought it would be a great idea to let Yue attend the sermon he had been requested to deliver at Harissa Cathedral. The invitation to address the worshippers had been extended to him by the Maronite Church. His Eminence found that appropriate to enable Yue to see other parts of the country and be closer to Beirut airport. She would be able to acquire more time to sleep before catching her flight on the next day.

Eventually, it was also the proper time to move back and reside in coastal areas as the cold season was deploying itself rapidly, particularly at high altitudes.

Yue was delighted to attend a sermon addressed by a renowned clergy, especially one who had become a dear friend, a colleague and above all a visionary.

# Chapter Four

Harissa cathedral was built 450 metres above sea level, overlooking the Mediterranean Sea and the bay of Jounieh. A scenic view reminiscent of the island of Capri.

The Maronite Archbishop had just finished mass. It was celebrated in the open air to accommodate thousands of worshippers who flooded the place for two reasons: attend Sunday mass and hear Archbishop Luigi delivering his sermon. People were getting accustomed to his thoughtful orations that differed greatly from regular discourses common to most clergy. People awaited his speeches, recorded them and played them in front of those who were unable to join the gatherings which rallied the faithful in their thousands.

Without fanfare, Archbishop Luigi appeared at the makeshift podium, wearing a black robe with a broad burgundy band around the waist and a pectoral cross worn across the chest, suspended from the neck. The sun was high in the blue sky, radiating warmth on the assembled crowds. Television crews who had broadcast the mass were all geared up and ready to cover the sermon. Several booths were set up with simultaneous translation of Italian into Arabic, English and French languages. Digital screens were mounted at convenient locations around the massive square and open car park.

Loud cheers could be heard everywhere. Yue and Paula were lucky to be seated on white plastic chairs in front of the podium, as most people had to stand shoulder to shoulder and tilt their heads upwards in an effort to watch the Archbishop closely on the screens.

Archbishop Luigi extended his hands seeking to appease the tumultuous crowd. Finally, the noise ceased in a gradual cadence. When silence fell, his Eminence cleared his throat and greeted all those present:

"Good day to all of you. I wish to thank Archbishop Najem for inviting me over and bestowing on me the privilege to address you in this prestigious sacred place. And I would like to extend my thanks to the local and foreign media for allowing viewers at home to participate with us."

"Today, we have among us a Chinese visitor: Mrs Huang, whose husband, a renowned astrophysicist, was a member of Explorer's crew. You all know the tragic end of the space mission. What's important now is to learn from our previous mistakes and self-criticise ourselves for the bad decisions that led to this ill-fated expedition."

"It should be known to all nations that interstellar travel and space exploration are farfetched issues. They have no potential to succeed. The vastness of the universe is beyond human reach. Scientists around the world realise the complexity of space travel but they find solace in unproven and wild speculations: that space curvature would bring two points closer to each other, therefore shortening the travel distance. Present theories and recent studies define interstellar space as a flat surface with slight curvature. That's a contradiction to previous conceptions as depicted in the relativity theory. So where is the truth?"

"Supposing the first theory were true, and that space is indeed curved and filled with wormholes, how many years, decades or centuries of travel would one still need to get from one star system to another?"

"Where is the fairness of all that to the crew? To their families? Is space exploration worth such illicit sacrifices? To achieve precisely what? Seek other civilisations? What makes us think we could do that: tamper with other life forms and societies? That's the essence of everything: God created small worlds within a wholesome universe, separating them from one another by humongous distances. He sought that, simply because we are not meant to tamper with each other's civilisation. Doing so would be a distortion of specific living and spiritual conditions beyond our jurisdiction. Before we have the nerve to intervene in this universe, let us first establish a common comprehension of who we are and why we are here."

"The answers to all questions have been conveyed to us through heavenly religions. Yet, we are still divided in their interpretation, trying to find ourselves elsewhere instead of comprehending the truth from within. It's similar to one of us, travelling to the United States for tourism purposes while completely ignoring the geography of his own country. We have to start from within: know ourselves, understand the purpose of being here on Earth. Only then would venturing outside the realm of our tiny planet be condoned. Exploring other star systems however, if doable, should be conducted in such a way that physical intervention with another exoplanet is totally forbidden."

"You have heard throughout history that Earth had been visited by aliens; that the pyramids of Egypt were built with alien assistance. Well, I can tell you bluntly that this is not true. Egyptian workers did the whole thing, like any other monument or shrine all over the world. I reiterate it is forbidden to disturb the intellectual and spiritual growth of any civilisation."

"Failing that, the universe would be a chaotic place relying on the teachings and guidance of the most advanced civilisations. But what is an advanced society? One with super technological knowhow? Is that sufficient to become a benchmark, a model for the less advanced? Certainly not. Imagine living under the rule of super intelligent aliens who are extremely advanced but devoid of purity and fairness. Would you consider that as the ultimate experience? Would you contemplate emulating them? Just reflect on it and you'll find it's totally unacceptable to adopt such a theory."

The Archbishop's voice was reverberating across the warm air that hung in the square.

People nodded amid complete silence, disrupted by harmonic noise from the speakers. He continued:

"Nations should rather focus on environmental improvements, explore the oceans and find medicinal cures for diseases and illnesses. Religion should be taught in a clear and unabashed way, with simplicity and sincerity; far from coercion. People have to comprehend that religion is not just a necessity; it's more than that; it's a precursor that lays the path towards a quicker understanding of oneself and the truth. Accepting religion is nevertheless not sufficient on its own: in parallel, one has to practice its teachings in order to earn God's forgiveness."

"Believe me, brothers and sisters, leading a life full of love and good deeds is the key to everything. Religion lays the foundation, we have to build the columns, beams and slabs in order to earn it. It's so simple. We cannot claim we are faithful to our religion if we don't tie our lives to that foundation. I would like to draw your attention to a fact I have experienced. I've known a person who erected columns on a semi-rigid foundation without completely omitting it. And he succeeded in his endeavour. Hence the superstructure is as important as the substructure and they complement each other. Reaching God in Heaven can only be achieved when both attributes are present. But always remember that one of the two has to be firm and sturdy; failing that, it wouldn't work."

Archbishop Luigi was delivering his sermon without written notes. Listeners were struck by his unwavering concentration and praised the clarity of his mind. After a slight pause in which he quenched his dry mouth with a glass of cold water, he addressed the crowd once again:

"I would like to dwell on a topic that often crosses your mind. It's about science and religion. People believe in their senses: you see a lion and you don't question its existence; you hear the wind blowing and you associate it with the swaying of tree branches. You have learned equations and formulae and you accepted them for granted, without questioning. Who are we to challenge Newton or Einstein? We can calculate a force by knowing just the mass or vice-versa. We can derive energy values knowing the power and the time. It's relatively easy to accept non-abstract, palpable material for they form part of our physical state."

"On the other hand, you have philosophical religious issues that evolve around the spiritual state. On the surface, they appear to form abstract material that humans cannot fully or even partially comprehend. Most of you have read Genesis, the Old and New Testaments and got confused by the narrative. Most probably you found yourselves much more at ease with the New Testament because of its simplicity and transparency: an account described by various disciples, addressing the life and deeds of our Lord Jesus. Nonetheless, Genesis and the Old Testament remain so vague at times, tale-like and mystically extreme some other times."

"Ambiguous material totally different from scientific equations which we can write down on a piece of paper and analyse. When did Creation take place? Is there life after death? How can we tally between Darwin's evolution theory and religion? Scientific evidence of early life millions of years ago? And so forth. I take the liberty to put forth to you my personal interpretation and reply to those questions."

"Earth is four and a half billion years old. Earth population stands currently at nine billion. That's a scientific fact no one can argue about. Also scientific is the calculation method to derive how long it has taken to reach that number. Therefore, starting with Adam and Eve, it would have taken around 35,000 years to reach our present figure. That is interesting, because once again and according to carbon dating, which is also scientific, human fossils have been dug going back 300,000 years for modern humans and 3 million years for early genus Homo. Non-human fossils dating 4 billion years have been found."

"So, how can we make sense out of it all? It's very clear scientifically speaking, that planet Earth had a life form since its creation. Humans, however, came at a much later stage and evolved through phases. We notice however, that in the event humans did exist 3 million years ago, the present population would have surpassed the trillion figure. We know that's not the case. So, what is the missing link?"

"On a personal level, and far from being the church's view, I reckon that human life has been cyclic. We currently belong to the latest cycle with Adam and Eve being our predecessors. I have to point out that in the beginning, the human cycle span was much longer than the present one, for a simple reason: cycles shrink in time as human intelligence evolves. For instance, the first cycle might have taken 500,000 years, the second 200,000 years and so on. Our cycle started 35,000 years ago and might continue for another 2,000 years until the next one is initiated. You might ask yourselves the question: What is a cycle and why does it have to end? Simply because our civilisation evolves at a certain rate, reaches alarming levels and ultimately leads to human annihilation through devastating wars and/or drastic population under-growth, as mortality rate surpasses birth rate. The cause for that could be the stifling automation impact on families, forcing them not to bear children. The consequence of that is the gradual reduction in population leading to nothingness."

"The Book of Genesis says that God created mankind in his own image. Animal life and vegetation came before that. It tallies therefore with the fossils dating sequence. Genesis however mentions only few days separation between the events and not billions of years as science reveals. Is there a discrepancy there? Not at all. God created the world in six days and rested on the seventh. A day in the Book of Genesis is not a usual day, it could have meant years, centuries, millions, billions of years."

"It is vital to understand that Genesis was probably written by Moses or Biblical scholars relying on conveyed revelations and accounts transmitted in primitive forms. That has nothing to do with their authenticity when one studies the core of the contents."

"All I'm asking of you is to trust God and not to be afraid of asking questions when your intention is to search for the truth and not to challenge it. Be simple and understand that complexity will never get you anywhere. In case you found yourselves in doubt, do not refrain from being good Samaritans. God loves you all. Whenever you love someone, you'll be loving Him as well. My advice to you is to have faith without questioning, for it renders your life much easier, knowing quite well that your search for the truth will always lead you towards Jesus, no matter how long you stall. Eternity is there for you to grab. God wants you beside him in Heaven. Do not disappoint Him. Take good care of yourselves. May God bless you all."

The sermon ended, leaving the crowds bewildered and dumbfounded. It took them one minute to realise the speech was over as they wanted to hear more. They clapped and clapped in a frenzy of shouting: "May God bless you too, Your Eminence."

People who sat on chairs had their line of view obstructed by the standing crowd, Paula and Yue among them. They had to rise and join the masses in their loud cheering.

Two thousand miles away in the Vatican, the Pope steered his eyes from the TV screen and stared at Archbishop Gambino muttering, "Isn't he great? At times I feel I'm watching and listening to my successor!"

# Chapter Five

Saying goodbye to his Eminence wasn't easy on Yue. Hanging around him had been a gratifying experience. She cried at the airport as he wished her well. The comfort of his hug was missed the moment he let go of her. She waved back at him few times before she disappeared into the outflow of travellers. Her sensations worried her. She was behaving like a teenager; she knew it but couldn't help it. Unlike the Archbishop who sought solace in his religion, Yue had to rely on their mutual promise to keep in touch and to visit periodically whenever deemed convenient. That would keep her going, looking forward to the "next time."

Archbishop Luigi returned home to Jounieh, just in time for lunch. Paula had prepared spinach lasagna: one of his favourite dishes. The table was already set with a large Pyrex baking dish in the middle, where a savoury scent wafted out of the sizzling lasagna, filling the air with a pre-taste of tomato sauce, parmesan cheese with a hint of oregano and garlic. Next to it, a bowl of tossed salad with thyme and rocket leaves glistened appetizingly, exhibiting the nice blend of olive oil and vinegar. Two empty glasses were placed next to two plates and two salad bowls, with an opened bottle of red wine that was left to breathe.

They sat quietly at the table, feeling the emptiness Yue had left among them. "We got used to her presence," said Paula while Luigi poured the wine.

"Yes. She is a nice and pleasant woman. Wish her husband could have been saved," replied Luigi with a sad tone. "Hope we'll see her one day."

"I'm sure we will," retorted Paula.

Lunch was heavenly. Luigi thanked his mother for the amazing lasagna. As they relaxed in the living room sipping espresso, he sighed with relief, realising how lucky he had been to have his mother close to him. Being next to him had made all the difference. He enjoyed his life but never stopped feeling lonely; deprived of female companionship and unable to express his emotions. He often had the urge to shout them out, to let them out. But all he did was to hide them out. It was a heavy price indeed, particularly when one had tried and experienced the joys of love and compassion.

That was true sacrifice. Luigi always believed that deprivation turned into a virtue when the temptation got high. Failing that it would lose its value and significance. An alcoholic who deprived himself from booze while the bottle was within reach had more virtue than one who stopped drinking because he couldn't afford one.

The same applied to everything else in life. It had always been a challenge to control one's lust and craving. Humans were assessed and appraised accordingly.

Paula was enjoying her afternoon nap when she woke up at the sound of Luigi's mobile phone ringing incessantly. She had apparently dozed off while sitting in her arm chair. Her son was not in his seat let alone in the living room. She called out his name few times but to no avail. She tried to get up and reach for the phone. The ringing had ceased, bringing peace and quiet back to the space around her. Paula looked at the screen and read the caller's ID name: Gambino. She searched the apartment for Luigi but he wasn't to be found anywhere. Paula peered out of the window and smiled when she spotted him lounging by the seashore, just about one hundred metres away from the back of the building where they resided. He looked vulnerable to the blowing sea wind that attacked his face, forcing him to adjust the locks of hair that covered his eyebrows. That was the scene as perceived by his mother. Yet from his perspective, the sea air was not waging a war on him; it was rather fiddling with him, trying to assert itself as a major player in a world ruled by God and Nature. The wind had a force to be reckoned with; it also brought along the salty smell of the water, carried by the waves that it hurled towards the shore, breaking and crashing on the rocks. The wind had a sound as well. It was an awesome living creature that breathed and spoke. It was also invisible. It ruled without appearing to the naked eye.

Luigi returned one hour afterwards and as soon as he unlocked the door, the aroma of freshly brewed coffee hit his nostrils. His mum was waiting for him as if she knew exactly when he would be back. It never dawned on him that she was taking glimpses out of the window. It was funny how one would believe living in total eclipse from the world when in reality every single move was actually observed and monitored. No one could hide from view.

"You missed a call from Archbishop Gambino," said Paula.

Luigi laid his coffee cup on the side table and picked up his phone. He retrieved the incoming calls list and pressed the latest ID number. A cheerful voice greeted him. Luigi switched on the video and speaker modes and Archbishop Gambino appeared on the screen wearing a hearty smile:

"Good day, Your Eminence," exclaimed Luigi. "I'm returning your call. Anything the matter?"

"His Holiness is requesting your presence in Rome on Thursday this week," replied Gambino. "He is convening a meeting at eleven am. Sorry for the short notice. Hope you have no other arrangements set up this week?"

"I can reschedule most of my appointments. Not a big deal. Any reason behind this sudden request?"

"Not a clue," responded Gambino. "All Vatican committee members were summoned too. I don't know what's going on, but his decision to meet was made at the spur of the moment, immediately after watching your sermon on TV. I meant to inform you yesterday but didn't fancy disturbing you on a Sunday."

"Thank you, Your Eminence! Please inform his Holiness that I'll be there."

The call ended, leaving Luigi in a daze. Why would the Pontiff request a meeting after hearing his sermon? Had he gone too far with his speech? Was his Holiness upset with him?

Paula jolted his trance and brought him back to the present world where a cup of coffee awaited him.

"I have to leave for Rome this Wednesday," he said. "The Vatican has called for a morning session on Thursday. I'm intending to spend an entire week. It would be beneficial to liaise with another clergy and keep abreast of what's going on within the Vatican City. Would you like to come?"

"If you're going to be away for a week, I'd rather leave for Milan and spend two or three weeks there," Paula replied. "I miss home and it would be nice to drop by the shop, visit friends and see Fabriano Junior."

"Good idea. Maybe I'll join you there for a couple of days. It's been quite a while since I've been to Bellagio, I miss the place."

# Chapter Six

Members of the Vatican committee consisted of cardinals, bishops and officials. Their presence in a singular conference room shed an austere environment that would scare any new comer. Despite his worldwide exposure, Archbishop Luigi felt a heavy weight squashing his shoulders. The Pontiff hadn't arrived yet. Archbishop Gambino seized the moment to introduce Luigi to the members, most of whom responded with appreciative nods, as they had heard a lot about him but had rare chances to get properly acquainted. Animated conversations ensued between the members who split into various clusters. Few were still standing while others were already seated. Despite their attempt to muffle their tone, it was obvious the subject of their side discussions focused on the purpose of the meeting.

The Pontiff's entry to the big room brought complete silence in its wake. Everybody stood up and bowed in respect. The Pope saluted the Council with the sign of the cross and nodded at Luigi who in turn paced the distance that separated him from his Holiness and kissed his hand.

"Good day, my brothers!" exclaimed the Pope. Static noise accompanied his amplified voice for a fraction of a second before receding. The sound reverberated off the walls but syllables were perfectly legible to the ear.

"We are all gathered here today to greet Archbishop Luigi, our Papal ambassador to the Middle East. His mission has succeeded in boosting Christian faith and has brought heavenly religions close to each other. As you know, Muslims and Jews alike have conducted open discussions with his Eminence and worshippers from all faiths are learning tolerance and acceptance of one another. That took dedication and sincere devotion to reach such levels of understanding and cooperation between the three major religions."

The Pontiff paused for few seconds and scrutinised the room with his piercing intelligent eyes. Each attendee had the impression of being analysed by his Holiness. The committee members shook their heads in concert showing their concurrence. Encouraged by their nods, the Pontiff continued:

"Furthermore, I'm sure you've been listening and watching his Eminence's sermons. The feedback we've been getting affirms that those discourses have captivated the hearts and minds of millions of people. His simplistic approach to tackle complex subjects and renders them plausible to the human mind has gained the respect of worshippers. People are no longer afraid of death and retribution. They have gained renewed hope that God was a good listener and a great fair judge with compassion and unconditional love for mankind."

"Those attributes my brothers cannot be neglected or considered as trivial. God has blessed his Eminence with a vision that I had trusted but couldn't defend or back up. Often, I tried to find some sense out of it, even requesting your assistance in studying his case."

"Unfortunately, the committee declined to hear out the young man who had just entered his discernment year. Time has proven that his visions were realistic in their nature and could be termed as close encounters with the spiritual world. That's the reason why he is different from any of us. Subsequently, his sermons carry deep meanings because he's able to relive his encounters and deduce some sense out of them, without revealing the sources of his information to the public. I'm certain you have noticed my choice for the expression "his visions were realistic" rather than "real." I wanted to emphasise that logic is realistic but not necessarily real. On the other hand, anything real is not necessarily logical, because reality depends on our acquired perception which is prone to change."

Once again, his Holiness stopped briefly to study the impact and reaction of his words on the attendees. The committee members stirred in their seats. Their refusal to hear Luigi out had given away their incapacity to deal with the supernatural. They were so immersed in earthly matters that any acceptance of the unexplained wasn't worth considering.

"As I'm getting old, rectifying what we have neglected to do is extremely vital. Archbishop Luigi has shown despite his relatively young age, unprecedented leadership and charisma. In order to be fair to the Catholic church and the Holy See, I hereby nominate His Eminence Luigi to become a member of the College of Cardinals."

Archbishop Luigi's heart raced amid loud cheers emanating from all corners as all members rose and clapped their hands in appreciation, shouting: "Cardinal Luigi! Cardinal Luigi!"

Luigi glanced at the Pope who had just joined the applauding group. He couldn't help noticing a wink directed at him by his Holiness, or was it a grimace? Luigi parted his lips and whispered: Thank you. The Pontiff nodded, realising the importance of his achievement.

Luigi came forth and bowed in front of the Pope who rested the palm of his right hand on Luigi's head and then made the sign of the cross, blessing the newly appointed cardinal. "I'm convinced I'm doing the right thing," the Holy See muttered.

"May God bless you, my son. Keep up the good work and continue with your present duties in the Levant for another year. But eventually, you're needed here. Time is passing by and I would like you to assert yourself here in Rome. A great future awaits you."

Paula was so happy for him, she was incapable of speaking. Her son would ultimately have the power to elect the future Pope or be elected himself.

"Well done! Well done!" It was the only thing she could say.

Paula had been in Eva's office when she received that call. She would never forget the look in her sister-in-law's eyes. That knowing look that she was behind her nephew's success and evidently being and playing the role of the proper advisor. Eva had snatched the phone away from her and yelled into the microphone, "Bravo, Luigi. I knew you'll make it. I'm glad you listened to me."

Luigi resented calling his mother at that particular instant. He hadn't known she would be at his aunt's office. He was unable to forgive Eva's evil deeds. As a clergy, he did, but not on a personal human level. She was a manipulator and a murderess. A cold person who abused others and claimed perfection. Should he deal with her based on her pre-confession or post-confession phases? As a religious man, he should opt for the second phase, for it had been through him that God had forgiven her sins.

# Part Eight

# Chapter One

At the age of forty-two, Luigi was unanimously elected by the Vatican College of Cardinals following the demise of the late Pontiff. He assumed the Papacy under the name of John Paul the Fourth. His predecessor had paved the way for the young cardinal, lobbying for him incessantly since his appointment in the Vatican College.

The whole world was surprised by the unprecedented swift election that took place within the conclave and was pleased to watch a young man heading the Holy See. Word of his earlier feats and sermons had spread rapidly across the globe, rendering him a figure to be reckoned with. Heads of all nations expressed their delight and paid their respect from the outset, forwarding their diplomats to the Vatican City, sending electronic mails and conducting live videoconference calls. Non-Christian and secular states joined the others in welcoming the Pontiff, wishing for continued workshops and dialogues between various religions and cultures.

Few weeks afterwards, United Nations envoys extended their invitation to John Paul the Fourth to address the General Assembly in New York. Tough security measures were enforced all around the UN Headquarters. Checkpoints and roadblocks were set up on all roads that led to the complex. Police patrol boats skimmed the surface of the Hudson river reflecting sunlight off their grey painted hulls. The whooshing sound of helicopter rotor blades slicing through the air could be heard from the streets beneath. The choppers were basically hovering rather than flying, acting as high-altitude observation posts. Unmanned drones were not allowed that day in the skies of New York.

The influx of motorcades came in waves, accompanied each time with blaring sirens and flashing lights. Dignitaries got out of their vehicles dashing towards the protected building entrances, giving the impression snipers on nearby roof tops were holding them at gunsight. The Pope's motorcade reached the UN Headquarters without fanfare, unlike most.

His Holiness was the last person to enter the large UN General Assembly Hall. A standing ovation welcomed him with big applause that lasted for two full minutes, in which the Pontiff examined the internal layout of the Hall while nodding in appreciation. Once the cheers subsided, the Secretary General made an introductory speech in which he praised the role of the Vatican, emphasising the wise guidance of the Holy See in fomenting peace and accord worldwide. He then introduced the Pope officially and passed on the floor to him. A second burst of applause flared up. His Holiness rose up from his seat and traded his place with the UN Secretary General. The Pope had brought along his laptop and held a folder that contained his handwritten speech which he deliberately composed in English. A huge video wall was set up for the occasion, giving his Holiness the flexibility to project through his laptop, vivid displays of regional maps, satellite pictures, graphs and list of action plans. The visual effect was supposed to be a complementary tool to support his discourse:

"Thank you, Mr Secretary, for the nice introduction. I had prepared a written speech with notes and highlights, but in the end, I decided to be informal and improvise. I thought that would render my plea to the respectful members of this assembly more effective and bring home my thoughts in a more direct manner. I shall select particular slides from my personal computer whenever the need arises. Please be patient with me once I scroll through them. I'm still a layman when it comes to automation skills."

Laughter could be heard throughout the spacious hall.

"Gentlemen, I've been elected to serve and not to rule. I've been appointed head of the Catholic church but I am still a simple human being: a fellow, a friend to all of you. I shall strive and make it my goal to be accepted worldwide by all humans, as a father, a brother and a son, regardless of one's religion and ethnic group."

"My duty is to spread God's teachings and instil his love in the heart of Christians. That's my prime responsibility. But I also have, like any other concerned citizen, a duty towards social and economic issues that plague this planet. I shall not rest until your governments sort them out. We are all children of God. Whether we belong to clergy, civic or governmental institutions, the same burden is shared by all. We need to help each other restore stability to this world; combat poverty; ensure medical care for all; open our schools and universities to all those who seek knowledge."

"Infants are dying by the millions in the African horn. Watch these spine chilling pictures of swollen abdomens, consistent with famine and starvation. Watch the huge eye sockets and the protruding bones of these boys and girls. Focus just for one second on their pleading and wandering eyes. These children have lost faith in us and have started to doubt the existence of God. That's where everybody goes wrong. God created us in His image and we are here on planet Earth to make our life meaningful, deserving and worthwhile. Stop blaming God for your wild fantasies and senseless adventures."

"Perform good deeds in His name and don't ever tell a poor hungry man, 'May God assist you!' Resorting to that approach is a meagre and devious try to alienate yourselves from direct responsibilities. Let us not fool ourselves anymore. Countries have no fixed boundaries any longer. Continents are linked together by skies and seas; yet their inhabitants are still regarded as foreign entities. Economy and financial strength fluctuates like any sinusoidal wave. The worldwide throughput is always the same but its distribution varies cyclically with each nation. Your turn may come one day and you won't have anyone to rely on."

"So much money is being wasted on Christmas and New Year decorations, so much food is being thrown unconsumed in garbage collectors. Billions of dollars are spent on mundane issues and yet, we hear about ten or fifty million-dollar donations to support our brethren. The irony of it all: those financial aids are committed by superpowers with annual budgets of trillions of dollars. Where is your compassion? How could you stare at those bloodshot eyes where tears have forged scars within their whiteness?"

"By the same token, millions of children are deprived from learning. It is unacceptable nowadays to find illiterate people. It is our combined struggle to build schools for them and lead them to become efficient and proficient in special domains where they would excel."

Slides of semi-naked children huddled in bunches underneath makeshift tents and hangar-type steel structures appeared on the video wall. The students were staring at their respective teachers who had no electronic boards, not even chalk boards to write on. The tents were in the middle of deserts, in valleys and rocky mountain areas.

The Pope showed the slides amid total silence within the auditorium. But his ears could hear intermittent sorrowful sighs and hums emanating from the audience. He drank some water from a glass deposited on the lantern and carried on:

"Talking about knowledge, God wants us to grow. The more we learn the closer we get to Him. Do not believe that querying something is a blasphemy. Do not be confused by the general conception that science and religion do not tally with each other. Science strives for a comprehension ruled by physical laws, whereby the governing perception is based on stimuli and reactions. Thus, nothing comes out of nothing. But is that a true statement? There must be an origin somewhere; a beginning that launched everything. If God was not the Creator, was the hydrogen atom then, the originator of life? In both cases though, there's a start. Just because we can't conceive the splendour of Creation, we shouldn't come up with wild theories that surpass the basic concept of believing in God. That dilemma will always remain unidentified until eternity."

"Having said that, we must believe in science to cope with our physical world. The more we grasp universal laws, the more appreciative we become of God and spirituality. Let us recall the space mission Explorer and how enthusiastic we had been. A craft was launched into deep space, travelling at the speed of light, breaking barriers that were unthinkable. We all know what happened afterwards. Science revealed itself in the technological advancements of the mission. The mission even with its failure has revealed to us the awesome power of the universe; something we shouldn't tamper with. The benefit we get is by learning from our mistakes."

"It is obvious that our attempts to strive to understand Creation and therefore the Beginning has taken us beyond our boundaries. We were and still are searching for the unexplained when everything had been explained to us, here on Earth, 2,200 years ago. We take a long leap to escape the Truth. The latter is in front of us but we neglect it and opt to steer away from it. A long leap, gentlemen, has a bitter uncertainty of not knowing where we would land and set foot. Even if we were to land solidly on our feet, a sudden unpleasant recoil effect is going to be felt. Never try to escape your inability to understand the Truth by undertaking such unfortunate leaps. They lead you nowhere. It is so simple to refute God's existence and so complex to acknowledge it."

"My advice to all mankind is to believe and adhere to religious teachings. One must practice those principles to earn Heaven. It would be ideal for you to combine both belief and practice into your daily lives; but should you find yourselves incapable of doing so, then my suggestion is that you opt for the implementation of goodness and virtues rather than pretending belief. Simply speaking: you cannot truly believe without making sacrifices. Those who claim belief and never practice it, will eventually abuse faith and establish pretexts to commit sins in the name of religion, based on false assumptions that God would forgive them regardless. Those who follow such path are normally mischievous and threatening to mankind. God might pardon an atheist with good deeds rather than an alleged believer immersed in sins."

The huge hall burst into applause with heads of states, ambassadors and dignitaries rising for a standing ovation that lasted several minutes. The Pontiff held up his hand, asking politely for calm and quiet. Then he continued:

"Few days ago, I came across an interview conducted with a renowned statesman priding himself with his country's vision of deploying robots in future military warfare. According to his account, wars will be waged by machines without human involvement except at command centres. Honestly, I cannot find a single advantage to that. Those futuristic robotic battalions will be disastrous to mankind because simply speaking, they'll be devoid of feelings and compassion. Destruction of the enemy, human or material will be a justified cause, evaluated by processors relying on logical circuits meant to emulate a human brain. Thus, any decision will be based on a digital output of either 0 or 1. Nothing in between will be acceptable to the artificial intelligence."

"The statesman saw an advantage in introducing robotic warfare. It would minimise human battlefield losses, he claimed. But what about peripheral losses, I would like to ask? Gentlemen. A big threat is facing us. Losses in the battlefields might be minimal but the expected damage within cities and towns would surpass by far any destruction encountered in conventional warfare. Machines take orders and execute them without questioning. Hence, the origin of all instructions would be diffused from the command centre and robotic battalions would analyse the pros and cons of such commands and relay their advice back to the centre for the eventual final order."

"But in that case, the human factor would be a singular input instead of the conventional way which involves two or more human entities agreeing on a common action. Few times in previous world wars, generals and lieutenants stood up and resisted military orders that could have annihilated a whole town with its inhabitants. Court martials were set up and many were vindicated. Nothing ever replaces a human compassion and verdict."

"Furthermore, common sense tells us that any threatened superpower would ultimately resort to nuclear warfare if its robots and machines were to be wiped out. That's the real danger. When soldiers die in the battlefield, nations think twice and reassess situations and conditions. Using robots instead would result in game-like wars devoid of human sensation."

"If you recall, decades ago, shares were bought and sold through brokers. Instructions were generated through telephone communication links and actions were taken after hours or even days. As technology advanced, people were able to watch the market on screens, issue immediate instructions through their computers and spontaneous actions were taken. The consequence of that had always been: a stock market crash."

"In the past, a shareholder reflected and took his time to initiate any buying or selling action. These days unfortunately, the realisation that the value of a share has dropped, would lead to further drastic crashes because of our capability to intervene and enact the selling process instantly from the confinement of our living room, from the wilderness, from anywhere for that matter. Relying on war machines is the same."

"By the same token, we are gradually losing our identity. Our handwriting has vanished, completely erased by characters on keyboards. People cannot express themselves anymore in a simple manner. Writing down our feelings on a piece of paper is becoming hard and difficult to achieve. We'd rather use social media to convey our emotions, trying to avoid typed text, relying instead on emoticon forms: smiley faces, weird abbreviations, likes and pulsing hearts."

"Incredible, isn't it? We have become so absorbed in social media to the point of self-neglect. Our privacy is being invaded. Electronic messages are floating left, right and centre; they are read but are misunderstood most of the time. Why? Simply because we tend to forget that one spoken word says more than ten lines of ambiguous abbreviations Our societies are collapsing as a result. Our children are dependent on machines and screens that display a lot but divulge nothing. Wouldn't you rather listen to the voice of your mother bidding you a safe journey instead of reading one hundred words and staring at various emoticons, that carry no sound, intonation or affection? You'll never be able to capture the sigh of your loved one and his or her emotional state just by using text."

"Thus, you switch to video mode wishing for vivid communication. But in reality, you are depriving yourselves from the real sensation of being with the other party. You won't be able to touch, to feel the warmth radiating. Your ethereal kisses will never leave their imprint on your loved ones."

"Finally, and in conclusion, I urge you to seek knowledge, useful knowledge, and put it in service to get closer to God Almighty. His love is everywhere but we need to find it and earn it. Love is the most powerful tool that ever existed. Learn how to love yourself through God and appreciate His blessings. Once you mastered that virtue, expand it around you; to your children, to your parents, to your friends and all those in need."

"Lots of things can be achieved in the presence of love. Telepathic meditation is a successful means of communication when love persists between the sender and the recipient. We could go on and on but there's an end to everything. Hopefully we shall increase the tempo of our gatherings in the future, hoping that we'll all work for the welfare of mankind."

"God bless you all. The Vatican will always be beside you and I shall be all ears and eyes to listen to your problems and play a supportive and reconciliatory role."

The General Assembly was filled with appreciative roars. Members rose in unison applauding incessantly. Oppressed and suffering nations were staring at a great religious leader who had finally dared to speak out openly on their behalf while asserting himself as their protector. Super powers knew from that instant that they were under scrutiny. From there on, the eyes of the Holy See were watching.

The Pope blessed the attendees with the sign of the cross. For the first time ever, he recognised the true meaning of his mission and was overwhelmed by the heavy responsibility he had to bear. But it was all worthwhile. He felt like crying out loud and telling everyone within the huge auditorium that the whole story began in a small village perched above the Valley of the Saints.

# Epilogue

In the North of Lebanon, a group of three foreign hikers walked vigorously along the winding dirt trails and steep rocky terrain, descending onto the lowest part of the Valley of the Saints. The ancient monasteries welcome them with their bells tolling.

They were in their late thirties. One was an atheist; one was agnostic; and the third a believer. The party of three decided to take a rest and have a quick bite. They heard the gushing flow of water hurtling down not far away from where they had stopped. They followed the magical sound of music until they noticed a running stream that forged its way through rocks and shrubs. The melody varied according to the number and size of pebbles that stood in the way of the water flow.

The hikers got rid of their knapsacks and stretched themselves on the dry soil which was covered with open pine cones. The hike had been enjoyable. The weather couldn't have been better: indigo cloudless sky; moderate ambient temperature, typical for the month of September. It only felt a little nippy in the shade.

Each one dug through his bag and retrieved either a sandwich or tinned cans of tuna and plastic forks. They sat there eating hastily as if they had been deprived of food for several days. They downed their food with fresh water collected from the nearby stream. One of them, the thinnest, lit a cigarette and puffed at it with delight. He gazed appreciatively at the natural beauty that surrounded them and pointed with his index to the monasteries and chapels that spread across the valley:

"Look at that," he cried out. "The scenery is awesome. So heavenly." Almost simultaneously, his friends burst out laughing.

"What's so funny?"

"Your choice of words, Steve," retorted the believer. "Coming from an atheist, the use of the word heavenly is kind of unexpected and surprising."

"Well, Paul! It's a figure of speech," the atheist said.

Five hundred metres away, carved into the steep northern mountain flank, a sizeable cave stood out among several smaller ones, with its gaping entrance blackened by the shadow cast on the valley by the sun that had started few hours earlier to move in an angular path. The mountain flanks were a contrast of light and dark colours.

"That's Heaven on Earth!" cried out the agnostic. "I'm interested to see what's inside that cave."

The other two smiled back at him as they got up on their feet. "Let's go, Pete," they shouted in unison.

As they got closer to their destination, Steve broke the silence uttering inquisitively, "I was wondering, Paul, I'm aware that your mum had suggested Lebanon was worth visiting, but how did she get to know about this valley? I'm really grateful to her. I wouldn't have contemplated undertaking such a journey on my own. I'm sure it goes without saying that the same applies to the three of us."

"My mother is Italian of origin. She lived in Milan and attended the same high school as Luigi Khoury who is nowadays Pope John Paul the Fourth. His father was of Lebanese descent. Actually, his dad was born in one of the villages that we've driven through before we began our hiking. Once my mother got married in Italy, she emigrated with my dad to Australia. She must have been very fond of Luigi because after the lapse of decades, she never ceased to mention his name, his origin, the tasty Lebanese food that Luigi's Italian mother had learned to prepare, Luigi's relentless description of Lebanon's natural beauty, mostly unknown to many people. It seems the Valley of the Saints was particularly highly praised by the Khoury family. My mum showed me lots of pictures of the gorge taken in various seasons. Awesome pictures that Luigi had taken personally while on visits to the country."

The group of hikers halted their advance and stopped ten metres away from the grotto's entrance. They stared at the wide orifice ahead and hesitated whether to venture inside the cave or just take some photos near its entrance. They consulted each other with their inquisitive eyes without uttering a single word. The grotto had a peculiar enigmatic attraction that held the observer under its spell. Paul took out his torch light and switched it on. His action prompted his colleagues to emulate him. The decision to enter the cave had been made on their behalf. No more hesitation.

One behind the other, they entered the grotto stooping low through the gap. Almost two metres forward, the cave passage widened considerably. The reflection of the torch lights off the grotto's walls diminished gradually as they widely converged into a large space where burning wall torches shed wavering light on the uneven stony floor and jagged rocky walls. The cave measured roughly ten metres by eight metres. The ambient temperature was relatively cold giving the hikers the shiver. At one corner lay a small makeshift wooden altar which faced a naturally smooth wall where a cross hung amid a dozen religious pictures and icons depicting Jesus Christ, the Virgin Mary, Angels and Saints.

A hermit was kneeling in front of the altar, holding a well-worn hard copy of the Bible whose open pages appeared tattered from prolonged reading and usage. Two candles witnessed his prayers, sending off sudden puffs of unsteady smoke whenever the breeze funnelled through the cave. At each waft of smoke, a peculiar burning smell of wax filled the space.

Realising he had unexpected visitors, the hermit made the sign of the cross, closed the Bible and put it down on the altar. He lifted himself up with a struggle and turned to face the group of hikers.

He looked in his seventies, judging by his stooping back and slumped shoulders. He wore a long beard of greyish-white colour. His eyes were like rubies, consequence of exhaustive hours of reading in darkly lit places. He seemed to be studying them, trying to figure out their origin.

"Hi," exclaimed Steve. "We are visiting from Australia. Sorry for barging in like that."

"Australia," the hermit replicated. "Welcome! Welcome! That's too far away!" The hermit spoke with a moderate English accent.

"We noticed the cave from far away and decided to explore it," said Pete. "We didn't realise it was inhabited."

The hermit ushered them to sit down on the stony floor. Unlike the way he stood up, he exhibited agility and suppleness as he crouched and assumed a sitting posture. The three men tried to replicate his moves, refraining to complain about the hardness of the uneven surface.

"This is my home," he said. "Sorry I have nothing to offer you. I can only pray for you. I've been in the valley for the past forty years. I was once an architect and a married man. French has always been my second language. As you're finding out, my proficiency in English is about average."

"You're doing fine expressing yourself," retorted Steve. "Wish we could speak foreign languages."

Paul swallowed his saliva and asked, in a shy tone, the question he was struggling to blurt out: "So, what made you decide to abandon everything and live in seclusion?"

The hermit's face hardened, and a sweep of sadness ravaged his features. "I lost my wife one year into our marriage. She got caught up in a car accident," he said. "I couldn't bear her loss. In the beginning, I blamed God for allowing it to happen. I even hated myself for not being there with her when it happened. My world had suddenly crumbled. I couldn't find any satisfaction at work, at home, with my parents, my friends. I loathed being pitied. One day, I was driving through the mountainous areas of this region and noticed the caves along the gorge. It was an invitation; a beacon telling me I belonged to those ridges. I informed my parents of my intentions and they genuinely thought I was losing my senses, or that it was a bad joke or something. I guess they never realised how serious I had been until I completely vanished one wintery afternoon. I had left a note expressing my final decision to live in seclusion for the rest of my life."

He gazed at the three hikers in a pensive way as if assessing the worthiness of divulging personal information to a foreign party who had just intruded into his life. But then again, he had already embarked in his account and he had to finish it, fearing that it might be otherwise misconstrued.

"I had stacked few woollen clothes and miscellaneous items in a small suitcase; took some change with me, enough to pay the taxi driver who dropped me at the nearest village from the valley, and then descended the steep terrain amid faint sunlight as dusk was setting. The wilderness was frightening, and I remember shuddering at the thought of being alone in a place that felt even lonelier as light fog started to form. The scary part was my obsession to head for the nearest grotto and dump myself inside its hollow cold emptiness. The closer I got, the more I realised I wasn't ready yet to surrender myself to the cavernous walls, especially not then, when surrounding trees and rocks became shrouded by darkness, unveiling frightening shapes."

"As a lighthouse guiding ships to their ports, candle and torch lighting reflected off the window panes of a nearby monastery, summoning me to head for its huge wooden door and bang the iron knocker in successive blows."

"An old obese monk threw the door open and stared at me inquisitively, studying me from head to toe. I was certain the monastery had never received before a visitor at that particular evening hour. He ushered me in without uttering a single word. Few minutes later we were in a room packed with dozen monks sitting on benches placed around a wooden table in what looked like a small dining hall. The smell of lentil soup caught my nostrils. Each monk had a bowl in front of him and a thick slice of brown bread beside it, obviously home baked from whole wheat. The wise-looking monk sitting at the head of the table spoke to me through tight lips concealed by the heavy beard he wore. His lips barely moved as he said: 'What brings you here, my son?'"

"I put my suitcase on the floor and recited my story, emphasising my yearning to seclude myself from the rest of the world. I even described the fear that overcame my senses earlier on, trying to justify my intrusion into the monastery. 'It's perfectly normal to be frightened', the senior monk said. 'That's a big transition in one's life. But what is more important is the reason behind your decision to isolate yourself. You need to be convinced you're doing that out of conviction. This valley is a spiritual experience that is indescribable. We find God in every rock, every tree, every stream and waterfall. We find Him in the wind and skies above; we find Him in the fog that lifts our prayers and spirits high up to reach Him'."

"The wise monk paused, glanced at the suitcase and continued: 'I see you have brought a few things for your journey. We shall assist you in your endeavour by offering you whatever goods you may need: food, material supply, clothing. Feel free my son to knock on our doors should you require anything. We are brothers and should be helping each other out. If you fall sick, call on us; if you are thirsty ask us for water. In the meantime, you can stay with us for as long as you need; on one condition, that you abide by the monastery rules'."

"'I cannot express my gratitude for your hospitality', I replied. 'I'll stay here for a fortnight and will leave afterwards for the cave. By then, I would have conquered my apprehension and fear. It would be the perfect transition before my complete seclusion'."

"'As you wish, my son. Brother Antonios will assist you during your stay in our monastery'. Antonios was the obese monk who had let me in. That night, I had the best lentil soup I had ever tasted. I wish the narrow bed were as good. But I learned afterwards how comfortable that bed had been compared to the hard-stony floor I lie on each night inside the cave."

The hermit sighed, straightened his posture and resumed his recitation:

"Before moving into the grotto, I spent a few hours each day assessing and scrutinising the living conditions that prevailed within those lonely rocky walls, benefiting from the two weeks I had set for myself to depart from the monastery. That gave me ample time to render my new residence functional and move few vital goods inside the cave, preparing myself to adjust to a new life full of austerity, self-denial and discomfort. I must admit that life in the monastery was a prelude, paving the way for an isolated life that had no mercy whatsoever."

"After saying goodbye to my brothers at the monastery, I headed for the cave on a beautiful morning. The natural beauty of the surroundings gave me an adrenaline surge and brightened up my morale. By the time I set foot inside the grotto, the whole thing dissipated. Reality sank in. I was finally inside my newly arranged home, my own fiefdom of prison cell: a small altar; a corner where wooden utensils rested on wall mounted shelving fixed through threaded nails, just above a wood-fired stove; a shallow mattress that laid three metres away from the stove; a corner for storing grains, flour, olive oil and olives."

"The monks ensured I had initially the right provisions to sustain myself and incited me to seek their assistance whenever the need arose. They even allowed me to have access to their monastery fields and gardens where fresh vegetables and fruits were grown. In return, I had to help out with the field work like any monk who lived in the monastery. Our pact is still ongoing despite the demise of the senior monk and the appointment since of two other seniors. The more I'm aging, the more lenient they have become. They do not expect me to work as hard as I used to. For that, I'm also eternally grateful."

The hikers were listening intently, completely absorbed in deep thoughts as if they were capturing the essence of the hermit's description, while adding to it animated scenes of how they perceived the ploughing of the fields, the sowing of the seeds and the harvesting of the crops.

Each one of them was experiencing a true fairy tale in which truth was stranger than fiction.

Steve stood up and paced towards the cave entrance. A thick carpet of greyish fog had enveloped the gorge, floating at almost the same level as the grotto's entrance. Mist seeped through the opening and tiny droplets of water grazed Steve's face. The sight unfolding beneath him and above him was surreal. Amid occasional clearances, one could glimpse the monasteries and pine trees beneath the thinning fog layer. The latter represented a demarcation line between the clear azure sky above and the overcast world that lay underneath. Steve checked his watch: it was three forty-five in the afternoon.

Steve called upon his friends to join him and admire the scenic view. They stared in disbelief. The nuance of colours was beyond any panoramic view they had ever seen. More than that, there was a peculiar feeling that the mystic view had captured more than their eyes: it captivated their mind as well. Time had seemed suspended and irrelevant. The valley was the past, the present and the future. Silently, the three friends returned to their initial places and sat on the hard floor without hesitation. This time the stone appeared to have softened somehow. The hermit smiled at them, realising their acceptance of his world.

"Tell us more about your spiritual experience," Paul said. The others nodded.

The hermit retracted his arms inwards, letting his dark brown robe cover them for warmth. Contrary to his expectation, he was enjoying the presence of strangers in his midst. He had occasionally chatted with humans upon his scarce encounters with people who visited the valley for touristic purposes. But he had never spent that much time talking, let alone revealing personal matters that he had kept to himself for decades. Nonetheless, the present company he was having seemed genuinely eager to know more about him. He relaxed his muscles and said with a soft voice:

"My isolation from the rest of the world was the consequence of my inability to face reality and to overcome my anger and resentment of what happened to my wife. I did not retreat myself because of my devotion to God or to consecrate my life for prayers. It was an act of pure evasion."

"That was how it all began. I kept questioning God about his fairness; about his abandonment? I couldn't fathom how a young woman with lots of expectations could just vanish in a split of a second. So many times, I asked God: Why her and not me? Gingerly, I started finding solace whenever I chatted with Hanna, the senior monk. My periodic visits to the nearby monastery allowed me to reveal to him my concerns, my apprehensions and my frustration. He would stare at me with his intelligent eyes, put on a comforting smile and speak softly: 'My son! You shouldn't be here if that's what is troubling you. You are running away from sadness and confrontation. Secluding yourself in a cave up here in the mountains would not grant you any relief whatsoever. On the contrary, your isolation would heighten the anxiety because you've created a rift between God and yourself. My advice to you is to head back home and resume your daily activities; nonetheless, you need to restore your faith in the Almighty and remember that God has created us to live but will never intervene to cause or prevent our death. It's very simple actually. We shall all depart eventually from this physical world but God has ensured that our souls shall live on eternally. Preventing death is therefore in itself a contradictory concept of the afterlife, as if elongating one's earthly life had more value than seeking eternity. I won't bother you with metaphysics and spirituality, but your seclusion has to be meaningful, otherwise return to your previous world'."

"'What do you mean by meaningful?' I enquired. Monk Hanna sighed and said: 'In order for your seclusion to be meaningful, resort to prayers and search for God. Inside the grotto, your body may be imprisoned but not your spirit. You've got to learn how to loosen up. Create a purpose for your stay and you'll find the truth soon enough'."

The hermit's face glowed with chastity and contentment. He was recalling events that had taken place forty years ago.

"Monk Hanna was absolutely right. I began attending mass at the monastery. Couldn't wait to hear the bells tolling. I had taken my watch off my wrist and church bells became my clock. I shared reading texts from the Bible and the contents revealed themselves in a way so different from the one I had perceived in my younger days. I would stop literally at every single word and enquire about its meaning, its message. My attitude changed. My anger vanished. I was ready for my hermitage."

"I can tell you without hesitation that my conception of life has matured a lot but hasn't reached a saturation point yet. I wonder at times if the latter existed. Will we ever attain the knowledge and subsequently the truth behind Creation, faith? The answer is negative because simply speaking we are not supposed to. Our bodies represent the biggest hindrance and our mind has various preoccupations that shield it from functioning flawlessly. The best we could do, is search for God. We can find Him everywhere: in Nature, in the air we breathe, in a child's innocence, in a woman's beauty. What's really important is to search for God before He finds us. We need to be prepared to meet Him one day and be accepted as eager scholars. Only then would we be ready to grasp the Truth. I am certain it is a wonderful truth."

The hikers left the cave after bidding the hermit goodbye. He was sad to see them exiting the grotto and followed them with his gaze until they disappeared into the mist. The atheist wondered if he had become an agnostic. The agnostic had turned into a believer. The believer was in a metaphysical state that took him beyond the Valley of the Saints.

After their climb, the group of hikers peered down at the valley beneath a rising fog that infiltrated the streets of the villages perched on the outer rim. The climb had been treacherous as the young travellers had chosen the shortest route, back to the asphalted road that linked the tiny villages overlooking the valley.

Youngsters were playing volleyball within the fenced court of a secondary school. Exclamations of cheers and boos could be heard periodically from the bleachers. The educational facility consisted of an L-shaped modern structure, unlike nearby red-tiled houses that were built from stone blocks. The name of the school was displayed on the front wall, just above the main entrance gate: KHOURY SECONDARY SCHOOL. The words were composed of big letters made of cedar wood planks. The building was apparently closed for the day.

Paul rested his knapsack on one of the granite steps. His colleagues followed suit. He walked towards the security booth at the car park entrance. There he found a yawning middle-aged man that looked bored and drowsy. The guard seemed too big inside the relatively tight space that enclosed him. He sat on a straw chair facing a wireless telephone receiver mounted on a pedestal. He rose politely from his chair the moment he laid eyes on the foreign visitor.

"I wonder if you could help me," Paul said in English.

The guard stared at Paul with furrowed eyebrows. Then he appeared to relax, put on a smile and replied in relatively good English and legible accent: "What can I do for you, young man?"

"I noticed the school is named after the Khoury family. Is this the Pope's native village?" Paul asked.

"Yes. It is. The funds were raised for decades since the Pope's father initiated the construction process."

"Can you show me on the Google map where the Khoury's property is situated?" asked Paul hesitantly.

"No need to. It's that villa over there." The sentry pointed at a rocky hill five hundred metres away. It was perched over the valley with lots of green field patches surrounding a red-tiled house. "You can walk the distance. You cannot miss it. The big garden is famous for its tasty cherry trees."

Paul expressed his gratitude to the middle-aged man. He waved at his friends to join him and they marched for seven minutes until they reached a beautiful house built on a recessed plot about one hundred metres off the main road. The sun was setting and birds were singing their last daily tunes as they huddled inside foliage and trees.

The external stone blocks were battered by the harsh winter weather over the years. But they stood solid as sentinels guarding their own legacy. Windows had their oak shutters closed. Concrete pathways formed geometrical patterns amid the turfed areas that joined the villa to the green zones around it. Creeping woolly thyme invaded their cracks. It was obvious though that someone attended to the landscaping as the ground cover growth along the walkways appeared to be well groomed and taken care of.

Towards the west, twilight exhibited wonderful colours, reflected by the sun setting behind the horizon. Paul had already excused himself and left his bewildered companions behind, before crossing the gate and advancing into the muddy soil. The earth was recently irrigated. He was able to hear the sound of a pick hitting the soil at regular intervals amid Arabic singing. The voice was that of a man, humming a folkloric tune. Paul followed the sound and turned left, finding himself facing the villa's southern elevation. On the far-right side, he could make out the silhouette of a crouched man wearing a kepi, working his pick around a pine tree. As Paul got closer, the gardener stood upright and gently laid his pick on the ground beside a shovel and a wheelbarrow.

"Marhaba! Min inta ya ibni?" The man said in Arabic, with a low-pitched voice.

Paul felt embarrassed like a trespasser would. He replied in a quivering tone, "I'm Australian. Do you speak English, Sir?"

"Yes, I do," said the tall man. "Have you lost your way, son?"

"No! No!" muttered Paul. "I was curious to check out where the Khoury family had lived. I've been down the Valley of the Saints and realised it was the village where the family hailed from."

"Any particular reason for your interest?" said the man as he extended his hand for a handshake. "My name is Jean Khoury."

"Oh I see." Paul was in disbelief. "Sorry, I thought you were the gardener."

"I practically am," said Jean jokingly. "I assume the role of a caretaker. My cousin the Pope has entrusted me with the property. He wants me to cater for the land, the house…requesting daily videos to be sent to him. He feels very close to this holy land and can't take it out of his heart and mind. You haven't told me why you're so taken by the Khoury family."

Paul cleared his voice. "My mother was Italian. She and Dad emigrated to Australia soon after their marriage. She had spent her youth in Milan and attended the same school as Luigi Khoury. They became friends and shared most of their time together. Not a single day passes by without her mentioning Luigi, his mum Paula, Lebanese food, the Valley of the Saints. She encouraged me to undertake this trip. I felt as if she wanted me to cover for her, to be the incognito visitor…she will definitely debrief me the moment I set foot on Australian soil."

"That's interesting," said Jean. At that instant, the stifled chiming sound of a mobile phone was heard. Jean fetched and took out his mobile device from the depth of his multi-pocketed fatigue trousers and watched the screen in disbelief.

"Unbelievable!" He cried out. "It's…It's Him! It must be past six already." Paul's heart skipped a few beats. He got closer to Jean and positioned himself for a good camera coverage. The screen popped open with a familiar face that Paul had often seen on television and other media devices. The Pontiff was live before them.

"Your Holiness! Please excuse my distraction. I should have been in touch earlier. I hope I didn't cause you any inconvenience."

Paul listened as his heart fluttered. He watched Jean nodding while conversing with the Pope. The latter's softly spoken words could be heard over the speaker. They were speaking to each other in English. Paul moved away in a polite manner, trying his best not to pry on a private conversation. The video call went on for quite a while. Paul could still make out the essence of the chat: Jean was requesting the Pontiff's consent to plant few apple trees and replace the cracked floor tiles of the sitting room. Paul decided it was about time for him to leave the property and return to his friends. He waved his hand at Jean while whispering a thank you. Jean cried out after him, "Just wait. I'll be through in a moment."

"Who's with you?" Despite the well-maintained distance, the Pope's voice came across loud, clear and inquisitive.

"Ah, that's Paul. He came all the way from Australia to visit the valley. He was advised and tipped by his mother. Very enthusiastic guy. It seems his mum was acquainted to you."

"Acquaintance of mine?" enquired Luigi. "Please put him through."

Jean beckoned Paul to come forth. "His Holiness would like to converse with you."

"Yes, she is. My parents have moved to the suburbs of Sydney. She spends most of her day out in the garden, growing vegetables, herbs and flowers. Whenever my sister and I visit her unannounced, she takes pride in fixing us tabbouleh salad, concocted from the garden produce. Most nights, she accompanies Dad to the pubs and attends social dinners. She's doing fine."

"Good to hear that! Give her my sincere regards and tell her that I still remember the good times we had. God bless you, my son."

The communication ended. Paul was filled with happiness. Luigi had an aching heart and a mind full of cherished moments reaching out from the past. That young man could have been his son. His dark auburn hair and green eyes were features he had watched with delight and affection. Paul reminded Luigi of his first and only love. So intense it had been he couldn't erase it from his soul. Luigi's veins tingled with the flow of blood circulating back to its lively source: the heart of everything. He had learned since the beginning that love was the most powerful and distinctive tool that ever existed.

Pope John Paul the fourth stared at his watch. It was seven in the evening. *How ironic,* he thought. Only this morning he had been reminiscing about his parents while sitting on the terrace of the summer papal palace of Castel Gondolfo.

Paul held the mobile phone in his palm and stared at a face he had often seen on television and other media networks. He felt serenity and peace overwhelming his soul.

"I'm pleased, young man, to see you in the midst of one of the most amazing places I have ever known. It makes me proud of my roots. I hope you had the chance to roam the entire valley and mix with its recluse inhabitants?"

For a brief moment, Paul trembled in awe of the great person chatting with him, even though the most influential man on Earth exuded moderation and an indescribable closeness. Paul recovered his calmness, but still found himself speaking agitatedly: "It's a great privilege, Your Holiness, to confer with you. I wouldn't have dreamed of such a moment. I'm honoured. My mother is going to be enthused by that. She has never ceased mentioning your name and her present life has not ebbed the past. Your Holiness please forgive me saying so, but she always refers to you as Luigi Khoury—"

The Pontiff interjected: "Oh! Are we acquainted then? Has she met me before?"

"Your Holiness, you attended the same high school in Milan. You were very close friends and she used to visit your home in Bellagio. She still mentions the tasty dishes your mother Paula used to make…"

Luigi's heart squeezed in anticipation of what was coming next: "What's your mum's name?"

Paul replied enthusiastically, "Gina Romano. Before marriage, her maiden surname was…"

"Mancini," said the Pontiff. "Is that right? You're Gina's son?"

"Yes! Your Holiness," blurted Paul with evident relief.

Luigi tasted the salty tears that covered his eyes and snaked down his cheeks. Tears converged to the tip of his upper lips and seeped through his mouth forced open by the astonishment he was experiencing.

"That's amazing, Paul," he said with a quivering voice. "Your mother was a special lady. She had left emptiness in our hearts after her departure for Sydney. Please tell her that she had always been on our mind. Tell her that her friendship meant and still mean a lot to me. Tell her that I shall never forsake her. Wish you all the best my son! May God bless you forever with your dear parents."

"Thank you, your Holiness. She's going to be greatly pleased…"

"One more thing before you go," said Luigi. "Is she happy and doing well?"